St. Giles, Durham, England Kepier Hospital , Durham, England St. Mary Magdalene Hospital, James Barmby

Memorials of St. Gile's, Durham

being grassmen's accounts and other parish records, together with documents

relating to the hospitals of Kepier and St. Mary Magdalene

St. Giles, Durham, England Kepier Hospital , Durham, England St. Mary Magdalene Hospital,
James Barmby

Memorials of St. Gile's, Durham
*being grassmen's accounts and other parish records, together with documents relating to the
hospitals of Kepier and St. Mary Magdalene*

ISBN/EAN: 9783337235529

Printed in Europe, USA, Canada, Australia, Japan

Cover: Foto ©Andreas Hilbeck / pixelio.de

More available books at **www.hansebooks.com**

THE
PUBLICATIONS

OF THE

SURTEES SOCIETY

ESTABLISHED IN THE YEAR

M.DCCC.XXXIV.

VOL. XCV.

FOR THE YEAR M.DCCC.XCV.

DURHAM:
THOMAS CALDCLEUGH, PRINTER.

No. 1.   A.D. 1189.

No. 2.   A.D. 1199.

No. 3.   A.D. 1291.

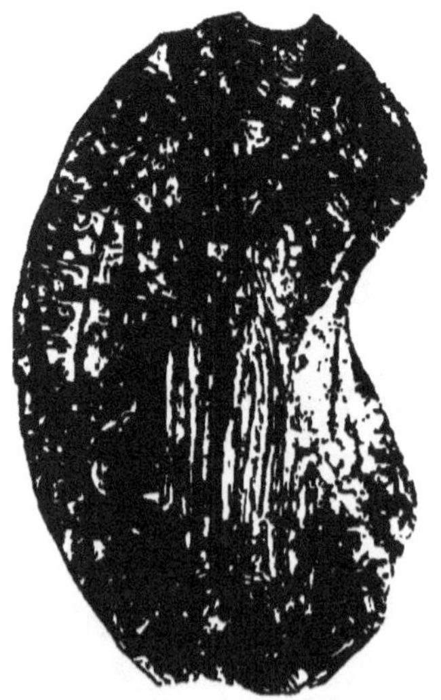

No. 4.   A.D. 1219-33.

No. 5.   A.D. 1335.

MEMORIALS

OF

ST. GILES'S, DURHAM,

Being Grassmen's Accounts and other Parish
Records, together with Documents
relating to the

HOSPITALS

OF

KEPIER and ST. MARY MAGDALENE.

Published for the Society

By ANDREWS & Co., DURHAM;
WHITTAKER & Co., 2, WHITE HART STREET, PATERNOSTER
SQUARE;
BERNARD QUARITCH, 15, PICCADILLY;
BLACKWOOD & SONS, EDINBURGH.
1896.

At a General Meeting of the SURTEES SOCIETY, held in Durham Castle on Tuesday, June 6th, 1893, the REV. W. GREENWELL in the chair.

It was ordered,

That a Volume relating to the Parish of St. Giles's, Durham, including Kepyer Hospital, be edited for the Society by the REV. J. BARMBY.

JAMES RAINE,

Secretary.

CONTENTS.

INTRODUCTION.

THE Borough of St. Giles is a suburb of the City of Durham, lying between the upper and lower portions of the River Wear, which approaches the city from the East and, after encompassing in a loop the hill on which the Castle and Cathedral stand, flows away towards the East again. The street called Gilligate is between the approaching and retiring streams, being a continuation of Claypath in the parish of St. Nicholas, and beginning where Bakehouse Lane on the one side and the narrow Tinkler's Lane on the other separate the two parishes, and where the Leaden Cross, shown in Speed's map of Durham (see Surtees' "History of Durham," Vol. iv, Part ii, p. 31), formerly stood. Thence the street ascends eastward in two successive acclivities to the summit of the hill on which the church stands, the ground sloping steeply down on each side to the river. The church, so situated, catches the eye of visitors to Durham with a pleasing effect, perhaps suggesting the thought to some of "the decent church that tops the neighb'ring hill." Its modest low tower, according so well with the surrounding scene, has happily been left unchanged by modern restoration. East of "the street" (as Gilligate is often called in the old records) the ancient parish extended far into the adjacent country, including a moor, which comprised, at the time of its enclosure in 1817, about 235 acres.

Minds sensible of the fascination of antiquarian research, when on the look-out for antiquities, cannot but long to go back beyond the time at which any definite history of a place begins. Hence, before attempting a sketch of what is historically known for the purpose of elucidating the records now published, it may be interesting to cast a brief glance into the times, so far as can be known or surmised, before there was any suburb of a city, or city at all, in the locality. Of pre-historic occupation of the vicinity there appear, indeed, to be but scanty traces so far discovered, though a stone axe is said to have been found at Sherburn Hospital, and two interments near Sherburn and Sacriston. There is, however, a significant intimation of British occupation in the term *Maiden*, applied to three places close to Durham, one of which was on Gilesgate Moor. This word, usually now combined with *Castle*, is believed to be British, and to denote some kind of fortified mound. The designation is not uncommon, being found in various parts. The following description by Leland of a structure so called may be cited in illustration :—" There is a Place an viii Mile plaine West from Bowis (*Bowes, on the edge of Stainmoor, in Yorkshire*) a Thorough-fare in Richemount-shire cawllid Maiden Castel, where is a greate rounde Hepe a 60 Foote in Cumpace of rude Stones, sum smaul, sum bygge, and be set *in formam pyramidis* ; and yn the Toppe of them al ys set one Stone *in conum* beying a yard and a halfe in lenghth. So that the hole may be countid an xviii Foote hy, and ys set on a hille in the very Egge of Stanemore. And this is a limes betwixt Richemontshire and Westmerlande " (" Itinerary," Vol. v, p. 122). The common addition of *Castle* to the old word *Maiden* cannot be taken as proof that the Romans had used the old fort as a *castellum*, though no doubt they have done so in some cases.

The three places thus designated near the city of Durham are (1) *Maiden Castle*, on the hill so-called, which rises abruptly above the Wear between Durham and Shincliffe ; (2) a mound, partly artificial, called *Maiden's Bower*, among the *Red Hills*, where the banner of St. Cuthbert is said to have been placed during the battle of Neville's Cross ; and (3) another *Maiden's Bower* (or *Maiden's Arbour*, or, as appears from the Grassmen's Books of St. Giles, formerly *Maiden Castle*), all traces of which have now disappeared, on Gilesgate Moor. The earliest known allusion to the last is in Wharton's continuation of the history attributed to William Chambre, the last of the " Tres Scriptores," where, in reference to a marble cross transferred to Durham Market Place in the time of Bishop Tunstall (d. 1571), it is said, " Crux marmorea, praeclara admodum, quae olim steterat in suprema parte vici de Gilligate, loco vocato *Maid Arbor,* data erat Gulielmo Wright de Dunelmo mercatori sua petitione per Dominum Armstronge[1] Scotum, dominum de Kepyere, ad constituendum in foro Dunelmi (Surtees Society's Publications, 1839, Vol. ix, p. 156). Surtees thus describes the place, as it was remembered when he wrote :— " Maid's Arbour, or Maiden's Bower. A few years ago a square platform, slightly elevated, was distinctly observable on the flat plot of ground within the angle formed by the roads diverging to Sunderland and Sherburn, at the West end of Gilesgate Moor " (" History of Durham," Vol. iv, Part ii, p. 69). At an earlier date, Cade (" Archaeologia," Vol. vii, p. 78 (1785), refers to it thus. After speaking of the entrenchment at Old Durham, supposed by him to have been Roman, he goes on—" A gentleman with whom I am acquainted has carefully surveyed the old road from this place by Kepyre hospital, and he assures me, that, in a dry season, the piers of a bridge are obvious in the bed of the river, seemingly of Roman construction ; and I have authority to say that coins have been formerly ploughed up here, and lately some of the lower empire have also been discovered within its vicinage. The ground-plot and ramparts of the watch-tower which served for signals to this station are visible and almost entire at the entrance of Gilligate Moor, and exactly correspond in form with those on the Roman Wall in Northumberland." Cade also alleges that there were traces of an "exploratory castrum" on the high ground, further north, near the present Newton Hall. Further, in the Grassmen's Books, published in this Volume, there are frequent allusions to a place on the Moor which is always called *the mayden castell* till the year 1598, when the designation is changed to *maiden bower,* though not uniformly so in following years.[2] It is shown by these books to have been an enclosure fenced

---

[1] Armstronge appears to be a mistake for Ormestone—a Scotchman, to whom Edward VI granted the suppressed Hospital of Kepyer in 1552. So says Surtees, and in the " Mickleton MSS.," No. 32, it is said, " Johannes Colborne, Dominus de Ormeston [non Armstrong, ut in Wh. fo. 783] Scotus."

[2] As to the change of the name from *castell* to *bower* see p. 25, note 4.

by a dike with a hedge of whins, which was regularly kept in repair till the year 1629, after which there is no more mention of it. It seems to have been utilized by the parish as an enclosure for milking cows in. For see entry in 1605 :—" For mendinge ye mayden castell, which was broken downe by the milkers of kye."

There is thus nothing beyond its name *Maiden* to intimate its origin. But the fortification similarly designated on Maiden Castle Hill is said by Canon Greenwell of Durham to be of the general character of such as were pre-Roman. Thus there seems to be enough evidence of some old race before the Romans having occupied the locality before us. Of Roman occupation there are the following traces. In the first place it may be held with confidence that a Roman road crossed Gilesgate Moor, passing the site of the *Maiden Castle* there. The whole system of Roman roads in the County of Durham is well shown in a paper, with a map, by Mr. W. H. D. Longstaffe, entitled, " Durham before the Conquest," published in the " Proceedings " of the Archaeological Institute, 1852, Newcastle, Vol. i, p. 41. It is there represented that a road from the south forked into two branches where Shincliffe now is, one of which crossed the Wear towards the north-west, passing by the fort on Maiden Castle Hill, while the other, keeping on the eastern bank of the stream, ran northward by Old Durham over Gilesgate Moor, and then crossed the river below Kepyer Hospital towards the important station at Chester-le-Street, which may have been Ptolemy's *Epeiakon*. Cade mentions, as we have just seen, that the piers of a bridge, apparently Roman, were obvious in a dry season in the bed of the river by Kepyer. Surtees confirms this statement, saying that in the dry summer of 1827 solid masonry was discovered on the north side of the Wear below the Hospital, believed by him to have been the piers of a bridge (" History of Durham," Vol. iv, Part ii, p. 91). Old Durham, of which mention has been made, is on the right bank of the river, opposite Maiden Castle Hill on the left side, where the ground begins to rise to Gilesgate Moor ; and there, on the flat, there are evident traces of an

ancient entrenchment, the " Pidding brook " (so called by
Hollinshed), which would naturally have entered the Wear
near Shincliffe, having apparently been diverted so as to
defend the entrenchment. Cade, as has been said, took
this to have been a Roman Camp ; and, by whomever it
was originally constructed, it is likely enough that both it
and the fortification on Maiden Castle Hill on the opposite
side of the river were in fact occupied by the Romans,
whose roads ran by them. If so, the other *Maiden Castle*
on Gilesgate Moor may well have been used by them (as
supposed by Cade) as a post for defence and observation
on the high ground beyond which their road northward
traversed. There is, indeed, a deficiency of distinct relics
of Roman occupation in this immediate vicinity. But
Cade speaks of Roman coins having been ploughed up at
Old Durham, and Surtees of a " fine old Nero found by a
woman hoeing turnips on Gilesgate Moor 14 years ago."
The latter alleges also that, " a few years ago, in removing
a portion of the rampart (*i.e.*, on Maiden Castle Hill
between Durham and Shincliffe) several squared stones
were found, and one which could scarcely be taken for
anything else than a rude and defaced Roman altar "
("History of Durham," Vol. iv, ii, p. 90). Mr. Longstaffe,
quoting this passage, adds in a note, " Mr. Raine
endorses this statement." Surtees says also (*Ibid.*, p. 69)
that " in the Minster yard Stukeley saw a Roman altar set
up as a gravestone, and that Dr. Hunter shewed him a
Roman head in a garden wall, apparently a portrait of
Marcus Aurelius," and alleges that " the head of St.
Oswald in the conventual seal was really that of Jupiter
Tonans, and an antique gem." The altar last-mentioned,
which is now in the Library of the Dean and Chapter, may,
it is true, have been brought from elsewhere, and so may
the gem ; nor do a few coins, found here and there,
actually prove Roman occupation. Such indications,
therefore, can only be taken as in some degree supporting
other better evidence. Among the places noticed in the
above survey as indicative of Roman or previous occupation of the locality, Maiden Castle (or Bower), on Gilesgate
Moor, was in the parish of St. Giles, and Old Durham,

though outside it, was closely connected with it as having belonged to the Rectory of St. Nicholas, appropriated by Bishop Nevill to Kepyer Hospital, and having consequently become afterwards the seat of the lords of the manor.

Between the relinquishment of Britain by the Romans, A.D. 427, and the foundation of Kepyer Hospital by Bishop Flambard, A.D. 1112, which was the origin of the borough and parish of St. Giles, well nigh seven centuries passed away. Meanwhile we find nothing to connect the exact locality with historical events, or invest it with any special interest. The Irish missionaries from Iona and Lindisfarne, under the leadership of St. Aidan, in the seventh century, may no doubt have passed close by, and evangelized to some extent the surrounding country. But such missionary station as they may have had seems more likely to have been in the locality of the present St. Oswald's Church, where relics of crosses indicative of their period have been found, than within the limits of the parish of St. Giles, where none such have been discovered. Then, when the Congregation of St. Cuthbert, A.D. 995, were returning after their wanderings to Chester-le-Street, it was at *Dunholm*, where the Cathedral now stands, that they stopped, and settled, and built their church ; and the city of Durham, thus originated, had its boroughs of Elvet and Framwellgate before there was any borough of St. Giles. It was in fact, as above intimated, not till the foundation of Kepyer by Bishop Flambard that the existence of the latter began.

KEPYER HOSPITAL.

In the year 1112 Ralph Flambard, Bishop of Durham, founded a church with a hospital attached in honour of God and St. Giles, and for the weal of his own soul, and redemption of the souls of William the Conqueror and Matilda his queen, who had nourished him ; of King William II, who had advanced him to the bishopric ; of King Henry I, who had confirmed him in it ; and of all who had bestowed, or should bestow, gifts or alms on the Church of St. Cuthbert. He himself dedicated it on the 11th of June, 1112, having endowed it with his vill of

Caldecotes hard by, and other emoluments, for the maintenance for ever of a clerk to serve therein, and of certain poor persons who were to dwell there. " Caldecotes " no doubt comprised the land near the site of the hospital, afterwards called " Kepyer Grange." *Cf.*, " De manerio de Caldecotes, vocato Kepiyer Grangie " (*Feodarium Prioratus Dunelm*. in Surtees Society's Publications, Vol. lviii, p. 77). This vill was granted with all its appurtenances and liberties, ecclesiastical and secular, in meadows, pastures, woods, wastes, and waters, with a mill at Milneburn. There were added two sheaves of corn from every carucate of the bishop's demesnes of Newbottle, Houghton, Wearmouth, Ryhope, Easington, Sedgefield, Sherburn, Quarrington, Newton, Chester, Washington, Boldon, Cleadon, Whickham, and Ryton. Finally the customary denunciation of eternal damnation was appended against any who should at any time disturb the Hospital in the enjoyment of its heritage. The Hospital was originally contiguous to the church, both being on the hill where the church now stands. There is no evidence of there having been any church previously, nor does that founded by Flambard seem to have been intended originally to serve any purpose but that of a chapel to the hospital.

It may be here noted that his original Deed of Foundation is no longer extant, having been destroyed, with all other charters of the house, when the Scots under Robert Bruce set fire to its muniment room (A.D. 1306) in the time of Bishop Anthony Bek. But the succeeding bishop, Richard Kellaw (1311–1316), issued a commission for ascertaining the rights and property of the Hospital ; and its old charters (of which there may have been copies elsewhere than in the muniment room), having been thus verified, were exemplified upon the Patent Rolls of Richard II in the year 1380, and again in the Close Rolls of Bishop Neville in 1445. Nineteen such charters, as exemplified in the Patent Rolls of Richard II (*per inspeximus*), are given in Dugdale's "Monasticon," Vol. ii, Part ii. In Appendix A to this volume the same are given as they appear, with preliminary and subsequent matter, in the Close Rolls of Bishop Neville now preserved in the

Public Record Office. It will thence be seen what Commissioners had been appointed by Kellaw, and how they had been directed to proceed, and also how subsequent bishops, Hatfield and Fordham, had confirmed to the Hospital all its rights and possessions as thus established, and finally how Bishop Neville had done the same, excepting only its right to tithes from the episcopal demesne lands, in lieu of which he appropriated to the Hospital the Rectory of St. Nicholas in Durham.

Though Flambard was the original founder of the Hospital, it was to Bishop Pudsey that it owed its subsequent constitution, as well as the privileges and a great part of the emoluments which it afterwards enjoyed. Meanwhile its buildings had been destroyed by fire during the usurpation of the See of Durham by William Cumyn after the death of Bishop Galfrid Rufus (the successor of Flambard), A.D. 1141. A short summary of certain events during that usurpation, so far as they affected the Church and Hospital of St. Giles, may here be in place. William de St. Barbara having at length been elected bishop, and consecrated at Winchester on the Sunday before St. John Baptist's day A.D. 1143, Roger de Conyers, who had been the leading opponent of the usurper from the first, and had already fortified his house at Bishopton, where he had been besieged by Cumyn without success, thought the time opportune, in concert with a few barons, for inviting the new bishop thither, and thence escorting him, with an armed retinue, to the city of Durham. He hoped, we are told, that Cumyn would by this time repent, or at any rate be deserted by his supporters. " But they were much deceived in their opinion. Not only did he not seek peace by repenting of his evil deeds, but he would not even endure the messengers of peace who were sent to him. Some he would not admit ; some he drove away ; others he vexed with threats and insults. Lastly, sending out the soldiers which he had with him, he attacked the adherents of the bishop who approached the walls. Consequently those who were with the bishop betook themselves to St. Giles, a church so called at a little distance from the walls, and there abode that night with the bishop"

(*Sym. Hist. Dunelm., Continuatio prima*). We read further in the *Historia Regum, continuata per Joh. Hagust.*, Vol. ii, p. 314, that "the bishop, having come with a great multitude to Durham, *endeavoured to surround the church of St. Giles with a rampart, so as to have that place for their defence*," and further, that "the monks who were shut up" (*i.e.*, in the Cathedral convent) "had prepared a secret access by which they had proposed to introduce the bishop with his adherents." Thus we see before us the two neighbouring eminences occupied as two hostile camps; that on which the Castle stands by William Cumyn, and that of St. Giles by Roger de Conyers with the bishop William of St. Barbara; while, close to the Castle, the monks, shut up in their convent, were scheming to get the true bishop clandestinely into his cathedral. But the usurper remained for the time triumphant. "Next morning, surrounded by a band of his satellites, he broke through the doors of the church (*i.e.*, of the cathedral, not of St. Giles, as Surtees seems to have supposed), and burst into it with armed men. And there were to be seen soldiers clad in mail with naked swords running to and fro among the altars; archers, some mingled among the weeping and praying monks, others standing over them and threatening them; and all the church filled with clamour and tumult. And indeed their hands hardly abstained from hurting the monks, one of whom they had nearly killed by a thrown stone. Nevertheless, leaving a guard of soldiers and archers in the church, they fortified it like a castle; and, as though dancing for joy at having done contumely to Divinity in a place of peace, the violators lighted fires, scenting the place with the smell of cooked flesh instead of the odour of incense; and for the voices of singers caused cries of guards and sounds of horns to be heard abroad. Meanwhile, sallying forth also frequently against the bishop's people, they did not suffer them to approach the walls " (*Sym. Continuatio*).

After this unsuccessful attempt to obtain entrance into Durham, Conyers, with the bishop, returned to Bishopton, relinquishing their temporary occupation of St. Giles; whereupon Cumyn is said to have ravaged the country and perpetrated atrocious cruelties. The contest went on, various places, including churches, being fortified and besieged by the opposing parties, and the whole diocese being in a state of civil war. It was in the earlier part of the year 1144 that the Hospital of Kepyer was burnt. On the approach at that time of Henry, Prince of Scotland and Earl of Northumberland, with the bishop St. Barbara to Durham, we read that " meanwhile the companions of William (*i.e.*, Cumyn) set fire to the hospital close by (*apud*) the church of St. Giles, and burnt the whole vill appertaining to it. They also committed to the flames the part of the burgh which belonged to the monks ; and the soldiers following on the track of the Earl consumed with fire what remained of the burgh " (*Sym.*, *ibid.*). It is evident from this account that the Hospital was then on the hill adjacent to the church, and not in its subsequent position on the bank of the river. It appears also that there was already a considerable number of inhabited tenements in the same locality, some of which belonged to the Convent of Durham, being the origin of the borough of St. Giles.

The eventual submission of William Cumyn and the entrance of William of St. Barbara into the See was on St. Luke's Day (October 18th), 1144. But nothing appears to have been done for the restoration of the destroyed hospital during his episcopacy. It was (as has been already said) to Hugo de Puteaco, commonly known as Hugh Pudsey, who succeeded St. Barbara in 1153, that its second foundation was due. He rebuilt the Hospital, removing it (perhaps for the sake of shelter and seclusion, as well as proximity to the river) to its subsequent lower position on the right bank of the Wear as it flows away to the east. The church he left on the hill, and probably added the chancel to Flambard's nave. The architectural features of the two parts of the church point to this conclusion.[1]

---

[1] An interesting association with Flambard's nave (the northern wall of which, with its original windows, happily escaped demolition when the church was restored not many years ago) is that of the noted hermit, St. Godric, who in early life, before retiring to his Finchale hermitage, spent some time at Durham, and, while there, used to frequent the then recently founded church of St. Giles for nocturnal devotion, and served there as *aedituus* and bell-ringer. " Ibi ecclesiam Sancti Aegidii, secus urbem

One peculiar feature observable in Pudsey's chancel is the large size of its side-door, which is on the north side. This may have been designed for the convenience of the brethren of the now separated Hospital when entering the church in procession from the north. Pudsey's ordinance for the reconstitution of the Hospital (which is given in Appendix A) provided, among other things, that there should be in it thirteen brethren (*conversi*), under the usual monastic vows, of whom six should be chaplains to officiate in the chapel and pray for the souls of Pudsey and Flambard ; the rest having special secular duties assigned them, to be fulfilled by them severally according to the discretion of the Master with the assent of the Prior and brethren. Provision is also made for an infirmary, for a common dormitory, and a common hall, in which all the brethren, not being sick, should have their common table, "unless the Master, for the accommodation of guests, or other honest cause, should at any time order otherwise." Also for an annual supply of decent clothing to all the brethren, with boots (*botis*) twice a year to the chaplains, and to the other *conversi*, who had more work to do, of foot-gear of a more serviceable kind (*socularibus cum coreis ligatis*) as often as might be required.

The endowments of the Hospital by the same Bishop Pudsey, with others in his own time or afterwards, till the destruction of the muniments in 1306, as shown by the Charters verified by Bishop Kellaw's Commission, may be summarized as below. They are here arranged in their conjectured chronological order, the Roman numerals showing the order in which they appear in the Patent Rolls of Richard II, and the Close Rolls of Bishop Nevill.

1. (I) Flambard's original Deed of Foundation.

2. (II) A Charter of Bishop Pudsey confirming all the donations of Flambard, adding a toft (for convenience, no doubt, of storing the corn) on all the demesne lands of the

positam, diutissime frequentavit ; et quantum literaturae novit libentissime devotus exercuit ; in qua nocturnas Domino vigilias celebrando, ipse ecclesiae minister et aedituus effectus est, et pulsandi ad horam divini officii ministerium adeptus est" (*Libellus de Vita et Miraculis S. Godrici, Heremitae de Finchale, Auctore Reginaldo Monacho Dunelmensi*, p. 59. Surtees Society's Publications).

See from which they already had tithes, and also granting free burgage in the street of St. Giles (*liberum burgagium in vico S. Egidii*), exempt from in-toll and out-toll, and from all aids and services, customs, vexations, and exactions, for ever. This was the origin of the Manor of St. Giles.

3. (III) Another Charter of the same granting to the Hospital the vill of Clifton,[1] a thrave of corn from every carucate in the demesne lands of the bishopric, with tithes of all his lands recently brought into cultivation (*de omnibus novalibus nostris*) ; and exempting the church of St. Giles for ever from " synodals and other customs which are wont to be exacted by the archdeacon or the dean or any of their officers."

4. (VII) Another Charter of the same, addressed to the Prior and Convent, confirms endowments of the Hospital in *Weardale*, comprising *Whiteleys* and *Swyneleys* (the boundaries being accurately defined) ; a mine of lead for covering the church of St. Mary and All Saints and also the Infirmary of the Hospital ; a mine of iron in *Rokehope* for making ploughs ; a toft designated as *De Laundene* ; the tithes of *Bradewode et Besunkedis usque ad Wycheles* ; the tithes of all *novalia* (*i.e.*, newly reclaimed lands) ; a thrave of corn from every *caruca* in *Werdale* ; and also pasture for all the cattle of the house, with the peculiar privilege—significant of the prevalent cruel custom, as well as of the wild state of the surrounding country—that the feet of the dogs were not to be maimed, but that the shepherds were to lead them bound for the protection of the flocks against wolves.

5. (XVI) A Composition was made, with the approval of Bishop Pudsey, dated 1197, between the Prior (Germanus) and Convent of Durham on the one part and Adam as Proctor for the Master and brethren of the Hospital on the other, whereby the latter were released from

---

[1] The Composition, which appears below [5. (XVI)], with regard to the tithes of Clifton payable to the church of St. Oswald, and to the sheaves of corn from the demesne land of Newton for which the same church had been liable, confirms the probability that Clifton and Newton were in the same locality, viz., on the opposite side of the river to Kepyer, in the old parish of St. Oswald.

all future claims on them for the tithes of Clifton (see III), formerly payable to the church of St. Oswald in Durham, on condition of their offering yearly on St. Oswald's Day at the altar of that church one bezant and two shillings, and also releasing to the church of St. Oswald the two sheaves from the demesne lands of Newton which had been included in their original endowment by Bishop Flambard.

[The two following benefactions, though not by Bishop Pudsey himself, appear to have been in his time, and supplementary to his.]

6. (XIII) Gilbert the Chamberlain (*Gilbertus camerarius*), who appears to have had land in his possession near the new site of the Hospital, granted the Master and brethren leave to make their mill-dam and mill-pool thereon. The language of his deed of gift shows him to have been contemporary with Pudsey, having been probably his own chamberlain. For he makes his grant " pro salute domini mei Hugonis Dunelm. episcopi, et pro salute animae Theobaldi fratris, et pro salute animae meae et uxoris meae Julianae Papedy, et haeredum meorum " (Referred to in Hutchinson's " History of Durham," ii, 301 *n.*). The same Gilbert, in a return made by the bishop to Henry II, in 1166, of the military service within his jurisdiction, with view to an aid for the marriage of the King's daughter, Maud, appears as follows :—" Gilebertus Camerarius [tenet] quintam partem 1 mil. & ex alia parte x partem unius " (*Lib. Niger Scaccarii*, p. 306).

7. (V) Gilbert Hansard, one of Bishop Pudsey's feudatories, gave his whole vill of Aymundeston (*Amerston, in the parish of Elwick*) and fifty oxgangs in Hurtheworth (*Hurworth*) for the support of a chaplain to celebrate for ever in the chapel of the Hospital for the souls of himself, his father and mother, and all his kin.

[This donation is what probably led eventually to the foundation of the Hospital of St. Mary Magdalen, with regard to which, and the negociations relating thereto, see below under " Magdalen Hospital," and documents in Appendix B.]

8. (XIX) " Stephanus Capellanus " gave to the Hospital all his land at *Southcrofte* in Gilligate.

[This donation, if not in the time of Pudsey, cannot have been later than the early part of the thirteenth century. For in a Composition between the Hospital and the Convent of Durham, apparently of that period, the Hospital is found to have been already in the possession of this *Southcrofte*. See Appendix B, I.]

Subsequent endowments, after the time of Pudsey, were as follows :—

9. (XV) Quenilda, wife of Richard de Lokes (or, properly, *cum lokes,* meaning " with the locks "), gave 12 acres of land in Medomsley, with common of pasture for 200 sheep, 40 cattle, and 40 swine. This gift may be assigned to the episcopate of Pudsey's successor, Philip de Pictavia (1195–1208) : for a deed of gift by the same Richard de Lokes, with the assent of Quenilda his wife and William his heir, of land in Medomsley to the Convent of Durham, is attested, among others, by " Americo archidiacono " ; and Aimerick de Talboys was a nephew of Bishop Philip de Pictavia, and appears as archdeacon in 1198 and 1214 (Hutchinson, ii, p. 280) ; *Cf.,* " Mickleton MSS.," No. 32, p. 44 :— " Americus [Homericus, Harmaricus] Archidiaconus Dunelm. et Carleol. tempore Bertrami [primi] Prioris. Vide in carta dicti Philippi Pictaviensis.—Fuit dictus Americus nepos ejusdem Philippi episcopi."

10. (VI) During the episcopate of Nicholas de Farnham (1241–1258) one Walter de Witton, Knight, granted to the Hospital all his land at Frosterley, to be held of the bishop on the accustomed service. Who this Walter de Witton was has not been discovered. The mention in his charter of " Nicholaus quondam episcopus Dunelmensis " as having confirmed it shows the donation to have been in De Farnham's time.

11. (VIII) Under the same bishop (described by the donor as " patris et domini mei"), John de Romesey, the bishop's seneschal, granted to the Hospital a rent of 65s., which Leoninus, son of William de Heriz, and William

de Leventhorp, had formerly paid to Walter de Monasteriis, together with the homage, services, ward, and relief, of half the vill of *Claxton*, to be held by the Hospital of Walter de Monasteriis by a yearly payment of 12*d*. The purpose of this donation was to aid in support of the poor resorting to the Hospital, and its condition was that at every mass said in the chapel thereof the Bishop de Farnham, and his predecessor, Richard Poor, should be commemorated. It thus appears that the family of Heriz, known as early possessors of Claxton, and who took its name, had succeeded an earlier family of De Monasteriis (or De Musters), and that Bishop Farnham's seneschal had acquired rights in half the vill, which he transferred to the Hospital.

12. (XIV) It might be about the same time that William de Heriz gave two oxgangs in his vill of *Claxton* to the Hospital. But there seems to be nothing to fix the date with certainty.

13. (IX) Also in the thirteenth century, Robert Corbeth and his daughter Sibilla, "for the love and brotherhood of the house," and on account of ten marks given by the Master, De Argentaneo, and the brethren, granted their whole vill of *Hunstanworth*, with all its liberties, which had been granted by a charter of Bishop Pudsey, to be held of the bishop for the twelfth part of a knight's service. The mention of De Argentaneo (or De Argentino) as Master of Kepyer intimates the approximate date. Hunstanworth is thus referred to in the Boldon Book :—" Robertus Corbette tenet *Hunstanworth* pro servicio suo in forest. sicut in carta sua continetur. . . . . Hospitale Sᵘ Egidii tenet ibi juxta divisam Walteri de Bolbec quandam assartam et pasturam ad nutrimenta pecorum et animalium ad opus pauperum quae Dominus Episcopus eis in elemosynam dedit."

The *assart* and *pasture* enjoyed there by the Hospital previously to Corbett's donation would be included in Pudsey's Charters. See above, 3 (III), and 4 (VII).

14. (X) The same Robert Corbeth further releases to the Hospital his claim to a parcel of land between Knock-

deneburn (*Newkton*) and the Derwent. By these last two
donations the possessions of the Hospital in the upper part
and to the North of Weardale became further extended.

15. (IV) Also in the thirteenth century, Ralph de
Epplyndone (Epplyngdon, Epplynden, &c. ; *hodie* Eppleton)
granted to the Hospital in fee farm a carucate of land in
Epplynden (whereof an oxgang contained fifteen acres),[1]
with the privilege of grinding at his mill next to himself
and his heirs, on the terms, "dabunt multuram ad
vicesimum vasculum" ; and, further, 20 acres in *Barnes*
and *Estwell*, 2 crofts specified, and common pasture for
240 sheep and 20 swine ; the reserved rent for all being 4*s.*

"Ralph, fil. Rogeri de Epplyngdene vixit tempore
Hen. III" (Surtees, I, p. 217 ; *Pedigree of Epplyngden*).
In the following century this possession was exchanged
for a perpetual rent-charge on the whole Eppleton estate.
For in a charter of Bishop Richard Kellaw, dated 24th
December, 1311, the Master (Hugo de Monte Alto) and
the brethren of Kepyer are allowed to grant to Robert de
Epplynden, the then lord, a messuage and two carucates
of land there, to be held by him and his heirs of the bishop
in capite, they paying to the Hospital for ever after an
annual rent of 113*s.* 4*d.* out of the said lands and the whole
manor of Epplynden, with power to the Master and
brethren to distrain (" Registrum Palatinum Dunelm.,"
Vol. ii, p. 1145).[2]

16. (XI) In the latter half of the thirteenth century
the Hospital also acquired possessions in the parishes of
Ryton and *Lanchester*, by the grant of Robert, Bishop of
Durham, who must have been either Robert de Stichill
(1260–1274) or Robert de Insula (1274–1283). He granted
to the Hospital his whole tenement of *Crawcrook* (parish of

---

[1] The oxgang, being as much land as an ox was supposed to be able to
plough in the year, varied in different localities according to the nature of
the ground.

[2] Surtees (" History of Durham," i, p. 217, under *Eppleton*) states
that Ralph of Eppleton's original deed of grant was, in his time, in the
possession of Francis Mascall, Esq., the rent-charge having been purchased
from the Tempests ; and that it bears the old seal of Kepyer Hospital, a
female figure supposed to represent the Blessed Virgin, whereas the later
seal of the house was St. Giles and his " goat." Surtees should have said
" his hind."

Ryton-on-Tyne), with mill and mill-service of the whole vill, the land which Adam de Ryton held, the millstream and fishery of the Tyne, &c., and also the whole vill of Yvestone (parish of *Lanchester*), which he had of the grant of James Latoun. The moiety of the vill of *Crawcrook*, comprised in this donation, was called after the Dissolution *Little Kepyer*.

17. (XVII) In the time also of Robert, Bishop of Durham (whether Stichill or De Insula), Henry Lyhtfot granted to the Hospital land at *Dernecrok*, with various privileges. Dernecrook is in the parish of Gateshead-on-Tyne.

The following charters are included, the dates of which the present Editor has not discovered :—

(XII). In *Elwick* Ralph de Amundevill granted a thrave of corn from every carucate in his vill of *Stotfold*.

(XVIII). The people of *Bedlingtonshire* commuted the thrave of corn due to the Hospital from every carucate of the bishop's demesne lands for 9*s*. a year, payable at Michaelmas, " for the support of the poor and strangers constantly resorting thither." The difficulty attending the carriage of the corn might be the reason of the commutation.

In addition to the benefactions above specified it appears from other evidence that (probably early in the thirteenth century) one Wido de Hotona (*Henry-Hutton*) had given lands to Kepyer Hospital, and that subsequently the Hospital had granted the same lands to the Priory of Finchale (see "Priory of Finchale," Surtees Society, 1837, p. 100). But this land having been parted with before the fire of 1306, the Charter referring to it is not among those afterwards verified.

Subsequent to the endowments and benefactions so far specified as having been verified by Bishop Kellaw's commission after the fire of 1306 we may notice the following :—

1. The same Bishop Kellaw, having in the first year of his episcopate (1311), probably for the convenience of the Hospital in its depressed state after the invasion of the

Scots, allowed (as above seen, p. xxiv) commutation of its possessions at Eppleton for a rent-charge on the estate, granted in his second year (1312) the tithes of all recently reclaimed lands (*novalium et novi assarti*) near *Gatesheved* (*Gateshead*), and *Brounsyde* in the parish of Auckland, until he should order otherwise concerning them ; which tithes had been held and received by his predecessor, Anthony Bek. The purpose of this subvention is alleged to be to relieve the depressed state of the Hospital, and enable it to continue and multiply its charitable works, and specially to provide two chaplains for daily divine service in addition to those already ministering (" Registrum Palatinum," Vol. ii, p. 1164).

2. Further, in his fifth year (1315), he assigned all such tithes of lands brought into cultivation since the eighteenth year of Bishop Bek and during his own episcopate in various places about Auckland and elsewhere, all definitely specified, to the foundation of " the Prebend of Kypier" in the Collegiate Church of Auckland, to be called the fourteenth Prebend, and to be appropriated in perpetuity to the Master of Kepyer for the time being, who was to have a stall in the choir, and all rights of a Prebendary. The conditions annexed were, that the Masters of Kepyer should provide one sub-deacon, with a stipend of 30s. a year, for the Collegiate Church of Auckland ; that there should be two additional chaplains maintained in Kepyer Hospital (making eight priests there always, inclusive of the Master) celebrating there for the bishop himself, his predecessors and successors ; that ten additional poor people should be relieved at the Hospital in the daily evening distributions ; that on the bishop's anniversary, which was always to be kept, thirteen poor should receive each, and be content with, one loaf of the weight of sixty *solidi*, pottage (*potagium*), drink, and three red herrings (*allecibus*, which *may* denote any kind of salted fish), each of the eight priests celebrating at that time on eight successive days for the donor's soul. In consideration of the burden thus laid on him beyond that of other prebendaries, the Master was to be exempt from attending synods, chapters, visitations, and the like ; but

he must always reside in the Hospital, unless at any time he should be in personal attendance on the bishop himself. For failure in the fulfilment of these conditions power was further reserved to the bishop for the time being to declare both Mastership and Prebend vacant, and to collate anew. (" Registrum Palatinum," ii, p. 1272).

At the same date, a mandate was issued to the Archdeacon, or his official, to induct Hugh de Monte Alto to the prebend personally or by his proctor, he having already been invested personally *per nostrum annulum* (*Ibid.*, p. 1277).

In the same year (2nd June, 1315) we find also a fresh and more formal assignment to the Master of the tithes of the *new assarts*[1] about Gateshead, this time with the assent specified of the Chapter of the Convent of Durham, and with the names of witnesses appended. The preamble to this Deed refers, as before, to the depressed state of the Hospital at the time, with especial mention of its spoliation and burning by the Scotch (*Ibid.*).

3. The same Bishop Kellaw granted licence to William Wilde to bestow in perpetuity on the Hospital a messuage and 42 acres of land at Plauseworth, to be held of the bishop in chief for the accustomed services (*Ibid.*, p. 1281).

4. Bishop Hatfield, in the same century (A.D. 1351), in consideration of the plague, known as the " Black Death," among the tenants of the Hospital, failure of crops, and murrain among cattle, granted an indulgence of 300 days to all who should contribute to its relief (See Appendix A, XIII).

5. In the same century the advowson of the living of Hunstanworth, where the Hospital already had possessions (see above, Charter IX), together with some other land there, was transferred from the Convent to the Hospital. As early as 1331 Bishop Beaumont had granted his

---

[1] In 1321 the tithes of the new assarts about Gateshead and of all the bishop's demesne lands there were commuted for a payment by the Rector of Gateshead to the Hospital of four marks at Pentecost and Martinmas. See Charter of Bishop Beaumont (*Durham Treasury, Reg.* ii, fo. 81).

licence for the transference in return for a rent-charge on the Hospital's manors at Caldecot and Clifton.   But it was not till 1352, under Bishop Hatfield, that the negotiation was concluded, the question of an adequate equivalent to the Convent for the grant having, as it seems, arisen meanwhile.   In 1335 Bishop Bury, who intervened between Beaumont and Hatfield, had granted licences, with this view, for the transference from the Hospital to the Convent of tithes at Pittington and Sherburn (See Appendix A, V, VI, VII, VIII, IX, XI).   It would seem that the bargain, however concluded, did not turn out altogether satisfactory to the Hospital.   For we find them obtaining leave from Bishop Hatfield to defer the appointment of a Rector to the living, there being no one found, as they alleged, to accept it, in view of its reduced revenues and the dilapidated state of its buildings (See Appendix A, X).

6.   Lastly, Bishop Nevill, in 1445, appropriated the Rectory of St. Nicholas in Durham, with its glebe at Old Durham, to the Hospital (See Appendix A, I).

Such, and so acquired, having been the possessions of the Hospital of Kepyer before the Dissolution, a brief notice only is called for here of their history after that event, a sufficient account being given in Surtees' "History of Durham," or elsewhere.   It may, then, be enough to note that on the 14th of January, 1545, they were surrendered by the last Master, William Frankleyn, to the Crown ; that Henry VIII thereupon granted them to Sir William Paget and Richard Cock ; that, having reverted to the Crown after the attainder and disgrace of Paget, they were granted by Edward VI (23rd May, 1552) to John Cockburne, Lord of Ormeston, a Scot, who sold them, after holding them seventeen years, to a Londoner, John Heath, Esq., Warder of the Fleet, from whom, through the marriage of Elizabeth, heiress of the Heaths, in 1642 to John Tempest, Esq., son of Sir Thomas Tempest, Attorney-General of Ireland, the lordship of the manor of St. Giles, with other possessions of the dissolved Hospital, has been inherited by the present Marquess of Londonderry.

Portions of the property had, however, been previously parted with by the Heath family, Kepyer itself having been sold to Ralph Cole, of Gateshead, in 1630, and the Tempests being consequently described as of Old Durham, not of Kepyer. With regard to Old Durham, it is to be observed that it was glebe of the Rectory of St. Nicholas in Durham, which Rectory, as has been already shown, was appropriated to the Hospital by Bishop Neville A.D. 1445. It was leased by Ralph Booth (Master of Kepyer) in 1479 to his relative Richard Booth and his descendants, on a lease of 99 years, and was consequently in the possession of the Booth family till 1578, when it would revert to the first John Heath as the then impropriator.

A list, with notices, of the successive Masters, or Wardens, of Kepyer will be found in Appendix D. They appear to have been usually men of mark, and to have been employed by the bishops in other honourable functions. The Hospital itself, being a well-endowed ecclesiastical corporation, was evidently regarded as an important foundation, the headship of which was a position of dignity.

MAGDALEN HOSPITAL.

A little to the north of the higher part of the street of St. Giles there still stands a chapel in ruins, which was formerly that of the Hospital of St. Mary Magdalen, and also a rectorial parish church, the land around it (about 23 acres) having constituted a separate parish. No distinct record of the origin of this Hospital and attached rectory has been found. Surtees ("History of Durham," Vol. iv, Part 2, p. 67) says vaguely that it "originated in some exchange of lands betwixt the Prior and the House of Kepyer; but the Master and brethren of St. Giles objected to any part of their estate being converted to a purpose not contemplated by their founder. The Prior therefore satisfied the scruple by building and endowing the Hospital of St. Mary Magdalen." Where he got this story he does not say. If he gathered it from the "Compositio inter Priorem et conventum et domum de

Kypyare," preserved in the Durham Treasury (See Appendix B, I), he must have read it very cursorily, though probably right in connecting that "Composition" with the origin of the Hospital. Its purport may be summarized as follows :—

The Hospital of Kepyer had lands at *Amerston* and *Hurworth*, which had been given by *Gilbert Hansard* for the support of a chaplain to celebrate for himself and his family (See Appendix A, I, Charter V). The Convent of Durham had property at *Chyrton* in Northumberland, which had been given by *John de Hameldun* for the support of three priests to celebrate for himself and his family on condition of his two brothers, Henry and Walter, being the *firmarii feodarii,* paying nine marks a year to the Convent. An exchange of these properties between the Hospital and the Convent had been proposed, but, after some contention, had fallen through, owing, apparently, to the Convent's unwillingness to maintain the three priests on the terms proposed in the exchange. Eventually, however, through the action of G. Hansard and Walter de Hameldun (the representatives of the two families whose souls were to be benefited), a composition was agreed to, one part of the conditions of which was that the Hospital should cede to the Convent certain land at Hurworth, together with twelve acres of " Southcroft " near the city of Durham, producing altogether an annual revenue of three marks, which were to be devoted by the said Convent to pious uses through the hands of its almoner in a certain place for the benefit of the souls of the said John de Hameldun and of all the departed. Now land and tenements at " Southcroft," described as being in Gilligate, had been given to Kepyer Hospital by " Stephanus Capellanus " (See Appendix A, I, Charter XIX), and, inasmuch as the " Composition " which has been summarized is headed " Hospitale S. Mariae Magd. juxta Kipyer," and as the Hospital of St. Mary Magdalen is known to have been ever under the almoner of the Convent, there can be little doubt either that " Southcroft " was the land surrounding it and held with other land for its benefit, or that to the "Composition" before us its origin is to be traced.

Other documents, also in the Durham Treasury, appear to refer to negotiations between the Convent and the Hospital on the same subject (See Appendix B, II, III, IV). Such transactions are interesting as showing how religious houses bartered with each other properties given them by benefactors for the repose of their souls, and were glad to transfer to each other the onus of providing masses for them.

Thus we may with probability assign the origin of Magdalen Hospital to John de Hameldun's donation to the Convent for procuring masses for himself and his family, and the date of its consequent foundation to about the middle of the thirteenth century.

There is, however, also in the Dean and Chapter Treasury a curious document (first published by the Rev. Francis Thompson in the "Transactions of the Durham and Northumberland Architectural Society, 1869-1875"), which may appear at first sight, though not really, to assert a different origin. It is in the form of a complaint (*Querela*), apparently *circa temp.* Edw. II (1307-1327), addressed to the Prior of Durham, of alleged wrong done to the Hospital of St. Mary Magdalen by an almoner of the Convent, and in its preamble it is alleged as certain that a knight, by name *John le Fitz Alisaundre*, had founded and endowed the Hospital for a chaplain and thirteen brothers and sisters of the same, who were to be needy persons of good character who had seen better days; and that his endowment consisted of lands lying near the Hospital and before the gate at Schirburn, and that for the sustenance for the chaplain and brethren he assigned to the Almonry of the Convent the vill of Rylley and the mill, &c., of the vill of Chilton. Now this document, being endorsed as "not containing truth for the most part," cannot, of course, be trusted as in all respects correct; but it seems at any rate possible that the "Sir John le Fitz Alisaundre" to whom the foundation is attributed

was the same as " John de Hameldun," who, according to
the " Composition," had given property at *Chyrton* to the
Convent, *Chyrton* and *Chilton* being supposed to denote
the same place. If so, the account given in the
Querela is not inconsistent with the inference from the
" Composition," since, according to the latter, it was the
donation of this John that originated the negotiations
which resulted in the foundation of the Hospital, and
it was for his soul especially that masses were to be
said there. (See Appendix B, V, for a copy and
translation of the *Querela*). The Hospital was further
enriched by benefactions of individuals (referred
to by Surtees, IV, ii, p. 67), including tenements in
Maudlingate; and, in 1391, Bishop Walter Skirlaw
granted an indulgence in its favour (See Appendix B,
VI). In 1449 the church, being in a ruinous condition
because of the watery ground (*terra aquosa*) on which it had
been built, was removed to a site further west under a
licence from Bishop Robert Neville to the Prior and
Convent. He granted also an indulgence of forty days to
all contributors to the new chapel, the ruins of which
remain. It was consecrated by a bishop, described as
Episcopus Holen., under a licence from Bishop Nevill
dated 6th May, 1451 (Appendix B, VII, VIII).

A rent of 3*s*. a year from a house in Crossgate was
given to the Hospital by a Vicar of Billingham (Appendix
B, IX).

Other benefactions, with a further account of the
property and position of the Hospital, are found in the
Hunter MSS., No. 37 (Appendix B, X).

In the "Transactions of the Durham and Northumberland Architectural Society, 1869-1875," above referred to,
will be found interesting references to entries in the
Almoner's Rolls, preserved in the Durham Treasury, about
the building and furnishing of the new chapel, and previous
repairs of the old one, as well as notes about the present
remains of the ancient buildings.

After the Dissolution the Hospital shared the fate of
other similar foundations; but its revenues, being vested

in the Almoner of the Convent, passed to the new Dean and Chapter, who continued to pay a stipend to the clerk officiating in the Parish Church of St. Mary Magdalen, till, some time after the Restoration, the Church having been allowed to fall into ruin, its services were discontinued, and the stipend of £4 annexed to the office of Librarian. It appears that before the Dissolution this Church had been served (wholly or in part) by the master of the school for poor boys who were maintained by the Convent and taught in the Infirmary outside the gates. Among the duties of their teacher was that of saying mass twice a week in the Chapel of St. Mary Magdalen near Kepyer, and once a week at Kimblesworth (Appendix B, X).

THE PARISH CHURCH AND LIVING.

As has been seen above, the Church founded by Bishop Flambard appears to have been intended originally as the Chapel of Kepyer Hospital ; but it came to serve the purpose of a Parish Church also as the population grew up around it. The Brethren of the Hospital, being an ecclesiastical corporation, would have the cure of souls, serving the Church in person, perhaps usually through one of their Chaplains appointed for the purpose. For from the Manor Court books (which commence in 1490) we find that in 1501 Thomas White appeared at an extraordinary visitation of the Archbishop of York as Parochial Chaplain of the Church of St. Giles. After the Dissolution, there having been apparently no separate endowment of a Vicarage, the lay impropriator would be responsible for providing a minister ; but how he did so there seems to be no distinct evidence to show. It may be observed that for some time we find the ministers of the parish designated as Curates or Chaplains only. So, in the Registers of Baptisms and Burials from which extracts are given in this volume, William Murray in 1591, 1592, and 1594, and Sir John Watson in 1604 and 1621, are called Curates ; and in the Register of Marriages, A.D. 1630, the latter is described as "*hujus ecclesiae capellanus.*" But in 1650, for the first time, as far as is known, we find a *Vicarage* spoken of, viz., in the "Book of Rates for the Co. Pal. of Durham."[1] Further, there is distinct evidence that in 1655 the Incumbents were entitled to tithes from certain lands in the parish. See " A note of lands paying tithe to the Church of St. Giles," preserved in the Parish Register and printed in this volume, p. 152. Then in 1704 William Done, though describing himself in the Registers as " Curate," signs the Church-wardens' Accounts as " Vicar " : and subsequently the Incumbents, though designated only as Perpetual Curates, have claimed without dispute tithes of corn, hay, green crops, &c., from certain lands or tenements in the parish. It is observable that William Cam, who was Incumbent next before the above-named Done and died A.D. 1682 (see Register of Burials), signs himself and is designated in the Register as *Rector*. This, however, is the only instance. How the right to tithes originated, and why the incumbents came to be thus variously designated, is a question that invites enquiry. Certain tithes may have been assigned to the living by one of the lay impropriators. In 1665 an Act of Parliament was passed enabling owners of impropriations to reunite tithes or portions of tithes to a parsonage or vicarage without licence of Mortmain ; and though this Act was subsequent to the dates above given, its intention may have been to legalize what had already been commonly done.

It may be observed lastly, in connexion with the subject, that in the Registers (Vol. III, p. 154) we find the following entry :—" A true Register of all the Orchards or yards that pay a modus to yᵉ Rector or his Curate at Easter . . . as they have been paid time out of mind in lieu of the tyth of hay herbs or fruit growing in yᵉ same . . . And received Anno 1693 per Wm. Done, Curate." Here the customary payments in lieu of small tithes are said to have been time out of mind due, not to the Curate,

---

[1] " The Book of Rates for Co. Pal. of Durham, as it was settled about the year 1650—Alsoe with some Augmentations & Ecclesiastical Revenues added since and with divers others—A.D. 1693." contains the following entry :—" St. Giles' Parish. The Vicarage—Augmentacion £0 2s. 0d."

Further, a valuation of lands in Durham for a subsidy to King Charles II in 1670 contains—" The Vicarage of St. Giles, £2 0s. 0d."
(*The Late Rev. F. Thompson's papers*).

but to the Rector *or* his Curate. This may be taken to imply that they had been originally due to the Impropriator of the Living, though perhaps usually allowed by him to be received by the clerks whom he deputed to serve the cure. At first after the dissolution of the Hospital, as will appear below, the curates appear to have been only unlicensed stipendiaries of the impropriator, who may have chosen in this way to provide them with a pittance, to which, by prescription, or legal sanction, they eventually acquired a claim; and, when this came to be so, they would suitably be called Vicars. Further, it may have been because of the endowment having been originally rectorial that Cam assumed the title of Rector.

A claim to other endowments was set up by the Rev. Francis Thompson, the Incumbent, when in the year 1851 a suit was instituted against the churchwardens with respect to certain property in the parish known as "the Church Estate." Mr. Thompson contended as follows :—

Though there appeared to have been no original endowment of a Vicarage, there had been from time immemorial a Guild, endowed with certain burgages or tenements in the parish, for the maintenance of a priest in the Church of St. Giles. In the Survey of Colleges and Chantries under Henry VIII in 1546 it is described as a Guild in the parish church of St. Giles, reported to have been founded to find a priest for ever for the maintenance of God's service in the said church; and in the "Valor Ecclesiasticus" of Henry VIII its possessions are defined as consisting of the site of the chamber of Richard Middleton the Incumbent, the chamber there, and 24 burgages in the street of St. Giles. Now there are still in the parish certain burgages or tenements, constituting what is called *the Gilligate Church Estate*, the rents and profits of which had till 1851 been for long received and applied to various parochial purposes by the churchwardens. In that year a Chancery suit ("The Attorney General *v*. Salkeld") was instituted against the churchwardens (of whom Salkeld was one) for maladministration of this estate. It was alleged that the Churchwardens had been accustomed to let the burgages or tenements on leases of 21 years corruptly and unprofitably, and in recent times had been content with a " Beefsteak Supper" given them by lessees in lieu of adequate fines for renewal. In the course of the proceedings Mr. Thompson laid claim to the profits of this estate for the living on the ground of it having originally belonged to the ancient guild. His supposition was, that after the dissolution of Kepyer in 1545 Richard Middleton, the incumbent of the Guild, had served the Church in the absence of any Vicar,[1] and that after his death the tenements in question, having belonged to the Guild, had been retained in trust by its four proctors, and from them passed to the Churchwardens, for its essential original purpose of " the maintenance of God's service in the Church of St. Giles," the impropriator being only too glad thus to save his own pocket.[2] It was further contended that, though Guilds and Chantries had by 1 Edw. VI, c. 14, A.D. 1547, been dissolved and their property given to the King, and though lands and tenements which had belonged to this ancient guild were shown by the *Ministers' Accounts* of the 3rd and 4th years of Edward to have passed into the hands of the Crown, and though some of them, so described, had been demised by the Crown under Elizabeth, yet that copyhold lands, which some of these were, had been especially excepted in the Act of Edward VI, and power had been given to endow therewith Vicarages in Churches where there were Chantries. There was, indeed, no evidence forthcoming of this having been done, or of the claimant's other suppositions as above-said ; but probability was alleged, and it was contended that, in the absence of any other known origin of the " Church Estate," the Church had, at any rate, an equitable claim. The circumstance of the lands having been held by the Churchwardens, and not by the minister of the parish, was accounted for by the allegation that Mr. Heath, having succeeded to the full rights of the Hospital, claimed to

---

[1] This supposition is confirmed by the fact that the plate, etc., of the Church, as well as of the Guild, was at first left in the charge of Richard Middleton, to be accounted for by him to the Crown. See Appendix C, p. 249.

[2] These suppositions receive confirmation from the fact that in the " Clavis Ecclesiastica " of Bishop Barnes (1575-77) the Guild, with revenue derived therefrom, is mentioned as still existing (" St. Giles Gilde in St. Giles Churche, vii*l.* iiij*s.* ij*d.*").

serve the Church by a stipendiary Curate removable at pleasure, and hence that there was no Incumbent in whom the property could be vested; that the Churchwardens were, in fact, sequestrators for the living.[1]

The Court, however, held that, in the absence of any proved identification of the property of the Church Estate with that of the ancient Guild, the claim could not be sustained, except with regard to one tenement, described as "Legge's Lease," which is at present occupied as "The Woodman" Inn. This alone, in the scheme sanctioned by the Court, was assigned to "the maintenance of God's service," its net income (estimated at the time as £20, but now, according to the accounts published in January, 1895, amounting to £50) being allowed to go towards the payment of assistant curates in the parish of St. Giles and in the then newly-formed district (now the parish) of Belmont.

The Editor of this Volume desires to express gratefully his obligation to the Rev. Canon Greenwell, Librarian of the Dean and Chapter of Durham, for important aid given him in the search for and transcription of ancient documents in the Durham Treasury; to the Rev. P. A. M. Sullivan, Vicar of St. Giles, for access to his parish books, together with much interesting information; and, last but not least, to the Rev. J. T. Fowler, Vice-Principal of Bishop Hatfield's Hall and Librarian of the University of Durham, for valuable assistance in the deciphering of MSS., interpretation of words and phrases, revision of proofs, and the preparation of the Index. Thanks are also due to Mrs. Thompson, of Warkworth, for her kindness in placing at the disposal of the Editor the valuable papers left in manuscript by the Rev. Francis Thompson, formerly Incumbent of St. Giles.

---

[1] This view is confirmed by the fact that in the "Clavis Ecclesiastica" of Bishop Barnes (1575-77) St. Giles is among "the Churches and Chappells having none Incumbents, but served by stipendiarye Preestes" (See Surtees Society's Publications, vol. xxii, pp. 5, 6); and that at the visitation held at Durham by Robert Swift, the Chancellor, in 1577, the curate of St. Giles who appeared was unlicensed;—"Robertus Prentize, curatus ibidem. Personaliter. No licence" (*Ibid.*, p. 46).

CORRIGENDA.

p. xi, note 1, l. 4, *read* " Cokborne."   " Armstrong " is printed
" Ormstrang " in Wharton's *Anglia Sacra*, pt. i, p. 783, and
" Ormstrong " in Mick. MS. 32, fo. 727, but the O has been
altered from A.

p. xi, note 2, for " note 4 " *read* " note 5."

p. xx, l. 22, *read* " De la Laundeue."

1, l. 13, for " note 2 " *read* " note 1."

7, note 1, l. 3, *read* " Lexicon."

55, note 2, l. 4, *read* " Thopas ": l. 11, *read* " Spenser's."

75, note 1, l. 1, *read* " Basire."

108, l. 4, " Ann " seems to be meant for " Anthony."

111, the notes should be numbered 1, 2, 3.

123, l. 30, *read* PA'ISHE.

146, note 2 wants the number.

180, l. 10, *read* " granam."

199, l. 3, *read* " Laundeue."

202, l. 18, *read* " Iuestan."

204, l. 18, " bladi di Cliftone " *read* " de."   *Ly* for *le* is common
in the writings of the school-authors.

226, l. 8, *read* " Thomas."

254, notes, l. 2, for " Tho. Grimston " *read* " W. de Wickwaine."

PARISH OF ST. GILES,
DURHAM.

PREFACE TO GRASSMEN'S ACCOUNTS.

THE office of Grassmen, whatever be the derivation of the name—whether from *grass*, or, as the better opinion seems to be, from *gersuma* (see p. 9)—was to take charge of the common lands of parishes. In the parish of St. Giles they were two in number, elected annually in Vestry on the Sunday after Ascension Day. They continued to be so appointed, certainly till 1790, to which year the two extant books of their accounts extend, and probably till the enclosure of the moor in 1817. The funds for which they were accountable arose mainly from "stents" (*i.e.*, rights of pasturage) on the moor, as well as in certain "townfields," which were subject to intercommon during the winter months (see p. 40, note 2). They also derived income from rents of certain common lanes which were available for pasturage, from "cavells," or allotments on the moor, from "tenter-rents" (paid for the privilege of bleaching on the common land), and, till the lord of the manor interfered, from the sale of whins. From time to time, also, they were empowered by parish meetings to exact "cesses" for various specific purposes (see pp. 11, 22, 25, &c.). Their expenditure was primarily for maintenance of the moor, its fences, gates, water supply, and the like, including prosecutions for trespass and law-suits respecting rights of commonage, and other expenses connected therewith. They met also out of their funds governmental requirements, as for bridges in the County, the house of correction, apprehension and conveyance of prisoners, maintenance of the parish armour, supply of soldiers for military musters, and provisions for the king's service. In the earlier years of their accounts we find, to a small extent, provision for the poor included, and in one year (1586) a contribution for casting a church bell.

The system of stinting (or stenting) on the common land appears to have been as follows. The right was confined to inhabitants of Gilligate after an initiatory payment. In the earlier years of the accounts the scale of payments seems to have varied ; but in 1701 the following rules were sanctioned for permanent observance:—

(1) All existing "stinters" were to be thenceforth "free of the common."

(2) Other inhabitants, or strangers coming to reside in the "Street," might acquire six "gates" (*i.e.*, free pasture for six animals) on payment of £6, *i.e.* £1 per "gate," except as below specified.

(3) Such as had served their apprenticeship in the "Street," or were qualified by "birthright," were to be entitled to the same privilege on payment only of 12*s.*, *i.e.* 2*s.* per "gate."

(4) Strangers coming into possession of a house in the "Street," whether by purchase or inheritance, and residing therein, were to pay £3, *i.e.* 10*s.* per "gate."

The qualification by "birthright" is shown by subsequent entries of payments to have included children and sons-in-law of existing "stinters" : but an eldest son and heir succeeded to his father's full right for an acknowledgement of 1*s.* only.

Prominent among the expenses in these accounts are those attending "Bounder Day," *i.e.*, the day of the annual perambulation of the boundaries, which took place in this parish always on Ascension Day, and that day only, the new Grassmen, as has been said above, being appointed on the following Sunday. A few words may be in place here for the purpose of drawing attention to the mode of its observance. Though, as is well known, the old Rogation processions were continued after the Reformation for the double purpose of giving thanks to God for the fruits of the earth and of defining boundaries, directions being given for their due religious observance in the Injunctions and in the Advertisements of Queen Elizabeth (see Sparrow's Collection, pp. 73, 125), and four of the authorized Homilies having been composed for delivery on these occasions, and though there is abundant evidence of the general continuance of the observance,[1] yet there is no allusion to it in these books till 1635, *i.e.*, the 10th year of Charles I,

---

[1] Among such evidences we may note as peculiarly interesting the account given by Walton, in his "Life of Hooker," of the careful observance by that great divine of "the customary time of procession" ("Life of Hooker," p. 184), and the strong commendation of it in Herbert's "Country Parson" (chap. 35). See also "Brand's Popular Antiquities," and especially on pages 202, 206 (Ed. 1873).

when we find, "The 23rd of May, Mr. Smeth and the Churchwardans with others of the parishe in Charges spent that day in goinge about the bounders, 4s. 8d." It does not indeed follow from the previous silence that the usage, prevalent elsewhere, had been neglected in this parish. It may have only been that cost attending it had not been included in the Grassmen's accounts. But still the form of the entry, as if the thing required some explanation, unlike subsequent entries in which "Bounder Day" is spoken of as a matter of course, may seem to suggest something then unusual. If so, "Mr. Smeth," who was evidently the leader of the ceremonial, was a likely man to have revived an ancient custom. For he was the same Elias Smith, incumbent from 1632 to 1665 and head-master of the Grammar School, who was noted for having preserved the books and vestments of the Cathedral in the troublous times of the Commonwealth (*Cf.* p. 62, note 2). He was thus likely to have had a love for old Church usages. After 1635, except during the period of Puritan ascendancy, "Bounder Day" evidently became a regular annual festival, with increasing festivities and increasing expenditure. What religious rites accompanied it, in Mr. Smith's time or afterwards, our books do not show. But the very prominence of "Mr. Smeth" on the first recorded occasion, with the continual mention afterwards of the "parson and clerk," lead us to conclude that there were some. Further, I am informed by Mr. Robert Allison, the present "Grieve" of the manor (who occupies an antiquated house in Gilligate attached to his office, and whose main duty now seems to be that of conducting the now septennial perambulations), that his father, who had been "Grieve" before him, had told him that "Parson Blackett" (a former incumbent) used to read prayers during the procession on "Whinny-hill"—a mound covered with whins between the Rainton and Sherburn roads not far distant from their divergence at the head of the "Street." This was no doubt a remnant of ancient usage.[1]

------

[1] In the "Injunctions of Queen Elizabeth" (1559) it is ordered that the curate, at convenient places during the processions, should exhort the people to thankfulness, saying Psalm ciii (*Benedic, anima mea*), with such sentences as "Cursed be he which translateth the bounds or dolles of his neighbour," or such other order of prayers as should be lawfully appointed. In the "Advertisements" (1564), it is further enjoined that "in the Rogation days of Procession they shall sing or say in English the two psalms beginning *Benedic, anima mea*, with the Letany and Suffrages thereunto, with one Homily of Thanksgiving to God." In Vol. lxiv of the Surtees Society's Publications (*Appendix*) will be found a very interesting

The following particulars of the observance after 1635, as shown by these Grassmen's books, may here be noted. In 1636, 1637, 1638, 1639, it is briefly noticed thus :—" For going about our bounders," the expenses being moderate, never amounting to more than 5*s.* After this there is no allusion to it till the year of the Restoration, 1660. The breaking out of civil war (of which these accounts show abundant signs) would in the first place account for the interruption, and then the prohibition of all such superstitious vanities under the Commonwealth. It should be observed, however, that for 1640, between 1643 and 1647, and again between 1649 and 1659, no accounts remain. Certainly at once on the return of the merry monarch the observance was revived, and went on year after year with increasing festivity and increasing expenditure. After a time the cost seems to have been complained of ; for in 1705 we find an order of Vestry limiting it in future to 16*s.* ; but, as the succeeding accounts show, without any permanent effect. As time went on, we observe as follows. The perambulation, except for the common herd, was on horseback, the parson, and often the clerk too, being mounted at the cost of the parish. Children, both " lads " and " lasses," always accompanied the procession, and were regaled on the route with bread, cheese, and ale.[1]

description of the Rogation Procession with solemn religious rites, which was retained at Ripon till about 1830. In it the vested choir, leaving and returning to the Minster during Matins, perambulated the town, chanting certain prescribed psalms and ending with the Litany, halts being made at three places, where the Gospel for the day was read. Such Gospel reading formed part of the pre-Reformation rite at crosses or trees, the latter being hence called " Gospel trees " or " Gospel oaks." *Cf.* Brand (p. 199, in Ed. 1873) for notice of such " Gospel trees " at Wolverhampton, where " processioning " with religious rites, as at Ripon, is said to have continued till 1796. My abovesaid informant, Mr. Robert Allison, the present " Grieve," speaks of an old oak on the lane to Pittington from the village of Broomside having marked a boundary in the Gilligate perambulation. This may possibly have been a " Gospel Oak." It will be seen in the account given below of the perambulation in 1895 that " the Oak " in this lane is spoken of as still marking the place where a halt was made, beer was broached, and sports were held. Elsewhere in the County of Durham the custom of perambulation is still continued ; notably so at Blanchland, where it is still, or certainly was very lately, conducted with much parade, lasting for two days, though not apparently at the proper Rogation season. But neither there nor elsewhere does there seem to be any retention of religious observances, though at Blanchland certainly (according to a graphic description, written by the parish clerk of the time, of the ceremonial in 1853) there has been no lack of potations and revelry. The original religious meaning of Rogation Processions has been lost sight of in our enlightened age, but by no means any old custom of eating and drinking.

[1] To the credit of the humanity of the good people of St. Giles there is no allusion in these books to the alleged ancient custom of whipping boys at certain places in order to impress on them a lasting remembrance of the

" Musicioners," a drummer and a fiddler being especially
mentioned, were always in attendance, being rewarded
both by "drinks" and payments. "Drinks" generally
were frequent during the procession, which terminated with
a dinner for a large number of persons at the cost of the
parish, "the parson's dinner," or the "parson's club," and
often the clerk's too, being in most years separately
mentioned. "Prunes," or "raisins," are occasionally
mentioned as provided, and in 1706, for the first time,
"tobacco." The first mention of a horse race is in 1688,
a saddle, or saddle and spurs, being for several years
provided to be run for ; and in 1720 and 1721 plates brought
from Newcastle are subscribed for. There were also races
for the boys, with a hat, or hat and ribbon, for the prize.   In
1698, and regularly afterwards, a "lass" with a "garling"
(*i.e.*, garland) appears on the scene.   In some years there
are two, 1*s*. being always paid to each "lass with y^{e}
garling." There were also competitions in dancing among
the girls, the prize being a pair of gloves.   See A.D. 1708 :
" For a pare of glufes to dans for, 1*s*.," and " Given to the
gerell that danst for the glufes and lost her part, 6*d*."
We may thus form for ourselves the picture of a pleasant
annual gala-day, in which all the parishioners took part,
on a flowery and breezy moor still in its primitive freshness,
with rites befitting the merry month of May, in which
Ascension Day most usually falls.   And if, as might well
be the case, the frequent and copious potations spoken of
led to some excess, this, too, it may be feared, was
characteristic of the manners of the age, and cannot be said
to be entirely obsolete.   See subjoined account of proceedings in 1895.   The custom of riding the boundaries is
still continued, but now only occasionally, usually once in
seven years, followed by a dinner, which is now provided,
not by the parishioners, but by the lord of the manor, his
manorial court being held on the same day.   The most recent
court and perambulation were on Ascension Day, 1895.
The following description of the latter, supplied by one
responsibly concerned in it, may be of interest, and worth
preserving :—

" The following is the route traversed in a perambulation of the Boundaries of the Manor on a Court Day,

boundaries, in evidence of which custom Brand cites an entry from the
old Churchwardens' books at Chelsea, " Given to the boys that were whipt,
4*s*." The presence, however, of children, usual at perambulations generally,
may be supposed to have had the purpose of keeping up a memory of the
boundaries in each rising generation.

the Steward, jury and posse comitatus keeping to the main road, whilst the Grieve and Constables traverse the actual Boundary when over cultivated or enclosed land :— viz., from the Britannia Inn to the corner of the Duck Pond; thence to the Sherburn Road at Giles Bridge; thence over the Old Durham estate, in a south-westerly direction, to a point on the old Wagon Way, about 300 yards west of Sherburn Road ; and thence to West Sherburn ; thence to Sherburn Grange, and thence to a point in Renny's Lane east of East House, and then back along Renny's Lane to Gilesgate Moor Cottage ; thence in a northerly direction to the Durham and Sunderland highway at a point a little east of the site of the old Toll Bar ; thence along the Durham and Sunderland Road, past Carrville to the trough beyond Belmont ; then back by the Durham and Sunderland Road to Belmont Hall, where a penny acknowledgement is paid for not going through from Belmont Hall to the Oak Tree in Pittington Lane ; thence back along the Durham and Sunderland highway to the Grange Inn in Carrville, and thence by the cross road to Pittington Lane ; and so to the Oak Tree in Pittington Lane. Here it is customary to tap the barrel of ale and partake of the refreshments supplied for the jury and friends, the posse comitatus being subsequently regaled, and spice distributed to the children, and prizes given for foot races ; after which the perambulation is resumed back to the Britannia Inn, and thence to a doorway of a house below the Britannia Inn, where 1*d*. is paid as an acknowledgement for not traversing the boundary through the premises; thence to a lane near the chain leading down to Ellis Leazes, and a stone is knocked off the wall at the foot of this lane, thus maintaining the right to traverse the boundary to the river, through the field past the Mayor's Well ; then back to Tinkler's Lane, and down Tinkler's Lane to the river, and along the river to Pelaw Leazes Lane, and thence past the Training School to Gilesgate, and then back to the Britannia Inn."

The following further details of the proceedings in 1895 have been furnished by the present Vicar, the Rev. Ponsonby A. M. Sullivan, and are, with his permission, here inserted, inasmuch as it is always desirable to preserve contemporary records of interesting old observances which might otherwise fade from memory :—

"I attended the Capital Court of the Lord of the Manor and Borough of Gilligate, Lord Londonderry. I heard the Jury solemnly sworn in ; also the " affearers,"[1] who had to amerce the fines, and the special constables. Mr. H. D. Wright, steward of the lord, presided. This was in a large upper room of the Britannia Inn. The Churchwardens were then called upon to produce the Church-plate, according to ancient custom. It was not, however, produced : we gave our testimony to its existence. We then paid through our churchwardens certain out-rents for messuages and land belonging to the Church. It being Church property, we were charged, for one year, 3s., instead of 21s. for seven years. After this the paying of out-rents by copyholders and others went on for nearly two hours. At 1.30 the procession started. First, two or three men, who had to walk the actual boundaries over hedge and ditch. Then the Steward's carriage and pair, containing himself and his clerk, myself, and Mr. Ralph Salkeld, while on the box by the driver sat *the Grieve*, old Allison, with his beard trimmed, and a grand new suit of clothes, but his old stick, with which he very emphatically laid down the law, pointing out to the walkers the course they should take. After this carriage came a large brake in which sat the Jury ; then various conveyances, and a number of men on horseback, and a very large and boisterous crowd of pedestrians. First of all we drove round the site of the extinct duck-pond ; then along the Sherburn road, stopping from time to time to watch the walkers, or to refer to the Steward's map for boundary points. Then it was discovered that it was not exactly the bounds of the parish, but of the manor, that were being perambulated. We drove along, pennies being thrown out at intervals for the boys, as far as the turn down to Sherburn House ; then back to Dragon Villa, and then down the " Green Lane " to Ravensflats. Here the Jury had to view two gates on the left, or north, side, thrown out illegally by Farmer Parnaby on to the Lord of the Manor's waste land, *i.e.*, the Green Lane. They were adjudicated illegal, I believe. Here the Jury ordered the beer cask to be tapped, and had begun to drink, but the Steward stopped this premature carouse.[2]

---

[1] " *Afferare.*—Multam taxare, temperare : hinc *afferatores*, apud Anglos, qui in curia nuncupata Leta multas recognoscunt et moderantur." D'Arnis' Lexion.

[2] If, however, the Steward had studied the Grassmen's books, he would have known that refreshment at this point had been usual in ancient times. *Cf.*, A.D. 1683, " For drinke in Pittington loninge from Ravensflat

We turned back, and on our way one of the horsemen charged with great violence into our carriage, and did some slight damage. Many of the horsemen were very wild and rowdy—some decidedly drunk. When we reached the Sunderland Road, I left the party and walked home. They went on to Belmont, where the beer was broached—by authority this time—and sports were held, chiefly races of various kinds.[1] The Steward told me that there had not been so large and excited a crowd in his memory. When they returned, I once more joined the Steward and a few on foot in the lower part of Gilligate, going with them down Bakehouse lane, and seeing the stone knocked off the wall to mark the right down to the Mayor's Well ; then down Tinkler's lane, up Leazes lane from the river, and so home."

Other matters of interest in these accounts, including historical allusions, will be pointed out in the notes. It may be observed here, with regard to the occupations of the parishioners, that the frequent occurrence of the designations "tanner" and "roper," shows that the industries thus denoted, which exist still, were of old standing in Gilligate, while changed circumstances have caused the "glovers" and "weavers," of whom there is frequent mention, to disappear. Among the latter the "challan-weavers," *i.e.*, shalloon-weavers, are prominent, shalloon being a kind of woollen stuff.

---

one the bounder day, 8*d*." "Pittington loninge" in this entry, and in the Grassmen's books generally, seems to denote what is now called the "Green Lane," or "Renny's Lane," leading direct from Gilligate to Pittington, and not that between Broomside and Pittington, as in the account given above of the perambulation in 1895.

[1] See above (page 6) for the place, viz., at "the Oak in Pittington Lane," which, as has been pointed out, was probably in olden times a "Gospel Oak." An oak, possibly about 150 years old, still marks the spot, being on the left side of the lane leading from the Village of Broomside to Old Pittington, outside the hedge of the plantation belonging to Belmont Hall, and 437 paces from the middle of the road bridge which crosses the railway at the end of Broomside Village. In an Ordnance Plan of 1857 the tree on this spot is distinctly marked exactly at the place where the present boundary between the parishes of Pittington and Belmont crosses the road. There is a tradition also of another Boundary Oak formerly existing on the Sunderland Road, some way beyond the "trough beyond Belmont Hall." This trough, in the account of the recent perambulation, given above on page 6, is said to be now the boundary in that direction.

PARISH OF ST. GILES,

DURHAM.

GRASSMEN'S ACCOUNTS.—VOL. I.

Expenses for this present yere 1579 beeing gyrsmen[1] John taylor & Robert Hudspethe.

Item paid to John burdes for dusson of haye. Item payde to Edward Symson wyfe for halfe a dussen stone of haye to the bull[2] xiid. Item payde to Rycharde gylson for syxe dayes vd. a day at the more dyeke for layinge up earthe to ye whicke[3] ijs. vid. Item payde to Rycharde Robinson for suche lyke ijs. iijd. Item payde to Rycharde Robinson for thornynge the wicke for saufegayrde of the shepe for seven dayes vd. a daye ijs. xjd. Item payd to Rycharde gylson eight dayes for suche lyke iijs. iiijd. Item payde to Roger Dyckenson for his mayre for cayriing a prisoner to Auckeland viijd. Item payde to Robert Smythe of petinton for up houlding of the yate in Petinton layne[4] vjd. Item payde to Rycharde Robinson one day for maykyn clene the punfolde and one daye for cuttinge of whins and two dayes for castinge of the grypp aboute the pynfoalde and whicke to the sayme[5] ijs. vid. Item payde

---

[1] So till 1590, when "grasmen" first occurs. Afterwards always "grasmen," or "grassmen." The original spelling supports the view of the connexion of the word with *gersuma*. See Surtees Society's Publications, vol. lxiv, p. 383.

[2] Continual mention will be found afterwards of the Parish Bull, kept for the use of the parish, being pastured on the Moor in Summer and housed in Winter. In 1605 a "Bull-house" was built for him, "house-room for the bull" having been previously paid for.

[3] The dike surrounding the Moor may have been planted for the first time this year with a quickset hedge, the young plants being (as appears below) protected by thorns. The "upholding" of this fence will be found to have required continual attention.

[4] Pittington Lane may be identified with the broad green one, now commonly called "Renny's Lane," which runs eastward in a direct line towards Pittington between the Sherburn and Rainton roads. There is still a gate at its eastern end separating it from the parish of Pittington. It will be seen that this as well as other lanes, being fenced on each side, were often let to individuals in successive years for pasturage.

[5] The parish pinfold remained till recent years in the open space on the South side of Gilligate near the Church. It appears from this entry to have been originally enclosed by a dike and hedge. Subsequently, as will be seen, it was fenced with wooden palings, then with a clay wall, and, in 1753, with stone and brick.

to Iohn Frankelayne for the retourne of the sesment money iiij*d.* Item payde for paper to this booke ———. It. paide to Richard Robenson for (*the rest illegible*).

Expences for this present yere 1580 who beinge gyrsmen Thomas Hudspethe Ingram taylor.

Item payde to Robert Smythe of petynton for up holdinge the yate in Petynton layne vj*d.* Item payde for two dussen stone of hay to the bull iij*s.* Item payde to Robert Smythe of petynton for up holdinge the gayte in petynton layne vj*d.* Item payde to Robert Smythe of petynton for maykinge of the two yates of the more newe[1] and for maykinge of a bryge at gyls bryge[2] iij*s.* Item payde to Rychard Robinson for maykinge of the poore folkes hedges of the more v*d.*[3] Item payde for Ses money to the briges for the use of y*e* parishe payde to the constable hands xiij*s.* Item payde to Rychard Robinson for maykinge of the dycke of the more perteanynge to the house that Rychard Jacson wont in ij*d.* Item payde to

———

[1] *I.e.*, Pittington gate, above referred to, and Sherburn gate, often afterwards mentioned.

[2] Gillsbridge is where a now insignificant brook crosses the Sherburn road, flowing down to the Wear, which it enters at the West end of Pelaw Wood. It will be seen from many subsequent references that there was a "carr," or pond, there, kept up by damming and "scouring" as a watering-place for cattle, from which a "gutter" flowed, over which a new bridge was made in 1735.

[3] It appears from this and other similar entries that certain widows and other poor people had houses and allotments on the Moor, fenced with dikes at the cost of the parish. *Cf.* (1582), "to william pavie for mendinge of the poore folkes dycke at the more one daye, v*d.*"; (1583) "For mendinge of the poore folkes dycke of the more, viij*d.*"; (1584) "For mendinge of wedow home dycke of the more ij*d.*"; "Wedowe Wilkinson and wedowe taylor do."; "Wedow Winter and for Malle Colson do."; "Wedowe Smythe and peter Crosbie do."; (1586) "Payd for the poore mens dycke that dwell att the pant"; (1590) "For mendinge of certayn poore folkes dickes on the more"; (1591) "For mendinge certayne porcions of the moire dicke belonginge to some poore about the pant"; (1593) The same; and other similar entries. It may be here noted that there appear also to have been formerly certain parcels of land in the parish called "poor's land," traces of which have now disappeared. Notices found of it are as follows. In the Accounts of the Churchwardens, which begin in 1664, there is in that year the entry, "Recd half a year's rent for the poore's land, £1 12 0"; and in 1683, "For dressing the poors land." In the Parish Register there is a memorandum stating that a legacy of £10 by Ralph Young for the use of the poor, A.D. 1636, was "laid out in a parcel of ground for the use of the poore in Gylligate." In the "Note of lands paying tithe to y*e* Church of St. Gyles," drawn up by Mr. Elias Smith (the Incumbent), A.D. 1655, there are two parcels designated as Poor's "land," viz., one of three roods, called "Midlan Poor Land," in "Pello Leas," and another of one acre in "Bakehouse Leas," *i.e.*, probably in Ellesleases, near the present Bakehouse Lane.

surviers (*surveyors*) of the hye wayes[1] ij*s.* iij*d.* Item payde
to Robert Smythe of petinton for the up holdin of the yeat
in petinton layne vj*d.* Item payde for sesmoney to the
taylor John cooke and to the Constable vj*s.* viii*d.* Item
payde to george Surtees for mendinge of the plankes of the
more yayte vj*d.* Item payde to Anthonye Cooke for
gaytheringe of stones iij*d.* Item payde to Rychard
Robinson and to Robert Wilson for . . . . . the lower
car[2] of the more xvj*d.* [*Caetera desunt*].

---

*The accounts for 1581 and 1582 are wanting, except
the following entry, which appears to have been the con-
cluding one for 1582.*

Item payde to william pavie for mendinge of the
poore folkes dycke at the more one daye, v*d.*

*On the back of the page on which the entries for 1583
begin there is a list of 65 surnames, each preceded by a
cross and a letter (presumably initial of Christian name),
and followed by a sum of money, the sums varying from id.
to* iij*s.* iiij*d.* ; *thus :—*

  ✗ E   symson . . iij*d.*
  ✗ J   atcheson . . ij*d.*
  ✗ g   brown . . iij*d.*
  ✗ R wilson . . iij*s.* iiij*d.*[3]

Then follows :—Sum xlij*s.* ix*d.* paid to thes above said
out of the xliiij*s.* viij*d.* which was resaved of the counstaples. This Indenture maid ——. Robert Hudspeth
de Gelegait in suburbiis de civitate Dunelm. Tanner.
Robert Hudspeth. M[r] Thomas Johnson and nephew.

Expences for this present yere 1583, These beinge
gyrsmen. Iohn burdies Cuthbart martyn for that present
yere. Item payd to Rycharde Robinson v*d.* a daye for

---

[1] *Cf.* "Pittington Churchwardens' Accounts," Surtees Society, vol.
lxxxiv, p. 88.

[2] A carr was a pool in marshy ground. *Cf.* "From Northcave to
Scalby 3 miles, al by low marsch and medow ground. This Fenne is
commonly caullid Waullyng Fenne, and hath many Carres of Waters
in it."—Leland, *Itin.*, vol. v, p. 124. On Gilligate Moor we find mention of
"the great Carr" and "the Lower Carr," both "dressed," or "scoured,"
and "dammed" from time to time for watering the cattle. One of them
seems to have been at "Gilsbrigg," where "the bog," "the car," "the
letch," and a "watering place," are elsewhere alluded to. For notices of
these carrs, see pp. 12, 13, 14, 16, 18, 26, 45. On pages 14 and 45, "the
lower carr" is mentioned in connexion with "gilles brige letche."

[3] The list appears to be one of persons among whom (as appears
afterwards) a sum received from the constables was distributed. The
purpose of the distribution does not appear.

skowringe of the great Carr of the more fower dayes the hole some is all togeather xx*d*. Item payd to Iohn thorpe for suche lyke v*d*. a daye fower dayes, xx*d*. Item payd to Thomas crayme (*Graham ?*) for suche lyke v*d*. a daye fower dayes xx*d*. Item payd to William Homble for mendinge of the gaytes of the more, vj*d*. Item payd for drinke that was gyven to the worke men that skowered the Carr, iij*d*. Item payde agayne for skowringe of the wather to Rychard Robinson v*d*. a daye two dayes, x*d*. Item payde to Thomas crayme (*Graham ?*) for suche lyke, x*d*. Item payde to Thomas tomson for suche lyke, x*d*. Item payde to fower men for bearinge of the cryple to sherborne, xvj*d*. Item payd to Thomas yonge for mendinge of the poore folkes dycke of the more, viij*d*. Item payd for kepinge of this booke, vj*d*. Item payd to Thomas yong for mending of the poore folkes dickes of the more, vj*d*.

1584.   Expences for this present is x*s*. ix*d*.

Thes beynge gyrsmen Iohn hubbock Raufe gayre. Item payde for a swall[1] to mend the yate of the more, xvj*d*. Item paid for a swall to mend the yate of the more, xvj*d*. Item payde to William homble for mendinge of the yates of the more, viij*d*. Item payde for carryinge of a cryppell to Shereborne, xij*d*. Item payde to the Sherobalaye concernyinge a wache,[2] xiij*d*. Item payde to Rycharde Robinson for skowringe of ducke pull,[3] v*d*. of the daye fyve dayes, ij*s*. j*d*. Item payde to william pavie for suche lyke fyve dayes, ij*s*. j*d*. Item payde to Rycharde Robinson for mendinge of the car of the more, v*d*. Item payd to Rycharde Robinson for mendinge of wedow home dycke of the more, ij*d*. Item payde to Rycharde Robinson for mendinge of Robert cornforth the wryght dycke of the more ij*d*. Item payde to william pavie for mendinge of wedow winter and for malle Colson dycke of the more, iiij*d*. Item payde to Rychard Robinson for mendinge of wedowe smythe and peter Crosbie dycke of the more, iiij*d*. Item payd to william pavie for mendinge of wedowe wilkinson and wedowe taylor dycke of the more iiij*d*. Item payde to william homble for

---

[1] See Glossary.

[2] Probably a watch, *i.e.*, for looking out for marauders. There are many signs in these accounts of an insecure state of things at this time. The *Sherobalaye* means the Sheriff's Bailiff.

[3] The "Duck pool" or "Duck pond" was, and remained till recently, on the space before the houses on the South side of the upper part of the street, where the pinfold, above-mentioned, also was.

mendinge of the yates of the more at two severall tymes, vij*d*. Item payde to william pavie for mendinge of william Coningam dycke of the more, ij*d*. Item payde to Thomas yonge for mendinge of william weathearell and James hodgson dycke of the more, iiij*d*. Item payde for kepinge of this booke, viij*d*. Item payd for a byll maykinge of a bill to the Constaples—

The somme of the expences is xj*s*. vij*d*.

[*No accounts are found for 1585*].

Expences for this present yere 1586 beinge gyrsmen Thomas marshall Edward Symson.

Item payd for the poore mens dycke that dwell att the pant[1] v*d*. Item payd to Iohn thorpe for mendinge of the hie wayes in the streat at the comman punfouuld, v*d*. Item payd to Anthonye cooke for certayne wood to mend the yate of the more xvj*d*. Item payd to william homble for mendinge of the sayde yate of the more, viij*d*. Item payd to Iohn thorpe for mendinge of the dycke of the more, v*d*. Item payd to Rychard Robinson for suche lyke, v*d*. Item payd to peter gelson for mendinge of the style of the common Rydge of ellesleyes,[2] ij*d*. Item payd to Thomas browne for his two horse for cariinge a prysoner to darton (*Darlington ?*) ij*s*. iiij*d*. Item payd to the castinge of the bell of this our money, xxxx*s*.[3] Item payd to Iohn thorpe for mendinge of the carr of the more, v*d*. Item payd to peter gelson for mendinge of the dycke of Ellesleyes, iiij*d*. Item payde to Iohn thorpe for mendinge wedowe taylor dycke of the more, ij*d*. Item payd to Thomas yonge for mendinge of Iohn Atkinson dycke of the more and for wedowe Wilkenson dycke, v*d*. Item payd to the

---

[1] "The pant" (meaning a conduit for water) is often mentioned. There appear to have been two; for see below, A.D. 1594, "bannds, &c., for the dowre of the *lower pant*." One of the fields on the South side of the street of Gilligate, a little above "Causey foot," is marked on old plans as "Pant Close," opposite to which on the North side of the street was, till comparatively recent years, a common well, resorted to by the inhabitants for water. In this locality may have been the "lower pant." The other may be supposed to have been on the Moor itself. *Cf.* below (A.D. 1591), "porcions of the *moire* dicke belonginge to some poore about *the pant*." Also (1593) the same.

[2] Ellesleases (still so called) was the tract of land descending towards the river on the North side of the street. The "Common rydge" (rigg?) might be a portion of the land there subject to rights of commonage.

[3] The bell thus subscribed to from the Grassmen's Fund may have been subsequently recast; for of the three bells now existing, the only one which is not of pre-Reformation date bears the inscription, "Soli Deo Gloria, 1640, A.E., R.T., R.C., T.D.," being thus shown to have been cast subsequently to this year.

hands george storie chutbart martyn beinge constaples for the byinge of certayne furnyture beloinge to this parishe,[1] vj*s.* iij*d.* Item pay'd for wrytinge of this booke, viij*d.*

[*The accounts for the years that here intervene do not appear*].

The new gras men for this yere of our Lord 1590 Iohn peirson & george cragg & they resaved in money declara at ther entrance————.[2]

———

Item Resaved of Frauncis browne fisher, iiij*s.* Item resaved of Anthoney trolope, ij*s.* viij*d.* Item Resaved of william mowbray iiij*s.* Item Resaved of george tompson Laborer, viij*d.* Item Resaved of peter nycholl for a horse, iiij*s.*

1591 (*Inserted here*).
[Thomas hewitson is maid free by the right of his father in law Iohn gaskin for so many gaites of cattell as his said father in law haith paid for in that *tyme* (?) he was inhabitant within this parish of S^t gilles and for no more the hole stent is vj . . . head and the foresaid Iohn haith paid but for iiij^{er}.
Resaved of Frauncis browne fisher for a horse, ij*s.* Resaved of Anthonye trolope for 2 kie, 2*s.*—— Resaved of william mowbray for a horse 4*s.*—— Resaved of georg tompson laborer for a koow 1*s.*—— Resaved of peter nicholl for a horse 4*s.*]

———

Expences laid furthe this present yere 1590.
Item paid to george tompson thomas prentisse Iohn thorpe Thomas thompson for skowringe of gilsbrige letche & the lower car & the springes that comes to yt3 vj*d.* a day, some ij*s.* Item paid more to thomas whitton Xp'ofer tompson thomas prentisse william mowbray for suche lyke,

---

[1] Meaning probably the common armour which parishes were required to have ready for use with a view to military service. *Cf.* " Pittington Churchwardens' Accounts," Surtees Society's Publications, vol. lxxxiv, p. 85. It will be seen below that such armour had to be inspected by the justices from time to time in various appointed places. See Index (*Armour*), and the direction of the Lord Lieutenant in 1594, given below, from which it appears that the parish was responsible for the equipment of three soldiers.

[2] The Grassmen's receipts, as well as expenses, begin now to be entered yearly. They were derived principally from " stents," *i.e.*, payments for the privilege of pasturing cattle on the common. For the system of such " stents," and of rights of common generally, see Preface, p. 1.

[3] *Cf.* above, p. 11, note 2.

ij*s*. Item paid to Robt cornforth for mendinge the yeat on the more, vj*d*. Item paid for skowringe of a gutter in the scrat lonnynge[1] iij*d*. Item delyvered to the hands of the counstaples Iohn smythe & Iohn hubbacke for certayn busines about the quenes affaires at houghton, v*s*. Item paid to thomas crame (*Graham ?*) for mendinge the mayden castell dicke,[2] v*d*. Item paid for mendinge of the more gaite & a gape to thomas whitton & Iohn pereson, viij*d*. Item paid to Iohn pereson for mendinge Elleslesse dicke, iiij*d*. Item paid to Anthoney trolope for mendinge of certayn poore folkes dickes in the more, vj*d*. Item paid for the wrytinge of our account, xij*d*.

The new gras men chosen for this yere of our Lord 1591 Iohn smyth & Artch connyngham & they receyved at ther entrie in money iiij*s*.

Item Resaved of Eliner cooke singilwoman for ij Kye accordinge to the order[3] ij*s*. viij*d*. Item Resaved of Isabell spurston wedow for a horse iiij*s*. Item Resaved of Iohn wardell for a cowe iiij*s*. Item Resaved of William murray curaite[4] for ij Kye, iiij*s*. Item Resaved of Isabell spurston aforesaid for a cow, ij*s*.

The hole Receites is iij*l*. xij*s*. viij*d*.

Expences this present yere 1591.

Item paid to thomas thomson Anthoney trolope Iohn thorpe for the skowringe of the doocke poole evere of them two days vj*d*. a day & ij*d*. to drink, iij*s*. ij*d*. Item paid to Edward symson for the kepinge & dightinge of the common

---

[1] This lane has not been identified.

[2] As to the " Maiden Castle," or " Maiden Bower," on Gilesgate Moor, see Introduction, and Index (*Maiden*).

[3] Some order, probably of the Parish Vestry, about " Stents," which is not recorded. *Cf.* Preface, p. 1.

[4] " Will's Murrey Clericus Parsona Ecclesiae praedictae [*i.e.*, Sci Egidii]. Admittitur Min. Can. A⁰, 1573. Natus Ille fuit 1 Januarii 154$\frac{2}{3}$. Rector fuit de Elton. Min. Can. fuit per 75 annos in simul. Sepultus in Eccl. Sci Oswaldi die Sci Mich'is 1649. Aliquando sub Matth. Cooper in Eccl. beatae mariae in Ballivo Australi officiavit. Pater ille fuit Rob'ti Murrey Clerici Vicarii de Kelloe. Qui Rob'tus postea Min. Can." (" Mickleton MSS.," No. 32, p. 52). He became Curate of St. Giles, 4th Feb., 1584, and afterwards Vicar of Pittington, in succession to his uncle Robert Murrey ; which living he resigned 11th Oct., 1621 (*Register of Bp. Neile, Dioc. Reg.*). In 1594, Sir John Watson appears below as having succeeded him as Curate of St. Giles. In 1591 (April 20th) he married Elizabeth Orde of West Orde (See Register), who after his death married in succession two prebendaries of Durham, viz., Henry Nanton and Ralph Tunstall. " Will's Murrey Clericus, Vicarius [*de Pittington*]. Cujus uxor fuit Eliza Ord de West Ord prope Barwick in Com North'riae. Post ejus mortem dicta vidua sua Eliza nupta Henrico Nanton IV prebendario D. et tertio nupta fuit Rad'o Tunstall X prebendario D. Nov. 1605 " (" Mickleton MSS.," No. 32, p. 124).

armor for the last yere past, iij*s.* Item paid to Rychard Robinson for skowringe the springs that feadethe the lower carr with water, xij*d.* Item paid for the common armor shewinge at houghton the xix day of august before the Justices to thomas prentisse thomas conyngham & Rychard tompson viij*d.* a man & the counstables charges vj*d.* a peace, the hole some, iij*s.* Item paid to william howell & his sonne for one hole day worke at the more yeat the vij of September, xv*d.* Item paid to Iohn thorpe for a burthen of rounges[1] to the said yeate, ij*d.* Item paid for one selme[1] to the same, iij*d.* Item paid to george tompson for makinge the dicke at the lower end of the Elless Leasses a little after S*t* cuthbert day, iiij*d.* Item paid to thomas prentisse for shewinge of one common armor[2] the xiiij day of october before the Justices upon the place grene, vj*d.* Item paid to Edward taylor for mendinge certayne porcions of the moire dicke belonginge to some poore about the pant, vj*d.* Item paid to george surtys for certayne buccles to the common armore which was wantinge, iiij*d.* Item paid for the booke kepinge & wryting our account, xij*d.*

The some of the expences —— xiiij*s.* x*d.*

The election of the new grass men for the yere of our Lord 1592. James mitchelson & Edward hall and they Receive in money at ther entrie ——.

Resaved of georg Allan for one cow as a outman ij*s.* Resaved of Andrew curro vij*s.* iij*d.* Resaved of William murra curate, vj*s.* Resaved of Isabell spurston wedow, ij*s.* Resaved of thomas baker for one cowe, ij*s.* Resaved of Edward wilkinson, xvj*d.* Resaved of Thomas orde, iiij*s.* Resaved more of georg Allan, ij*s.*

The hole Some of the receats is iiij*l.* ij*s.* iiij*d.*

Expences laid for this yere 1592.

Imprimis for the more dicke, xviij*d.* Item more my selfe ij dayes & the hurd iiij dayes, xviij*d.* Item for the more yeat mendinge, viij*d.* Item paid for oyle to the common armore, iiij*d.* Item for kepinge the Elless leas dike, xij*d.* Item paid for the drissinge of the armore & caringe of yt to the muster, ij*s.* Item paid for kepinge the armore, xij*d.* Item paid for nailes & buckles to the

---

[1] See Glossary.

[2] "One common armor" may mean one soldier's equipment. It is observable that this year armour was exhibited twice—in August at Houghton, and in October on the Place (*hod.* Palace) Green. One of the suits may have been found defective at the first inspection, and so had to be shown again. It appears below that certain buckles had been wanting.

armore, viij*d.* Item paid for gettinge of 800 slates to cuthbert stokell laid out by me James mytchelson, iiij*s.* viij*d.* Item delyvered to the churchwardens for the mendinge of the pant, ix*s.* Item delyvered to georg cragg counstaple, ix*s.* iiij*d.* Item paid to Iohn thorp & thomas prentiss for skowringe the water surves (*service*) on the more, xij*d.* Item paid to the hurd for makinge the dike on the more the tyme of winter when it was nedefull, ij*s.* viij*d.* Item paid to thomas tompson for repayringe the mayden castell, iiij*s.* xj*d.* Item paid more to the hurd for mendinge certayn gapes in the more dike, iiij*d.* Item paid for kepinge of the booke & wrytinge our account, xij*d.*

Some of the expences, xlij*s.* vj*d.*

Remayninge to the new grasse men Iohn taylor & Edward wilkinson for this yere folowinge, 1593, xxiiij*s.* vj*d.* (*erased*).

Resaved at this account of georg cragg for ij kye, ij*s.* viij*d.* Resaved for Xpofor swinney, iiij*s.* Resaved of Andrew curro at this tyme ix*d.* in full payment of all his hole stent after xvj*d.* a cowe.

The grass men Iohn taylor & Edward wilkinson Resaves at ther entre in money xxxj*s.* ij*d.*

Resaved of Thomas cowlson for one cowe, xvj*d.* Resaved of Iohn tyerman for one cow, ij*s.* Resaved of Rowlan tompson for one horse, iiij*s.* Resaved of Edward wilkinson for ij kye, ij*s.* viij*d.* Resaved of thomas baker for one horse, iiij*s.* Resaved of george allan for one horse, iiij*s.* Resaved of Iohn Anderson for one horse, ij*s.* viij*d.* Resaved of Anthoney Ranaldson for one cow xvj*d.*

The some of the Receits——lj*s.* x*d.*

The grassmen for this yeare 1592 Resaved at ther entrens in monie i—ij.

Resaved of Thomas coulson for one cowe, oo–ii . 4. Resaved of Iohn tyerman for on cowe, o-2—. Resaved of Rowland tompson for on horse, oo–4—. Resaved of Edward wilkingeson for 2 kye, oo–2—. Resaved of Thomas baker for one horse, oo–4—. Resaved of georg allan for on horse, oo–4—. Resaved of Iohn Anderson for on horse, oo–2—. Resaved of Anthoney Ranaldson for on cow, oo i—.

Expences laid furth for this yere 1593.

Item paid to Thomas whitton for vi stoupes & settinge of them for the cattell to rubb on the common, vj*d.* Item

2

paid to Iohn thorpe for mendinge of certayn porcions of dicke belonginge to some poor about the pant, vj*d*. Item more to Iohn thorpe for mendinge the yeate on the more, ij*d*. Item paid for mendinge a band of the dore at the pant, ij*d*. Item paid for latt brodes bought at darnton for M[r] heaith bawcus,[1] x*d*. Item paid to thomas tompson for castinge of the car iij dayes & a halfe, xxj*d*. Item paid to Iohn thorpe for such lyke, xxj*d*. Item paid to Rychard Robinson for two dayes, xij*d*. Item paid to thomas whitton for two dayes, xij*d*. Item paid to thomas Grame for one day, vj*d*. Item paid for a gallan of ale to the workmen, iiij*d*. Item paid to thomas whitton for makinge the hedge upon the ellessless, iiij*d*. paid more to the said thomas for thornes to the same, iiij*d*. Item paid to Iohn thorp for makinge certayn places at the lower car for the cattell to dringe (*drink*), vj*d*. Item paid to thomas Mitchall for the building of Rychard morlan bawcus,[2] xij*s*. Item paid to Robt. hudspeth for wryting our account & the booke kepinge, xij*d*.

Some of the expences xxij*s*. viij*d*.

-- --

[1] Mr. Heath's bakehouse ; *i.e.*, that of the lord of the manor, at which the tenants were required to bake their bread, as well as grind their corn at his mill. *Cf.* Copy of Court Roll, A.D. 1600 (given below in this volume), in which Mergaret Smithe, tenant of a burgage in Gilligate, is bound "molere granam suam ad molendinum domini, et pinsere panem suum ad Communem pistrinam domini." In a suit instituted in the year 1726 by John Tempest, then lord of the manor, against certain inhabitants for alleged trespass on the common and other infringements of his manorial rights, he asserted the obligation of freeholders as well as copyholders of the borough to use his bakehouse only, even to the exclusion of their right to bake their bread in their own houses. See below, p. 39. It would seem from the entry before us that the parishioners had to keep the lord's bakehouse in repair, as well as resort to it. In the Manor Court Book is found as follows :— "11 Oct., 13th Car. I.——Pain—That all who bake white bread within the parish shall bring it into the bakehouse between 6 & 7 in the forenoon & their household bread between 10 & 11 upon pain of 3*s*. 4*d*. each offender." The lord's bakehouse may be supposed to have been where a bakehouse existed till within living memory, viz., the last house on the North side of the street, where a lane, still called "Bakehouse Lane," bounds the parish on the West ; the adjoining land being also designated as "Bakehouse Leazes" ; as in the following extract from the Manor Court Book, 3 Nov., 11 Car. I. :—"Pain—That none shall misuse the Bake-house-Well or Bake-house-Leazes-Well upon pain of every one so offending—6*s*. 8*d*."

[2] This appears to have been a new bakehouse, distinct from Mr. Heath's manorial one, which has been already mentioned. It may be that such inhabitants as were not bound by their copyhold tenures to use the lord's bakehouse only were now resolved to have one of their own, at which they could bake on their own terms. We find subsequently in 1610 (p. 39) a specified rate of charges not to be exceeded by the "backhouse-man."

New grass men chossen the Sunday next after the Assencion day[1] in the vere of our lord 1594 william cornforth & thomas hewitson & they Resave in money at ther entre ——.

Resaved of Robert connyngham for a cowe, wever,— xvj*d*. Resaved of Xpofor tompson laborer for two whyes, iiij*s*. Resaved of Rychard thompson sonne of william tompson sagerston (*i.e.*, *sexton*) for thre gaits, iiij*s*. Resaved of Robert conyngham wever for one cowe, xvj*d*. Resaved of Iohn watson curaite[2] for thre gaits, vj*s*. Resaved of Iohn tyers for a cow, ij*s*. Resaved of the said Iohn tyers for A horse, iiij*s*. Resaved of the foresaid Robert coningham for a horse, ij*s*. viij*d*. Resaved of Rychard frissell the last end of his hole stent, iiij. Resaved of Iohn smyth tanner the last end of his hole stent, iiij. Resaved of Rychard chilton, ij*s*. viij*d*. Resaved of Iohn smyth challanwever[3] for two whyes, ij*s*. viij*d*. Resaved of Iohn Anderson roper for a cow, xvj*d*. Resaved of William hilton for ij kye, ij*s*. viij*d*. Resaved of Thomas crame for a cow, ij*s*. viij*d*. Resaved of the foresaid william hilton for a horse, ij*s*. viij*d*. Resaved of A gentlewoman which is dwellinge in Mr Raphe conyars house which he dyd taike of Iohn tyerman for a cow paid ij*s*. Resaved of Thomas cornforth challanwever for iiij^er graits, v*s*. iiij*d*. Resaved of Thomas marshall tanner the last end of his hole stent ——. Resaved of Xpofer shereton for the last end of his hole stent ——. Resaved of georg Cragg for ij gaits, ij*s*. viij*d*.

Some of the Receits iiij*l*. 8*s*. 2*d*.

Expences for this yeare 1594.

Item paid to thomas crame for mendinge the more yeat, xij*d*. Item paid to Robt. cornforth for mendinge the same yeat, iiij*d*. Item paid to georg Surtiss for bannds & other nedefull things to the dowre of the lower pant, v*d*. Item paid for the drissinge of the common armoure, xx*d*. Item paid to Iohn Johnson for caryinge the railes to the

---

[1] This was the usual day for choosing the Grassmen for the year, the perambulation of boundaries having been, as at present, on Ascension Day.

[2] Curate of the parish after the removal of William Murrey to Pittington; called "Sir John Watson" in 1597. *Cf.* "Mickleton MSS.," No. 32, p. 52 :— "Johēs Watson [al. Sr John Lack-Latin] fuit Min. Can. Ao 1598." His title of "Sir" associates him pleasantly in one's mind with Shakespear's curates of the period; while his nickname might well have suited some of them. For some further notice of him see under "Extracts from Registers."

[3] See Glossary.

new yeat of the moure, vj*d*. Item paid to thomas crame for upholdinge the more dicke for the hole yeare, iiij*s*. Item paid to Robt. hudspeth for wrytinge our account, xij*d*. Item paid to William homyll (*Humble?*) for makinge A new yeat to the more hym selfe & his sonne ij dayes xiiij*d*. a day, some, ij*s*. iiij*d*. paid to georg allan for kepinge of the common armor, xvij*d*. Item paid for a common purss to the grass men, ij*d*.

Some of the expences —— xij*s*. x*d*.

grass men chosen for this yeare followinge 1595, Thomas hudspeth & Andrew curray, and they Resave at ther entrance in money iij*l*. xv*s*. iiij*d*.

Resaved of Iohn pearson the yonger for two kye, ij*s*. viij*d*. Resaved of Iohn Johnson for a horse, ij*s*. viij*d*. Resaved of Rychard tompson for A horse, ij*s*. viij*d*. Resaved of William hilton for a cowe, xvj*d*. Resaved of Rychard Chilton for two kye, ij*s*. viij*d*. Resaved of Iohn smyth challan weaver for a cowe, xvj*d*. Xp'ofor Jarvice carpenter the first newincomer after the last order and haith paid acordinge to the same for one cowe, iiij*s*. Resaved of Iohn homyll glover for one horse and two kye after the Raites of the same order, xvj*s*. Resaved of Thomas marshall laborer for two kye after the same raite & order, viij*s*. Resaved of Leonard whelden for one cowe, ij*s*. Resaved of James cowtman for one cowe, xvj*d*. Resaved of Thomas hewitson for a cowe, xvj*d*. Resaved of george tompson for two kye, ij*s*. viij*d*. Resaved of Iohn pearson the yonger for two kye, ij. viij*d*. Resaved of Thomas Snawball for one cowe, xvj*d*. Resaved of Ingram taylor for two kye his hole stent, ij*s*. viij*d*. Resaved of Thomas marshall Laborer for two kye, viij*s*. Resaved of Iohn homell glover for one cowe, iiij*s*. Resaved of Iohn watson curate for two kye, iiij*s*. Resaved of Rychard chilton for one cow, xvj*d*.

The Some of all the Receaits is vij*l*. viij*s*.

A copie of A dereccion from the lord Lieftenantt to the Justices appointed for Esington warde concernyng the repayringe of the common armore in everie parishe. 1594.

Wheras the right honorayble the lord Lieftenantt of thesse north p'ts haith bene informed that the common Armor in Esington warde is out of repaire and not so kept for hir ma^ties service as yt ought to be for remedie wherof his lordship haith geven dereccion unto us to geve commaundement unto yowe to se that the said armor be repaired and kept in good case that therwith hir ma^tie may be well and trulie served and your selves discharged yor bounden duties, wherfore for that Esington warde is in our division I have Apointed one Robt. heslopp to vewe all the Armore and what is a miss and not servicable that he shall dress repaire and amend the same yowe agreinge with hym for everie armore iij*s*. iiij*d*. when they ar maid servicable And afterwards for kepinge the said armore in reparacion to pay hym for everie armore xij*d*. in the yere hereafter Thus much upon his lordships derection to us [*wc*] will and charge yowe to se this our warrantt performed : geven under our hands and scales the iijth of September Anno Regni Elizabeth &c. xxxvj^{tie}.

Rychard belassis[1] ⎱
Henry Anderson ⎰

Imprimis Resaved of M^r heith of kepeyere iij*s*. iiij*d*.
Item Resaved for the far graunge ...   ...   xx*d*.
Item Resaved for Ramsyde ...   .   xx*d*.
Item Resaved for old durham   ...   ...   xx*d*.
Item Resaved for gelegaite ...   .   xx*d*.

wch p'teculer somes was paid for the dressinge of ⎱
the thre common armore wch this parishe is charged ⎰ x*s*.
wth to Robt. heslop appoynted by my l. leifteannt ⎰
& the Iustices as his warrant doith here testefye. ⎰

[*The above, which appears as a later page of the book as now bound up, is shown by its date to belong to this year 1594*].

Expences for this yere 1595.

Item paid to Rychard morlans man for the carage of a tre for a stoupe to the new yeatt, iiij*d*. Item paide to william homyll for dressinge of yt & settinge of yt, x*d*. Item paid to the hurde for helpinge of hym the same day——. Item paid to the counstaples for makinge a paire of new stocks to Iohn hutcheson & Xpofor Jarvis, iij*s*. ij*d*. Item paid to Rychard Robinson for makinge the dicke of elleslese, v*d*. Item paid to Rychard Robeson & his

---

[1] *Cf.* (A.D. 1597), "For dressing of the common Armar at the Commandement of Mr Richard Bellasses" ("Houghton-le-Spring Vestry Book," Surtees Society, vol. lxxxiv, p. 272). Richard Bellasis, of Morton House in the parish of Houghton, being a justice of the peace, was also a governor of Kepyer Grammar School in that parish with John Heath of Kepyer, who, together with Bernard Gilpin, Rector of Houghton, had founded it. The original governors were the two founders, Heath and Gilpin, with power to either of them to appoint successors. John Heath had apparently appointed Richard Bellasis after the death of Bernard Gilpin in 1583. Henry Anderson, also a justice of the peace, originally of Newcastle, was the owner of Elemore and of Haswell Grange (the latter being in the parish of Easington), and lessee under the Chapter of Durham of Hallgarth Manor in the parish of Pittington, in succession to Christopher Morland, whose daughter and heiress he had married.

daughter for gettinge of stones out of sherborne borne one day, ix*d*. Item paid to Thomas crames daughter for one day for such lyke, iiij*d*. Item paid to Daniell hudspeth for one day & a halfe, vij*d*. Item paid to the husbands of sherbourne for carrage of x foother of stones from ther borne to the cawcie,[1] vj*s*. viij*d*. Item in bread & drinke to the waynmen, viij*d*. Item paid to Roger Ezeike (?) for an Iron bolt to the stocks, x*d*. Item paid to Rychard Robeson for mendinge the dicke on the more, viij*d*. Item paid to Edward brantingham for rep'racion the more dicke, xx*d*. Item paid for dressinge the common armore belonginge to the parish, vj*d*. Item paid to Thomas Crame for makinge the hedge aboute the mayden castell, vi*d*. Item paid to the counstaples for a sesment for the quenes affaires, vj*s*. viij*d*. paid to Thomas marshall counstaple for a sesment to the Salt peter man[2] a penne of the pound, x*d*.

---

[1] The paved way called the "cawcie" (or "causey"), for which we find stones again led in 1599, was probably from Gillsbrig (See above, p. 10, note 2) on the Sherburn road to the bottom of the upper declivity of Gilligate, still called "Causeyfoot," for keeping which in repair one Margaret Hall in 1622 left 30s. in her will (See "Extracts from Registers").

[2] Curious information about the "saltpetre man" will be found in *Notes and Queries*, 1st Series, VII, 376, 433, 460. It appears that any soil impregnated with animal matter, such as that of stables, cow-houses, and dove-cots, was claimed by the Crown with a view to home production of saltpetre, to be used in making gunpowder; and the Government Official for this purpose was called the Saltpetre man. In a proclamation of Charles I (1625), "for the maintaining and increasing of the saltpetre mines of England for the necessary and important manufacture of gunpowder," it is set forth "that our realm yields sufficient mines of saltpetre without depending on foreign parts. Wherefore for the future no dovehouse shall be paved with stones bricks nor boards, lime sand nor gravel, nor anything whereby the growth and increase of the mine of saltpetre may be hindered or impaired, but the proprietors shall suffer the ground or floors thereof, as also all stables where horses stand, to lie open with good and mellow earth, apt to breed increase of the said mine. And that none deny or hinder any saltpetre man, lawfully deputed thereto, from digging taking or working any ground which by commission may be taken & wrought for saltpetre, &c." Another proclamation in 1627 (with reference to a patent that had been granted to Sir John Brooke and Thomas Russel for making saltpetre by a new invention) gives them power to collect the animal fluids, which were to be preserved by families for this purpose, once in 24 hours in Summer, and once in 48 in Winter. It seems that the saltpetre-men were apt to abuse their powers: for Lord Coke, in a "Speech & Charge with a Discourse of the Abuses & Corruptions of Officers" (8vo, London, N. Rutter, 1607), says, "There is also a Saltpetre man, whose commission is not to break up any man's house or ground without leave; and not to deale with any house but such as is unused for any necessarie employment by the owners, &c., and not to digge in any place without leaving it smooth & level, in such case as he found it. This Saltpetre man under shew of his authoritie will make plaine & simple people beleeve that he will without their leave break up the floore of their dwelling house, unless they will compound with him for the contrary, &c." Further, in 1656 an Act was passed forbidding the saltpetre makers to dig in houses without leave of the

Item paid to the counstaples for another sesment of a penne of the pound for the kepinge of A sluhound,[1] xd. paid to Edward brantingham for repairinge the dicke of the more, xxd. Item paid for wrytinge our account & the booke kepinge, xijd.

Some of the receats - - xxixs. iijd.
paid fourth in expences— iijs. iiijd.
Some of the hole expences— xxxijs. vijd.

Some declara to the hands of the new grass men Iohn smyth and Iohn trype which they resave at ther entrance for this yere 1596.

Resaved of Edward cornfourth Ropper for two kye, ijs. viijd. more Resaved of the forsaid Edward cornfurth for other two gaits, ij. viijd. Resaved of Robart conningham wever for one cowe, xvjd. Resaved of Xp'ofor Jarvis carpinter for a cowe, iiijs. Resaved of Iohn wilson sonne of Raphe wilson Rop' (*roper*) for his hole stent, viijs. Resaved of Iohn whitfeild for two kye smyth of sherborne house, viijs. Resaved of Thomas cowlson cooke the last ende of his hole stent, ixd. Resaved of Robart cowlson for one gate, xvjd. Resaved of george tompson for one gaite, xvjd. Resaved of Leonard whelpton for one gaite, ijs. Resaved of Thomas carnfourth challan weaver for two gaits, ijs. viijd. which is the last of his hole stent.

Some of the Receats is——7l. 9s. 9d.
Some of the receats——vijl. ijs. 9d.

Expences for this yere, 1596.
Item paid to Rychard Robinson for up holdinge the Dicke of the more for one halfe yere, ijs. Item paid to Thomas marshall and Iohn howell counstaples for a sesment concernynge the day of truce (?) the xvij day of august 1596, vjs. ob.[2] Item paid to Rychard Robeson for mendinge of certayne capes (*gaps*?) on the ellesslease, iiijd. Item more paid to the foresaid Rychard for the same

owner. The " Sesment to the salt peter man " in the text may have been for the purpose of a composition with him as intimated by Lord Coke.

[1] The keeping of a *sleuth-hound* for hunting culprits, the previous provision for a " watch," and the number of prisoners conveyed to various places about this time, appear significant of a state of insecurity, from social or political causes, at this period of Elizabeth's reign.

[2] In this year (1596) a treaty was concluded between Elizabeth, Henry IV of France, and the States against Philip after the taking of Calais by the latter, which was followed by the expedition to Cadiz (See Lingard, vol. vi, p. 273). This may be the " truce " alluded to.

dicke, ———. Item paid to daniell hudspeth for caryinge of
a creaple to Sherborne, iiij*d.* paid for charges at the court
for suyinge of Robt. barro, vij*d.* Item paid for dressinge the
common armor november 28, 1596, xij*d.* Item delyvered
to the Churchwardens for the releife of wedow wilson
lyinge sicke at the mercie of god, xij*d.* Item paid to Iohn
howell counstaple for the Releife of william grene taylor
when he was suspected to have y[e] playge.[1] Item paid to
Thomas mitchell for cariinge of a prisoner to ferrie hill, x*d.*
paid for the booke kepinge & wrytinge of our account,
xij*d.* Item paid to Xp'ofor Jarvis for mendinge the more
gate, xvj*d.* paid to Rychard Robeson for the more dicke
the last halfe yere ———.

Grass men chosen for this yere followinge 1597   Symon
alderley & george tompson & they Receive at ther entrance
declara (*the sum erased*).

Some vj*l.* xv*s.* iiij*d.* ob.

Resaved of Robert hudspeth for two gaits, ij*s.* viij*d.*
Resaved of Edward brankingham for two gaits, iiij*s.*
Resaved of Iohn tripp for two gaits paid his hole stent,
ij*s.* viij*d.* Resaved of george Thompson for one cowe,
xvj*d.* Resaved of george tayleyr glover for iiij[er] gaits,
v*s.* iiij*d.* Item Rec[d] of Robt. Barry for his fredom of the
common for all his gaites viij*s.* and there is geven him
back of this said some with the consent of the whole
parishe—iiij*s.* and so Rec[d] for all his hole stent.

Some of all the receyts vij*l.* x*s.*

Expences paid out this present yere 1597.

Item paid to patricke garrie for caryinge a prisoner
to aukland, vij*d.* Item paid to Xp'ofor jarvis for mendinge
the yeat of the more, viij*d.* Item paid to Iohn homyll for
his horse for the quenes servis, x*d.* Item paid to Iohn
anderson for mendinge ellessleise dicke, vj*d.* Item paid for
dressinge the common armore, vj*d.* Item paid to george
tompson for the upholdinge of the more dicke for the hole
yere, iiij*s.* Item paid for the wrytinge of our account, xij*d.*
Item for our charges at the seute of Robt. Barrow, xxj*d.*

---

[1] This is the first allusion in the Grassmen's books to the contagious
sickness, usually called "the plague," which was prevalent in the North
during the latter years of Elizabeth, as to which, and its fatal effects in and
about Durham, see Surtees Society's Publications, vol. iv, pt. 2, p. 7. It first
affected the parish of St. Giles in 1589, and, after a cessation, broke out
again in 1597, ceasing finally in 1604 (?). (See Register of Burials).
But it will be seen below that there was again a suspected case in 1605.

Delyvered of the grasse money in the tyme of the visitation[1] to Sr Iohn watson curaite and Iohn smyth with others as followeth.

Item paid to the counstaples for a sesment, vi*s*. viij*d*. Imprimis first delyvered to Sr Iohn watson, viij*s*. more delyvered to hym at another tyme vj*s*. viij*d*. Item delyvered to the hands of Iohn Smyth, x*s*. Item delyvered to Rychard chilton counstaple for makinge of two lodges to Andrew curro, iiij*s*. Item more delyvered to the said counstaple for the relevement of James cowtman the tyme he was on the moore, v*s*. Item paid to Raphe Robeson for buryinge of James cowtmans wyfe, iij*s*. iiij*d*. Item delyvered to william cowtman to by vitalles to the clengers (*cleaners?*) when they were dressinge James cowtmans house, viij*d*.

Somme of the expences xliiij*s*. j*d*.

(*In another hand*). Some is in all l*s*. ix*d*.

Grass men chosen for this yere followinge 1598 Iohn wilson & Thomas Snawball and they receyve at ther entrance declara v*l*. xxiij*d*.

Iohn fressill haith paid to the hands of Iohn wilson & thomas Snawball for iiij^er gaits of the common v*s*. iiij*d*. Resaved of william newton tanner for fyve gaites of the common accordinge to the order servinge his apprentiship within the said parishe, x*s*. Resaved of Iohn smyth challan weaver for two gaits, ij*s*. viij*d*. Resaved of Robt. browen for two gaits, ij. viij*d*. Resaved for the common bull, l*s*.

Some of the hole receyts viij*l*. xij*s*. vij*d*.

Expences for this yeare 1598.

Item paid for vj horsses to Ferrie hill for cariinge the pledges,[2] ijs. Item paid to the churchwardens for solger money, iiij*s*.[3] Item paid for dressinge the common armor, xij*d*. Item paid for cariing of a prisoner to new-castell, xvj*d*. Item paid for the kepinge of the bull,[4] iij*s*. Item paid for drissinge the maiden bower,[5] ij*s*. viij*d*. Item

---

[1] *I.e.*, the plague aforesaid, which was commonly so designated. We observe in the entries that follow the sanitary provision of huts or "lodges" on the Moor for the seclusion of infected persons, and the careful purification of infected houses.

[2] Sureties, or hostages? The purpose is unknown.

[3] For "Soldier money" see "Churchwardens' Accounts," Surtees Society, vol. lxxxiv, p. 19.

[4] There has been no mention of a bull since 1580. The parish may be supposed to have done without one of its own. For the purchase of a new one now see first entry of 1599.

[5] This is the first occurrence of "bower" instead of "castle." (See

paid for upholdinge the more dicke for the hole yere, iiij*s*.
Item paid for vij stone of hay to the bull xiiij*d*. Item paid
for wrytinge our account, xij*d*.

The some of the expences xxj*s*. vj*d*.

Grass men chosen for this yere following chosen the
next sounday after the assencion day Rychard storie &
william hilton and they receive at ther entrance declara
vij*l*. xj*s*. j*d*.

Resaved of Iohn frissell for two gaits which is the full
end of his hole stent, ij*s*. viij*d*. Resaved of william
newton for one gait which is the end of his hole stent, ij*s*.
Resaved of Rychard tompson for one gaite the last of his
stent, xvj*d*. Resaved of Robert cowlson for one gaite,
xvj*d*. Resaved of Edward cornfourthe for two gaites the
last of his hole stent, ij*s*. viij*d*. Resaved of Edmond
smyth Rop' (*Roper*) for his hole stent ij*s*. a cowe, xij*s*.
Resaved of the hole parishe everie cowe ij*d*. for bull hay
the hole some, xiiij*s*. viij*d*. Resaved of Rychard chilton
for iiij^er stone of the bull hay, xij*d*.

Some of the hole receates ix*l*. 8*s*. ix*d*.

Expences laid out in this yere 1599.

Item paid for a common bull, xl*s*. Item paid for hay
to the said bull, xxj*s*. Item paid for the carage home of
the same, xvij*d*. Item paid for charges to the waynmen,
vj*d*. more paid for bercinge yt in, iiij*d*. Item paid for
leadinge of stones to the cawcie,[1] xxj*s*. ix*d*. Item paid for
mendinge of the more gaite, vj*d*. Item paid for scowringe
of the bridge letch,[2] ij*d*. Item paid for mendinge of
pittington yeat, vj*d*. Item paid for mendinge of ellessleise
dicke ix*d*. Item paid to Edward brantingham for mendinge
brode close dicke,[3] ij*d*. Item paid for Roge money,[4]
ij*s*. iiij*d*. Item paid to george Rowell for kepinge the bull
& servinge hym all the winter, iij*s*. Item paid to Thomas

Introduction). But the older designation is resumed next year, and
continued till 1623, in which year and in 1624 it is again called *bower*; but
in 1625 once more *castle*; then *bower* till 1629, after which it ceases to be
mentioned. It would thus seem that its later name of "maiden's bower"
had come into use certainly by the end of the sixteenth century, though still
used interchangeably with "Maiden Castle." The substitution would be
natural when the real meaning of the old word *maiden* was unknown, while
the bower of a maiden had become a familiar idea, especially in the poetry
of the time.

[1] See p. 22, note 1.

[2] *I.e.*, At Gillsbridge. See above, p. 10, note 2.

[3] The "Broad Close" was a field belonging to the parish to the North
of the divergence of the Rainton and Sherburn roads.

[4] For "Rogue Money" see "Churchwardens' Accounts," Surtees
Society, vol. lxxxiv, p. 19.

crame for upholdinge the more dicke for the hole yere, iiij*s.*
Item more for pittington yeat & mendinge the maden
castell, vj*d.* more paid for the same yeat for nayles, j*d.*
Item paid for a saile to the bull, j*d.* Item paid to Edward
brantingham for caringe a cripple to Raynton, vj*d.* Item
paid to Andrew curro for carringe a prisoner to ferrie hill,
viij*d.* Item paid to Robt. hudspeth for wrytinge our
account, xij*d.* Item laid fourth of the grass money more
then was resaved for the foge of brod close, iiij*d.*[1] Item laid
out in the lower end for the lyke, j*d.*

Some of the expences v*l.*

Grass men chosen for this yere following 1600 the
sounday next after the Assencion day Iohn Smyth and
Andrew curro. And they Resave at there entrance declara,
iiij*l.* vij*s.* vij*d.* Resaved of Thomas marshall for iij stone
of hay, ix*d.* Resaved of William cornfurth for ij stone, vj*d.*
Resaved of Rychard Storie for ij stone, vj*d.* Resaved of
Edward cornfourth for ij stone, vj*d.* Resaved of the hole
parishe everie cow ij*d.*[2] the hole some for the bull hay,
xiiij*s.* ij*d.* Resaved of william dawson for the bull, xxxiij*s.*
Resaved of Iohn helcotes laborrer for one cowe gaite on
the common, iiij*s.* Resaved of Rychard chilton the last
of his hole stent, xvj*d.* Resaved of Iohn smyth challan
weaver y*e* last of his stent, xvj*d.* Resaved of Thomas
prentice for one gaite, xvj*d.* Resaved of wedow smyth for
iiij*er* stone of hay, xij*d.* Resaved of william deanam for
ij stone, vj*d.* Resaved of george tompson for ij stone, vj*d.*
Resaved of Iohn Smyth for vj stone, xviij*d.* Resaved of
Robert cowlson for one gait, xvj*d.* Resaved of Iohn
blaxton for all his hole stent after the order for strangers
iiij*s.* a gait the hole some, xxiiij*s.* Resaved of George
Cragg for one gaite, xvj*d.* Resaved of Edward harle for
two gaits on y*e* common, iiij*s.*

Some of the receits viij*l.* xix*s.* 2*d.*

Expences Laid furth for this yere 1600.

Item paid for mendinge of a weyskale,[3] ij*d.* Item paid
to thomas snowball for daminge the lower carr, iiij*d.* Item
paid for skowringe lviij roode of the more dicke ij*d.* a roode
the hole some, iiij*s.* x*d.* Item paid for one armore dressing
which the streat is charged with yerely, vj*d.* Item paid to
thomas tompson for mendinge of pittington yeat, vj*d.*
Item paid to Rychard Storie for one foother of hay to the

---

[1] For explanation of this payment, see below, p. 40, note 2.
[2] Viz., for hay for the parish bull, as appears below.
[3] *I.e.*, a weigh-scale, which would be required for weighing the hay.

bull, price xiiij*s*. vj*d*. Item paid for the carrage home of yt & drinke to the waynmen & bereinge in of yt, xvj*d*. Item paid to thomas snowball for settinge the stoupe of the more yeat & mendinge certayn places of the dicke, iiij*d*. Item paid to william howell for makinge a capp for y*e* said yeat, vj*d*. Item paid to thomas baker for damminge of the water at gilsbrige, ij*d*. Item more for mendinge the dicke at the foote of the seven akers,[1] ij*d*. Item paid to thomas baker for mendinge the dicke on the lower ende of elless Leasses, vj*d*. Item paid to Rychard frissell for his horse to carrie a prisoner to the whyt cross of spanimore, vj*d*. Item paid to Edward cornfurth for suche lyke, vj*d*. Item paid to y*e* churchwardens for makinge up the roge money, ij*s*. iiij*d*. Item paid to george rowell for servinge the bull the tyme of winter & housrome for the hay, iij*s*. Item paid to M*r* wansworth for the bull, xxxiij*s*. paid for bringinge hym home, ij*d*. Item paid to Thomas snawball for mendinge the more dicke wher yt was nedefull & for mending the yeat stoupe, xviij*d*. Item paid to george tompson for dressinge the mayden castle & the dicke, viij*d*. Item paid to the said george tompson for makinge a defence to kepe the water in the lower car for the better servinge of the cattell & for mendinge of pittington yeat two dayes, xij*d*. Item paid to thomas snowball for mendinge certayn gapes in the more dicke, ij*d*. Item paid to thomas Thomson for mendinge pittington yeat with suche neds is yt dyd lacke, vj*d*. Item paid to the hurde for mendinge certayn gapes in the more dicke & mendinge yet where yt ys nedefull unto our count day, ij*d*. Item paid to Rychard farreless for A coppie of y*e* articles, iiij*d*. Item paid to Iohn litlephare for wrytinge us ij presentments,[2] viij*d*. Item more paid to Rychard farreless for copiynge them all in to one when they were given to the Justices, iiij*d*. Item paid to Rychard Stone for carrynge of a prisoner to chester, vj*d*. Item paid to Robert hudspeth for wrytinge our account, ij*s*.

Some of the hole expences iij*l*. xij*s*. j*d*.

New gras men chosen the sounday next after the assencion day Thomas hudspeth & Rychard glover and they receive declara at ther entrance in money v*l*. ij*s*. iiij*d*.

------

[1] The "Seven Acres" was one of the "Town fields" in Pellowleases, now Pelaw Leazes. See p. 40, note 2.

[2] Probably of recusants, the previous "articles" having reference to the same. *Cf.* "Churchwardens' Accounts," Surtees Society, vol. lxxxiv, p. 48, and "Recusants" in Index of that volume.

Item Resaved of the hole parishe everie cowe ij*d*. towards the bull hay the hole some xiiij*s*. Resaved of George Rowell for one horse gait, viij*s*. Resaved of George Wilbie for one cowe, iiij*s*. Resaved of James hodshon for ij horsses gaits, v*s*. iiij*d*. Item And a stress (*distress?*) delyvered for George wilbie for one horse gait paid & discharged, viij*s*.

receits vij*l*. j*s*. viij*d*.

Expences laid foorth for this yere last past.

Item paid to the counstaples for the dressinge of the common armore the vth of June, vj*d*. Item paid to the hurde for dammynge the water at giles bridge & for skooringe some part of the leche, vj*d*. Item paid for a heade peece o^{r} murrion y^{t} was lost, ij*s*. vj*d*. Item paid to the hurde for skowringe xx^{tie} roode of the more dicke & for upholding ye said dicke for the hole yere, iiij*s*. Item paid for one foother of hay to the bull price, xviij*s*. Item paid for the carrage of yt home, xij*d*. Item paid in charges to the waynmen & for bereinge in of yt, ix*d*. Item paid to Thomas tompson for mendinge of pittington yeat a hole dayes worke, viij*d*. Item paid for two shelmes^{1} caryinge to the same, j*d*. Item paid to the counstaples concernynge a sesment for elvett and framwelgait bridges, xx*d*. Item paid to the hurde for mendinge of ellesleese dicke & the lower ende of vii akers dicke, iiij*d*. Item paid to the hurde for servinge the bull in the tyme of wynter, xij*d*. Item paid for vj^{th} horsses to chester with certayn prisoners one horse vj*d*. the hole, iij*s*. Item likewyse for two to branspeth with a prisoner y^{t} was executed for a murther 4*d*. a horse, viij*d*. Item paid to the churchwardens for makinge up ther hole some to the Justices for Roogemoney, ij*s*. viij*d*. Item paid to wedow smyth for howsrowme for the bull & for standinge of his hay for this last yere, ij*s*. Item paid to Thomas tompson & his wyfe for dressinge of the mayden castell, xvj*d*. Item paid to the hurde for castinge of the dooke poole and for dammynge the water at giles bridge, xx*d*. Item more paid to the said hurde for castinge of the poole next the pinfold, ij*s*. Item paid for wrytinge of our accounts, ij*s*.

Expences xlvj*s*. iiij*d*.

The grass men elected the sunday next after the Assencion day for this next yere 1602 Thomas cornfurth & Thomas marshall of the lower end & they Resave at ther entrance declara iiij*l*. xv*s*. iiij*d*.

¹ See Glossary.

Item Resaved for a bull xxxiij*s*. iiij*d*. Resaved of Iohn whytheade for two horse gaits on the common, xvj*s*. Resaved of George wilbie for a horse, viij*s*. Resaved of Iohn Johnson for a horse, ij*s*. viij*d*. Resaved of Edward harle for one cowe, ij*s*. Resaved of James hodshon, xvj*d*. Resaved of George tomson for a cowe, xvj*d*. Resaved of Rychard Artcher for ij horse gaits & one cowe, xx*s*. Resaved of the hole parishe everie cowe ij*d*. for the bull hay the hole sum, xiij*s*. j*d*. Resaved of Rychard Artcher at this count makinge of this foresaid xx*s*. puttinge hymselfe in the parishinges well (*parishioners' will?*). they ar content to taike vj*s*.

Expences Laid fourth for this last yere 1602.

Item paid to the hurd for upholdinge the more dicke for the hole yere, iiij*s*. paid to the counstaples for the dressinge of the common armore, vj*d*. more paid to the same counstaples for a sesment for wolsingham & newton bridges, ij*s*. vj*d*. paid for settinge of a stowpe of pittington yeat, j*d*. paid for one foother of hay to Thomas Snowball for the bull, xij*s*. paid for the carrage home of yt, xij*d*. paid to Rychard Skirfeild for his drinke, iij*d*. paid to Catherin tomson for ye gettinge in of yt, iiij*d*. paid to Iohn peerson for makinge the dicke in ellessleases xij*d*. paid for Restinge of Umphray garrie to the court for a horse gait, iij*d*. paid to the churchwardens for Rooge money, iij*s*. vij*d*. paid to the hurde for mendinge the mayden castell dicke, iiij*d*. paid to the hurd for hantinge of the bull to the common, ij*d*. paid to Thomas tomson for dressinge the mayden castell, xvj*d*. paid to Thomas Snowball for xxj^tie stone of hay for the bull, price iij*s*. ij*d*. paid to xp'ofer tomson for makinge up the pellowlese dicke[1] next his howse, ij*d*.

[*Caetera desunt, till A.D. 1605*].

Expences laid out for this last yeare 1605.

Item paid for the bull that was bought, xl*s*. Item p for my maire & my charge to darnton xviij*d*. Item p to Thomas snawball for a stone of hay to ye bull when he cam home, ij*d*. Item p to Nycholas sparke for scowringe the wateringe place at gills bridge, iiij*d*. Item p to Xp'ofor tomson for mendinge ye mayden castell which was broken downe by the milkers of kye, v*d*. Item paid to the counstaples for A sesment of ij*d*. the pound for certayn

---

[1] "Pellowleases." See below, p. 40, note 2.

bridges decayed, xx*d*. Item p when we cam from Mr Coksons beinge to se A bull which we should have bought in drinke, vj*d*. Item p for a Fother of hay to the bull, xij*s*. Item p for leadinge home of yt, xij*d*. Item p to the leder of yt & for ther drinke when yt cam home, vj*d*. Item p for for the lainge of yt in the howse, iiij*d*. Item p to william Kent for upholdinge of elleslease dicke, viij*d*. Item to the counstaples for ye dressinge of the common armore, xij*d*. Item p to three men which careed them to vew on ye place grene before the Justices, xvj*d*. Item p to the churchwardens for makinge up ye hole some of the Rogemoney, ij*s*. ix*d*. Item p to Nell Robson for howsrome for ye bull his hay & for servinge of hym the tyme of winter, iij*s*. Item p for ye dressinge of the mayden castle, xij*d*. Item p for certayn gapes mendinge at ye lowe ende of vij acres, iiij*d*. Item p to Margarett tomson for one dosson stone of hay to ye bull, ij*s*. ij*d*. Item p for charges of the court for ye sute of George wilbie deseased, xv*d*. Item p for paper for this booke, ij*d*. Item p to Nycholas sparke for upholdinge ye more dicke the hole yeare, iiij*s*. Item paid for the wrytinge of this our account, ij*s*. Item paid to william Kent for mendinge the dicke at pittington loninge, iiij*d*. Item paid for a hupe to the more yeat, iij*d*.

Expences iij*l*. xviij*s*. ix*d*.

So Remaynes declara——iiij*l*. xiij*s*. vj*d*.

Newe grass men chosen the First day of June A° 1606 Rychard Storie & Iohn Frissell & they have Resaved declara iiij*l*. xiij*s*. vj*d*. dew to ye use of the parishe.

Item rec^d of George Tayler Tanner for thre gaits on the common, iiij*s*. Item rec^d of Thomas Colson for one horse gait, ij*s*. viij*d*. Item rec^d of George wilbie concernynge the sute, vj*s*. Item rec^d of Sander Little for two kye gaits, viij*s*. Item rec^d of the parishe for bull hay ij*d*. a cowe, xij*s*. Item rec^d of Thomas colson for a horse gait, ij*s*. viij*d*. Item rec^d of Iohn colson cooke(?) for A horse gait, ij*s*. viij*d*. Item rec^d of Xp'ofor Bowmer (*Bulmer*) for a cowe gait, ij*s*. Item rec^d of Xp'ofer Jarvis carpinter for a cowe gait, iiij*s*. Item rec^d of daniell hudspeth for one horse gait, ij*s*. viij*d*. Item rec^d of henry Arresmyth for lij fother of whinnes[1] ij*d*. a fother the hole, viij*s*. viij*d*.

---

[1] It thus appears that at this time the parishioners assumed and exercised the right of disposing of the whins on the moor. In 1726 John Tempest, then lord of the manor, in his suit against the parishioners alluded to above (p. 18, note 1), disputed this right, maintaining that the whins were his.

Some lvij*s.* iij*d.*
Some totall vij*l.* ix*s.* x*d.*

Expences laid out for this last yeare by the said gras
men.

Item paid for thre horsses to Ferrie hill with prisoners,
xviij*d.* Item p to wedowe hodshon, vj*d.* Item paid to
Thomas cornforth for the articles, viij*s.* Item paid to
Thomas Baker for the more dicke for the hole yere, iiij*s.*
Item paid to Rychard storie for A lode of hay to y*e* bull,
xij*s.* Item paid to y*e* counstaples for y*e* harnes scowringe,
iiij*d.* Item paid for gettinge in of the bull hay, iiij*d.*
Item paid to George wilbie for the carrage home of yt, xij*d.*
Item paid for our drinke & the wayne men, vj*d.* Item
paid for charges of Jarett swanes daughter beinge in
suspecion of the plauge,[1] xiiij*d.* Item paid to william
homble & his sonne for ther worke concernynge the
settinge up of the bull howse,[2] vij*s.* iiij*d.* Item paid to
george wilbie for the carrage of ij lode of timber, ij*s.* Item
paid for ther drinke, iiij*d.* Item paid for nayles to the
doore, iij*d.* Item paid for roge money ij*s.* Item paid to
Thomas baker for mendinge of the dickes about y*e* closes,
vj*d.* Item paid to Nycollas sparke for diginge of clay to
y*e* bull howse, vj*d.* Item paid to george Rowell for suche
lyke, vj*d.* Item paid to Rychard tripp for suche lyke, vj*d.*
Item paid to ix bearers of clay & water one day to y*e* said
howse, ij*s.* iij*d.* Item paid to william kent for workinge
at y*e* bull howse, v*s.* iiij*d.* Item paid to his sonne for his
worke, ij*s.* iiij*d.* Item paid to george Rowell for 3 dayes
worke, xviij*d.* Item paid to Iohn helcott for 3 dayes,
xviij*d.* Item to Charles harrison for 3 dayes, xviij*d.* Item

---

[1] See above, p. 24, note 1.

[2] A bull-house appears to have been erected for the first time this year,
" house-room " for the bull having been previously paid for in successive
years. It was not a stone erection, timber, wattles and clay having been
alone employed. The following appears to have been the whole cost, the
timber used having been got for nothing :—

		£	s.	d.
Straw	...	0	5	1
Wattles & carriage of the same	...	0	1	2
Broom for gavel end	..	0	0	6
Carriage of timber	...	0	2	4
Carriage of straw, flags, rails, & posts	...	0	1	11
Digging clay, & other work	...	1	15	1
Door, lock, & nails	...	0	1	11
Hecke	...	0	0	4
		£2	8	4

to wedowe cooke for ij dayes, vj*d*. Item p to Thomas baker for mendinge the dicke, iiij*d*. Item p to margreet walker for 3 dayes, ix*d*. Item p for drinke to them, iij*d*. Item p to Rychard storie for 4 thrave of strawe, xvj*d*. Item p to hym for A planke that was for gills brigg, viij*d*. Item p to Kent for gettinge of wattles & carrage of them home, xiiij*d*. Item p to hym for a thrave of otte (*oat*) straw for Ropes, iij*d*. Item p to Iohn wilson for ix thrave of Rye straw & vj of bigg straw, iij*s*. vj*d*. Item p to charles herryson for the carrage of ŷ straw to ŷ bull house & for the drawinge[1] of yt, 14*d*. Item p to hym for a gutter makinge at the bull house, vj*d*. Item p to Iohn Kent for bannes crokes a locke & other nedefull things to the doore, xx*d*. Item p to Xp'ofer Jarvis for ij dayes worke & a halfe, ij*s*. j*d*. Item p to Kent for a hecke making to ŷ bull, iiij*d*. Item p for ŷ carrage of ij horse lodes of flages, iiij*d*. Item p to peter baker for ŷ carrage of Rales & postes, v*d*. Item p to one that dyd Ryve them, ij*d*. Item p to charles herryson for brome to ŷ gavell ende of ŷ house, vj*d*. Item p to hym for servinge ŷ bull & for housrome of ŷ hay, ij*s*. Item p to george browne for makinge ŷ mayden castell dicke, vj*d*. Item p to william homble & his sonne for mendinge ŷ moore yeat, vj*d*. Item p to Anthoney homble for layinge downe ŷ planke at gills brigg, iiij*d*. Item p to Kent for removinge the dore & makinge a peace of wall, xij*d*.[2] Item p for mendinge of pittington yeat, iiij*d*. Item p to Iohn maughams wyfe for hir horse to chester, vij*d*. Item paid for wrytinge this our account, ij*s*.

Some of ŷ expences iij*l*. xix*s*. v*d*.

grase men chosen the xvij[th] day of may 1607 Iohn wilson & Robt. marshall And they have rec[d] declara iij*l*. x*s*. v*d*. to the use of the parishe.

Item Rec[d] of Edward harle Tanner for three gaits on ŷ common which is the last of his stent, vj*s*. Item Rec[d] for the bull that was sould, xlvj*s*. vj*d*. Item rec[d] for bull hay everie cowe ij*d*. the hole, xiiij*s*. ij*d*. Resaved for hay that was sould $\overset{xx}{\underset{iij}{}}$ (*i.e.*, 60) stone & three at ij*d*. a stone the hole some, xv*s*. ix*d*. Rec[d] of George Taylor glover the last payment of his hole stent for the common, ij*s*. viij*d*.

---

[1] *I.e.*, Drawing it out straight for thatching. The word in this sense is still in use. *Cf.* "Memorials of Ripon," III, 102 (Surtees Society's Publications, vol. lxxxi):—"A.D. 1379-80, j mulier auxil. ad tractand. dictum stramen et portant. aquam per idem tempus, 2*s*. 1*d*."

[2] See p. 10, note 2. It would seem from this entry that there was some sort of building in connexion with the watering-place at Gillsbridge.

3

Rec^d of Rychard carr for a horse gait, viij*s.* Rec^d of Xp'ofer Jarvis for a cowe gait, 5 paid for, iiij*s.* Rec^d of henry Arrasmyth for xxviij fother of whines ij*d.* a fother the hole, iiij*s.* viij*d.* Rec^d of Iohn orde for A horse gait, 5 paid for, viij*s.* Rec^d of Xp'ofor Bowlmer for iiij^{er} gaits on the common the last payment of his hole stent, viij*s.*

Some ix*l.* viij*s.* ij*d.*

Expences laid forth for this yeare 1607.

Item paid to wedowe hodshon, vj*s.* Item p to william Kent for upholdinge ye moore dicke, iiij*s.* Item p to Rychard cornforth for a lode of hay to the bull, price xvij*s.* iiij*d.* Item p for A bull that was bought, xlj*s.* Item p for scowringe ye lowe carr to Kent & browne, xij*d.* Item p for a stobb & settinge of y^t at the more yeat, viij*d.* Item p for mendinge of pittington lonyng end & for settinge a stobe at ye yeat & mendinge ye maden castle dicke, xij*d.* Item p to wedowe alderley for standinge of ye bull hay, xij*d.* Item p to georg browne for scowringe gills brigg letche, viij*d.* Item p to ye hurde for kepinge & hantinge ye bull to ye common, iiij*d.* Item p for wrytinge this our account, ij*s.* It. p to william Kent for servinge the bull ye foreend of winter, xij*d.*

Some of the expences is iij*l.* xvj*s.*

Some declara v*l.* xij*s.* ij*d.*

Newe grass men chosen the viijth day of may for this yeare 1608 Robt. heighington & Rychard carnforth and they have resaved for the use of the parishe v*l.* xv*s.* viij*d.*

Item Rec^d of Sander litle for one gait of ye common, iij*s.* vj*d.* the other vj*d.* rebayted by ye consent of the parishe. Item Rec^d of Nycholas newbie for a bull that he bought, xl*s.* Item rec^d of william dawson for a bull that he bought, xl*s.* Item rec^d of Robert baker for thre gaits on ye common, xij*s.* Item rec^d of M^r watson for hay that was sould, v*s.* Item rec^d of Silvester maugham for vj gaits on ye common, xxiiij*s.* Item rec^d of Thomas wan for one gait on ye common, ij*s.* Item rec^d of Mr Robt. Selbie for thre gaits on ye common, xij*s.*

Some of Receyts xij*l.* xiiij*s.* ij*d.*

Expences.

Item p to Edward hall for a sesment which he laid out for the parishe, v*s.* Item p for a warran to hym, xij*d.* Item p to wedowe hodshon, vj*d.* Item p to Edward harle for his horse to newcastell, xij*d.* Item p to William

Newton for such lyke, xij*d.* Item p to Cuthbert cornforth & Iohn burdus for ther chargs for the servinge of ye same warran, xviij*d.* Item p to Cuthbert cornforth for his horse to eaghton (*Heighington?*) with a prisoner, x*d.* Item p to Robt. hudspeth for making two presentments maid to the counstaples for ye last yere, vj*d.* Item p to ye counstaples for dressinge ye common armor, x*d.* Item p for mendinge of pittington yeat & the maidin castell, vij*d.* Item p for mendinge the more dicke one dayes worke, vj*d.* Item p for scowringe the gills brige letche, ij*s.* iij*d.* Item p for upholdinge the more dicke ye last somer, xij*d.* Item p for scowringe the doocke poole to george browne, ij*s.* iiij*d.* Item p to nycholas sparke for upholdinge the dickes of elles leases & other places belonginge to the common, ij*s.* vj*d.* Item p to Rychard wanles & Andrew currey for them and ther horsses to chester with ij prisoners, xij*d.* Item p for one that stood with the bull in ye markett on St Cuthbert day, iiij*d.* Item p to Robt. hudspeth for making a bill of all ye naymes in the parishe concernynge a generall muster, iiij*d.* Item p to william Kent for straw & thackinge ye bull howse, xvj*d.* Item p william Kent for scowringe certayn roodes of ye more dicke & makinge all the dicke sufficient, iiij*s.* Item more for a stile to ye said dicke, iiij*d.* Item p to Nycholas sparke for scowringe ye maiden castell dicke, xij*d.* Item given to Nycholas newbie agayn concernynge the bull that was sould, iiij*d.* Item paid to Thomas yong of wharington (*Quarrington*) for a bull that was bought, xl*s.* Item p to the hurd for fetchinge home ye said bull & for hantinge hym to the common, vij*d.* Item p to sparke for mendinge pittington yeat, iij*d.* Item p to the counstaples for articles that they resaved of the Justices, xiiij*d.* Item p for a locke to the bull howse, vij*d.* Item p to peter baker for servinge the bull, xij*d.* Item p to Rychard chilton for dressinge ye maden castell, xiiij*d.* Item p to sparke for mendinge pittington yeat, vj*d.* Item p to Iohn Robson counstaple, vj*d.* Item given agayn to william dawson for ye bull, iiij*d.* Item p to M^r wanles for one fother of hay to ye bull, xx*s.* Item p to the wainmen for ther drinke, iiij*d.* Item p for bearinge in of yt, iiij*d.* Item p for wrytinge this our account, ij*s.*

     expences v*l.* iiij*s.* viij*d.*
     So remaynes declara vij*l.* ix*s.* vj*d.*

Newe gras men chosen the sounday next after the Assencion day beinge the 28 day of maii 1609 Thomas

marshall & Cuthbert cornforth & they have rec[d] for the use
of the parishe, vij*l.* ix*s.* vj*d.*

The accompt of the foresaid Gras men as followeth.
Item Rec[d] of the parishe everie cowe ij*d.* for bull hay, xij*s.*
viij*d.* Item Rec[d] of George hubbucke for two gaits on y[e]
common, viij*s.* Item Rec[d] of Launce wilkinson for one
gait, iiij*s.* Item Rec of Iohn Greme for two gaits, viiij*s.*
Item Rec of Iohn colson carpinter for two gaits, ij*s.* viij*d.*
Item Rec of George Rowell for one gait, v paid for, iiij*s.*
Some totall ix*l.* viij*s.* x*d.*

expences.
Item p to Annas hodshon, vj*s.* Item p for a purse to
y[e] gras men, ij*d.* Item p to George browne for mendinge
y[e] moore dicke, vj*d.* Item p for a common bull at darnton,
xliiij*s.* viij*d.* Item p for my horse & my chargs for
bringinge home of the bull the same tyme, xviij*d.* Item
p to George browne for scowringe y[e] letche at gills brigg,
xxj*d.* Item p for a fother of hay to Robt. marshall for the
bull, xv*s.* vj*d.* Item p for bearinge the said hay home
gettinge y[t] in to y[e] howse, xvj*d.* Item geven to the counstaples to pay for the common armore, vj*d.* Item p for
hantinge the bull to the more to the hurde, ij*d.* Item p for
the Fogg more than we dyd resave of y[e] parishe, xviij*d.*
Item p to George browne for servinge y[e] bull the tyme of
winter, xx*d.* Item p to william Kent for scowringe and
upholdinge y[e] more dicke, iiij*s.* Item p to y[e] pyper for
plainge to the more when yt was dressed, iiij*d.*[1] Item p to
Iohn grene for mendinge ellessleise dicke, vj*d.* Item p to
Thomas cornforth for one dossen stone of hay to y[e] bull,
ij*s.* vj*d.* Item p to william Kent for scowringe dickinge &
dressinge y[e] mayden castell, xx*d.* Item p for mendinge
pittington yett & mendinge the dicke, vj*d.* Item p for
wrytinge the statute for the hyewayes anewe, xij*d.* Item
p for wrytinge this our account, ij*s.* Item p to Raphe
pendreth yonger for A sesment for the Reparinge of
witton on weare bridge, xx*d.* Item p for arreaste & entry

---

[1] This is the first reference to the custom of calling out the inhabitants
once a year to join in "dressing" or "scaling" or "moulding" the moor,
to which frequent allusions appear afterwards. Those who "scaled," *i.e.,*
scattered the deposits of the cattle, &c., were called the "mouders." They
appear to have been summoned by music, and regaled with "drinks." The
"pyper" here may have served, not only to summon them, but also to
cheer them in their work. *Cf.,* below (A.D. 1674):—"To George Pearson
for playing to the mouders," and (A.D. 1695) "For playinge to the mouders
when they mouded the moore."

of Iohn greene, iij*d*. Item p for iiij horsses to fishborne with a prisoner, ij*s*.

Some totall iiij*l*. xj*s*. viij*d*.

Newe Grass men chosen for this yere followinge 1610 George Taylor glover and Thomas snawball and they have Resaved for the use of the parishe at the accounts of ye old gras men, 4*l*. 7*s*. 2*d*.

It ys agreed by the parishe at this account that Nycholas sparke shall have one gait Allowed on the common for and in consederacion of his duetefull service & paynes takinge in lokinge well to the common beinge appoynted punder upon his well doinge yf not yt must not be allowed yf he be slowthfull and negligent to looke to ye more & common As well in winter as sommer for the more saiftie of ye said more especially in winter for shepe & other cattell beinge not of this parishe.

The accoumpt of the foresaid grasse men for the last yere as Followeth.

Item Resaved of the hole parishe everie cowe ij*d*. for bull hay the hole some, xiij*s*. iiij*d*. Item Rec^d for the bull that was sould, xlvj*s*. vj*d*. Item which was saved by the bull that was bought, xviij*d*. Item Rec^d of George hubbucke for three gaits on the common, xij*s*. Item rec^d of Iohn harryson fuller for three gaits, xij*s*. Item rec^d of xp'ofer symson Tanner for two gaits, iiij*s*. Item Rec^d of James sutton for two gaits on the common, ij*s*. viij*d*. Item Rec^d of Rob'te baker the last payment of his stent, viij*s*. Item Rec^d of Thomas ludworth for iiijth gaits on ye common, xvj*s*. Item Rec^d of Thomas wanne for one gait, ij*s*. Item Rec^d of Nycholas sparke for one gait, iiij*s*. Item Rec^d of Rychard Martyn for two gaits on the common, ij*s*. viij*d*. Item Rec^d of George Rowell for his hole stent, iiij*s*. Item Rec^d of the hole parishe for the new dicke,[1] xxxxiij*s*. vj*d*.

Some vij*l*. xviij*s*. viij*d*.

Some of the Receyts ys xiij*l*. iiij*s*. iiij*d*.

expences.

Item p to Robt heighington for charges of the courte, xxiij*d*. Item p to wedowe hodshon vj*s*. Item p to william newton for his horse to carrie a prisoner iiij*d*. Item paid for the bull that was bought, xlv*s*. Item p for mendinge

---

[1] A new dike round the Moor for its protection appears to have become necessary. See above, p. 9, note 3. The cost of the work will appear below.

the dicke in vij acares to william kempt, iij*d*. Item p for hantinge the bull to the common, iij*d*. Item p for sekinge the bull when he was strayd away, iiij*d*. Item p for dressinge the armore dew to this parishe, vj*d*. Item p to george browen for castinge a gutter at the bull howse, iiij*d*. Item p to Edward hall for the releife of Iohn Atcheson in the tyme of the vicitacion,[1] vj*s*. iiij*d*. Item p to george browen for servinge y*e* bull all y*e* tyme of winter, ij*s*. Item p to william Kent for upholdinge the more dicke the hole yere, iiij*s*. Item p to N sparke & Thomas ludworth for ther mendinge the far more gait, iiij*d*. Item p to G browne for two Railes to mend the bull stall, iij*d*. Item p to hym more for ij burthen of Rise[2] to lay under the hay, iij*d*. Item p for ij spikings to the bull howse, j*d*. Item p to xp'ofor Jarvis for one dayes worke at the bull howse, x*d*. Item p for hay to the bull to Iohn Tripp, xix*s*. Item p for winnynge & driynge of the said hay, xij*d*. Item p for carage home of the said hay, ij*s*. Item p for drinke & bread to the waynmen, iiij*d*. Item p for Rakinge after the wayn & gettinge in of yt to y*e* bull howse, x*d*. Item p to Thomas ludworth for mendinge the far more gait, ij*d*.

Expences for the new dicke as Followeth.

Item first p to certayne workmen for castinge the dicke, x*s*. Item p to Cuthbert cornforth for wood to the gaits, ix*s*. vj*d*. Item p to Thomas snawball for wood, ij*s*. Item p to Iohn colson for two peaces of wood, xij*d*. Item p to Iohn Burdus for certayn peaces of wood, xvj*d*. Item p to Iohn colson for wood to maike ij capes for the yeats, vj*d*. Item p for hupes & ij pickes to y*e* said gaits of Iron, xxj*d*. Item p to certayn workmen for breardinge[3] the dicke, x*s*. Item p to ij wrights iiij*th* days xj*d*. a day the hole some, vij*s*. iiij*d*. Item p to Rychard chilton for one peace of wood, ix*d*. Item p to Thomas snawball for ij peaces of wood, xvj*d*. Item p to Thomas snawball for j stoupe & a raile, iiij*d*. Item p to Kent his sonne & N sparke for ij dayes worke, ij*s*. Item p to Cuthbert dent for one days worke, vj*d*. Item p to George Rowell for one days worke and a halfe, x*d*. Item p to N sparke for one dayes worke about the yeats, vj*d*. Item p to Rychard cornforth for lokinge to the common, ij*s*. vj*d*. Item p to Thomas Casick for nayles, j*d*. Item p to xp'ofer Thomson for a litle Jobb mendinge about the gait, j*d*.

---

[1] *I.e.*, The plague, which is usually so referred to.
[2] *I.e.*, Brushwood. See Glossary.   [3] See Glossary.

Expences for y*e* bull hay.

Item p to Thomas snowball for vj dossen stone of hay to y*e* bull ij*s*. a stone the hole xij*s*. Item p to Rob'te heighington for a rope to hould fast ij stoupes in the bull howse, iij*d*. Item p to Rob'te hudspeth for wrytinge this our accompt, ij*s*. Item p for our fower dinners & our clarke, ij*s*. vj*d*. Item p to Nycholas sparke for mendinge certayn gapes in Ellesleise, vj*d*. Item p to Edward cornforth & to Cuthbert cornforth for ther horsses to gaitside (*Gateshead*) to bring prisoners from newcastell, ij*s*.

expences ys viij*l*. iiij*s*. xj*d*.

Some declara iiij*l*. xixs. v*d*.

The following appears on a later page of the book as now bound up :—

The 29 daye of Aprill 1610.[1]

M*d* it is consented and agreed the daye and yere abovesaid by the assent and consent of the 24*tie* of the parishe of S*t* Geles that the Backhouse man that is Silvester maugham shall have the whinnes growing on the common more belonginge to S*t* Giles parishe for this yere next cominge for iiij*s*. ij*d*. rent to cutt and take the said whinnes for the said yere at the appoyntment of the Churchwardens of S*t* Giles chosen in the said parishe for the said yere followinge for so manie as he shall nead to the same backhouse for one whole yere, and none to be sold by the said Silvester to any other. provided that the said Silvester maugham shall without any pennie receyveing bake to everie housholder three pyes or three Caks on the sabothe daye that is everie sabothe daye throughe the yere free, except Easter sondaye Whit soandaye and Christmas daye, and the housholders to paye for thes three feastes & dayes to the backhouse man as hathe bene usually payd, and also everie housholder shall paye to the said Backhouse man for the bakinge of spyce Cakes for there owen house for five cakes one half pennie, tenn A pennie, and so furthe as they are in number, and for the said spice Cakes to paye to the said bakhouse man for everie threteene Cakes one Cake[2] and no more, and the backhouse man not to demand any further thenn is heer sett dowen.

The new Grasse men chosen for this yere followinge 1611 humphray garrie & Robt. colson And they have Resaved at this account of the old Grasse men the some of iiij*l*. xixs. v*d*.

<hr>

[1] See above, p. 18, note 2, and p. 31, note 1, with reference to the vestry order which follows.

[2] *Cake* is written above *penny* erased. A "baker's dozen."

The accompt of the said Grasse men as followeth maid the 24 day of May 1612.

Item Rec^d of wedowe Foster concernynge ye new dicke, xij*d*. Rec^d of Thomas Trewett servant to Iohn Booth for two kye gaits on the common, viij*s*. Item Rec^d for the bull that was sould to william dawson, xlviij*s*. Rec^d of the parishe for bull hay everie cowe ij*d*., the hole, xij*s*. ij*d*. Rec^d for fogg of pellow leases[1] everie cowe vj*d*., the hole xxxij*s*. Rec^d for fogg in brode close[2] everie cowe vj*d*., the hole xxviij*s*. Rec^d of Iohn colson carpinter for one gait, xvj*d*. Rec^d of Nycholas sparke for one cowe gait, iiij*s*. Resaved of James sutton for a horse gait, ij*s*. viij*d*. Rec^d of Thomas dawson for iijth gaits, iiij*s*. Rec^d of Rychard martyn for one gait, xvj*d*. Rec^d of Anthoney duckett for iiij^{or} gaits on ye common, xvj*s*. Rec^d of Iohn brantingham for one gait, ij*s*.

Some totall xij*l*. xviij*s*. xv*d*.

Expences for the last yere 1611.

Item p to wedowe hodshon, vj*s*. Item p to Rychard Tripp for ij sakes of cooles to Iohn atcheson, viij*d*. Item p to william Kent and Rychard Tripp for one dayes worke at the lower carr, xij*d*. Item p to Edward hall Bailiffe for an old Sesment behynd unpaid for Reparinge of Briges, v*s*. Item p to Iohn colson carpinter for mendinge of pittington yeat & Sherebourne yeat, xx*d*. Item p to william stobbs for servinge at that tyme, iij*d*. Item p to william Kent & Rychard Tripp for scowringe the lower carr, xij*d*. Item p to william Kent for mendinge the moore yeat, iiij*d*. Item p to Nycholas sparke for up holdinge of Ellesse leise dicke, ij*s*. Item p to Iohn frissell for mendinge of ye Railes in pellow leise chare, iiij*d*. Item p to Rychard glover for ij Thrave of straw to ye bull howse xij*d*. Item p to william Kent lainge on the said straw, xij*d*. Item p to George

---

[1] Pellowleases. The enclosed fields on the South of the street, between it and the river, are so designated. These, with others, were called *Town fields*, being subject to commonage during the winter months:—"Whereas there are within the Manor of Gilligate and Parish of St. Giles certain *Town fields* or enclosed lands, which are subject to Commonage thereon, calld ' Right of Intercommon,' from 15 Sept. in each year to 31 March in the year following" (*Act for Enclosure of Gilligate Moor, 1816*). It appears that the fog, as well as the hay, of these fields, till the right of Intercommon began in September, belonged to their " owners," and had to be paid for, if used for pasturage. It will be seen among the "Expenses" of this year that the Grassmen paid the "oweners" 33*s*. 4*d*. for the use of Pellowleases fog, and 30*s*. 6*d*. for that of " Broad Close," which was also apparently a Town field, being on the North side of the Rainton road above the top of the street.

[2] See last note.

Tayler Tanner Counstapple for a sesment for the house of correction,[1] v*s*. Item p to the counstaple for dressinge the common armore belonginge to the parishe, — . Item p to Rychard chilton for dressinge the maiden castell within & without ——. Item p to Iohn Creme for mendinge of pittington yeat & scowringe the dicke, x*d*. Item p to Iohn grene for puttinge on a hupe & mendinge sherborne yeat, vj*d*. Item p to M*r* Iohn heath the elder for brigges, v*s*. Item p to George cragg for bull hay, xxij*s*. vj*d*. Item p for the carage of the same home & drinke to y*e* wainmen, xij*d*. Item p for gettinge in of the said hay, vj*d*. Item p to william Kent for upholdinge the more dicke & scowringe so many Roodes of y*e* said dicke, iiij*s*. Item p to william Kent for servinge the bull y*e* tyme of winter, ij*s*. Item p to Thomas cornforth for one dossen of hay to the bull, iij*s*. Item p to Rob'te Baker for halfe A dossen xviij*d*. Item p for the bull that was bought, xxxix*s*. Item p for poundlawes[2] for the bull to Iohn Booth, vj*d*. Item p to Cuthbert cornforth for his horse to darnton to buy the same bull, xvj*d*. Item p for my charges & the horse, x*d*. Item p to Thomas baker for mendinge the dicke at the lowe end of vij acres,[3] vj*d*. Item p to the oweners of the fogg in pellow leise, xxxiij*s*. 4*d*. Item p to the oweners of brod close fogg, xxx*s*. vj*d*. Item p for wrytinge this our accoumpt, ij*s*. Item p for charges of the corte at the sute of Iohn Tripp, vij*d*.

Expences viij*l*. xix*s*. ij*d*.
Some declara iiij*l*. j*d*.

On a later page of book is found as followes :—
The iij*th* day of may A° 1611. Resaved of the hole parishe concernynge the new dicke & the yeats everie horse iiij*d*. & everie cowe ij*d*. as Followeth. *After this there is a list of 69 names with the sums contributed by each person named, varying from ij*d*. to xij*d*.; and at the end, some xxxviij*s*. vj*d*.*

[So far all entries have been transcribed in full, as they appear in the original Grassmen's accounts. Henceforth, for the sake of brevity, many which recur regularly every year will be alluded to only. The headings also of each year's accounts, except in case of any peculiarity, will be

---

[1] For reference to 7 Jac. I, c. 4 (A.D. 1610), for establishment of Houses of Correction, see Surtees Society's Publications, vol. lxxxiv, p. 82.

[2] See Glossary.

[3] One of the enclosed fields of Pellowleases.

curtailed, and such phrases as " Item received," or " Item paid," before each entry suppressed].

Grassmen for 1612, Edward cornforth & Rychard cornforth. Resaved of the old grasmen, the 24th day of May, iij*l*. i*s*. ix*d*.

Accounte maid the xvjth day of May 1613.

Item Rec^d of the hole parish everie cowe ij*d*. for bull hay, the hole, xiiij*s*. Of Rychard hunter for the bull that was bought to Thomas snawden, xxxj*s*. vj*d*. Of the parishe everie cowe vj*d*. *ob*. for the fogg in brodeclose which some ys in the hole xxix*s*. vij*d*. For pellowleese fogg everie cowe vj*d*., xxviij*s*. vj*d*. Of Rychard hunter for the branded bull, xxxix*s*. vj*d*.

[*Payments received, as usual, for cow and horse gaits, amounting to £1 0s. 8d.*]

Item yt ys allowed by the parishe at this account that Iohn helcott shall be free on the common for ij*s*. a cowe gaite and so haith paid for ij gaits iiij*s*.

Expences.

Item p to Iohn Tripp for fogg in brode close for the last yere 1612. To wedowe hodshon, vj*s*. To Iohn garrie for his horse to ferrie hill with a prisoner, vj*d*. To Iohn grene for scowringe gillsbrige letche, vj*d*. To Xp'ofer boolmer and George Rowell for ther horsses to Ferrie hill, xij*d*. For a quaire of paper for the use of the parishe, iiij*d*. For scowringe of the lower carr, xviij*d*. For nayles, j*d*. For a hupe to the more yeat, ij*d*. To Iohn Frissell & Rychard Tripp for settinge the Railes in pellowlease chare, iiij*d*. To Rychard Tripp for settinge Railes at the layne ende next to Iohn colsons, iiij*d*. To Iohn grene & Rychard Tripp for makinge up of Elleslease dicke, xij*d*. To Iohn Frissell for wrytinge some busines for the use of the parishe, ij*s*. vj*d*. To George cragg counstaple for a Sessment, x*d*. For dressinge the common armore, xviij*d*. To nycholas Barrey for his worke doyn of ye pickes, vj*d*. To the new counstaples xp'ofor sympson & John harryson ij*s*. viij*d*. To Mr Barnes for articles, xij*d*. For thre burthen of ryse to lay under ye bull hay, iiij*d*. For ij thrave of straw to ye bull howse for carrage home of yt drawinge of yt & thickinge of yt, ij*s*. vj*d*. To Thomas snawden for a bull, xxxv*s*. To william Kent for servinge the bull ye tyme of winter, ij*s*. More for a saile[1] to the bull, ij*d*. For vj stone of hay to ye bull, xiiij*d*. To william

---

[1] See Glossary.

Kent for dressinge the maden castell & mendinge the hedge about yt, xij*d.* For the bull bought at darnton & for my charges and my horse, xl*s.* For a fother of hay to y*e* bull & charges to the waynmen & gettinge in of yt, xx*s.* iiij*d.* For wrytinge this our account, ij*s.* To George cragg counstable for a sesment, xx*d.* For the Fogg in brode close & Anthoney duccotts close, xxxj*s.* For the Fogg in pellowleise, xxviij*s.* iiij*d.* For the sute of humphray garrie, iiij*d.* More then the fogg cam to in brod close, xvij*d.*

[*Other entries, as usual, for upholding the moor dike, making up gaps in dikes, mending gates, &c.*]

Expences x*l.* v*s.* iiij*d.*

The hole some declara dew to the parishe, xxxix*s.* ij*d.*

M*d* that at the Receyt of this account the two counstaples xp'ofer sympson Tanner & Iohn harryson fuller have Receyved these parsells followinge thre lynyngs of stell capes edged with Reed ij sortts girdles (*sword girdles*) iij daggers & ij swords thre pickes & thre full common Armore & thre head peaces j old —— pece. 16 May, 1613.

Grasse men for 1613, George Tayler Tanner & Iohn Claxton. Resaved of the oulde grasse men the xvj*th* day of may, xxxix*s.* ij*d.* Item Rec*d* of the hole parishe everie cowe ij*d.* for bull hay, xiij*s.* vj*d.* For the fogg of brode close everie cowe vj*d. ob.* to y*e* number of lv gaits the hole ys xxx*s.* For the fogg of pellowlease everie cowe vj*d. ob.* lvj gaits the hole ys xxx*s.* ij*d.*

[*As usual, for gaits on the common, amounting to £2 2s. 8d.*]

Some of the hole Receyts ys vij*l.* xv*s.* vj*d.*

Expences for this yere 1613.

Item paid to wedow hodshon, vj*s.* To xp'ofor symson counstaple for A Sesment iiij*d.* of the pound, iij*s.* iiij*d.* To Rychard skirfeild for a fother of hay to the bull, xvj*s.* For the carrage home of yt, xij*d.* For gettinge of yt in to y*e* house, iiij*d.* To george browne for settinge y*e* yeat in brode close, vj*d.* To william Kent for Reparinge y*e* mayden castell, xvj*d.* To dame Wilbie for thre stoupes & thre Railes set at the baccos layn,[1] vj*d.* To xp'ofor

---

[1] Bakehouse-lane (still so called) was the Western boundary of the parish on the North side of the street. See above, p. 18, note 1. The railing of various lanes at this time—Cf. above, "Railed in Pellowlease chare," and "at the layne ende"—may possibly have been with the view of letting such lanes as were grassy for pasture, as we find done in subsequent years.

symson for A sesment j*d.* of y*e* pound, x*d.*   For ij dossen of hay to the bull, iiij*s.*   To the counstaples for a sesment j*d.* of the pound for captayn hodshon, x*d.*   To william Kent for a saile to the bull, j*d.*   For dressinge y*e* common Armore belonginge to us, vj*d.*   To the oweners of the fogg in pellowleise, xxix*s.*   More than the fogg cam to, xviij*d.*   To Rob'te hudspeth for wrytinge this our accoumpt ——.

[*Other payments for mending dikes, gates, and the like*].

Some of the expences ys v*l.* ix*s.* iij*d.*

The hole some dew to the parishe ys xlvj*s.* iij*d.*

Grasse men for 1614, Iohn burdus & Iohn smyth weaver.   Resaved of the ould gras men, June v*th*, xlvj*s.* iij*d.*

The accounte of the said grasmen maid the 21 of May.

Rec*d* for the bull that was sould to Robte peacoke, price iij*l.* iij*s.* iiij*d.*

[*Receipts, as usual, for* gaits *on common and in* fogg].

Some of the hole receyts ys xij*l.* ix*s.* j*d.*

Expences for 1614.

To wedowe hodshon, vj*s.*   To Thomas cornforth for caryinge a prisoner to chester, xviij*d.*   For shewinge the common armore on shinklife more, iij*s.*   For one thrave of spartes[1] to the bull house & for lainge on of them, vij*d.*   To the counstaples for articles, xij*d.*   To the counstaples for a sesment, xx*d.*   To william Kent for skowringe giles bridge letche, iiij*d.*   For one fother of hay bought of M*r* wanles & y*e* carrage home, xx*s.*   To Thomas cornforth for the armore shewinge on the place grene & for dressinge of yt, ij*s.*   To Rychard martyn for the armore scalinge, xij*d.*   To Rychard tripps manghe[2] for halfe a dayes worke at y*e* more dicke, iij*d.*   For a saile to the bull, j*d.*   For wrytinge this our accounpte, ij*s.*

[*Payments also for mending dike and gates, and to owners of fog in* Brode *close and* Pellowlease *close, and for serving the bull*].

---

[1] See Glossary.

[2] A word probably equivalent to *meyne* (as in Chaucer), or *meiny* (as in Bailey's Dictionary), meaning a company or family of household servants. *Cf.*, Surtees Society's Publications (1845), cccxxxviii, in Will of John Wood, of Eldon, A.D. 1587, " I will command my *meneyi* that they be good to the," where, in another deposition, instead of this word, " folkes " is used.

Some of the expences, v*l*. iiij*d*.

So Remaynes of this accoumpte viij*l*. iiij*s*. ix*d*.

Taken out of this account to george Tayler for that he paid for Cuthbert prentice at the last account, xvj*d*., and iiij*d*. given backe in y*e* price of the bull, iiij*d*.

deducted out of this account not paid by Cuthbert comynge for iiij*or* gaits, xvj*d*.

The 21 day of may. Grass men for 1615, Rob'te heighington & xp'ofor symson. Rec*d* vij*l*. vij*s*. j*d*. The account of the said grass men for ther yere maid the xij*th* day of May, 1616.

Item Rec*d* for the bull which was sould, xlviij*s*.

[*Receipts, as usual, for* gaits *or* stents *and for fog in* Brode *close and Pellowleases close*].

Some of the hole receyts, xv*l*. xviij*s*. vij*d*.

Expences for 1615.

Item p to wedowe hodshon, vj*s*. For A bull, liij*s*. iiij*d*. To the hurde for hantinge hym to y*e* common, ij*d*. To wedowe wilbie for hir Releife in tyme of hir siknes, xij*d*. To Raiphe symson for iiij*or* thrave of strawe to the bull house, ij*s*. viij*d*. To Rob'te bambrough for y*e* carradge home of yt & for watringe of yt, x*d*. To the counstaples Iohn smyth & Iohn burdus for a sesment for bridges xij*d*. on y*e* pound, x*s*. To thre men for cariinge the thre common armors to vew upon shinkliffe more the xx*th* day of September, iij*s*. vj*d*. For makinge a peace of dicke at y*e* lower end of vij acars belongyng to the parishe, vj*d*. For dressinge the common armore belonginge to y*e* parishe, vj*d*. To Rob'te bambroughe for scowringe the lower carr & gilles brige letche[1] thre dayes, xviij*d*. To Iohn frissell for findinge Rounges & nayles for mendinge of pellowlease yeat, iiij*d*. To Rychard Tripp for mendinge of moores chare, ij*d*. To Andrew currey for hymselfe & his horse to fearie hill with a prisoner, x*d*. To the counstaples for two sesments, xx*d*. To Iohn burdus for Repayringe the mayden castell laid out by hym the last yere, xij*d*. To Rob'te hudspeth for wrytinge our accoūnt, ij*s*.

[*Some other payments for work at dikes, gates, and the bull house, for serving the bull, and for fog in* Brode *and* Pellowlease *closes*].

Expences vj*l*. xviij*s*. xij*d*.

---

[1] This entry confirms the supposition that "the lower carr of the moor" was at Gillesbridge. See above, p. 11, note 2.

1616. M^d the xij^th day of may Rob'te heighington &
xp'ofor symson haith maid ther account the day & yere
Aforesaid before the parishe just & right.

The xij^th day of may 1616. Grass men chosen for this
present yere Rob'te Reneson tanner & Iohn harryson fuller
& they have receyved for the use of the parishe at this
accounpte the some of ix*l*. In witnes wherof they have
sette ther hands.
                              Iohn harison.
                              Robert Renoldson.

Rec^d of Rychard Robeson Seaver for a horse gait,
viij*s*. Rec^d of wedowe hall of crawcrooke, iiij*s*. Of Iohn
Claxton for two laynes, viij*s*.[1] For a bull which we sould,
xlv*s*. viij*d*.

[*Other receipts for* gaits, *bull-hay, and fog in the
two closes*].

Receyts xvj*l*. vij*s*. ij*d*.

Expences.

Item p to wedowe hodshon, vj*s*. To Rob'te bambrough
& Edmond smyth for Repayringe ye maiden castle for one
dayes worke, xij*d*. To ye counstaples for articles given by
ye justices,[2] xviij*d*. For A bull at darnton to ye use of y^e
parishe, xxxviij*s*. For charges for gettinge hym home to
Thomas cornforth & Rob'te Kent & for one stone of hay, iij*s*.
To the hurde for hantinge hym to ye common, ij*d*. To
Ambros butler Rob'te Kent for thre dayes worke & a halfe
at mayden castle, iiij*s*. To Rob'te bambrough for ringinge
yt aboute with whines, xij*d*. To the workmen for drinke
to ye said worke, vj*d*. For a lock to ye bull house, iiij*d*.
To Rob'te Carr & william burton for skowringe giles brige
letch, xij*d*. To George cragg for foure Riges in ye lyme-
kill close & ye third part of iiij^or riges, xvij*s*. x*d*.[3] For
mowing of them xx*d*. For winninge & ledinge of y^e
same home, xxij*d*. For drinke & bread to ye wainmen &
bearears in of yt, x*d*. To Thomas cornforth for changinge
of A bull, vj*s*. viij*d*. To Iohn grene & Rob'te bambrough
for vj dayes worke at the over ducke poole vj*d*. a day, iij*s*.
To Anthoney duccott for iiij^or Thrave of bigg straw to y^e
bull house, xij*d*.(?) To Nycholas yonger for lainge on of
yt ——. To Iohn grene for servinge of hym & for ther

---

[1] See above, p. 43, note 1.

[2] See above, p. 28, note 2.

[3] No doubt for making hay for the bull. It was sometimes, as appears
from other entries, bought ready-made. Observe the division of the closes
into " rigs."

drinke, ix*d*. To Rob'te bambrough for mendinge the dicke at the lowe end of vij acars belonginge to y⁰ parishe, vj*d*. To sparke for sekinge y⁰ bull when he was wantinge, vj*d*. To Iohn grene for a saile & settinge of his heake, iij*d*. To the counstaples for a sesment to Captayn hodshon, xx*d*. For a bull for y⁰ parishe, lij*s*. viij*d*. For fetchinge hym home from whitworth, viij*d*. To M* peter blaxton for a peace of hay to y⁰ bull, iiij*s*. ij*d*. For carradge of yt to y⁰ bull house, viij*d*. To Nycholas sparke for his maire to Aukeland with a prisoner, viij*d*. To Iohn patteson for a Iron hupe to y⁰ moore yeat, v*d*. To y⁰ churchwardens for a copie of an Inditement & for a petecion, iij*s*. viij*d*. For dressinge y⁰ common Armore, vj*d*. To Rychard Tripp for mendinge the layn ende in moors chair, iiij*d*.[1] For paper for this booke, ij*d*. For wrytinge this our account, ij*s*. [*A few other payments of the usual kind*].

Expences x*l*. xviij*s*. v*d*.

Grass men for 1617, Rob'te baker & Rychard martyn. Received at entrance £6*l*. 8*s*.

Richard X martyn, his marke.
Rob'te X Baker, his marke.

Rec*d* for the bull sould to Rob'te peacoke, xlxvj*s*. (*sic*) viij*d*.

[*Receipts for* gaits, *fog, and* the ij lonyngs]. The hole Receyts ys xiiij*l*. iiij*s*. ij*d*.

Expences 1617. To wedowe hodshon vj*s*. To Robert bambrought for castinge Aboute the mayden castell & for lainge yt about with whines & the stile, xx*d*. To Iohn blaxton for a warant from y⁰ Justices concernynge for y⁰ collectors of y⁰ poore of this parishe,[2] iiij*d*. To the counstaples James foster & Rob'te Ranardson for A sesment of xij*d*. y⁰ pound for bridges, *Julii 13*, x*s*. To xp'ofor symson for a fother of hay to y⁰ bull, xvj*s*. To Thomas Tompson for his horse to chester with A presoner, vj*d*. To Nycholas sparke for makinge up the gavill end of the bull house, ij*s*. viij*d*. To Anthoney duckett for 16 Thrave of bigg straw iij*d*. A thrave the hole, iiij*s*. ix*d*. To Nycholas sparke for thekin (*thatching*) 4 dayes viij*d*. a day and for a server of hym 4 dayes the hole, iiij*s*. For mendinge y⁰ yeat in pellowlease chare with certayn rounges lackinge & a sweard, ij*d*. To the collectors of the hye wayes Iohn hall and Thomas

---

[1] Presumably some narrow lane known as "the Moor chare."

[2] See "Pittington Churchwardens' Accounts," Surtees Society, vol. lxxxiv, p. 46, note 1.

patteson, vij*s*. viij*d*. To the counstaples for givinge in ther Answere for certayn articles given them by the head counstaples, x*d*. To Iohn hall one of y^c survaers for the hye wayes, xv*s*. To Rychard Tripp for a heaspe & a stapple to pellowleese chare & for mendinge of moores chare, vj*d*. To the counstaples for the house of correction, x*d*. For iiij^or stone of hay to the bull, ix*d*. For a bull that we bought, xlvij*s*.

[*Other entries of the usual kind*].

Expences ys ix*l*. 5*s*. iij*d*.

Declara, iiij*l*. xix*s*. j*d*.

Grasse men for 1618. George Tayler glover And Andrew Currey.

Receyved iiij*l*. xix*s*.

Rec^d for the bull that was sold, xlvj*s*. [*Also for fog, bull hay*, the lonyngs, *and one* horse gait]. The hole Receyts ys xj*l*. viij*s*. vij*d*.

Expences 1618.

To wedowe hodshon, vj*s*. To Iohn Tripp for his horse in y^c kinges affaires,[1] viij*d*. For the articles, viij*d*. To Rob'te Kent for mendinge y^c mayden castell, viij*d*. For a fother of hay to the bull, xvij*s*. For a locke to the bull house, iij*d*. For vewinge the common Armor on Raynton more, iij*s*. To the counstaples for A sesment for ye becones, x*d*. For dressinge of A sworde, viij*d*. To Rychard Littlepher for oure comynge up to vew the harnes, iiij*d*. To the counstaple Rob'te Carr for thre men that carried the harness to Raynton more the ij^th tyme, iij*s*. To Rob'te carr for the dressinge of the common Armore, vj*d*. For two sesments iiij*d*. the pound, vj*s*. viij*d*. More to the counstaples for ij sesments 1*d*. of ye pound xx*d*. For one dossen of hay to the bull to James foster, ij*s*. To George cragg for one dossen, ij*s*. vj*d*. To Nedd waller for dressinge y^c armore, vj*d*. To Iohn burdus for one dossen of hay to ye bull, ij*s*. vj*d*. For the bull that was bought at darnton, li*s*. To Thomas dawson for a warrant, vj*d*. For two dayes for dressinge the common vennell in Raynton Loninge, vij*d*. [*Other usual payments*].

Expences ix*l*. vj*s*. ij*d*.

---

[1] This entry, together with the following reference to "beacons," and repeated inspections of the armour this year and afterwards, seems significant of the political state of things at this time ; also, and still more, in 1622 and subsequent years. The projected intervention of England at this period of James's reign in the contest on the Continent between the Protestant States and Spain may account for such military activity.

Grasse men for 1619, Anthoney duccott and James Foster. Received xlij*s*. iiij*d*.

Item Rec*d* for the bull that was sould, x*l*. xiij*s*. iiij*d*. [*Other usual receipts*]. Some ix*l*. x*s*. vj*d*.

Expences.
To Nycholas sparke for scowringe y*e* common vennell in Raynton Loynynge, xij*d*. To M*r* blaxton counstaple for articles, xij*d*. For a fother of hay to y*e* bull to Rob'te heighington, xxiiij*s*. For A bull to y*e* use of y*e* parishe, xlvj*s*. For scowringe the springs at giles brige, xiiij*d*. For ij stone of hay to y*e* bull, v*d*. For makinge ye dicke at y*e* foot of vij acares, xiiij*d*. For makinge y*e* dicke betwene the moore & brod close, xij*d*. To Iohn grene for kepinge y*e* bull in y*e* markett, iiij*d*. To Rob'te hudspeth for his wages, ij*s*. To M*r* blaxton constaple for caryinge the common Armore to Raynton more y*e* first tyme, iij*s*. More to M*r* blaxton the second tyme to vew on Raynton more, iiij*s*. For A saile to the bull, ij*d*. To M*r* blaxton constaple for Roge money, ij*s*. xj*d*. To george greson for dressinge the maden castell, xviij*d*. For iiij*er* stone of hay for the bull, xij*d*. To Iohn greene, ij*s*. vj*d*.

Somme, viij*l*. ij*d*. Remaines clear, xxix*s*. iiij*d*.

Grass men for 1620, Thomas cornforth and Rychard Robeson. Received xxix*s*. iiij*d*. [*Receipts for* gaits, *fog in the two closes, and for the two* Lonynges, *amounting to £7 5s. 6d.*]

Expences for 1620. Account maid 20 May 1621.
To the counstaples for a sesment iii*d*. *ob*. on the pound, ij*s*. xj*d*. For articles to Rob'te bambroughe counstaple, xij*d*. For dightinge the bull house, j*d*. To Thomas snawdon for A fother of hay to the bull, price, xxij*s*. x*d*. To george Rooel for makinge y*e* gapes up in vij aceres at St. Cuthbert day, iij*d*. To Rob'te bambrouge counstaple for the vewinge of the armore of Raynton more before y*e* Justices in charges for 3 Times, vj*s*. vj*d*. To Isbell wilson for a dossen stone of hay to the bull, ij*s*. To Anthoney duckett for hay to the bull, vj*s*. To Rob'te baker for A dossen stone of hay to y*e* bull, ij*s*. To Iohn Rackett for 4 stone, x*d*. To Rob'te bambroughe counstaple for y*e* kinges kitchen,[1] ij*s*. iiij*d*. To Rob'te hudspeth for

___

[1] James I, in his progress to Scotland in 1617, had passed through Durham, arriving there on Easter Eve. Was this payment in 1620 of 3*s*. 4*d*. to the constable for "the King's Kitchen" arrearage of an impost on parishes for entertaining him on that occasion; or was it part of some

4

wrytinge our accompte, ij*s.* To Roland Robson & Thomas miller for hay loding & bringing home, iiij*d.*

[*Other payments of the usual kind*].

v*l.* xvij*s.* vij*d.*

Grasse men for 1601 (*sic*),[1] George Tayler Tanner and Thomas wanne. Received at entrance, £1 · 7 · 11.

(*Signed*) George Tailer Tanner.

Thomas X wane his marke.

Account made June 2, 1622.

Rec^d of Thomas cornforth for the bull that he bought, xxxix*s.* x*d.*

[*Receipts, as usual, for* gaits, the lonyngs, *and* pellowleise *and* brode close *fogs*]. Sum tot. 12*l.* 3*s.* 3*d.*

Expences for 1621.

To Robert heighington counstaple for the vewinge of the armore at Raynton moore before the Justices in charges, ij*s.* viij*d.* To Iohn grene for fetchinge the bull home from murton, vj*d.* To william shakelocke of murton for the bull which we bought, xxxvj*s.* viij*d.* To george cragg for A fother of hay to the bull, xx*s.* To the counstaples for a sesment of iiij*d.* of the pound, iij*s.* iiij*d.* For a locke to the bull house doore, vj*d.* To Edward hodshon for weights for weainge of bread xij*d.* To the countaples for a sesment of iij *ob.* on the pound, ij*s.* xj*d.* To Iohn patteson for spikines (*spikings for the moor's gate*), j*d.* For two stone & a halfe of hay to the bull, vj*d.*

[*Other payments of the usual kind*].

Sum tot' 6*l.* 18*s.* 3*d.*

Grassmen for 1622, Robert Barmphught (?) and Iohn herrison chosen 23 April. Received £5 2*s.*

(Signed) Rob'te X bambrough, his marke.

Iohn harison.

Rec^d for the bull, xxxiij*s.* iiij*d.*

[*Receipts, as usual, for* gaits, *fogs, and* the lonings].

Som. vij*l.* xvj*s.* iij*d.* totall, xij*l.* xviij*s.* iij*d.*

Expences for 1622.

For a muskett to the parishe p by ye grasmen, xiiij*s.* For dressinge the common Armore the vij^th of July, ij*s.*

---

general subsidy for maintaining the royal establishment? It is well known that various expedients were resorted to for relieving his impecuniosity. *Cf.,* below, p. 51, note 2.

[1] Perhaps a clerical error for 1621, there being otherwise no accounts for this year, and accounts for 1601 having appeared in their proper place.

To the iiij[er] men which ys appoynted soldgers, iiij*s.* For powder & mache, v*d.* For the articles, xij*d.* To george Tayler for his horse to wirmeth (*Wearmouth*) vj*d.* To Rob'te heighington lyke wyse for the same, vj*d.* To Rob'te bambrough for a maire to chester, vj*d.* For a locke & a key, ij stapples & heast (*hesp ?*) x*d.* For soldger money matche & powder, iiij*s.* ix*d.* To Rob'te hudspeth his wages, ij*s.* To george cragg for hay growed in clifton[1] for the bull, xij*s.* vj*d.* For ledinge the bull hay from clifton, ij*s.* vj*d.* To the counstaples iiij*d.* of the pound, ij*s.* iiij*d.* all the aforesaid laid out by Iohn herrison : more paid by Iohn herrison to captan hodshon, ij*s.* vj*d.* All laid out by Iohn hereson : paid for A Sword belte, iiij*d.* To Iohn haryson for the foge in pellowlese, xxiiij*s.* x*d.* For the foge in brodelose, xxj*s.* xj*d.* To fower men for goinge to chester at the commandement of the Justices, iiij*s.* For the bull price which we bought, xl*s.* To Rychard tripp for a sesment ij*s.* xj*d.* To william burton for hantinge the bull, ij*d.* To Rob'te bambrough for kepinge the foge in brode close, xx*d.* [*Other usual payments*]. viij*l.* —*s.* v*d.*

Grasmen for 1623, chosen 15 Ap., Richard Tripp and Robert Baker, Received at entrance iiij*l.* xij*s.* xj*d.*

Item Rec[d] of walter Jackson for one gait, 4*s.* For 60 kyne for the bull haye 2*d.* for everie Cowe that is, x*s.* For 53 gaites in Pellowe Lees fogg 13*d.* two gaites, that is 27*s.* 6*d.* For 52 gaites in the brodeclose fogg 6*d.* A gaite is 26*s.*

[*N.B.—These are all the receipts entered this year, among which it is observable that only one gail on the moor is paid for, the stock having apparently been transferred to the fog of the entercommon fields (See above, p. 40, note 2), and to other fogs, which were paid for*].

Som' iij*l.* viij*s.*—Som' totall viij*l.* vj*d.*

Expences for the same year.

Imprimis to George Tayler for the kinges purveiors,[2] iij*s.* More for the same use, ij*s.* iiij*d.* For a pounde of gunpuder, and a yearde of matche, xxj*d.* For Articles,

---

[1] For the locality of Clifton, see Introduction.

[2] Were these purveyors for the purpose suggested above in note 1, p. 49? "Purveyance" is defined by Bailey, "Providing of corn, fewel, victuals, &c., for the King's house." *Cf.* (A.D. 1627), "Purvey money." But sessments for the king's "provision" recur henceforth continually till the Commonwealth, being, we may suppose, for his general requirements for the king's service.

xij*d*. For carreing the Armour to Rainton more, iiij*s*. For a paire of skailes for weinge the bread, iij*d*. For three dossen and A halfe of hay ij*s*. A dossen, vij*s*. More for three dossen and A halfe of hay at ij*s*. 8*d*. the dossen ix*s*. 4*d*. For makinge A pertition betwext the bull and the haye and mendinge the old worke, viij*d*. To M*r* Heath for the fogge of his sexe rigges, xviij*d*. To George Rowell for the fogge of the Abbey land, 12*s*. To Thomas cornforth for his fogge, viij*d*. To Rob't Bambrough for his fogge, viij*d*. To Hengse (?) man for his fogge, 6*d*. To william hilton for his fogge of 2 rigges, 4*d*. To Robert baker for the fogge of 10 rigges, ij*s*. vj*d*. To Margart Snoball for her fogge, viij*d*. To william Atcheson for his fogge, 12*s*. To Richerd Tripp for his fogge, xj*s*. To M*r* Smythe for his fogge, ij*s*. To george Tailer glover for his fogge, ij*s*. To william Sheraton for the fogge of the brigge land, ij*s*. To Charles Boothe for his fogge, ij*s*. To Robert Skaithlock for his fogge, xij*d*. For makinge the hedge in Colsons laine, ij*d*. For A booke of the size of bread, v*d*. For 3 stone of haye to the bull, ix*d*. For dressinge the maidens bower, xvj*d*. For a stone of haye to the bull, ij*d*.

Som'— iiij*l*. x*s*. vij*d*. — and so remaines ij*l*. x*s*. iiij*d*.

Grasmen for 1624 —— Bulmer & Henric Johnson. Received on entrance, iij*l*. x*s*. iiij*d*.

Rec*d* for 44 gaites in the brode close, 6*d*. A gaite ——. For 18 gaites in the pellow leeses, 7*d*. A gaite —. [*Other receipts for gaits, &c*.].

Som' xj*l*. xj*s*. x*d*.

Expences in the same year.
Brode close fogges.
Payd to M*r* Heath for his fogge, 18*d*. [*Other payments for fogges, varying from 6d. to 3s. 2d., to nine persons, including Mr. Heath: and finally*, Paid for Almner[1] Leeses, 12*d*.].

For pellowlees fogges.
[*Payments varying from 6d. to 2s. to nine individuals for fogges, but including*, Payd for the common rigge, 6*d*.].

Payd for a bull, lj*s*. For dressinge the harnes, 2*s*. To the counstables for A sesment, 3*s*. For a sesment to

---

[1] "Almner" here must mean Almoner; the land denoted being that anciently belonging to St. Magdalen's hospital, and in the hands of the Almoner of the Convent.

the brigges, 5s. For halfe A pound of gunne puder, vijd. To M' Warde for vewinge the Armor at the Churche, vjd. To the 4 souldiers for goinge to Rainton more, iiijd. To the counstables for gettinge the pykes dressed, vjd. To the counstables for dressinge the muscott, vjd. To the constables for A sesment for A sesment for the kinges provision, 3s. 4d. To the 4 soulgers for goinge to be trained at rainton more, iiijs. To the counstables for A sesment at houghton, iiijd. For salve to the bull, ijd. To 3 men for scowringe the lowe carr one day, xviijd. For scowringe the ducke pull and Gills brigge 6 daies & one day more, iijs. 6d. For a stocke to the muscott, xijd. To Capten hodshon for a sesment, xd. To the constable for A sesment, xijd. To the counstable for kepinge Raphe Applebie one night, 7d. To the counstables for Another sesment, 8d. To Richerd Tripp for Articles from the head counstable, iiijd. To Nicholas Bulloc counstable for a sesment, vs. For dressinge the Armor, ijs. For mendinge the maden boore, vjd. For 9 stone of hay to the Bull, ijs. For wrytinge the statutut (*sic*) for the ways, 12d. For a bull, xliijs. iiijd.

Som' ixl. xixs. ijd.

Grasmen for 1625, chosen 19 April, Richard Welberie and Thomas daweson. Received at entrance xxxijs. viijd.

Rec'd of Iohn Sarvant for one beast gaite, iiijs. For lijtie gaites in the fogg in Pellowleases att vijd. p gaite, xxxs. ijd. For xlviij gaites in the brode Close in the fogg, xxvs. vijd. For Bull hay money att ijd. a beast, ixs. ijd. [*Other receipts for* gaites].

Some vijl. xiijs. vijd.

Disburssments for ther whole yeare.

Imp. paid for a lock and a stapple to the brode Close yeate, iiijd. ob. To the Cunstables for a Cesment to Branspeth in the vesitacoun,[1] xd. For fower pound of gunpowder and 6 yardes of match, vjs. iiijd. To the Cunstables for makinge their answere to the articles to them in Charge givine, viijd. For a stake to the bull, ijd. For kepinge the bull to our ladie daie in lent, viijd. To the Cunstables for wrytinge ther answere to the articles, vjd. To the Cunstables for the Burgases of the parlament

---

[1] The Plague being usually so called, it may be supposed to have broken out again at Brancepeth after its cessation in Durham, A.D. 1604. See above, p. 24, note 1.

house,[1] vs. To the Cunstables for soulgeers money,[2] iiijs. To fower soulgers that went to Rainton more to be trayned and for Carryinge the armore, iiijs. The same tyme for halfe a pound of gunpowder, vijd. To xp'ofor Simpson for one fother of hay for the bull, xvs. For articles, viijd. For old raiesse[3] to laye under the hay and dressinge the house, iiijd. For a Capp to the pellas lease yeate, ijd. For the kinges provesioun, iijs. iiijd. For Rogg money,[4] ijs. xjd. To Mr Thomas Heeth for his fogg in the brod Close, ijs. For halfe a pound of gunpowder, viijd. For one yard of match, ijd. To the Cunstables for the solgeers that went to Rainton more that tyme, iiijs. To Richard Tripp for the fogge in pellow leses, xviijs. [*Payments for* fogg, *1s. or 2s., to seven other individuals*]. To mendinge the hedge betwene old durham and 7 Akers, iijd. To the Cunstables when the soulgeers went another tyme to Rainton moore to be trayned, ijs. viijd. To the Cunstables for another tyme for the saide soulgeers trayninge att Rainton moore, ijs. viijd. To the Cunstables more for the burgases of the parlament, vs. To Thomas Cornforth for the payinge of the soulgeers that they weare behind with their wages : the tyme Thomas Cornforth was Cunstable when he went forth of his office, xvjs. viijd. To Tymothie Hubbock and Henry Johnson Cunstables for dressinge the Common armore, ijs. To the Cunstables for a Sesment att ijd. per pound the 19° of maij 1626, xxd. To Richard Tripp for 3 daies work att maden Castell dicke, xxjd. To Henry Cowlson for makinge the yeate with new Railes in pittington loninge, viijd.

Pd by Mr Wellomy, fogges [*Payments follow, varying from 6d. to 3s. 2d., to eight persons for* fogges *in* Brod Close].

To Mr Iohn watson for wrytinge upp our accoumpts for the whole yeare, ijs.

Somme disburssed vijl. js. iiijd. ob.

Grassemen for 1626, chosen 19 Ap., Iohn peakocke and nicolas Bullocke. Received xijs. ijd. ob.

[*Receipts for gates and fogs* = £4 4s.]

Expences for 1626.

[*Payments, from 6d. to 12s., to eight persons for* brode close fogge. *Ditto, to four persons, and* for the brigland fogge,[1] *and for* Pellowe leases fogge].

To the Constables for y⁰ kings provision ixs. ijd. For mending the backhouse laine hedge, iiijd. To the soldiers, ijs. iiijd. For a peice of wodd for mending y⁰ brodeclose gate, ijd. For A sparr to y⁰ same, ijd. To william Maugham for bringing sheepe to the pinfold of the common, ijd. For A sparr to Shereburne gate, iiijd. To George Rowle for standing with the bull in the markett, iijd. To the Constables, iiijs. vijd. For gunpowder & match, xiijd. For A bagge, ijd. To Antho: Thrislewood for a harr kutt,[2] vijd. To Xp'ofer Bee for hay, xjs. iiijd. For writing thes accompts, xijd. To the Cunstables for the solgers, iiijs. viijd. For gunpowder & match,———. [*Other usual payments*]. 4*l*. ijs. 4d.

Grasse men for 1627, chosen 13 may, Richard martin and Thomas dobison. Received ij*l*. vjs. xd.

Richard **X** martine

marke

Thomas dobbysonn.

[*Receipts, as usual, for gates and fogs* = £9 15s. 6d.]

Expences for 1627.

To the Constaples for drissing the harnes, ijs. For souldeers wages, ijs. More the same day for powder, os.— For a bull, ij*l*. iiijs. To the heard for two entering pennyes———. To the Costaples a ses for the Correction house, iijs.———. To Robert Car for mending of the backhouse leases hedg, iiijd. To Christopher simson for a load of hay to the bull, xvjs.———. To Christopher bulmer for a Cap to the pellow leases gate, ijd. To william bentley and his man for two dayes worke, ijs. To thomas dawson for twentie stone of hay, vs. For writing of our accounts, js. [*Other usual payments*]. o*l*. 17s. 9d.

---

[1] The " Brigland fogge " may possibly have been that of a close at Gillsbridge.

[2] " Harr Kutt." Apparently some part of a soldier's equipment. Can it be meant for " haketoun " (or " Hacqueton "), a word defined in the Glossary to Chaucer's Poetical Works (London, G. Bell, 1888) as "a short-cassock without sleeves " ? *Cf.* " The Tale of Sir Mopas " (" Canterbury Tales ") :—

" And next his schert an *aketoun*,

And over that an haberjoun,

For persying of his hert."

See also Johnson's Dictionary :—" HACQETON. Some piece of armour. ' You may see the very fashion of the Irish horseman in his long hose, riding shoes of costly cordwain, his *hacqueton*, and his habergeon.'— Spencer's ' State of Ireland.'"

Grasse men for 1628, chosen 15 Ap., george Tailer, Tanner, & Robert heighinton.   Received ij*l.* xv*s.* ix*d.*
George Tailler, tanner,
Robert X Heighington's
marke.

The new Grasse men gave out of the somme a bove saide x*s.* j*d.* to maintaine the sute Against Robart wan for overstint of the Common contrary to the orders—x*s.* j*d.*

Item laid forth for a cessment and paid to Tho: Dobison Constable, iij*s.* iiij*d.* Paid for a warrant touching our high waies, ij*s.* ij*d.* For drissing our harnes, xij*d.* To the common souldiers, ij*s.* For the peticion to the bench, vj*d.* To Lancelot Dawson for a peticion to the Judges, xij*d.* To Richard Tripp for mending the maiden bower dike, iij*d.* To Thomas Simpson for purvay money, iij*s.* iiij*d.* For a hing locke, iiij*d.* For mending the porterclose dike, iij*d.* Item 1*d.* on the pound for the Captaines, x*d.* For writing this accompt, xij*d.* To the common soldiers for ther wages for caryeing the common Armore to chester moore, ij*s.* viij*d.*

[*Other payments for mending gates and dikes, fog, &c.*]

Receits for 1628.
Imprimis of M*r* Traviniam Collingwood for a Cow gait, iiij*s.*

	iij*l.*	iiij*s.*	vj*d.*
	ij*l.*	xv*s.*	ix*d.*
Receits	v*l.*	xix*s.*	iij*d.*
Disbursed ...	4*l.*		
So Remayneth ...	j*l.*	xix	iij*d.*

[*Other receipts for* gates *and* fogg].

Grasse men for 1629, chosen 7 Ap., Thomas Cornfoorth & Thomas Coolteman.   Received j*l.* xix*s.* iij*d.*

Receites.
Imprimis received of henerie Johnson for the last of his whole stent, 2*s.* 8*d.* For 60 gates in our fogges, 4*d.* *ob.* p cowe, in alle xxv*s.* For 55 gates in pellow leses, 5*d.* p gate, in all xxij*s.* x*d.*

[*Other receipts for* gates, *amounting in all to* £5 9*s.* 1*d.*].

Item Resaved for the Loones (*lanes*) att Thomas Dobbesons, vij*s.*

Disbursments.

To Richard Tripp for casting the lowe carr, 6*d.*
To M*r* Pleasant for counsell concerning the high wayes, 5*s.*
To M*r* martin his man for his fees, 2*s.* 4*d.* To Robert
Bambrough for scouring the mayden bowere dicke, 6*d.*
To George Taylor Constable for artickles, 10*d.* To the
Constables for the Kings purvayer, 3*s.* 4*d.* For a hespe
and a stappell to the brode close gayte, 3*d.* For making
the pellow leeses gaite, 2*s.* For a hespe and a stappell to
it, 3*d.* To M*r* Martin Ian. 15 for scire-facies, 2*s.* 6*d.* To
M*r* Pleasant for counsell, 5*s.* Payed Timothie Cumming
Sherife for his fees, 6*d.* Spent at Richard Stories, 6*d.*
To George Taylor Constable for Rogue monie, 3*s.* 4*d.*
Spent at Richard Stories, 4*d.* To M*r* Martin for a writ
called scire-facias, 2*s.* 6*d.* To M*r* Comming Sherife,
6*s.* 8*d.* To M*r* Pleasant for Counsell, 5*s.* To Richard
Tripp for making the bakehouse leeses dicke, 6*d.* For
writing our accounts, 1*s.* [*Other payments of the usual
kind*].

New Grasse men chosen the xvj of aprill 1630 ; Peter
booth & giles atkinson. Received of the laste grasse men,
0 . 12 . 9.

[*Receipts, as before, for* gates *in* Pellow lease *and*
Brode Close *fogs, with a few others, and* of Thomas
dobbeson for madlane lane vij*s.* ; *amounting in all to*
iij*l.* xviij*s.* vij*d.*].

Expences.

To the Constapples for souldgers and the Howse of
Correction, vj*s.* viij*d.* To Robert Baumebrough for
mending the moore gaite and a staile (*stile?*) to it, viij*d.*
To the Constapples for artickles, viij*d.* To Iohn Cowlson
for mending the Brood Close yett and for a Raile a hespe
and a stappell to it, xij*d.* To Richard Welburie for a
presentment for the Recusants, 4*d.* To Robert Baume-
brogh for mending the more gaite and a Capp to it, vj*d.*
To Richard martyn for artickles, xij*d.* For the Bacckus
gaite mending, iiij*d.* For pellease yet mending a hespe
and a stappell, vj*d.* In expences, viij*d.* For writing our
Countes, xij*d.* [*Other payments for looking to the bull and
repairs of gates and dikes*]. ij*l.* xix*s.* iiij*d.*

1631. Grasse men Timothy hubbucke & Robart
dobson. Received xvij*s.* iij*d.*

Resaved for the fogge in the brood clooce, xxiiij*s*. ij*d*. For the fogge in the pellesse, xviij*s*. Of M*r* Langbrag (?) for 3 gates xvj*s*. of Thomas dobbesone for madelane lone, vij*s*.—Summe total. 3 . 18 . 5.

Expences.
To the Counstaples for the house of Correcshon, iij*s*. iiij*d*. To the Counststaples for the Kinges parvesion, iij*s*. iiij*d*. To Richard trep for mening (*mending*) backas dicke, ij*d*. To Nicklaye bullock for upholeng the backas lease dicke, vj*d*. To Thomas tompson Cunstaple for a sesment for the brigges, xx*d*. For writing of our accountes, xij*d*. For wardes to a hinge locke, ij*d*. [*Other payments for repairing gaps, gates, &c., and for fog in* Pellowlease *and* Brode Close]. Summe 2 . 13 . 10.

Delivered to y*e* new grasmen may third 1632 beinge Robart baker & Iohn nelson. Resaved the Some of j*l*.——.
Resates.
[*Receipts for 43 gates in* pallese[1] *at 6d., 51 in* brood close *at 6d., for* Madlane lone 9*s*., *for* pallese lane 3*s*., *and for several other gates; in all £7 6s. 8d*.].

Expences.
Iohn ball for a yet to petinton loone, 5*s*. For bringe of it, 1*s*. 4*d*. To peter baker for bringe home the owlde yet, 2*d*. More to him for makeinge the dicke a boute the yet, 3*d*. For Roge monie to the Cunstaples, 3*s*. 4*d*. For a heade pece to Sherborne yet and makeinge it, 1*s*. 8*d*. To the Cunstaples for the Artickles, 8*d*. More to Cunstaples for the Kinges proveseon, 3*s*. 4*d*.
For fogge in the brode Close.

[*Payments, from 6d. to 12s., to seven individuals for their* fogge *and for* the fogge of the brege land,[2] 2*s*.].
fogge in the pelleese.
[*Payments, from 6d. to 12s., to five individuals for their* fogge, *for* the fogge of the Common wey 6*d*., *and for* fogge of the breges land 2*s*.]. To the Cunstaples for Artickles at howton, 1*s*. 4*d*. To the head Cunstaples 2*d*. the pound for a sesment for bregges & the house of Corectione, 1*s*. 8*d*. William Atkinson for a olde Rekenge of a olde sesment, 3*s*. 4*d*. For paper to this booke, 2*d*. For writinge of our accountes, 1*s*. For a sesment Conserninge the hiewayes, 1*s*. 8*d*. For Artickles to the Cunstaples, ——. To Thomas dobesonne for scouringe y*e*

---

[1] *I.e.,* Pellowleases.   [2] See above, p. 55, note 1.

laine, ——. to Robart bamebrough for scouringe of the dammes on the more, ——. For stopes and stappells to pallelese yet, js.

Summe total, 3 . 16 . 1.

Grassmen for 1633 Iohn Smith and Geo. Taylor. Received at entrance £3 10s. 8d. [*Other receipts, in which there is nothing peculiar, amount to £6 8s., making in all £9 18s. 8d.*].

Expences.

Paide for a bull to Richard Owen, xxxvjs. To Richard barnefather for Artickles, viijd. For 2 stone of hay to the bulle ——. To Richard barnefather for the house of Correcsion a penye of the pound, iijs. iiijd. To Richard Cornforth for a penie of the pound to Captane ward, xd. For a fouther of hay to the bul, xxs. For leding it home, xijd. For drinke to the waynmen, iijd. To George Renell for geting it in, vjd. To Richard barnefater for the kinges purvaer, vjs. To Iohn patteson for a hupe to the more gate, ——. To Iohn Colson for makenge ye stox (*stocks*) and ———— of it, ijs. vjd. To Iohn patteson for towe stapples and a haspe to the broade Close yet, iijd. To Crestefere bee for satenge (*setting?*) the brode Close yet, iiijd. To Richard barnefather for a sesment a penie of the pound for fishburne bregs, xd. To George Roule for sarvinge of the bull and huserume for the hay, vs. To M^r heeth for wood to the stox, iijs. vjd. For hay to the bull, vs. xd. For a sale to the bull, ijd. For writing our accountes, xviijd. To Richard barnesfather for a sesment of a penie of the pound to a louetanant (*lieutenant*), xd.

Disbursed—*l* . 7 . 0 . 9.

Delivered by Georg tailer & Io. Smith oude grassemen to Richard Corneforth challonweaver and Richard tripp the somme of 2 . 17 . 11.

A Note of the outlaie that hath bin disburst by the Grasse men this yeare 1634. Rich. Tripp & Rich. Cornfurth the younger.

Imprimis given back againe of the 2*l*. 17*s*. 11*d*. when we enterd on to Iohn Bambrough by the parish consent, ——. For a paire of stiles[1] & a back & doore threshold, 3*s*. Given to the Captaine for Marking the harnish the 15 day of October, 3*s*. To Rich. Tripp & Iohn Brantingham for 10 days laboring worke at the Bull house, 5*s*.

---

[1] For meaning of *pair*, see Glossary. *Cf.*, below, "a paire of wards."

To Robart Cooleson Carpinder for one days worke at the Bull house & drinks to the laborers, ———. For ten board Nailes a pennie. For water carriing to the laburers a day ———. A pike for the Moore gate, j*d.* To Iohn Brantingham for straw for litter ———. To willyam Bell for the Javill (*Jail*) & house of Correction, 3*s.* 4*d.* For a stapple, i*d.* For a dayes worke at the low Carr, 7*d. Ditto* at Gylls bridge, 7*d. Ditto* at Bull house, 7*d.* To 4 shouldiers, 8*d.* A pound of powder for the Shouldiers, i*s.* 2*d.* Item 2 Muscats dressing, i*s.* For 7 burden of wattles to the bull house, ———. 2 days worke at scowring the duck pond, i*s.* 2*d.* To willyam Bell for the artickles 8*d.* To the Counstopples presentment, 8*d.* 2 spikings for the Bull house, i*d.* Disburst for the Kings provision, 3*s.* 4*d.* To willyam Bell for a Briddge mending, i*s.* 8*d.* Mending Ellisleases low hedge, i*s.* A stapple for hangin on the lock of Pelloleases yeet & scowring of Porter Close hedge ———. For mending & varnishing the Common Muscats, 4*s.* vj*d.* To 4 Shouldiers the 15 of October, 2*s.* 8*d.* For setting the yeet & the stupe of Pelloleasses, 4*d.* For a paire of wards to the locke of Pelloleases gate & mending the lock, 4*d.* A stapple, j*d.* 4 spikings, 2*d.* To the new Captaine, ———. A quart of Ale to the writer,[1] 2*d.* Disburst for the fogg of Pellowleases, 1*l.* 4*s.* To Richard Johnson the 15 of fabruarie 1634 five groates to the house of Correction & ten pence for the bridgs mending ———. To will : bell for a sesment of one pennie of the pound, ———. For layinge the wattles of the Bulhouse, ———. For goinge aboute in the parriche disburste for drinke, iij*s.* x*d.*

[*Receipts*].

After receipts from individuals for gaites, *eight in all*, Receaved by Richard Corneforth of gorge taler for whins,[2] ix*s.* of Edward smythe for the laines, x*s.* Of Mat. Charlton for y^c bull, £2 2*s.* Summa totalis, 4*l.* 8*s.*

Richard Corneforth payd to george Rowell for brod closse, xij*s.* [*Five other payments for* fogge *follow*]. To Robert baynbrough for makinge the yeate in the brod

---

[1] See also below, "disburst in drinke." Such expenditure, not hitherto entered, except for "waynmen" or other workmen, will be found very frequent and considerable afterwards ; and, not least, in the jovial days of the second Charles.

[2] *Cf.,* above, p. 31, note 1. We find also a large clearance of whins from the Moor in 1637, and still more afterwards in 1700. Their growth may have been one reason for so many "fogs" having been taken about this time by the grassmen and let in gaits to parishioners.

close ——. To the wrytter for kepinge the booke, xij*d.* To Master wright fogg, vj*d.* More y*e* abovsayd yeare for pellaleases fogge, 1*l.* 7*s.* It. RS for y*e* broad Close fogge, 1*l.* 9*s.* Sum. 2 . 16 . 0.

RS for all receits for the yeare of our lord 1634 ... 10*l.* 2 . 9
Disbursed in all y*e* sayd yeare   ...   .   5 . 7 . 5
Remayning to be payd to y*e* new collectors[1] for y*e*
        yeare 1635 ...   .   4 . 15 . 4

RS of Richard Corneforth & Richard Trippe y*e* old Collectors for y*e* yeare of our lord 1634 y*e* sum of 4*l.* 15*s.* 4*d.* by Richard Corneforth & Thomas Morland Collectors for y*e* yeare 1635.

Receits for y*e* yeare 1635.
Rec*d* of Richard trippe and Richard Corneforth grasmen for the yeare of our lord 1634 y*e* sume of 4*l.* 3*s.* 10*d.*
[*Receipts for* gates, *including* Resaved of Antonie Embersun for his hole stent, 1*l.* 4*s.* 0*d.*, *amounting to* £2 8*s.* 8*d.* Resaved for the fogge in the palese, 1*l.* 5*s.* 0*d.*]
[*Receipts for* fogg *in* palease, *in* breg-land, *and from two individuals, amounting to* £1 4*s.*]
Resaved by Raph grene for the fogg in the brod close, 18*s.* [*Payments to five persons for* fogge, *amounting to 19s. 9d.*] It. RS of Ralph Green for y*e* Lonings, 10*s.* Received 2*s.* for y*e* Loning. Layd out to y*e* mouders,[2] 1*s.* 6*d.* To mending of blind lane dike, 3*d.*

Disbursements for y*e* yeare of our Lord 1635.
To the Cunstaples a groot of the pound for the huse of Correction and bregges, 5*s.* 4*d.* Paid mor to the Comstaples for the repairing of the bekens (*beacons*) ij*d.* the pound, 2*s.* 8*d.* More to the Comstaples for Artickels, 8*d.* For a hupe & a picke and nales & workmenshep to yets, 11*d.* More to the foresaid Comstaples for drisenge of the harnes and a bick to one of them & the band delerowes [3] 18*s.* More to the forsaid Comstaples for the foore solgers wages, 2*s.* 8*d.* *Ditto* for 8*d.* of the pound for workinge

---

[1] Presumably "collectors" for the poor. See Surtees Society's Publications, vol. lxxxiv, p. 46, note 11.

[2] *I.e., Moulders;* those who "dressed" or "scaled" the moor annually by scattering the mould. "MOULD, earth mixed with clay" (Bailey). See above, p. 36, note 1.

[3] *I.e.,* Bandeliers. See Glossary. The word "bick" preceding may possibly be meant for *buckle.*

of the Kinges wood,[1] 6*s.* 8*d.*   For a presentment, 4*d.*   For
Reparinge of the breges 2*d.* the pound, 1*s.* 8*d.*   For the
Kinges provesione a groot a pound ——.   Mor to the
mustermasters a penie a pound ——.   For makinge of the 7
akers dicke betwext the he (*high ?*) feeld and it, 4*d.*   To
Richard barnefather for a sword belt, 1*s.* 6*d.*   To Iohn
brantingeham for menenge (*mending*) the bakers lease dicke,
8*d.*   For Thomas Dawsons Dinner at Auckland, vj*d.*   For
Carregh (*carriage*) of the kinges wood to Lampton staeth
11*s.* 8*d.*   For wardes to the lock of palleise yet, 2*d.*   The
23th day of may M[r] Smeth[2] and the Churwardans with

---

[1] See also entries below for carriage of the same. The reference is to
Charles I's notorious ship-money, which was levied this year (1635) on the
country generally by writs to the Sheriffs, as well as on the sea-port towns.
Cf., "Churchwardens' Accounts," Surtees Society's Publications, vol. lxxxiv,
p. 97.

[2] Mr. Elias Smith succeeded Sir John Watson as Curate of St. Giles
A.D. 1632. He was also Minor Canon and Precentor of the Cathedral,
Head Master of the Grammar School, and at one time Vicar of Bedlington.
To him was due the careful preservation of the books of the Cathedral
Library, and the vestments belonging to the Church during the Common-
wealth. See "Mickleton MSS.," quoted below. It will be seen from the
extracts from the Registers of the parish of St. Giles, which are given below,
that after 1642 the entries are irregular and few, and for many years there
are none ; but that in 1667, the seventh year after the Restoration, a new
Register book was bought, in which regular entries were made, and that
Elias Smith is there specified as still minister of the parish. We may
suppose him to have had to relinquish his ministrations during the troublous
period. The Bishop, and the Cathedral clergy, with the Dean, Walter
Balcanqual, fled from Durham when the Scotch Covenanters, after defeating
Lord Conway at Newburn-on-Tyne in 1640, had entered the Bishopric, and
seized the tithes and rents of the clergy. Smith, however, may have
continued in the locality, viz., at Old Durham, then in the possession of
the Tempest family ; for there is in the new Register book a copy of a
Terrier, said to have been found in the study at Old Durham, and "writ by
Mr Elias Smyth" in 1655. The following notices of him appear in the
"Mickleton MSS.":—"*De Canonicis minoribus* [petit Canons].—Elias Smith
Clericus A.M., Min. Can. erga finem Ai 1628. Fuit Archididasculus
Scholae Gram. infra mentionatae Dec. & Cap. D. post Ric'um Smelt
Clericum Archid. Scholae predictae. Fuit Rector de Bedlington. Fuit
precentor Eccl. Cath. predict. durante vita sua. Et sepult. in Eccl. predict.
9 Dec., 1676" [No. 32, p. 52].

   "*De Schola Gram., &c., Dunelm.*—Elias Smith Clericus A.M. Ac unus
Canon. Minorum in Cath. Eccl. D. Qui Scholam Gram. predictam adiit
circa Festum Sti Petri ad Vincula Ao 1640. Sed Discipulos & Scholares in
Area Collegii docuit, scilicet aliquando in domo pertinente ad tertium
prebendarium Eccl. predict. juxta le Guest Hall ibidem (Vide de Hospitum
Aula seu Aula Hospitalitatis predicta, p. 139). Aliquando etiam in domo
pertinente ad primum prebendarium D. docuit. Ejus discipulorum Unus,
quem docuit dictus Elias in prefatis separalibus Domibus fuit I.M.
Collector hujus operis. Curam habuit idem Elias in temporibus nequissimis
post occisionem Regis Caroli Librorum in Bibliotheca Dec. & Cap. D., ac
etiam omnium Caparum & vestimentorum et aliarum rerum ad dictam
Ecclesiam pertinentium, salvaque omnia in eisdem temporibus custodivit.
Fuit etiam Parsona Vicarius de Bedlington. Predictus Elias Scholae
Gram[is] Civitatis D. Pedagogus & recepit 40*s.* medietatem An[tis] (*Annuitatis*)

others of the parishe in Charges spent that day in goinge about the bounders, 4*s*. 8*d*.[1] Paid more to nickholas Carr Cunstappel for a sese of towe pence the pound for the bregges, 1*s*. 8*d*. More to nickholas Carr for carregh of the kinges wood to lambton staieth, 6*s*. 8*d*. Wrytinge of our accountes, 1*s*. 6*d*. Given to Iohn Wilkinson back againe, 2*s*.

[*Other payments for repairs of gates and dikes*]. Somme is iij*l*. 2*s*. iiij*d*.

Mistaking the account of Raph grene ix*d*.

RS. By Peter Booth & Giles Atkinson of Richard Corneforth & Ralph Green May 29 1636 for Grasse mony y*e* sum of 2*l*. 16*s*. 3*d*.

[*Received for six* gates, 31*s*.; *and for* ye Lonings, 10*s*. = £2 1*s*.].

Expences as foleth, paid unto nickholas Car and Iohn Cragges Counstaples.

Item paid the 28th of may for Carrech (*carriage*) of his magestes shep timber 8*d*. the pound, 6*s*. The 4*d* of June for the preson and the house of Correeseon a 4*th* the pond is 3*s*. 2*d*. The 11*th* day of Jun for the infeckted pepell 2*d*. the pound is 1*s*. The 20 day of June for the infeckted pepell of gatsied (*Gateshead*) 12*d*. the pound is 10*s*. The 16*th* day of October for his magestes proveseon 4*d*. the pound is 3*s*. 4*d*. For the infickted pepell the 20*th* of September 6*d*. the pound is 5*s*. More the same day for the bekens (*beacons*) a 1*d*. the pound is ——. The 11*th* day of desember for the infeckted pepell 6*d*. the pound is ——. The 30 of Januarie to the infickted pepell 6*d*. the pound is ——. The —— of march for yarme bregg 4*d*. the pound is 3*s*. 4*d*. For the decayed bregges 2*d*. the pound is 1*s*. 8*d*. To william Atkingsun for a strass (*distress?*) for the parish, 1*l*. 2*s*. To peter baker for manenge (*mending*) of petintun loinge yet and the dick a picke to the yet, 10*d*. To gyles Atkeinsun for upholeng the backase

predictae ab Ep'o D. Et Samuel Martin Magister Scholae puerilis ejusdem Civ. recepit alteram medietatem ejusdem Annuitatis ad 40s. Vide in Rotulis Audit. Epī D. A⁰ 9 transl. Ejusdem Epī. Iste Sam. fuit primus ejusdem I.M. preceptor. Prefatus Elias Smith Ludi Magister Scholae Grammatical. apud D. Cui 40s. per an. de Ante (*Annuitate*) predicta soluta. Et alia summa 40s. dicto Samueli Martin altero Magistro Scholae Puerilis ibidem soluta." Vide (*ut antea*) [*Ib.*, p. 61].

" *Patroni, &c., Ecclesiae Sti Egidii.* Eleas Smith Clericus A.M. Parsona. Qui etiam Unus Min. Can. Cath. Eccl. D., ac Magister Scholae Gram. Dunelm. Ac Vicarius de Bedlington " [*Ib.*, p. 73].

[1] This is the first allusion to the custom of riding the boundaries on Ascension Day. See Preface, *Bounder Day.*

leese dick, 1*s*. For our Charges the xv^th of may for goinge about our boundres, 2*s*. 8*d*. For writeng of our accountes, 1*s*. 6*d*. To the Counstaples of Shenklie for a Carrech a grot the pound is 3*s*. 4*d*. To M^r heath for Cunsell, 10*s*.

RS. by Richard Trippe & George Greeveson of Giles Atkinson & Peter Booth ye sum of 10*s*. j*d*. grassemen May 21. 1637.—0 . 10 . 1.

Grasmen for 1637, Richard Tripp and George Greson. Received at their entry, x*s*. j*d*.

Receyved for xxxix gates in pellow leyes fogge, xx*s*. ix*d*. For xlvi gates in ye broad close fogge, xij*s*. Of Robart barker for pellowlese lane, vj*s*. Of Iohn smeth for madlen lanes, v*s*. Of the nighbours towards the boul (*bull*) paing for vj*s*. viij*d*. [*Other receipts for* gates, 2*s*. *or* 4*s*. *each, except* wedowe Ranton, *who pays for a gate* 1*s*. 4*d*.]. Some is in all v*l*. 1*s*. vj*d*.

Expences 1637.
To the Constables for the kings provision, iij*s*. iiij*d*. For the house of Correction, iij*s*. iiij*d*. For Yarm bridge, iij*s*. iiij*d*. To George Greson for skowring the Carr in the lowe moore one Day, vij*d*. To Richard Tripp for one day more, vij*d*. To Richard Tripp for mending the hedge betwixt the vij Acres & the hyefield, vij*d*. For cutting of whines thre Daies and for bringing them to bull house, xxj*d*. To Peter Baker for mending pittington loning Dike & for Damming of water, vij*d*. To Richard Tripp for two burden of wattles for the bull house and whinnes, vj*d*. To Richard Tripp & A lasse for carrying water ix*d*. To George Greeson for thacking of it two daies, ij*s*. To Richard Tripp for one Day, vj*d*. To Iohn Wilkinson for one day, vj*d*. For Drinks to them, viij*d*. For hay for ropes & litter, iiij*d*. For A resting men to ye Court, xiiij*d*. To the Constables for A penny the pound to Captaine Mallery, x*d*. For charges in the Court, x*d*. To Thomas Dobyson for fogge in ye brodeclose, vij*d*. Out of this foresaid receypt to Richard Tripp, iiij*s*. For setting the water in Maudlen laine the right course, ij*d*. For the fogge in Pella leazes to Mr Maior, xij*s*. iiij*d*. For writeing of our accountes, xvij*d*. For our Charges the 30th day of Aprell for going about our boundders, iiij*s*. vj*d*. For a Risteng (*arresting*) of Iohn gray to the Court, ij*d*. For a Risteng of Raph nobell to the Court and for other Charges thar in the Curt, x*d*. For william hilton Thomas Chater

wedow hallcat and wedow hunter for making of thar Cavels[1] on the more, viij*d.* For maineng (*mending?*) the moore stie and sateng of it up, iiij*d.* For a ston of hay to the boull, iiij*d.* To peter baker for loukeng to him, iiij*d.* For a boull for the parish, xxxix*s.* [*Other payments for mending gates, dikes, and the like*].

The Some of Expences is v*l.*, viij*d.*

RS. Anno 1638, May 24. By the grassemen chosen for this yeare viz. Nicolas Carre & Richard Cornforth of the old grassemen—0 . 0 . 10.

Receipts of the usual amounts, 2s. and 4s., for gaits ; *including* Resaved of Iohn gray fisher of the last of his hole stent, 2*s.* of Willam wheldon for on best (*beast*) gat, 4*s. Also*, Resaved for the toowe lones of Iohn gray and Cuthbart swanbourne —. Resaved of the hoole parish for to paied for hay to the bool —.

Some is iij*l.* xvij*s.* vj*d.*

Expences (1638).

To the Cunstaples for towe severell sesments on at xij*d.* the pound and the other at a penie the pound, 10*s.* 10*d.* For making of divers of the powre mens dicke on the Comon that is to saie nickolas barrow Robart Colsun willam hilton Thomas Chater wedow halcot wedow fresell and Iohn Nalson ——. For a saill to the boull ——. To Richart treep for hay to the booull 1*l.* 2*s.* To peter baker for kepeng the booull, 2*s.* 8*d.* For a warring (*warrant*) for facheing (*fetching*) the booull, 1*s.* Paid in Charges the 22 day of may for goinge about our bounders, 4*s.* 6*d.* To peter baker for faching the booull out of woriceshire (*Yorkshire*) 6*d.* To peter baker for skowring of watter hooles on the Common, 6*d.* To nickholas barrow for helinge of his beeth (*beast's?*) heed, 4*s.* Paid unto Temothe hubock and to Richart marting for the parish use, 1*l.* 1*s.* 4*d.*

Expences is in all laid out, 3*l.* —*s.* 6*d.*

Grasse men for 1639 ; Henry Johnson and Thomas Dawson ; " and they Resaved at ther entrens no things."

---

[1] This word occurs again A.D. 1660, and 1661, meaning apparently allotments on the moor. "CAVEL, or KAVEL, a lot, a share. Teut. *kavel.* To CAST CAVELS, to cast lots, to change situations, Teut. *Kavelen. Cavil* is the place allotted to a hewer in a coal mine by ballot. It means also an allotment of ground in a common field."—BROCKETT. The word is still in use among the Northern miners for the parts in the mine allotted to each for hewing.

5

Receipts, 1639.

[*For 8 gates at 2s. and 4s. each*]. Of the whole parrish for thre score and fyve beasts every beast 4*d*. in all j*l*. js. 8*d*. Of Gyles Atkinson for madline lone, 8s. For lone of the bull, 10*d*. For pelles lane, 5s.   2 . 10 . 6.

Expences 1639.

For one fother of hay to the Bull to Robert Tweddell, xvij*s*. 4*d*. To Robert harwell for bull hay standing in his house, xx*d*. More for hay to the Bull, viij*s*. For a harr tree to the mooregate, viij*d*. For carying of it, ij*d*. More for a rale to it, vj*d*. To Iohn Colson for workman-shipp to it, viij*d*. For paper, iiij*d*. In Charges the 11th of may goinge aboute our bounders, 5s. For writeng our accountes, 1s. 6*d*. [*A few more payments for making dikes and mending a gate*]. Sum 1 . 19 . 10.

Remaines 10s. 8*d*., & payd by ye Churchwardens for Nicolas Carr (?) to ye new Grassemen in all 1*l*. 10s. —*d*.

May 17, 1640. Delivered by Thomas Dawson & Henry Iohnson to Richard Barnfather & Iohn Colson, j*l*. ij*s*. 2*d*. [*No further accounts appear for this year*].

Grasmen for 1641 ; Richard Barnfather and Iohn Colson.

[*Receipts for* gates *as usual, eight in all*]. Resaved of Iohn gray fisher for pallalease lone, 5s. —*d*. Of Mr Iohn lianes for his time beinge heare, 7s. Resaved at our Enterences in monie, j*l*. ij*s*. 2*d*. *Total* £3 . 8 . 6.

Expences, 1641.

Paied to Richard Trep for 4 dayes at geals bridg, 2s. 8*d*. To Richard Treep for workin at the low car 4 dayes, 2s. 8*d*. To petter Baker for workin at Sherburn gat & seting a stoup, 6*d*. To petter Baker for mending the pinfould, 1s. To petter Baker for filling a cooll pit on the mouer, 1s. To the sayd petter for stopin thre wedowes gapes, 6*d*. To the counstapell for the gale & the correkcion house, 3s. 4*d*. Payd to gyles Atkyson with the parrish consent, 1*l*. [*Other payments for* gates, gaps, *&c.*]. *Total*, £1 . 15 . 0.

1642 (?) the 27 day payd to Thomas Browen & Iohn Butley for carring the armes for the parrish, 10*d*. (?). September 4. payd to them more for ther wages, 10*d*. (?). payd for a vayg to newcastel, 10*d*. (?). payd for thre vayge [1]

---

[1] What is meant by "thre vayge" is not apparent. It may possibly mean three *voyages, i.e.* journeys, the word *voyage* having been used formerly (as in French still) for travel by land as well as by sea.

for metting the Justeses 18*d.* Item payd for half a carrag Joyned with Shinkley for the kinges tresure, 6*s.* To the head counstapel for the gaiell and the hous of correckcion, 3*s.* To M[r] willson for writt artikels conserning the skots[1] 8*d.* For louking to pellees foug making the stile 2 stobes & a raiel, 1*s.* For allaslees hedg and harpers close, 1*s.* For drinkes when they brought wood to the pinfould, ——. For waiting the commishiners at newcastell, 2*s.* For a sut conserning for ye bull for the parrish, 6*s.* Paid & spent for carges about the parrish, 1*s.* For writting oure accounts, 1*s.* 6*d.*—1 . 9 . —.

Resates by the grasemen Richard Barnefather . . . in the yeare 1643. [*Receipts for* madland *and* pellayley *lanes, and for two gaits only*].

Disbursements, 1643.

To the head Counstapell for the house of (*correction*) ——. To petter baker for skouring the low carr ——. For mending pettinton yeet ——. For mending the enter common heges ——. For skouring geele bredg, 4*d.*

Received for ye yeares 1641 & 1642 the sum of 4*l.*—. Disbursed ye sayd yeares ye sum of 3*l.*—. Remaines——.

disspursmentes laid forth by the gresmen (*date illegible; probably 1647*). For a fother of haige (*hay*) for ledinge and getening it in, 1*l.* 4*s.* For a hang loocke for foowld. For drawing the Common in Expences, 2*s.* To Iohn barker for makinge the backaslease dicke, 2*s.* For Restes (*arrests*) to the Courte, 2*s.* For writinge of our acounte, 1*s.* 6*d.* To Edward bartingham 1*l.* 6*s.* For house Roume and sarvinge the boule, 8*s.* To Iohn Colson for a stile to the more dicke, 8*s.* To Iohn harison for making madland (*Magdalen*) dicke, ——. For 4 stone of haige for the boule. To Cristefore man for . . . . the Clooke ——. For Execusones for Thomas foster and . . . trotter paid to the bale, 2*s.* —.

[*A few other entries, some being illegible*]. Som is 3*l.* 16*s.* 2*d.*

Remaines 7*s.* 6*d.*

4 April 1648. Grassmen Robert Dobson and (*illegible*). Received at entrance, 6*s.* (7*s.* 6*d. being erased*).

---

[1] *Cf.*, below, " the commishiners at Newcastell " ; and " Churchwardens' Accounts," Surtees Society's Publications, vol. lxxxiv, pp. 103, 303. After the occupation of Newcastle by the Scotch Army under Lesley, the commissioners there were waited on by the High Sheriff of Durham, Sir Wm. Belasyse, and Sir Wm. Lambton, to give security for supplying provisions. A subsidy of £850 daily was eventually exacted.

Resceites (*for nine gaites, from 1s. 4d. to 4s. each*). Of Richart barnscfather for pales lone (*Pellowleases lane?*) 3s. For the boulle, 4l. 5s. 8d.

Some of Resates is 5l. 18s. 8d.

Disspursments as foleth.

To william Rumfoute for a fouther of haye to the boull, 18s. For breng it home and geteng it in, 4s. 2d. To peter baker for makinge seven dicke,[1] 6d. For writen our accountes, 1s. 6d. To Jain patteson for stanenge (*standing*) of the haie and sarvinge of the boule, 5s. To Richard treep for makinge up the gapes belongenge to the Enter Common, 6d. Geven backe to frances Embeerson, 1s. 6d. Geven to Antonie Emberson for the use of waliam Rumfutes Chelldren, 1l. 3s. For the more dyke makeng up, ——.

dispursments is 2l. 10s.

Grasmen for this yeare follinge [1649] Crestofore bee and Iohn ——. *Received at entrance, 3l. 0s. 6d.*

[*Receipts for* 17 gates, *for* horses, *and* bestes, *varying from 1s. 4d. to 8s. each*]. Resaved of Richard barneffather for palese lone, 3s. ——. Of Robart dobson for madlan lone, 3s. Some of Resates is 6l. ijs. 10d.

[*Disbursements*].

Paid for a boule, 2l. 10s. For towle (*toll*) for the bule, 2d. For skouring of geles bredges and the lowe Car and filling the peet (*pit*) up, 3s. 9d. To Antonie Emberson for a fother of haie to the boule, 2l. 6s. 8d. For a saale for the boule and wood for a stalle for him, 6d. For making up the Entercommoes dickes, 6d. To the gresmen for gooeng a bout for byenge the hay for the boule, 1s. [*Other usual payments*].

Dispursments is 5l. 19s. 10d.

Between 1649 and 1659, i.e., from the first till the last year of the Commonwealth, no accounts are extant, except the following, which has been crossed out.[2]

---

[1] Perhaps meaning "Seven Acres dike," *i.e.* the dike of the Close or common field so called in Pellow Leases.

[2] It seems probable that such accounts as do follow now, previous to 1661, were not entered till 1660, the year of the Restoration. For they are confused, as well as scanty, as though there had been difficulty in making them out and squaring them. We may observe also the payment of 2s., instead of 1s. 6d. as previously, for "writtinge our accompts," and an additional 1s. for "rectyfinge" them. An illiterate person seems to have been employed. Perhaps none more competent was at that time available. The learned Elias Smith had not returned to his cure. Similar

The Grasmens accompts for the yeare 1658 as followeth

Recaved this yeare in all for gates upon the Comon, and the money wch entred upon at first, 3*l.* 12*s.* 5*d.* More recaved for stubing the whins in all the sum of 5*l.* 2*s.* 3*d.* The sum in all is 8 . 14 . 8.

Disbursments this yeare 1658.

inprimis for stubing the whins and other things which you may see heare sett downe the sum of 9*l.* 10*s.* 3*d.*

dew to us upon this yeares accompts, 15*s.* 7*d.*

Receits 1659.

Rec^d for the bull now solde, 2*l.* 18*s.* 6*d.* [*Receipts for* horse *and* cow gates]. The somm is 4*l.* 10*s.* 2*d.*

1660. Received of William Willson for thre gates at on time to the grassmen, 12*s.* Of George Crukes for tow gates, 4*s.* For the Pellolese loninge, 4*s.* For Maudlns loninge, 5*s.*——1*l.* 5*s.* 0*d.*

Recaved this yeare 1659 in all the sum of 6*l.* 17*s.* 2*d.*

Disbursements 1659.

Paid for a bull, 2*l.* 9*s.* 0*d.* For hanting the bull, 1*s.* For makeinge the moore Ditch, 4*s.* For Dressinge giles bridge & mendinge the Ditht (*dike?*) about the bogge, 1*s.* 6*d.* For mendinge shearburne yeate, 2*s.* 4*d.* For writting our accounts, 2*s.* 6*d.* For Railes and mendinge pittington yeatt, 2*s.* 4*d.* P^d Mr Hauwden about William Watsons sute and in expenses, 1*l.* 1*s.* 0*d.* To Iohn Pattison for the bull standing and fetching the hay, 7*s.* 6*d.* For the hay standing, 2*s.* 6*d.* To Andrew Rudderford for hedging Gillsbrig bog, 6*d.* For making 2 gaps upon the sands, 6*d.* To Katheren Hugall in pt of payment for carrying the stoupe to Pittington lane end, 4*d.* For

remarks apply to the parish registers of the period. Since 1640, indeed, the scantiness of the accounts had shown signs of the disturbed state of things. It is interesting to note what had since then occurred in Durham. In 1640 the Scots had been there, and again in 1643. In 1644 a great sickness had prevailed throughout the year. In 1646 the King had come to Durham attended by the Scottish Commissioners, and later in the same year the see had been dissolved and the episcopal estates ordered to be sold. In 1649 the Castle was sold to Robert Andrewes, Lord Mayor of London, and the Cathedral left desolate. In 1650 the Scotch prisoners after the battle of Dunbar had been confined therein. At once after the Restoration our books show a return to the old order of things. Parish affairs are again regularly seen to, and regularly recorded, and all seems to have gone on as before the troublous times. We note, further, a cessation of vexatious political imposts, and a characteristic growing tendency to spend the money of the parish in potations and festivity. We may well conceive how welcome to the general population the change would be.

mending and hanging Shearburn moore yate, 6*d.* For 9 stone of hay for the bull, 3*s.* 9*d.* For a lode of hay, 1*l.* 11*s.* o. For leading, 1*s.* 6*d.* For the wayn mens dinners and getting in the hay, 1*s.* For rectyfying accoumpts and writing, 1*s.* For writtinge our accoumpts, 2*s.* the somm is 6*l.* 14*s.* 8*d.*

Disburst this yeare 1659 in all the of 6*l.* 17*s.* o*d.*

Remaines in our hands in all for this tow years accoumpts the sum of o . o . 1.

Receaved of georg hutcheson for a hors gait, 4*s.* More Receaved of Elsebeth tod for a hors gait, 4*s.*

(*Alia manu*) paid by me mary Bluitt thre shillings the last part of pament for tow cow gats.

Grassmen chosen this yeare 1660 Iohn Burdas and Thomas Foster and they reccavd at their enteringe a penny——o*l.* o*s.* 1*d.*

Recaits.—Receaved of Iohn Hayes for a horse gate Being the last of his hole stent, 8*s.* Of Iohn Herrinson for tenter rent,[1] 8*d.* Of Iohn Atkinson for the loninge at leadancross,[2] 1*s.* For the tow common lonings, 9*s.* For the Cavells, 13*s.* 2*d.* [*Other receipts for* gates]. Receaved in all, 3*l.* 4*s.* 11*d.*

Disbursments 1660. Disburst upon the bounder day, 15*s.* 2*d.* To William wilsons for goinge to Renton, 3*d.* To Nichollas Ladler for bull hay, 10*s.* To walter Jackson for keepinge the bull, 8*s.* For makinge the moure dike, 18*s.* 8*d.* For makinge sum gaps and scoweringe gils bridge, 1*s.* 6*d.* For writtinge our accounts, 2*s.* 6*d.* Paid to the hird, 4*s.*

disburst in all, 3*l.* o*s.* 1*d.*

Grassmen 1661, Mathew Borrow and Petter Booth (*the name of the latter erased*). *Received at entrance,* 9*d.*

Recaved for tow coman lonings, 11*s.* 6*d.* Of George Maugham for the loninge, 6*d.* For the Bull, 2*l.* 16*s.* 4*d.*

---

[1] This is the first entry of "tenter-rent," *i.e.*, of payments for bleaching ground on the common or elsewhere. It became common afterwards.

[2] "Leaden Cross." It stood in the middle of the street, at the junction of the parishes of St. Nicholas and St. Giles, and is shown in Speed's map of Durham engraved in Surtees' History of Durham, vol. iv (City of Durham, p. 54). Surtees there says, "Beyond this (*i.e.*, the old city gateway), the street of Claypath stretches Eastward, and, climbing about two-thirds of the first hill, joins Gilesgate at the spot where the *Leaden Cross* once stood. When Hunter wrote, the pedestal of the cross was still standing in the middle of the street at the top of the Beast-Market." Also, in a note, "In the rentals of the Commones of the Abbey in 1454 an entry occurs, 'De uno tenemento ad Crucem Plumbeam, vis. viii*d.*'—*Hunter.*"

For Reshes, 9*d.* Of William Jurdinson for a cow gate, 4*s.* Of Henry Johnson for tenter rent, 8*d.* Of Richard yates for a cow gate, 4*s.* Of Ezi Story for tow gates, 1*l.* o*s.* o*d.* Of Iohn Atkinson for the loninge, 1*s.* Of Iohn Herrinson for tenter rent, 1*s.* 4*d.* Of Ezi Story for one cow gate, 10*s.* Of the Neibors for every cow threepence, 12*s.* 6*d.* For Cavells for the mower dike, 6*s.* 8*d.* For the Bull, 2*l.* 3*s.* o*d.* Sum 8*l.* 13*s.* o*d.*

Disburements, 1661, by the grasmen Mathew Borrow and Anthony dobson.

Disburst upon the bounder day, 13*s.* 6*d.* For a stapell for the pinfould and a lock & key, 8*d.* For leedinge home the bull hay and gettinge in, 8*s.* For the Bull, 2*l.* 3*s.* 4*d.* More spent when we bought the bull, 4*d.* For makinge dike at the sands, 1*s.* 10*d.* For the bulls gras and fetchinge home and gettinge him cailled in the Markett, 6*s.* 8*d.* To Walter Jackson for keepinge the bull, 8*s.* To George Robson and William Jurdinson for stubinge the whines, 6*s.* Paid to the hird when he was hiered, 6*d.* To Walter Jackson when he was hiered, 6*d.* To Walter Jackson for gatheringe the whins to geether that was stubd, 4*d.* Given to Mr Heeth for confirminge the Order and to Mr Phillaps for writinge it and expences goinge about it, 1*l.* 9*s.* 2*d.*[1] Geven for helpinge to drive the moore[2] in drinke, 1*s.* To Mathew Borrow for seekinge draughts and helpinge home with the hay for the bull, 2*s.* To Nicholas Ladler for Bull hay, 10*s.* For writinge our accounts, 2*s.* 6*d.* [*Several other payments of the usual kind for mending dikes and gates, &c.*]. Disbursments are 8*l.* 4*s.* 11*d.* Remaines in our hands 8*s.* 1*d.*

Grassmen 1662, Thomas Reedhead and George Crukes.

[*Receipts for 21* horse *and* cow gates, *at* 1*s.* 4*d.*, 2*s.*, 4*s.*, 10*s.*, *and* £1, *for* Pellowlesses loninge, loninge at

---

[1] The expenses here attending the gathering of the stubbed whins on the Moor, with the obtaining of an order from Mr. Heath with regard to them, seems to imply that the lord of the manor had now asserted his claim to them. See above, p. 31, note 1.

[2] "Driving" the Moor, which seems now to have been annual, would be for the purpose of discovering the beasts grazing on it, and detecting interlopers or diseased animals. There is frequent mention afterwards of "scabbed horses," which were eliminated or impounded. Among the Receipts of 1734 we find, "To the scabbd Lane, 8*s.* 6*d.*"; and Robert Allison, the present grieve of the manor, speaks of a field below Magdalen Chapel, which is, or was, called "Scabgarth" from scabbed animals having been impounded in it.

Causefoute, *and* Maudlan loninge, *and three* tenter rents at
8*d. and* 1*s.* 4*d.*]. 7*l.* 6*s.* 0. Rests in our hands, 2 . 4 . 3.

Disbursments 1662. Disburst on the boundery day,
6*d.* To the Collectors, 5*s.* For a lode of hay, 1*l.* 6*s.* 8*d.*
For leedinge it home, 4*s.* For gittinge it in in drinke and
wainemens drinks, 2*s.* For gettinge draughts and helpinge
them that day 1*s.* 6*d.* For the Bull, 2*l.* 6*s.* For mendinge
the mower yett and wood and tarringe the wood, 5*s.* 6*d.*
For six stone of hay, 2*s.* For six stone of hay for the bull,
2*s.* For our accoumpts makinge, 2*s.* 6*d.* In drinke when
we maid our accoumpts, 6*d.* To the belman for callinge
the bounders, 4*d.* For our diners one the bounder day,
14*s.* Paid at Thomas Grymes for drinke that was geven
to the childer, 1*s.* Geven to the musick that day, 1*s.*
[*Other payments of the usual kind*]. 7 . 6 . 0.

8th of June, 1663. Receaved by us Robert Jackson
and Antony Wharton new grasse men this yeare the sume
of 2*l.* 4*s.* 3*d.* More recaved from the ouerseers, 5*s.*
Recaved for the Bull, 2*l.* 7*s.* 6*d.* Of Thomas Snawdon for
whins, 2*s.* Of Mr Marcham for six loode of whins, 2*s.*
Of Henry Wilkinson for whins, 11*d.* Of Nickolas Ladler
for whins, 1*s.* Of Iohn Keenleside for seven loode of
whins, 2*s.* 4*d.* For Cavells of the moore dike, 6*s.* 4*d.* For
stubinge the whins at sixpence a gaite the sum of 3*l.* 4*s.* 6*d.*
[*Other receipts as usual, for* 6 *gates, at* 1*s.* 4*d. and* 10*d., the*
loninges, *and* tenter rents]. Sum, 11*l.* 4*s.* —*d.*

Disbursments 1663. For the bull, 1*l.* 17*s.* For
stubbinge six akers of the moure, 3*l.* 18*s.* 0*d.* To James
Reed for takinge up the younge whins, 6*d.* Disburst to
them that mesuered the ground that was stubd in drinke,
6*d.* Spent when we got the scrowell drawen of all the
gates in the street, 1*s.* To the hird for hantinge the bull,
1*s.* For callinge the bull, 1*s.* For a loade of hay to the
bull, 1*l.* 6*s.* 8*d.* For wainemens drinkes and gettinge in
the hay, 2*s.* To Iohn davinson for stubbinge, 16*s.* To
Mr Haudon for his Fee at Entering the sute against Henry
Wanles, 3*s.* 4*d.* More to the clarke of the court, 6*d.*
More to the bailliff, 1*s.* 6*d.* More for drawinge the order
and Lookinge aboute that sute, 1*s.* To Richard Coulson
for mendinge the pinfould and for wood to mend it, 1*s.* 6*d.*
To William Wilkinson for arrestinge severall parsons for
stubbinge whins, 1*s.* Spent when we went aboute
Mr Wanles suite, 8*d.* For writtinge our accomptes, 2*s.* 6.
[*Other entries of the usual kind*]. In all—11*l.* 1*s.* 9*d. ob.*

Rests in our hands, 2*s.* 3*d.*

September the 21th 1663.

It is ordered concluded concented and agreed by and with the consents and assents of the inhabetants of ye parishe of S^t gyles that they will all Joyne and stand firmly one to another and pay every sess and taxation that shall be Laid one for to try sute against Mr Henry Wanles Alderman for Eetinge with us in our Entercommons and he saith he will and we the inhabetants are all consented and 'greed to try sute with him wheireunto we have heareunto set our hands the day and yeare above written Anno Dom' 1663. Iohn **X** Coulson, *&c.*, *&c.* [*There follow twenty-five signatures, four only of the signers writing their own names*].

Grassmen 1664, Ouswand Bell and Thomas Allinson. *Received at entrance, 2s. 2d. [Receipts, as usual, for* gates *and* lonings ; *also,* Recaved for whines, 3s. 4d. Of Iohn Rennesid for 5 lods of whines, 1s. 8d. At 3 pence a cow for the Bulle hay, 10s. 3d.].

In all 5l. 15s. 9d.

Dispursements 1664.

For the lode of the Bull hay, 1l. 6s. 8d. For Ledden it home, 3s. 6d. More for getting it in in drinkes and wainemens drinkes, 2s. 6d. To the museck and for drinke and for calling out the moudders,[1] 1s. To the museck and for drinke and for calling out the moudders, 2s. For our dinners one our bunder day, 1l. Paide more for drinke one the bounder day, 6s. 8d. paide more for museck, 2s. 6d. For driveing the moure, 1s. 4d. For writting our accounts, 2s. 6d. [*Other payments for repairing* dikes, gates, *&c., of the usual kind*]. Sum 5l. 1s. 2d. Remaines, 14s. 7d.

Grasmen 1665, Thomas Snawdon and Richard yaits. *Received 14s. 7d. [Receipts for* gates, *for* Madglin *and* Peleases loninges, 10s. *and* 6s., *and for* the ould Bull, 1l. 12s. 0d.]. Total sume 4 . 19 . 7.

And Thomas Snawdon and Richard Yates doth ingage to pay other ten shillings for another gate if he keepe him upon the Comon tow dayes after the date heareof June the 4th 1666.

Disspurcments 1665. Dispursed by the consent of the fower & twentie to Edward Brantinham, 2s. 7d. For scouringe the pound to Geo. Robson, 1s. 4d. For

---

[1] See above, p. 61, note 2, and p. 36, note 1.

hay to the bull, 5*s*. 6*d*. For driveing the more, 1*s*. 4*d*. For the Bull that we bought, 1*l*. 1*s*. and in drinke when he was sould & for driveing him to the market, 1*s*. 6*d*. For our dinners and for drinke on the bounder day, 1*l*. 1*s*. More for drinke at Tho. Grames the same day, 1*s*. 9*d*. For driveing the more 1*s*. 4*d*. For writinge our accounts, 2*s*. 6*d*. [*Other payments for* uphoulding dikes, repairs, &c.]. 4 . 19 . 6.

Grasmen 1666, Robert Chamers and Iohn Herrinson. *Received* 1*d*.

[*Receipts for* gates *at* 4*s. and* 10*s.* ; *for* Maudlane loninge, 10*s.* ; *for* Pellowleeses loninge, 5*s.* ; *for* the loninge at the Cawseefoute, 1*s.* ; *for three* tenter rents, 8*d. each; for* whins for Shearbourne house, 5*s.*]. *Sum,* 5 . 18 . 11. Rests in our hands, 7*s*. 5*d*.

Disbursements, 1666. Paid to the hird for bringinge a horse to the fould, 4*d*. For 4 Stoupes for the mouer for the Beese to Rub one and Leedinge them and lyinge them, 6*s*. 8*d*. For drissinge the duke poole and in drinke to them, 4*s*. 10*d*. For scoweringe gills Bridge and for stakes for it and in drinke, 3*s*. For driveinge the mower, 1*s*. 4*d*. To William Wilson for Mendinge the dike adjoyninge to the Sands, 2*s*. 6*d*. Paid about the parishe busines, 1*s*. 4*d*. In Charges againest Robert Heighington, 6*s*. 2*d*. More in expences about the same sute, 1*s*. 7*d*. For Makinge the Moure dike and more in drinke, 1*s*. Paid for the Bull, 1*l*. 7*s*. Paid one the Bounder day for our diners and in drinke, 15*s*. 9*d*. For the Minesters diner and the Clarke one the Bounder day,[1] 8*d*. For the Minester and Clarke in drinke one the Bounder day,[1] 1*s*. For driveinge the mower, 1*s*. 4*d*. For our accompts makinge, 2*s*. 6*d*. [*Other usual entries*]. 5 . 18 . 5.

December the 4th 1666.

It is Ordered Concluded Consented and agreed by and with the Consents and Assents of the inhabetants within the parishe of St Gyles that they will all Joyne with the Grasmen and pay all Sesses and Taxations that shalbe Laid upon them for the tryinge and mentaininge sute againest

---

[1] This is the first notice, since the mention of " Mr. Smeth " in 1635, of the minister and parish clerk (as afterwards constantly) on the " Bounder Day," implying perhaps the retention of some religious functions. As to the designation " minister," instead of " curate " as previously, and usually " parson " afterwards, due perhaps to puritanical influences, see " Church-wardens' Accounts," Surtees Society's Publications, vol. lxxxiv, p. 98 note 2.

Robert Heighington for inclosinge and Barringe up a Close Called the five Akers which is entercommon and belongeth to the said inhabetants for the winter Season and he saith they shall not put any goods their for he will try sute with the parishe and we the inhabetants are agreed to maintaine sute againest him and unto this agreement have set our hands the day and yeare above writtne.

Robert Dobson, *&c. &c.* [*Fifty-four more signatures follow; seventeen write their own names*].

No accounts for 1667 remain.

Grassmen 1668, William Wilson and William Herinson.

Due to the old grasmen, 4*s.* 5*d. ob.* Recaved of Mr Matthew for 14 loode of whines, 4*s.* 8*d.* For 50 gaites in the fogg of Pellowleeses at 10*d.* p. gate, 2*l.* 1*s.* 8*d.* For 55 gates in the fogg in Broode Close at 8*d.* p. gate, 1*l.* 16*s.* 8*d.* Of Doctor Bazeer[1] for Pellowleese yets, 1*s.* 9*d.* Of Francis Callehane for the same, 1*s.* Of Robert Bell for fower gaites which he haith paid at his entring on the comon, 2*l.* Of Ralph Nicholson for Maudlan lane, 10*s.* Of Iohn Herrinson and Robert Faierfax for Pellowleese loninge, 6*s.* Of Ralph Richard for tenter rent, 8*d.* For the Cavels of the Mouer dike, 6*s.* Of Iohn Nelson for tenter rent, 8*d.* Of William Wilson for the comon loninge at Causee foute, 8*d.* [*Other receipts for* gates].

Disbursments this yeare. For Leedinge the Bull hay and gettinge it in, 4*s.* For a lock for the pinfoold, ——. For Makinge the dike adjoyninge the sands, 2*s.* For Mendinge the pinfoold fower times and wood and Nayles for it, ——. For the fogg in Pellowleeses, 2*l.* 1*s.* For the fogg in Broodelose, 1*l.* 16*s.* For a sayle and band to ty the Bull in, ——. For mendinge the yet at the Backhouse and for Crukes and bands and Rayles for it, 1*s.* For drivinge the Moure, 1*s.* For gills Bridge scoweringe and a rayle for it, 1*s.* For the bounder diner, and in drinke to it and to the Musick, 1*l.* 5*s.* 6*d.* For the Minesters horse that day, 6*d.* Paid at Thomas gryemes for drinke for the boyes upon the bounder day, 6*d.* Spent at Robt. Bells when we got his money for his gaites, 2*s.* For makinge the Mouer dike, 13*s.* 4*d.* And in drinke to them at the bargaine making, 6*d.* For our accompts, 2*s.* 6*d.* [*Other payments for repairs, &c., of the usual kind*]. Disburst, 7*l.* 6*s.* 11*d.*

---

[1] Dr. Isaac Bazire, divine and traveller; Archdeacon of Northumberland, and Canon of Durham: died 1676.

Grassmen 1669 Iohn Wilson and Robert Faierfax.
[*Entries of the usual kind; but no expenses entered for the* Bounder day]. Receipts, 2*l.* 8*s.* 9*d.* Disburst, 2*l.* 12*s.* 1*d.*

Aprill 22th 1670 (?). It is agreed concluded consented & agreed by & with the consents & assents of the Inhabitants within the parish of St Giles that they will all Joyne with the Grasmen & pay all sesses & taxations that shall be laid upon them for the trying & maintaining suite agt James Rodham of the parish of St Gyles ; he deniing to pay what our said order doth expresse as it is accustomed & unto this agreement have set our hands the day & yeare above written. [*There follow fifty-two signatures, twenty-two writing their own names*].

Grasmen 1670, Richard Hopper and Henry Johnson. Due to old grasmen, 4*s.*
Received for the bull, 1*l.* 10*s.* Received Iohn wilson when he was reasted (*arrested*) for the order, 4*d.* [*Receipts for* gates, lanes, *including* hy *and* low ends of Pellelease lon, the Cauvles (*cavells*) of the moure dike, 6*s.*, *and two* tenter rents *at* 8*d.*]. Somme, 4*l.* 16*s.* 2*d.*

Disbursmentes 1670. Paid to willam shaw for keping the mouredycke, 4*s.* For drynk when we gread with william shaw for keping the moure dike, 6*d.*[1] To M^r georg mourcroft for his charges that he wanted when the Inhabetant was indited for renton lon, 2*s.* More payd to georg more croft In drynk, 1*s.* For drynk when we sould the bull, 1*s.* To edward brantingam for reisting the old grasmen, 4*d.* To the hyrd for making the more dike, 15*s.* For drink to the hird when he mad the more dike, 1*s.* 2*d.* To the hird for brynging James roddam horse to the fould, 2*d.* For reaysting James roddem, 2*d.* To Iohn wilson for draining pellelease lon, 6*d.* For mending the dick about the bog at gyles brig, 8*d.* For drink when we recaived humphfry houbdon money, 3*d.* To thomas alleson for seking the regester boke, 4*d.* For our accountes making, 2*s.* 6*d.* Disburst on the bounder day, 15*s.* For drynk when we drave the more, 1*s.* 4*d.* To the musik on the bounder day, 1*s.* Spent when we bought the bull, 1*s.* [*Other payments of the usual kind*].
The Somme in all is 4*l.* 11*s.* 1*d.* Remaines 5*s.* 1*d.*

---

[1] Observe at this period, and subsequently, the prevalence of "drinks" on all available occasions.

[In the years that follow, until 1798, in order to avoid unnecessary repetition of customary receipts and payments, only such entries as are unusual or otherwise interesting will usually be transcribed. But the names of the grassmen for each year, the whole sums each year received and expended, all entries connected with the " bounder day " and " scaling " or " driving " the moor, and all such as show the prices of labour and things, will still be given].

1671. Grassmen, Iohn Daveson and Nicholas Hutchesson.

Received. For the bull, 1*l.* 7*s.* Of Thomas Keenleside for wheens, 11*s.*

Disbursed. For driveing the moor, 1*s.* 3*d.* For pound-louse[1] for y'e bull, & for drinke when we sould the bull, —. Spent when we went to receive mune (*money*) for the wheenes, 1*s.* Spent when we went to speek with Curnill Tempest[2] about thame that wad not pay for there gats, 1*s.* To Iohn Colson for a hartre for Sherburn get and seting it one, 3*s.* For the bull, 2*l.* 5*s.* For driveing the moure, 1*s.* For drinke dispursed on the bounder day, 17*s.* For grasse to the Bool, 2*s.* To Nicholas pearsson one the bounder day, 2*s.* 6*d.* To Simond Marttin for drissing of the bool when he was el, 2*s.* 6*d.* [*Other entries*].

Receipts, 7l. 2s. 2d. Disbursements, 6l. 8s. 11d.

1672. Grassmen, James Snowden and Nicolas Sparke.

Received. For a bull that wee soulde to Iohn Coulson, 1*l.* 13*s.* For whines, 2*s.* 4*d.* [*Other entries*].

Paid. For voweing (*viewing*) Iohn Fosters dikes to thame that wee got to vowe thame in drinke, 1*s.* 6*d.* To Robart Coulson for one Raile and a Sworde for Pittington yeet, 1*s.* 2*d.* For the boule that wee got at Branddon, 2*l.* 1*s.* For grase to the boule, 1*s.* 6*d.* Giveing Hugh Hutchinson agane in drinke, 1*s.* For a stile a Joining to the sands and for a bowe for the boule (*bull*) to Robart Coulson, 1*s.* 6*d.* For a meare at was of oure moure to Robart Headly for calling of hir, 4*d.* To Robart Richardson for a lousse[3] for the poundfould, 6*d.* Giveing in drinke to them that helpe to put in the picke and put one the houpe

---

[1] See Glossary.

[2] Colonel Tempest, *i.e.*, John Tempest of the Isle, through whose marriage with the heiress of the Heaths the Tempest family acquired Old Durham. See notes to Registers.

[3] Apparently the payment for loosing, or releasing, an animal that had been impounded. *Cf.* " Pound-lowse " above.

of Shirbrune yett, 8*d.* For driveing of the moure, 1*s.* 3*d.*
For the bull that wee bought, 1*l.* 18*s.* 6*d.* To Nicolas
Pearson for the bunder day, 1*s.* For driveing the moure,
1*s.* Disbursed of the bounder day in drinke, 8*s.* [*Other
entries.*] *Receipts,* 7*l.* 16*s.* 7*d.* *Disbursements,* 7*l.* 15*s.* 11*d.*

1673. Grassmen, Robert Colson and Iohn Nelson.

Received. For the Bull, 1*l.* 6*s.* 8*d.* Of Iohn Keenele-
side for whins, 10*s.* For the first Bull, 1*l.* 16*s.* [*Other
entries*].

Disburst. For the Bull, 1*l.* 18*s.* Spent at Shawes
when we greed aboute the moure yett, 1*s.* 2*d.* For mendinge
the pinfould, 1*s.* For gras for the Bull to Iohn Dawson,
1*s.* 2*d.* For penyworths of grass for the bull, 1*s.* 2*d.* For
Buter and Milke for the bull, 4½*d.* Spent when we sould
one bull and bought the other bull, 1*s.* 6*d.* Spent about
getting a order, 1*s.* 2*d.* To Simond Martin for Mendinge
the Bull, 2*s.* 6*d.* For settinge the moure yett and in drinke
at Will'm Shawes, 2*s.* Spent at Thomas watsons when
we agreed with the Hird for uphouldinge the dike, 1*s.*
Paid to him that went about with us for the Caules (*cavells ?*)
4*d.* Spent at Iohn Keenleside when we got money for
whins, 1*s.* Geven to the hird in drinke when we went to
vew the moure dike and agreed for makinke them, 1*s.*
Spent at severall times when we got things set downe,
1*s.* 6*d.* For drivinge the moure, 1*s.* 4*d.* For makinge the
moure dike, 16*s.* For mendinge the moure yet and for
Nayles and Rayles for it, 3*s.* For Scoweringe gills bridge
and for a Rayle for it, 1*s.* For tow peeces of wood for the
pinfould and Nayles, 6*d.* For arrestinge M^r druery to the
Courte, 2*d.* Spent that day about that bussenes, 6*d.*
Spent upon the bounder day, 8*s.* 4*d.* To Nicholas Pearson
that day, 1*s.* 6*d.* and in drinke to him, 6*d.* Spent at
Will'm weemeses when we recaved for his Cowgate, 1*s.*
For drivinge the Moure, 1*s.* 4*d.* More in drinke for the
lads one the bounder day, 2*s.*

Rec^d in all 7*l.* 1*s.* 6*d.*—Disburst, 5*l.* 5*s.* 2*d.* Rests in
our hands, 1*l.* 16*s.* 4*d.*

June the 14th 1673.

It is Ordered Consented Concluded and agreed by and
with the Consents and Assents of the fower and twenty and
the Inhabetants of the said street that Every Inhabetant
there man or woman that at this time haith any Cowes or
whyes upon the Mower or Coman that they shall pay to
the said grasmen for every Cow graysing there at this time

the sum of sixpence for kepinge the bull and for all that shall have any Cowes upon the said Coman twixt this and Michaellmas day the said sum and in Case any man or woman doe refuse to pay this said sum that we the said fower and twenty and inhabetants of the said street will keepe harmles the said grasmen of all parson or parsons that shall Contend against them wheirunto we have set our hands the day and yeare above writen.

Tho: Emerson, &c., &c. [*Fourteen signatures; six write their own names*].

1674. Grassmen, Thomas Booth and William Weames.

Rec^d of Iohn Beelly for 3 gats, 6s. Of Mr Iohn Dury for parte of his gates, 3s. Rec^d of nighboures . . . . hay by Jug^1 the sume of 17s. 4d. For the Bull that we soulde, 2l. 10s. For the Cavells for the moure dike, 7s. 6d. Of Ralph Nickolson for oure yeares rent for the longing, 10s. Of Robart Fairfax for parte pelowleazes longing, 2s. Of Thomas Bell for the lone and of the pellowleeszes longing, 5s. 6d. Of Christopher Kellsoe for two gates, 4s. Of George Banckes for one gate, 10s. Of William Wilson for the longing, 6d. Of Ralph Richardson for tenters, 8d. Of Iohn Nelson for tenters, 8d. Of Robart Richardson for tenters, 8d. [*Other entries*]. Rec^l in all, 7l. 15s. 8½d.

Disbursements 1674.—Spent at William Shawes when wee greed with him aboute the moure yett, 1s. Spent when we bought the Bull, 1s. To Ralph Jackson for hay that was gote of him, 1l. Paid for the hay leading home and getting it Jug to them, 7s. 2d. For grase for the bull, 2s. 6d. For uphoulding the dike adjoyning unto the Sandes, 2s. 6d. For driveing the moure, 1s. 4d. To Thomas Browne one serving the bull getting in to his Close, 1s. 8d. To Thomas Bell for hay at he gave the Bull at was his Owne, 12s. 6d. To George Pearson for playing to the mouders, 1d. To Thomas Bell for keaping the Bull, 5s. Spent upon the bounder day, 10s. Giving Nickolas Pearson that day, 1s. 6d. For driveing the moure, 1s. 4d. To Robart Richardson for a crouke for the poundfolde, 6d. [*Other entries*]. Disburst in all, 7l. 5s. 4d.—Rests in our hands, 10s. 4d.

---

¹ *Cf.* below, "Getting it Jug to them." "JUG (from Latin, *jugerum*, an acre), a common pasture or meadow (*West Country*)"—Bailey's Dictionary. Also, "A load, or small load, of hay"—Ditto, 1763. Can it mean that the hay was bought and delivered by load? The word in the text between "nighboures" and "hay" has not been deciphered. It may perhaps be intended for a proper name.

1675. Grassmen, Iohn Herrison and Georg Robson.

Rec^d of Robert Faierfax for one horse gate, 8*s.* For Maudlane Loninge, 10*s.* For Pellowleesses Loninge, 5*s.* 6*d.* Of Iohn Belley for a Cowgate, 1*s.* 4*d.* For the Caveles of the mouer dike, 6*s.* For the Bull, 2*l.* 3*s.* 6*d.* Of Iohn Nelson for tenter rent, 8*d.* Of Rob't Richardson for tenter rent, 8*d.* Of William Willson for the Coman (*common?*) at Cawsfoutt, 6*d.* Of Iohn Belley for one gate, 1*s.* 4*d.* Rec^d in all 4*l.* 6*s.* 6*d.*—Disburst in all, 4*l.* 6*s.* 9*d.*

Disbursments 1675.——For Stopinge the water at gills Bridge, 6*d.* Restowed of Robert Coulson when he went to vew the yets to see what they did need, 6*d.* For Makinge the dike at gills Bridge, 8*d.* Spent upon the Bounder day, 12*s.* For seekinge the Bull, 1*s.* To Nicholas Ladler for the Bull when he Impounded him, 1*s.* Paid for the Bull, 2*l.* 2*s.* For gras for the Bull, 6*d.* Geven to Peeter Greveson in drinke when he entered upon the Bull, 6*d.* Geven to George Pearson for playinge to the Mouders when they mouded the moure, 6*d.* To Nichollas Pearson on the bounder day, 1*s.* 6*d.* Spent when we Impounded Robert Faierfax horse, 6*d.* Geven to the hirds Lad for helpinge me to get Robert Faierfax horse to the fould, 1*d.* [*Other entries for upholding and making* dikes, *mending* yets, *&c.*].

1676. Grassmen, Thomas Hugall and Richard Hutchinson.

*Receipts, of the usual kind—*2*l.* 14*s.* 2.

*Disbursements—*Paide to Petter Grevson for dicking up Mr Wanelise yet at Normouer (*North moor?*) ——. To Rob. Branttingam for a troueke and a stapel for the pounfoueld, 4*d.* Spent for driveing the mouer, 1*s.* 4*d.* Spent upon the bounder day, 16*s.* 6*d.* For a hores (*horse*) for the parson, 6*d.* To Nick: Pearson for playing on the bounder day, 1*s.* 6*d.* [*Other usual entries*]. *Sum,* 2*l.* 13*s.* 8*d.*

June the 4th, 77.—Memorandum that it is Consented Concluded and a greed by and with the assents and Consents of the Four and twenty that noe man that hath any tenters in the Coman Loninge or any man that shall sett any their shall after the date hearof but he shall pay to the grasmen yearly and every yeare for soe many yeards as every man hath their the sum of 1*d.* p. yeard and to this we have sett our hands heare under written. [*Twenty signatures; ten write their own names*].

1677. Grassmen, Iohn Coulson and Robert Richardson.

Receipts, of usual kind, 3l. 12s. 0d.

Disbursements. Spent when we resaved the ten shilling of Will Hunter for maudlane loning, 4d. To Petter Grevesson for uphoueld (*upholding*) mouer dicke, 4s. To Petter Grevesson for makeing the mouer dicke and for giell bridge, 12s. 10d. To Iohn Foster for leding the wood, 7s. To Iohn Coulson for 7 dayes for mending the puenfould and maikeing thre (?) yetes and at the woode, 10s. 6d. To Rob. Richard son for carring the wood to pettington yet and Shirburn yet and in the wood, 4s. To Rob. Richardson for a crouke for the punfould, 2d. To Petter Grevesson for maiking the dicke at Will Willson shop end and in Poter lo'ing,[1] 1s. Spent when we went abuet the orderes, 1s. 6d. To Mr Hadan for his advice, 1s. 8d. For driveing the mouer, 1s. 4d. Spent upon the bunder daye, 16s. To Nick. Paerson for plaing, 1s. 4d. For a hores for the parson on the bunder daye, 6d. Spent when we went to demand the mueny of Edward Denton and when we resaved his mouny and mathew Denton his mouny, 2s. To mending blind Laine hedge,[2] 3d. To making water holes for the bees (*beasts*), 1s. 6d. To mouding the moure, 1s. 6d. [*Other entries*]. Disburst in all—3l. 14s. 2. Restest out in our hands, 0l. 2s. 2d.

1678. Grassmen Thomas Watson and William Wilson.

Receipts of the usual kind.

Disbursements. For stoupes and rayles and nayles for Sheerburne yett and pittington yett and takeing up the stoupe and settinge it againe and woorkemanshipp, 3s. 9d. For scoweringe gills Bridge and findinge a rayle for it, 10d. For driveing the moure, 1s. 4d. To Robart Richardson which was owne them when they went out of grasmens place the last yeare, 2s. 2d. Spent aboute fouldinge Will'm Hunters Mayer and in contention about getinge the ten shillings for the loninge belonginge to Maudlns, 1s. For scoweringe Maudlen loninge, 1s. When we recaved Thomas Burnapps moneyes and Thomas Bayles and Iohn

---

[1] Meaning perhaps "Potter's loning" (or *lane*), which may have been identical with "Tinker's (or *Tinkler's*) lane," still so called. See below, p. 90, note 1.

[2] "Blind Lane," not unfrequently mentioned, has not been identified with any existing lane.

6

Millers for their gates, 2*s.* For a writter for oure yeare, 2*s.* 6*d.* Disburst on the bunderday, 18*s.* 6*d.* Disburst at Will'm Shawes, 1*s.* 6*d.* Paid to Nichollas Pearson and Thomas Wilson one the bundere day, 1*s.* 10*d.* For a horse for the parson that day 6*d.* For a Cap to Sheerburne yett and for mendinge it, 1*s.* 8*d.* For driveinge the Moure the bounder day, 1*s.* 2*d.* For our accompts, 2*s.* 6*d.*—— Rec^d in all this yeare, 3 . 9 . 10. Disburst in all, 3 . 6 . 11.

1679. Grassmen, Iohn Maston and Iohn Maior.

Receipts, as usual, 5l. 5s. 1d. No disbursements preserved.

1680. Grassmen, Tho. Readhead and Edward Dentton.

Receipts, as usual, including Cawcy foot Loning, 6*d. Sum, 5l. 10s. 2d.*

Disbursements. To Peter Grevson for Stoping ye water at Gills Bridge, 1*d.* For driving the Moor, 6*d.* When we Rec^d ye mony of Tho. Gelson Spent, 1*s.* 6*d.* When we Rec^d Tho. Burnops Mony Spent, 6*d.* When we Rec^d Tho. Willds mony Spent, 6*d.* For our drawing our order against Rob't Cornfourth, 1*s.* For Bayles fees, 1*s.* 8*d.* For entering ye Plea, 3*s.* For our Aturnays fees, 1*s.* 8*d.* For our Aturnays fees more, 1*s.* 8*d.* For Attending ye Court ye first Court day, 2*s.* For Attending ye Court ye Second Court day, 2*s.* For Attending ye Court ye 3 Court day, 2*s.* Spent upon our Witnesses upon that day, 3*s.* 8*d.* In expences in going about Severall Times for ye Parish against Robert Cornfourth, 2*s.* 6*d.* For driving ye mouer upon ye Bounder day, 1*s.* 4*d.* Upon ye Bounder day for meat and Drinke, 1*l.* 1*s.* 10*d.* Upon ye Bounders to Nicholas Pearson, 1*s.* 6*d.* To david Sharp upon ye Bounder day, 1*s.* Spent at Will'm Shaws upon ye Bounder day, 6*d.* Spent at Robt Woods upon ye Bounder day, 6*d.* For Scouring ye venall into ye Blind Loning, 1*s.* [*Other payments of the usual kind*]. *Sum,* 4*l.* 18*s.* 6*d.*

November 10, 1680—It is ordered concluded consented and agreed by and with the assents and consents of the inhabetents of the street of Gylligate that they all joyn and stand firmly bound to keep harmless the grassmen in trying suite against Robert Cornfourth and that they shall pay every sess and tacsation for ye said grassmen Thomas Readhead and Edward Denton which shall be laid on for ye mentaining of ye same sute for breaking our Entercomans[1] upon St Cuthbart day being ye fourth of September and y^t all we the inhabetents doe freely declare y^t we freely will pay every man ye said sess or tacsation unto ye said grassmen at any time upon demand be it more or less and y^t for the better confirming the said order we have all hereunto set our hands ye day and year first above written Anno domini 1680.

William Cam Rect^r[2], &c., &c. [*Forty-two signatures in all; twenty-two write their own names*].

1681. Grassmen, Richard Martin and Thos. Gelson.

No receipts preserved.

Disbursements. Spent one oure bouner day at Nicho: Ladlares, 14s. 2d. Spent at Tho: Allinson the same day, 2s. 6d. Given to nicholas person that day, 1s. 6d. Spent one oure bounder day at william Shawes, 1s. 4d. For driveinge the moure one the bounder day, 1s. 6d. Spent when wee lade the ses at Rob: dobsons, 6d. Spent when i receved Mical Ladlar silver, 1s. 6d. For the cawsee at Madland lonnen end and stones and sand and worke mand shep and drinke for the workeme, 1l. 4s. 1d. and of that gilbart Snowdan has in his hand for stones, 6s. 8d. [*Other payments as usual*]. Received in all 4l. 4s. 8d. Desburst—4l. 12s. 10d. Wantinge that wee are out of purs, 8s. 2d.

1682. Grassmen, George Ewbanke and Mathew Denton.

Receipts for 15 gates, at 2s. and at 10s. each; also, Received of Charles Howard, Esqr., the 17th day of Aperrill one thousand six hundered eighty and three for two gaits on the enter Commans, 1l. Of Tho: Allinson for Mardland (*Magdalen*) Lo'inge, 13s. 6d. Of Iohn Nelson for Tenter-

---

[1] Allusions to "breaking our Entercommons" on St. Cuthbert's day (*i.e.*, 4th Sept., the feast of his Translation, his principal feast being 20th March) occur in 1683 and regularly afterwards. It would seem to mean entering the enclosures called "Town-Fields," in Pellowleases or elsewhere, which were subject to commonage during the Winter months. See above, p. 40, note 2. St. Cuthbert's Day was eleven days previous to September 15th, when, according to the Enclosure Act of 1816, the right of commonage in these fields began.

[2] He was incumbent of the parish till Sept., 1682, when his burial is recorded in the Register. For notice of him see appended list of Curates of St. Giles. His peculiar designation as "Rector" will be found alluded to in the Introduction, under "the Parish Church and Living." Surtees, in his list of incumbents, erroneously calls him Thomas.

ing, 8*d*. Of Rob't Richardson for Tentering, 8*d*. For Kavells of the mower dike, 6*s*.—Rec*d* in all—7*l*. 18*s*. 10*d*.

Disbursements. To Tho: Graime for Scouring the Gutter into Mardlands Loninge, 6*d*. Spent upon St. Cuthbart day for Driving y*e* Mower, 1*s*. 6*d*. When we made Searsh through the book, 1*s*. For a man at Pitinton yet (*gate*) for his days worke, 1*s*. For y*e* dike Joyning to y*e* Sands in Alis Leesees, 2*s*. 6*d*. For Scouring A gutter in Pellow Leesees Loning, 6*d*. To Iohn Robinson for Paveinge the Cawcy beloing to y*e* Common Lo'inge, 3*s*. To Richard Nicholson for Higning (*hanging*) Shearburn yet, 1*s*. 4*d*. For mending y*e* Punfold and for two Railes, 1*s*. For Driveing y*e* Mower, 1*s*. 6*d*. Spent when we delivered y*e* wafe mear to y*e* Baliff, 6*d*. Paid for 50 mens Dinners one the Bounder day, 1*l*. 5*s*. More in drinke one y*e* same day, 14*s*. For bread and Cheese for y*e* Lads, 4*s*. 6*d*. For driveing y*e* Mower on y*e* Bounder day, 1*s*. 6*d*. Spent at Will'm Shawes y*e* Same day, 2*s*. 8*d*. More at Rob't Woods y*e* same day, 6*d*. Spent for Searcheing y*e* book at Severall times for severall people, 3*s*. To Nicholas Pearson upon y*e* Bounder day, 1*s*. 6*d*. Paid for bread more, 2*s*. [*Other payments, as usual, for* dikes, yets, scouring Gills Bridge, *&c.*, spent *on various occasions, &c.*]. Disburst in all, 5*l*. 12*s*. 10*d*.—Rests in our hands, 2*l*. 6*s*.

1683. Grassmen, Anthony Wharton and Edward Ridley.

Receipts, similar to those in 1682. Sum, £4 13s. 8d.

Disbursements. For two dailes, 3*s*. 6*d*. To Richard Nicholson for a stoop and a sord tree[1] and making the yett, 7*s*. 6*d*. And in drinke, 1*s*. Paid to Rob't Richardson for Iron worke for Shirburn yet, 2*s*. 4*d*. For wood for two stiles, 1*s*. 6*d*. For making y*e* stiles, 1*s*. For three days worke about y*e* yet, 3*s*. For a man to help him y*t* day y*e* yett was Hung, 1*s*. Spent upon S*t* Cuthbart[2] when we broke our Enter commons, 2*s*. For driveing y*e* Mower y*t* day, 1*s*. 6*d*. To Rob't Richardson for Iron worke, 1*s*. 6*d*. And in drinke, 6*d*. To Thomas Grame for Scouring y*e* venall in y*e* howle way,[3] 6*d*. In Charge at y*e* Court against

---

[1] Swordtree. See Glossary.

[2] *I.e.*, St. Cuthbert's day. See above, p. 83, note 1.

[3] *Cf.* below (1685), "For scouring the Vennall coming down the Howleway into Mardland Loning," and (1687) "Scouringe the Vennall goinge into Mardland Loninge." The "Vennall" might apparently have been either a narrow passage or a gutter. It seems most commonly to have the former sense, as now. *E.g.*, the narrow passage between the houses on

Edward Denton, ——. For Scouring Gills bridge and makeing ye Dike about ye bogg, 2*s.* 6*d.* For driveing ye Mower one ye bounder day, 1*s.* 6*d.* Spent at Shawes on the bounder day, 1*s.* 6*d.* Spent y^t day at Rob't Woods, 1*s.* For drinke in Pittington loninge from Ravensflat[1] one the bounder day, 8*d.* To Nicolas Pearson one the bounder day, 1*s.* 8*d.* For a horse one ye bounder day for ye hird, 8*d.* Spent upon bounder day, 1*l.* 1*s.* 4*d.* Spent at Severall times for seartching ye booke, and Seting things down, 2*s.* 6*d.* [*Other usual payments*]. Disburst in all, 4*l.* 16*s.* 2*d.*—Rests due to us, 2*s.* 6*d.*

1684. Grassmen, Thomas Lang and William ——

Receipts for gates, pellalesis *and* maddellen lonings, tenter rents *and* For Cafels for makeing the moure dike.[2] *Sum,* 4*l.* 19*s.* 4*d.*

Disbursements. For skowering out the Duke Pool, 7*s.* 6*d.* For scowring the venall on the sand twice, 2*s.* 6*d.* For a cap to Pittington Gate, 1*s.* 6*d.* For scowring out Gills Bridge, 4*s.* 9*d.* Spent when we broke up the Enter Commons, 1*s.* 6*d.* For haineing the moor hedge & Pittington Lone end, 10*s.* For an iron bolt for ye top of Shirburne Gate, 1*s.* For a sneck for the said Gate, ——. For 2 dayes heging the moure dike, 1*s.* 8*d.* Spent one the bounder day at Robert Woodes, 2*s.* 6*d.* Spent at William Shawes, 1*s.* Spent at Ravensflat, 1*s.* 6*d.* Spent in drink on the bounder day, 15*s.* 3 pound of preanes (*prunes*) one the bounder day, 6*d.* P^d George Pearson one the bounder day, 1*s.* 6*d.* Spent when

the north side of Gilligate opposite the Church is still called "the Vennell." But see two entries above (A.D. 1618), "For dressinge (or scouring) the common vennell in Raynton Loninge," where the sense of gutter seems more likely. Also (A.D. 1684), "scowring the venall on the sand"; and (A.D. 1691) "for mending sands hedge and scouringe ye vennell"; and especially (A.D. 1692)," for scouring the venal water course on the Mour." Where exactly the "Houleway" was is not known. It evidently led into or was near "Mardland (*i.e.*, Magdalen) loning," which was the lane leading out of Gilligate to Magdalen Hospital, where is now the road to the Goods-station; and in a "Draft Appointment of S. M. Magdalen," among the papers left by the Rev. Francis Thompson, "Houleclose" is marked among the fields in that small parish, near the now ruined chapel. Can the name be a corruption of "Holy way"?

[1] The farm-house and farm still so called, between the Rainton road, a little to the west of Belmont Church, and the old lane, further south, to Pittington.

[2] The meaning of this entry is obscure. "Cafels" may mean *Cavels,* which seem usually to denote allotments on the Moor (see p. 65, note 1). Could it be that certain persons had such allotments assigned them near the "Dike," on condition of their maintaining the latter? *Cf.* below, A.D. 1691, "For the Cavels of the moore hedge, 5*s.* 10*d.*"

we drafe the mower, *2s.* For bread and chease, *3s. 6d.* For fetching Christopher Celses hors out in madelloning, *2d.* For 60 mens diners and the accountes makeing up, *1l. 5s. 3d.* [*Other payments for repairs*]. *Sum, £4 19s. 4d.*

1685. Grassmen, Tho. Robinson and Rob. Johnson. *Receipts as usual. Sum, £4 15s. 10d.*

Disbursements. For wood for y⁰ Punfold, *2s.* To James Coulson for mending y⁰ Punfold and his drinks and nailes, *2s. 2d.* Spent when we did break y⁰ Entercommons, *1s. 6d.* For the suit against Eadon and Paxton the sum of *1l. 12s. 6d.* For Scouring the Vennall, *1s.* For Searching the booke att severall times, *2s. 6d.* For Casting a Tranck for turning the Carts, *1s. 6d.* For Hedging about Gills Bridge, *1s. 6d.* For making the Hedge at Pittington Longing end, *4d.* For Scouring the Vennall coming down the Houleway into Mardland Loning, *1s. 6d.* To Thomas Nicolson for Iron work for the Mower yett, *1s.* Spent on them that Scald the mower, *2s.* Giveing to musick that day, *1s. 6d.* Spent a bout the Parish business, *1s. 6d.* For making up Marlands Lonings Hedges, *1s. 6d.* For driving the mower, *1s. 6d.* For Casting A Pound at the low end of the Moure, *2s. 6d.* Geven to the Musicke one the bounder day, *2s.* For A horse for the parson that day, *1s.* Spent at Will'm Shaws that day, *1s.* Spent when we recaved Ralp Lumleys money and upon the parson their, *2s. 6d.* [*Other payments*]. Disburst in all, *5l. 6s. 5d.* Rests due to us to be Pᵈ by the next Grasmen, *9s. 5d.*

1686, Grassmen, Robert Dobson and Robert Jackson.

[*Receipts, as usual, for* gates, lanes, tenter rent, Cavells, *and* of Mʳ Edon and Paxton, *5s.*].

Disbursements. A new yett for Maudlan lo'inge and stoupes for it, *5s.* Two Styles for the mower dike, *1s. 6d.* Pᵈ at Robart Woods upon the Bounder day, *3s. 2d.* For Meat and drinke upon the Bounder day, *10s.* In drinke and bread to the Lads, *4s. 2d.* Pᵈ to the Musicke and drummer that day, *3s.* For Making the mower dike, *1l. 1s.* Spent when we broke the Entercommons, *1s.* Spent when we drave the mower, *1s. 6d.* For scouring the Vennall, *6d.* [*Other payments of the usual kind*]. Recᵈ in all, *6l. 10s. 0d.* Disburst, *4l. 18s. 0.* Rests due, *1l. 12s. 0d.*

1687. Grassmen, Peter Grieveson and James Rodham. *Receipts as usual.*

Disbursements. For makinge a Staple and a houpe for the Pinfold, 1*s.* For goinge about Margrat Corbyes horse, Spent, 6*d.* For breaking the Entercommons, 1*s.* For drivinge the mower, 1*s.* 6*d.* To Iohn Maston for dressinge ye duke powle, ii*s.* To William Willson for scouringe the vennall joyninge to Pellowleses Loninge, 1*s.* 6*d.* To William Willson for Scouringe the vennall goinge into Marlland Loninge, 6*d.* For mendinge the gaps goinge into Francis Thompsons pasture, 1*s.* 8*d.* For a Turnepike joy'inge to Francis Francis Thompson, 3*s.* For a Lock for the Pinfold, 1*s.* For a dale and nailes and a forehead for the mower vett, 2*s.* 2*d.* For Scouringe Gills bridge, 2*s.* 6*d.* For makinge ye hedge about it, 1*s.* Spent at Shaws and Woods, 4*s.* 11*d.* For meat upon y^t day at Peter Grievson, 9*s.* Given to ye Lads in bread and drinke, 1*s.* Given to ye Drummer and ye fidlers, 6*s.* And in drinke to them, 6*d.* Driveing ye mower, 1*s.* 6*d.* Spent at James Rodham's upon ye bounder day, 12*s.* 9*d.* [*Other payments for hedges, &c., and* spent *on various occasions*]. Rec^d in all 6*l.* 14*s.* 0*d.* Disburst in all, 5*l.* ii*s.* 8*d.*

1688. Grassmen, Richard Maugham and George Blackelocke.

Receipts as usual for gates, lonings, *&c., including* For the Cables, 5*s.* 6*d., and* Of Mr Eden & Mr Paxton for Averidge, 5*s.*—*Sum,* 6*l.* 17*s.*

Disbursements. For driving ye moore at our entry, 1*s.* 6*d.* For breaking ye entercommons, 1*s.* For making Gylsbridge when we enterd, 6*d.* For scouring Gylsbridge pond, 2*s.* For mending gaps in Thompsons hedge, 1*s.* For mending the Moor gate & a new foot stoone, 1*s.* 6*d.* To Peter Grievson for wood & mending ye pinfold, 6*s.* For a new gate & Iron gear for pittington lane, 13*s.* For making Maudlan lane hedge & hanging ye gate, 9*d.* For scouring ye gutt where Crts got into ye moore, 6*d.* For scouring Burdons pond, 1*s.* For making Guils bridge hedge, 1*s.* For Saddle bridle & Spurs, 7*s.* For ye Drum & vyolin, 3*s.* 6*d.* For Ale one ye Moore, 5*s.* For bread Chease & drink for ye Children, 4*s.* For eighty mens Dinners, 1*l.* 6*s.* For drink at Dinner, 13*s.* For a horse for ye Parson, 1*s.* For Arresting Mr Emerson & witness charge, 10*d.* [*Other usual payments*]. Disburst, 7*l.* 1*s.* 1*d.* Out of purs, 4*s.* 1*d.*

1689. Grassmen, Ralph Richardson and Walter Haire.

Receipts of the usual kind, but including, Rec^d of
Iohn Haire, Bakhouseman for his two Gates, 1*l.*   Of
Andrew Milner for Chap^{ll} Loning,[1] 7*s.* 6*d.*   Of Wid
Nickolson for Aleason lane,[2] 1*s.*   For 60 Fother of Whins,
1*l.*   For Wm Wilson Loning, 6*d.*   Of Rob't Dallavill
Esq^r3 for shearbur house whins, 10*s.*   *Sum, 6l. 12s. 6d.*

Disbursements.   For two new stoops for ye moore,
1*s.* 8*d.*   For setting them, 4*d.*   For 2 new Rales for y^e
Pinfold, 1*s.*   For Nales For mending ye Pinfold & workmans wages, 4*s.*   P^d Shaw for keeping Shearburn Lane,
5*s.*   Mr Smith for letting his men keep Pittington Lane,
8*s.*   For driving ye moor 2 times, 3*s.* 6*d.*   Sp^t when we
went 3 times to Robt Wood & Burdons Hind con-
sering ye moore hedge, 3*s.*   For scouring Burdons pond,
6*d.*   For setting a foote stone at Shearburn gate & seting
ye stoop, 1*s.*   For Iron Cotrells for Shearburn gate & a
new pike, 1*s.* 2*d.*   For 2 new Crooks, 2*s.* 3*d.*   For two
Crooks when ye first was brok, 3*s.*   For a new Hartree
& one dayes wage, 2*s.* 6*d.*   For Altering both stoops, 1*s.*
For a saddle & Bridle, 9*s.*   For Counsell when we tried
sute with Richardson, 3*s.* 8*d.*   P^d ye Drummer & Violin,
3*s.* 6*d.*   Spent when we tryed sute with Richardson, 1*s.* 8*d.*
For aresting Robt Rickeson & Court fees, 10*d.*   P^d for
drink one ye bounder day, 15*s.* 6*d.*   For bread & Drink
for ye boyes, 4*s.* 9*d.*   Sp^t when we bought ye saddle, 9*d.*
Sp^t when we receved money for ye whins, 6*d.*   Sp^t when
we gathered ye Cavell, 6*d.*   Spent when we sold ye whins,
6*d.*   Given Robt Johnson for taking a scabb hors from y^e
Common to ye fels, 6*d.*   [*Other payments of the usual kind,
including* spent, *on receiving money and various other
occasions*].   Disburst in all, 6*l.* 19*s.* 10*d.*

1690.   Grassmen, Danniall Kaye and Robt. Welsh.
Receipts as usual, including, Recev'd of Capten Baker
for Whins to Shearbur house, 6*s.* 8*d.*   Of Mrs Sutton for
ye winter halfe years Grass, 5*s.*   Of Eliz. Nicholson for
Neasoms Laine, 5*s.*   For Loning Betwixt Mr New house
& George Burdon, 6*d.*   Of Mr Edon & Paxton for one hors

---

[1] Was "Chapel Loning" the same as "Magdalen Loning," called so
from the chapel of the hospital of St. Mary Magdalen, the ruins of which
still remain?

[2] Lanes seem now to be called sometimes by the names of persons,
who may have been in some way connected with them.

[3] Robert Delaval was Vice-Master of Sherburn Hospital.   Among the
records in the keeping of the present Master of the Hospital is a Latin
document signed by him, 4th Aug., 1682, depriving John Lawes, Thornley
Brother, for recusancy and being a convicted papist.

fogge, 5*s*. Of W*m* Baker for S*t* Magdalen Loning, 4*s*. 6*d*. Rec*d* in all 4*l*. 4 . 10.—P*d* in all—4*l*. 8*s*. 1*d*.

[*Disbursements for this year not preserved*].

1691. Grassmen, W*m* Hunter and Richard Hutchinson.

Receipts, including Rec*d* for Tinkers Lane going down to y*e* Ware (*Wear*), 1*s*. Rec*d* for the Loning adjoyning to M*r* Newhouses house, 6*d*. For the Cavels of the moore hedge, 5*s*. 10*d*. Of M*r* Paxton for a hors grass in y*e* entercommon, 5*s*. *Sum, 3l. 19s. iid.* Rec*d* of M*r* Hodgion after accomp, 10*s*.

Disbursements. For seting y*e* water out of y*e* Pellow Leazerd's Loning and scouring, 1*s*. 6*d*. For dressing y*e* old scouring in y*e* Loning, 6*d*. For driving y*e* moore, 1*s*. 6*d*. For Breaking y*e* Entercommons, 1*s*. 6*d*. For making y*e* moore hedge and upholding untill ye Bounder day, 1*l*. 0*s*. 6*d*. For mending sands hedge & scouring y*e* vennell, 2*s*. 6*d*. For mending Gilsbridge hedge, 1*s*. 6*d*. For y*e* tree thatt was made into rales for y*e* Pinfold, 2*s*. For footing y*e* stoops nailes & workmans wages, 5*s*. 1*d*. For a bolt for y*e* Turnpike and a lock for y*e* Pinfold, 1*s*. 6*d*. For the Person & Clark one y*e* Bounder day, 1*s*. For the Bounder dinner & drink, 1*l*. 10*s*. For Chease bread & drink for y*e* boyes, 9*s*. For Railes for Gilsbridge hedge, 6*d*. [*Other usual payments*]. *Sum, 5l. 5s. 7d.*

1692. Grassmen, George Blaclock and W*m* James.
Receipts as usual, including Rec*d* for the loning adjoneing of M*r* Newhowse, 6*d*. Of M*r* Paxton for a horse Grasse in the entercomons, 5*s*. Of Capt. Baker for Whins, 5*s*. 4*d*. *Sum, 2l. 16s. 6d.*

Disbursements. Payments of the usual kind, including For bread and Chease one y*e* Bounder day and for Meat all together, 12*s*. For y*e* person a horse to ride one, 1*s*. For drink at Elizabeth Robinsons, 1*s*. 6*d*. For y*e* persons drink one y*e* Bounder day, 6*d*. To y*e* drumer and violin, 3*s*. For driveing y*e* mour one y*e* Bounder day, 1*s*. 6*d*. To Christpher Vinson for scouring y*e* venal water Course one y*e* Mour, 6*d*. For scouring Madland venall, 6*d*.—Despursments—4*l*. 9*s*. Out of purss, 1*l*. 12*s*. 6*d*.

Anthony Nelson not p*d* his tentur Rent. Robert Richardson not p*d* his tentur Rent.

July y*e* 1*t* day in —93. Rec*d* of Iohn Browne and Tho*s* Fosster being Grassmen instant y*e* sume of 1*l*. 10*s*. 0*d*. in full by me W*m* James.

1693. Grassmen, Thomas Forster and Iohn Browne, and they are to pay to ye old Grasmen 1*l.* 12*s.* 6*d.*

Receipts. May 23 —93 Rec^d of Henry Hutchinson A miller ye some of Three pound for his six gates one Gilligate moore, 3*l.*

July 1693. Iohn browne paid for his six gates on gilegate moure in the parish of sente giles the som of thre poundes.

July ye 23 —93. Rec^d of Willm Hill in full for six gates 3*l.* [*Several other receipts for* gates]. Rec^d for Whins of Mr Baker, 12*s.* For 3 years Cavels, 10*s.* 2*d.* Of Wm Willson for ye lane 3 years, 1*s.* 6*d.* Of Rich^d maugham for ye common lane, 17*s.* 6*d.* For 3 years Rent for Tinkers Lane,[1] 3*s.* Of Wm Hunter jun^r for 3 y^rs Tenter Rent, 2*s.* 6*d.* Of Nicholas Paxton for 2 y^rs horse grass, 10*s.* Of Thomas Hutchinson for 2 gates, 4*s.* (*Alia manu*) in Abraham Allinsons Chamber being ye last of his stint.

(*Alia manu*). Mamarandom that Iohn simpson stinted no more but 3 gats tell after his Fathers dessease.

May 1696. Thomas foster resaived of Iohn simpson for three gates on gilegat moure the som of 6*s.*

July 1694. Of Willyam broune for six gates of gilegat moure, resaived by me Iohn browne, 3*l.*

September ye 13th —94. Of Rowland Brown for his six gates, 12*s.*

December 1694. resaived then of abraham aleson for his six gates of gilegate mour the som of twelve shilings I say resaived by us grasmen Iohn broune and Thomas foster by ekewel proporshon, 12*s.*

August 1695. resaived of Iohn busbe the som of 2 poundes ninten shilings sixpence in —— for his six gates on giligat mour I say resaived by me Iohn browne, 2*l.* 19*s.* 6*d.*

May the 12, 1696. Thomas foster resaived of Richart mensforth the som of four shilings for 2 gates on gilegat moure, 4*s.*

---

[1] Tinker's (or Tinkler's) Lane is that which leads down from the South side of the street to the river, nearly opposite Bakehouse Lane, and forming the Western boundary of the parish on that side. It now seems to have had gates to it, and to have been let like other lanes. If it was as narrow as now, it could not, one would think, have been of much use to any one. But only 1*s.* per annum was paid for it, under the name in after years of "acknowledgement," which may have been only for right of way, the expression in 1696 being " for ye acknowledgement *down* Tinker's loan."

July 1694, the 10 day. Resaived of mister baker for 18 fother of whins, 6s.—October 95. resaived of mister baker for 25 fother of whins, 8s. 4d.

Recd of Richard mensforth for 2 gaits, 4s., being ye last of his six gaits by us grasmen Peter Greveson and Wm Haire.

Ino Brown & Tho. Forsters disbursments.

Pd to Wm & Robert Baker for 4 dayes work, 6s. 8d. More pd to Wm Baker for 1 day & halfe, 1s. 3d. To Robert Baker for 4 dayes, 3s. 4d. For A stoope & Cape at Sherburn gate, 10s. To Wm Baker halfe a day, 5d. For a heed for ye moor gate, 1s. To Wm Wilson for ye new hedge, 18s. For mending ye Low hedge, 10s. For A plank for ye Gutter, 2s. Pd Rich. Anderson for 1800 & halfe of quicks, 6s. 4d. Eliz. Robinson for Ale, 4s. To ye sadler for 2 saddles & Bridle, 13s. 4d. Pd for a hatt, 3s. 6d. & gave to ye boy yt came second, 6d. Pd about Wm Hunters Assize Tryall about his six gate one ye moore, 28l. 13s. 4d. In expence one ye Bounder daye, 8s. For mending ye Pinfold & Lock & stapple, ——. Spent one ye bounder day more, 10s. 3d. Pd for boyes Drink, 4s. For mending ye moor hedge & driving ye moore, 4s. 3d. For ye Persons horse & Clarks, 2s. For breaking ye Entercommons 2 Times, 3s. For making my Accomptes & Writing for me, 5s. For making a hoope & pike for Shearburn gate & for mending ye gate & mending Pittington gate, 4s. 7d. For keeping ye Sands hedg in repaire 3 years, 7s. 6d. Pd at the Charg of Two bounders for drink, 9s. 2d. For Gilsbridge boge mending & 2 rales, 1s. 6d. Spent in Collecting Cavels & receiving small somes, 2s. 9d. Spent when I went to get my notes made, 6d. For making our Accompts, 2s. 6d. [*Other entries of usual kind*].

Received in all, 23l. 0s. 2d. Recd by bond 9l. 0 . 0.

1696. Grassmen, Thomas Forster and Thomas Hutchinson.

Disbursements of the usual kind, including—To Ion Coulson for mending ye Pinfold broken by Henry Wanles & for Iron work & mending ye blind Loaning gate, 6d. For Repairing Pitting gate, with a new sheath & a head, 3s. Spent about Letting & paying ye workmen for breaking ye moore hedges, 1s. For a horse for ye Person & for his dinner, 3s. 6d. To ye drimmer & to Nicholas Peirson, 1s. 6d. Spent at Margery Allinson in drinke & bread for ye Boys & some of ye Inhabitants, 3s. 1d. Spent at Nicholas Sparker in drink & bread amongst y*e* Boys = with diverse of y*e* Inhabitants, 7*s.* P*d* for y*e* Halt (*halter*) & y*e* Sadle, 7*s.* For mending Pittington gate was broken by M*r* Shaws servants, 1*s.*

Disburst In all, 3*l.* 11*s.* 7*d.*

Receipts of the usual kind, including—Received of M*r* Baker for Whins, 5*s.* Of M*r* Paxton for a horse eatage for y*e* last year, 5*s.* Of Martin Nicholson for y*e* acknowledgement down Tinkers Loan, 1*s.*

Received In all, 2*l.* 13*s.* 10.—Rest due to me, 17*s.* 3*d.*

1697. Grassmen, Thomas Lowther and Iohn Martin.

Disbursements include—Paid Last Martinmas for mending y*e* more hedge, 2*s.* 6*d.* More paid for making the moore hedge this spring, 1*l.* 1*s.* Spent when we gathered In the Cavels, 3*d.* Spent when we Skaled the Moore, 9*d.* Spent when we drave the moore, 1*s.* 6*d.* Paid for the p'sons dinner and horse to ride the bounders on, 3*s.* 6*d.* Paid the drummer, 1*s.* 6*d.* Spent with severall neighbours on the bounder day, 2*s.* 6*d.* Paid at Simond Litefouts for drink on the bounder day, 6*s.* Paid for on Saddle on the bounder day, 6*s.*—Disbursed this yeare, 2*l.* 18*s.* 6*d.*

Receipts include—We Receved att our Entrance nothing. Rec*d* of Martin Nicholson for Tinckler Laine, 1*s.* For the Cavels, 5*s.* 6*d.* Of M*r* Baker for 13 load of Whins, 4*s.* 4*d.*—Rec*d* this year, 2*l.* 4*s.* 10.—Due to us, 13*s.* 8*d.*

1698. Grassmen, Rowland Brown and Henry Robinson. And they payed to Iohn martin & Tho. Lowther 13*s.* 4*d.*

Receipts include—Received of Rob't Cornforth for not breaking y*e* peice of Enter Common y*t* George Wilkinson hath a garden in at y*e* Top of his close & before y*e* Court & Collenell Tempest[1] he did agree y*t* upon nonpayment the

---

[1] *I.e.*, William Tempest, of Old Durham, bapt. 1653 (See "Register"), bur. at St. Giles 1699—1700. He was the son of John, the first possessor. The question before the manorial court seems to have been thus:—Robert Cornforth had a close which was subject to "Entercommon" in the winter months. He had allowed George Wilkinson to make, and fence, a garden at the top of it, rendering that part unavailable as common pasture. He is required by the court to pay an acknowledgement, or break the garden up. It appears below that he elected to pay, for we find in 1689, "Of Robert Cornfourth for his acknowledgment for not breaking his garth above his Cloase, 6*d.*" A similar acknowledgement appears in 1704 as paid by "the Shewmakers," for having grown corn at the head of their close. The Mr. John Tempest mentioned below was probably his son, who succeeded him, and who contested his manorial rights in the parish. See below.

parish is to break it up, *6d.* Rec^d of Richd Maugham for Blind Loning which we lett him ye 12 day of June for *5s.* (?) & now being eaten with scabd Horses he hath only paid us, *2s. 6d.*

We agree y^t ye Grassmen shall be reimburst their Charges or stand an other year.   Richard Maugham.

his mark
Anthony **✕** Dobson.

Disbursements.   Paid for ye repairing ye moor Hedges in summer, *1l. 1s.*   Paid Tho. Lowther & John Martin, *13s. 4d.*   Spent at receiving the moneyes, *2s. 6d.*   For mending ye Pinfold & Rales, *10s. 6d.*   For ye Bounder Dinner, *1l. 10s.*   Paid David Sharp for Druming, *1s. 6d.*   Paid ye vyalin, *1s.*   For Repairing ye Hedges in Summer, *4s.*   For Repairing ye Hedge adjoyning to Robt Hixon y^t at Michalmas Court Mr John Tempest Amarsed us for, *2s. 6d.*   For scouring Gils bridge Gutter, *5s.*   For making Gils Bridg Hedge, *1s.*   Spent when we mouded ye more, *9d.*   Spent with neighbours one ye Bounder day, *2s. 6d.*   Spent at Simond Light footes, *2s.*   For driving ye moor 3 times.   For driving ye moor Two times to vew scabd Horses, *3s.*   For A Saddle one ye Bounder day & Furniture, *8s. 6d.*   Given ye Lasses with ye Garling,[1] *1s.*   Paid for ye Persons horse one ye Bounder day, *1s.*   For mending Shearburn gate & ye Blind Loning Gat, *5s.*   For 2 new stapples & one hesp, *6d.*   Paid for searching ye books about Stents, *1s.*   Spent at making up our accomps, *1s.*   For Writing our Accompts.   For making Blind Lonyng Hedge, *6d.*   Spent when we received Hastans *5s.*, *6d.*   Spent when we received Fandons *10s.*, *6d.*   Spent when we gatherd ye Cavells, *6d.*   Paid for the Person one ye Bounder day, *2s.*   Paid Robert Johnson Se^{or} (*senior*) for keeping Sands Hedge, *2s. 6d.*

Rec^d in all *4l. 14s. 6d.*—Disburst in all, *6l. 11s. 1d.*—Rest due to us, *1l. 16s. 1d.*   [*N.B.—The disbursements this year have been transcribed in full*].

Whereas the many Whins that Grow on Gilesgate moor doe very much Damnify ye same, We the foure & Twenty of ye Parish of St Giles doe Order & fully Agree that from henceforth All & every person qualifyed to stint ye s^d Moor shall pay Threepence per Gate yearly for each Gate they shall stint to ye Grassmen for the yeare being, for

---

[1] First mention of the "Garling," *i.e.*, garland.   See Preface, on "Bounder Day," p. 5.

stubing ye s^d Moor for ye Improvement of ye same. And further it is hereby Ordered by us ye s^d Foure & Twenty that ye s^d Grassmen shall have full Power to Impound the Goods of all such as Refuse to Pay ye s^d 3d. per Gate. As Wittness our Hands this Eleventh Day of June in ye yeare of our Lord God 1700.

his mark

Ralph Maire.   William X Hill.   John Martin.

1699.   Grassmen, Henry Parkeson and William Fawdon.

Imp. May 7, 1700, Rec^d of John Atteshon for 6 gates being in behalf of his wife, 12s.   Of George Hastines for a fogg gate, 5s.   Rec^d of them which stented ye moor at 6d. p. house, 1l. 2s.   Of Robert Shafty for 6 fudder of whines, 2s. Of Robert Cornfourth for his acknowledgment for not breaking his garth above his Cloase, 6d.   Of Mr George Dickson for one fudder of whines, 4d.   [*Other receipts for gates and the common lane*].   Rec^d of Rob^rt Maugham in behalf of His wife for his wife hath p^d for four gates & he hath p^d onely for 2 gates which is ye last of his 6 gates, 4s. Received in all, 2l. 19s. 4d.—Disburst in all 3l. 1s. 1d.— Rests due to us, 1s. 9d.

Disbursements.   Paid David Sharp for Druming, 2s. 6d.   Paid ye violine, 1s.   Spent when we measured ye moor hedg, 1s. 3d.   Spent when we breake ye Entercommons, 1s. 6d.   Spent when we search ye book 3 times, 1s. 6d.   Spent with John Coulson for going to vew ye gates, 1s.   Paid to two workemen one day for mend ye hedg adjoyning to Robert Hickson in winter and gaps, 2s.   Spent when we went to Collect ye Sess for ye moor hedg, 6d. Spent at Simond Lightfoots one ye Bounder day, 2s. 6d. Given to ye Children one ye Bounder day in drink, 1s. 6d. More given ye Lasses with their Garlines one ye Bounder day, 1s.   Paid for ye Parson for meat and drink on ye Bounder day, 2s.   P^d for David Sharp & Walter Hair on ye Bounder day, 6d.   P^d 4d. for ye Lads bread Given on ye Bounder day, 4d.   Spent when we went to meet ye 24 about ye 6d. order[1] & spent at Receiving Wm Maughams money, 6d.   Spent when we went to demand ye money of Elizabeth welsh for ye whines with some neighbours which were there, 6d.   [*Other usual payments*].

1700.   Grassmen, Anthony Dobson and John Martin.

---

[1] See order of year 1686, entered on page 95.

*There follow here a few memoranda of receipts for gates,
&c., this year: but the accounts for the year are found
entered afterwards in what appears to have been a new book
procured this year, but now bound up in one volume with the
foregoing. See next page. Next comes a list of 75 names,
with sums varying from 4d. to 4s. opposite each ; but with no
intimation of their purpose. Then as follows—*

P^d towards the suit Concerning William Watson
agreed by the four and twentie. *Below this heading
there is a list of 22 names, with similar sums opposite them.
Of this list the former one may be a continuation, displaced
in the bound volume. Then came the following memoranda,
referring, as will be seen, to former years.*

October 22th, 1685.

Memorandum that it is concluded consented &
agreed by the assent and Consent of ye fower antwenty
and all ye rest of ye inhabitants of ye street of Gilligate y^t
we will save and keep harmless our Grassmen that is
Rob't Johnson and Thomas Robinson in trying of a Suit
against Edward Eadon and Nicolas Paxton Junior in y^e
behalf and right of our Entercommons and in defence of y^e
Grassmen in doeing their office. Further it (*is*) concluded
and agreed that if their be any need for moneys to try this
suit that ye fower antwenty upon demand of ye s^d grassmen
shall lay a Sess as much as shall Clear ye Charges of ye s^d
suit and to be Collected and levyed by ye s^d Grassmen and
we the inhabitants do declare that if any man assessed do
refuse to pay that he shall be suied forthwith and we ye s^d
inhabitants will save and keep harmless ye s^d grassmen
where unto we have sett our hands ye day and year above
written. [*This is followed by ten signatures, eight of the
signers writing their own names*].

Aprill 6, (1686).

Memorandum y^t it is Concluded Consented & agreed
by ye assent & Consent of ye fower & twenty & all ye rest
of ye inhabitants of ye street of Gilligate y^t every inhabitant
which stints in ye Common pasture shall send a mowder to
scayle ye s^d Common pasture ; or otherwise shall pay
sixpence when ye Grassemen shall give notice, & if any
refuse to send or pay ye Grassemen shall sue them to the
Lords Court, or fold their goods, & the fower & twenty to
keepe ye Grassemen indempnified. Witness our hands y^e
day & yeare above writen. [*Ten signatures ; five write their
own names*].

THIS BOOKE WAS BOUGHT BY IOHN MARTIN & ANTHO DOBSON GRASSMEN FOR Y^e PARISH OF St GYLES ANNO DOM. 1700.

Whereas the many Whins that groweth on Gilligate Moor (or stainted Pasture) do very much damnifie the said moor or Pasture, We the Twenty four and ye rest of ye inhabitants free of the same moor or Pasture by a Generall Consent & Assent do order & fully agree that from the day of the date under named all and every person qualified to stint the said moor or Pasture shall pay Three pence per gate yearly for each Gate they shall stint. And it is further agreed that if any Forraner or Freeborn Come to stint our said moore or pasture that they shall pay ye said sum of Threepence per gate so soon as they stint To the Grassmen Chosen for that year and the stints so Collected to be employed for ye stubing of ye s^d moor & for ye improvement of the same. And further it is ordered by us whose hands are underwritten That We the said Twenty four & parishioners doe hereby oblage ourselves to defray any Charge or Charges the said Grassmen shall be putto in impounding the goods of those that are obstinate & refuse to pay. Given under our hands this Eleventh day of June Anno Dom. 1700.

Twenty Four and inhabitants that do stint.

[*Forty-six signatures; twenty-eight write their own names*].

July ye 27th, 1701.

We ye four and Twenty & ye Inhabitants of ye Street of St Giles's who are free of ye Stinted pasture Call'd Gilligate Moor, by our generall assent & Consent—and for ye better and more sure Testimony to our succeeding Generations, have ordered and Unanimously agreed y^t all these present Inhabitants, or who hereafter shall Come to inhabit in our s^d Street—not booked as Stinters, or y^t have not paid for his or their Gates on our stinted Pasture call'd Gilligate Moor, shall have no right there without paying to us or our Grassmen for ye time being **Six pounds** in hand for their six Gates, Excepting such as have served their Apprentiships in ye said Street or are otherwise qualified by their Birthright &c. Such to pay twelve shillings.

Mem. Those Strangers or foreigners having a house left or buying one (living in our s^d Street) to pay three pounds for their freedom for their six gates, as heretofore.

Mem. We further agree y* no Child or Children now borne or y* hereafter shall be borne in y* s* Street of S* Giles's by Strangers (their parents not being free on y* s* Moor nor pay'd for their Gates shall have Liberty to Stint y* s* Moor but upon y* Terms above mention'd for Strangers. Witness our Hands. [*Thirty-eight signatures; twenty-two write their own names*].

January y* 16, 1701—Rec* of Ralph Robinson In full for his six gates on gilligate moor y* sum of 3*l.* Rec* by us grasmen ; Iohn Martin, Anthony Dobson.

Aprill y* 25, 1702—Rec* of thomas Nicolson for 3 gates, 6*s.*

May y* 10, 1702—Rec* then of anthony Burdon In full for his six gates on gilligate moor y* sum of three Pounds.

Rec* by us gras(*men*) ;   his

Iohn Martin ; Anthony **X** Dobson Sen*.

Test. W* Dunn.   mark

Grassmen for y* year 1700, Antho. Dobson & Iohn Martin. [*Receipts include nothing unusual*].

Disbursements include—P* W'm Wilson for stubing 7 Acres & 3 Ropes, 2*l.* 7*s.* P* W'm Wilkinson for stubing 1 Acre, 6*s.* For four Rubing soups[1] for y* moor, 3*s.* 4*d.* For a horse and cart 3 dayes Leading manner (*manure*), 3*s.* 4*d.* P* W'm Wilson for scouring at Gils & Normour Bogg, 3*s.* 8*d.* For making y* hedge at Gils Bridge, 1*s.* Spent when I let y* 2 Common Lanes, 1*s.* 6*d.* When I went to M* Smith & M* Salvin about y* order, 1*s.* 6*d.* For a new booke to place our Accompt in, 3*s.* For 3 rales for y* Pinfold A Crook & loop nailes & wages, 3*s.* 8*d.* For A lock for y* Pinfold, 1*s.* Given in Ale when I agreed for y* hedge one y* moore, 1*s.* Spent when I came about y* street to get y* order sygnd, 2*s.* Spent when I agreed with Wil'm Wilkinson to stubb to y* Windmill, 1*s.* Spent about y* parish business in going about our orders, 9*s.* 9*d.* P* for y* Persons Horse one y* Bounder day & his Clubb, 2*s.* P* y* drum & vialinns, 5*s.* 6*d.* Spent one y* Bounder day at Simond Light footes, 3*s.* 4*d.* Given y* Girles y* had y* Garlands, 1*s.* 6*d.* Given in Drink to y* boyes & Girles & Brad & Chease, 4*s.* P* for A Saddle, 10*s.* For A hatt, 3*s.* For y* Bounder Dinner, 1*l.* 19*s.* 9*d.*

---

[1] *I.e.*, Posts for the cattle to rub themselves against. *Cf.* above, "stonps for the bees (*beasts*) to rub on."

7

Memorandum that Robt maugham took pellewleases Loning & is not to eat or cutt yᵉ same after Ladyday which shall be in yᵉ year 1702 : **as Witness my hand** —— price 6s.

Item Ino Davinson tooke yᵉ Lane caled magdalens yᵉ 9ᵗʰ of June & is to give it up from Eating & Cuting yᵉ 25ᵗʰ of March in yᵉ year of our Lord 1702 price 5s.

1701. Grassmen Antho. Dobson & Ino. Martin. The parish was indebted to them the sum of 3l. 12s. 9d.

Receipts for gates *and* lanes, *including* Recᵈ of Wᵐ Wilson for his Lane adjoyning to his yard, 6d., *amount to* 7l. 3s. 6d.

Disburst 5l. 9s. 4. Due to me yᵉ Last year 3l. 12s. 9d.—Rests due to me, 2l. 1s. 1d.

Disbursements include—Pᵈ Richᵈ Martin for dresing & scouring Gyls bridge Gutter, 8s. Spent when we measured yᵉ Stubing, 1s. 6d. Spent when we received Ralph Robinsons money yᵗ is pᵈ, 3s. 0d. Spent when we received Antho. Burdons moneyes, 3s. 4d. Spent at breaking yᵉ enter Commons & about Cornfoths peice, 3s. Paid for drawing yᵉ new Whins & spent, 8s. 6d. Spent when we mouded yᵉ moore burnt yᵉ offall whins 2 times, 3s. Spent at Simond Light foots one yᵉ bounder day, 4s. Given to yᵉ Girle yᵗ had yᵉ Garland, 1s. 6d. Paid for yᵉ Persons horse to ride yᵉ bounders, 1s. Paid for yᵉ Persons Ale in Company one yᵉ Bonder day, 1s. Paid yᵉ Drummer, 2s. 6d. Paid yᵉ vyaline, 1s. 6d. Paid for Ale for yᵉ Person Drummer & Vyaline one yᵉ bounder day in yᵉ morning, 1s. 6d. Given to yᵉ boyes (*and*) Gyrls in bread & drink, 3s. 6d. Paid for yᵉ Persons Dinner, 2s. 6d. Paid for a Chese 2s. 6d. & Bread 1s. 6, 4s. Paid for mending yᵉ Pinfold, Pitingtongate a new, & Shearbur gate a new, 16s. 6d. Paid for Antho. Dobson & Iohn martins Drinke one yᵉ bounder day, 2s.—Disburst this year, 5l. 11s. 4d.—Rest due last yeare, 3l. 12s. 9d.— Recᵈ this year, 7l. 3s. 6d.—Rest due to me, 2l. 1s. 1d.

Cavels unpaid.—Simond Swalwell, 2 : Ann Nicholson, 2 : Edw'd Ridley, 2 : George Blaclock, 2.—Tot. 8d.

May yᵉ 28ᵗʰ 1705.—Widow Dodshon excused by ten votes against four from paying yᵉ Rent of yᵉ Common Lane for this year.

his mark

test. Wᵐ Dunn : Antho. X Greivson : Ralph Maire.

[No accounts remain for 1702 and 1703].

1704. Grassmen, Iohn Davison & Wm Wilkinson.

Recev^d of Martin Nicholson for tinar (*tinker's*) lane, 1*s*. Recev^d of the shewmakers' for an acknowlidgment on the heade of Corn for the close head, 6*d*. Rec^t for ye cavels, 6*s*. Of Iohn Davison for Magdalen lane, 5*s*. Of Judith James Tenter Rent, 3*s*. Of Rowland Brown for Tenter Rent, 1*s*. For the Lane at Causey foote, 6*d*. [*Other entries*.] Rec^d in all, 5*l*. 4*s*. 2*d*.—Disburst in all, 5*l*. 3*s*. 10*d*.—Rest in our hand, 4*d*.

Disbursements include—For mendin the peenfould at oure enterance for wood & nales & workmanship, 2*s*. 6*d*. Spent when we got the books of Iohn Martin, 6*d*. For scouring the gutter in pellowlis lonin, 6*d*. Spent when we drave ye more one ye bounder day, 1*s*. 6*d*. Spent when we drave ye moor about over stents, 1*s*. 6*d*. Given ye Two Garlings, 2*s*. P^d ye Drummer, 2*s*. 6*d*. Spent at Simon Light footes, 6*s*. 3*d*. For A Bounder Dinner for 43 men, 1*l*. 4*s*. 7*d*. P^d for Ale & bread & chese for ye boyes & Girls, 4*s*. 6*d*. P^d for ye Persons horse one ye Bounder day, 1*s*. P^d for ye persons Clubb in Ale, 6*d*. For making ye Blind Loning hedge, 6*d*. For mending ye hedge about pryars Stable, & scouring ye Gutter, 1*s*. For stubing Whins & drawing whins, 3*s*. 4*d*. Spent on ye Bounder day after Dinner, 2*s*. Given ye Drummer in Ale, 3*d*. P^d for claring ye stubing 4. Receed in all 5*l*. 4*s*. 2*d*.

Mem^d that Wm Wilson shall Receive one shilling due for Stubbing. Witness our hands [*fourteen signatures; twelve write their own names*].

1705. Grassmen, Iohn Simpson & Ralph Robinson.

Receed for stubing by 3*d*. p gate, 2*l*. 8*s*. 6*d*. Rec^d for Iohn Rawling whins, 8*d*. Receed for Whins to Shearburn house, 8*s*. a by fother of whins, 4*d*. Receed of Thomas Cummin the summ of six pounds in full of A new order for his six gates & he having but four Gates desygnd to stint we Lend him Two pounds of ye six by order of ye Twenty four & Stenters untill he stent a fifth Gate at which Stint he promiseth to pay ye Two pound Lent

---

1 See above, p. 92, note 1. One of the Companies of the City of Durham was that of "Cordwainers." They seem, as abovesaid, to have owned a close which was one of the "Town Fields" of St. Giles, and as such subject to commonage. In Forster's Map of the City of Durham (1754) a field East of "Tinkler's Lane" is marked as "Close belonging to the Cordwainers' Company."

we say receed four & Lent Two by us Grasmen, Iohn Simpson & Ralph Robinson. Witnesses hereof: [*four signatures*]. *Other receipts for lanes and cavels, ending with*—Magdalen Lane Voyde by Scabd horses.

Rec^d in all, 9*l.* 16*s.* 4*d.*

Disbursements. Paid for stubing 5 Acress of Whins, 1*l.* 18*s.* 6*d.* For drawing the Young Whins, 8*s.* 3*d.* For stubing 3 Acress, 1*l.* 1*s.* 0*d.* For stubing one Acre, 7*s.* 3*d.* P^d Wm Baker for 2 dayes Stubing, 1*s.* 6*d.* P^d him for five yards of morter wall for ye pinfold, 9*s.* 9½*d.* Spent at 2 times Dressing ye Stubing 2 times measuring the stubing 2 times mouding ye moor & 2 times burning ye Whins, 9*s.* 6*d.* For ye Turn Pike, 2*s.* Spent when we gatherd 3*d.* p. gate, 2*s.* 6*d.* Given Rob't Ellot in Ale, 4*d.* For nailes for ye Pinfold & mending it, 7*d.* Spent about geting ye order for manner (*manure*) at 3 times,[1] 3*s.* P^d Ellioner Lawson for 4 dayes of scaling, 1*s.* 4*d.* P^d Robt. Ellet for dressing & scaling ye burnt heaps, 3*s.* 6*d.* Spent when we met ye Showmakers about ye parish Right, 6*d.*[2] For a hatt for ye boyes, 2*s.* For driving ye moor for scabd horses & overstents at 2 times, 3*s.* P^d for bread & Ale for ye boyes & Drummer, 2*s.* 7*d.* Paid our Clubb at Dinner, 6*d.* P^d for a bounder Dinner, 15*s.* 9*d.* P^d ye Drummer, 2*s.* 6*d.* For ye 2 persons Club & Clarke,[3] 1*s.* 6*d.* For 2 horses for ye persons, 1*s.* 6*d.* Lent to Thomas Cumin, 2*l.* For Leading 4 Cart Load of manner for Wellby Hare, 1*s.* For 4 Cart Load of manner for Matt Renton, 1*s.* Spent when we let ye Stubing, 1*s.* Spent when we Collected for ye Cavell, 2*s.* 1*d.* Spent when we agred for Leading manner, 1*s.* 10*d.* Spent at severall meetings about ye orders, 2*s.* 6*d.* [*Other entries of the usual kind*].

Disburst in all, 11*l.* 3*s.* 1*d.* qr. —— Rest due to us, 1*l.* 3*s.* 9 qr*d.*

May ye 13th 1706. These seen & Allowed ye above s^d Acc^t by us [*Eight signatures; six write their own names*].

Mem^d That Judith James is to pay to ye Grassmen of St Giles his Parish for her Tenters in ye Common Lane in Pellow Leazes for ye year 1706, 2*s.*

---

[1] See below, p. 102, for the Order referred to.
[2] See above, p. 99, note 1.
[3] We observe that this year two "persons" (*parsons*) are provided for, as well as the Parish Clerk.

1706.   Grassmen, Iohn Simpson & Ralph Robeson.

Various receipts for gates, tenter rents, whins, *&c.,* *including*—Rec^d for Whines to Shurben house, 4*s.* 4*d.* Aperell ye 22, 1707, Rec^d then of Iohn Hewert for his six gates on oure stinted paster In ye Right of his wife by us grasmen, 12*s.*   Rec^d then of William Roads for 2 gates on oure paster one pound by us grasmen, foure gates wass p^d for before by his wifes first husband, 1*l.*   Rec^d for Whens to Shurborne house, 6*s.*   Rec^d at thre pence p. gate, 2*s.* 3*d.*   May ye 22th 1707 ; Rec^d then of Anthony Allenson for six gates of our Stinted Pasture Gilesgate Moor he being born in ye Parish, 12*s.* [*The same of Thomas Snowdon*].   Rec^d of y^m y^t run for ye saddel, 2*s.* Rec^d of Richard Maugham for ye lane at ye Cassefut, 6*d.* Rec^d of Mr Whittingam for whins, 4*s.* 4*d.*—Rec^d in all, 9*l.* 10*s.* 2*d.*

Disbursements.   P^d Simond Lightfoot for keping Sherburn gate 1705, 2*s.* 6.   P^d him for ye same 1706, 2*s.* 6*d.*   For drawing 15 Acres of Young Whins, 10*s.* For drawing 22 Acres of Young Whins, 14*s.* 8*d.*   Spent at mouding ye moor 2 dayes, 3*s.*   For a new gate for magdalen Lane, 1*s.*   Given ye Labourers in stubing, 10*d.* Spent at Iohn Martins about proving ye mare to be Mr Lambs, 1*s.*   For scaling ye manure over ye moor, 1*s.* P^d our Arrears, 1*l.* 3*s.* 9*d.*   Spent at Collecting 3*d.* p. gate, 3*s.* 1*d.*   Spent in Collecting ye Cavell, 1*s.* 9*d.*   Spent about ye old by Lawe & search, 11*d.*   Spent about going to Shearburn house for ye parish mony 4 times, 1*s.* 1*d.* For 5 Summonses to ye Court, 10*d.*   P^d Iohn Riply in proofe to all the Action, 1*s.*   P^d in Suppeny (*Subpoena*) & Charge of our Witness, 1*s.* 2*d.*   For a stoope for ye Cows to Robb one, 1*s.*   For ye Bounder Dinner, 16*s.* For Bread and drink for ye boyes, 2*s.* 6*d.*   P^d ye Drummer, 2*s.* 6*d.*   P^d ye Garlands, 1*s.* 6*d.*   For a saddle for ye Course, 8*s.*   For ye persons horse, 1*s.*   For ye Clarks mare, 6*d.*[1]   P^d ye persons Clubb at Dinner, 6*d.*   P^d for ye Drummers Ale, 3*d.*   For Tobbacker & pipes, 9*d.*[2]   Spent upon ye Person & Clark after bunder diner, 1*s.* 6*d.*   To Ino. Miller for Ale at ye high Stoope, 2*s.* 1½*d.*   P^d in private expence when absent, —— [*This entry erased*].   P^d for Stenters that came & did not pay their due in ye Reckoning, 1*s.*   P^d Robert Ellet for stubing 3 Acres of

---

[1] Observe here the commendable distinction between parson and clerk with regard to the cost of the steeds provided for them to ride.

[2] The first allusion to smoking.

Whins, 1*l.* 1*s.* Spent at making this accompt, 1*s.* P^d for making our accompts, 2*s.* 6*d.* [*Other entries*]. Disburst in all, 9*l.* 9*s.* 6*d.*—Rest in our hands, 7½*d.*

June ye 2^d, 1707. Then seen & Allowed this Account by us [*Thirteen signatures; all but one write their own names*].

Whereas Iohn Simpson & Ralph Robinson Grasmen for the street of St Gyles by order of the Twenty four and the rest of the stenters on Gilligate moor or stinted pasture have stubed severall Acres of Whins on the said more or stinted pasture We the Twenty four and the rest of the stinters unanimously agree to Give for every Stint we keep one ye said moor or pasture a Large Cart Load of manure Commonly caled a Water Cart or four pence a Cart for buying every Cart for every Stint we have to the said Iohn Simpson & Ralph Robinson & their Successors Grasmen from year to year. And we further agree to pay all & all manner of Charge that the Grasmen shall be at in Leading & Scaling the said Cart Loads of manure and we unanimously agree to pay all & all manner of Charge expended by ye said Grasmen or their successors Grasmen for the time being that they shall be att in Collecting the said severall sums for every Gate of all & Singuler the stinters. And upon Refusall of any Stinter or Stinters to pay according to their equall proportion as they stint to impound ye Goods of the party neglecting to pay either the four pence a Cart Load for every Cart Load of manner for every Gate or for not paying their Assessment for Leading & scaling ye manner. And for ye better encoraging the Grasmen aforenamed & their successors in the improvement of our said moor or stented pasture We fully & absolutely agree to keep harmless the said Grasmen & their Successors from any Charge or Charges they shall be att by reason of any Sute or Sutes that may happen by ye impounding ye Goods of ye refusers to pay as aforesaid.

And further we agree that no Grasmen that now is or hereafter shall be shall expend any monyes one ye Bounder day Commonly cald Holy thursday without our Bounders at ye stinters Charge.

And Likewise we agree that no Grasman hereafter shall be Allowed above sixteen shillings for Bread meet and Drink & all other Charge one ye Bounder day for ye Dinner. Given under our hands this Tenth day of September Anno Dom. 1705. [*Forty-five signatures; twenty-nine write their own names*].

1707.   Grassmen, Thomas Hastans & Wm Brown.

Receipts include—Rec^d for 3*d*. p gate, 2*l*. 5*s*.   Rec^d for ye Cavels for ye more hedge, 7*s*. 11.——Rec^d in all 6*l*. 13*s*. 4*d*.

Disbursements   include—For   stubing   the   young Whins, 1*l*. 10*s*.   To Robart Ellet for Casting for water at priers stabel, 1*s*. 4*d*.   Paed the Drumer for druming and given him in aell, 3*s*.   Paed to William Wilson and Edward Ridle for mending the Clay wall in the pondfould, 1*s*. 4*d*.   For the persins Hors on the bound day and his club, 1*s*. 6*d*.   Given to the 2 Garlings, 2*s*.   To the boyes and gerels for bread and alle, 1*s*. 6*d*.   For Collecting the 3*d*. per gate and the Cavels, 4*s*. 6*d*.   For our bound Diner, 16*s*.   To ye dikers for making the mour dike and prier stabel hedg and gils bridg hedg, 1*l*. 0*s*. 10*d*.   To John Milner for aell and bread in the mour on ye bound day, 3*s*. 6*d*.   Disburst in all, 5*l*. 12*s*. 4*d*.

Agreed with Rob't Ellett for stubing 3 Ackers of Whins one ye moor at 7*s*. p. Acker, 1*l*. 1*s*.

1708.   Grassmen, William Brown & Thomas Hastings.

Receipts include—Rec^d of William Ayre of pettenton hallgarth for 19 fother of whins, 6*s*. 4*d*.   [*Other receipts for whins at the same rate*].   Rec^d of William Lasenbe in part of his six pound and hath given his bill to pay the other pound to the next Grasmen he did pay 3*l*. the first year and one pound the next year, 1*l*.—Rec^d in all, 7*l*. 7*s*. 6*d*.

Disbursements   include—Paed to Robart Ellet for draying (*drawing*) the young Whins, 1*l*.   To Robart Ellet for stubing there (*three*) Akers of whins, 1*l*. 1*s*. Spent when we meshered the 3 akers of stubing, 1*s*.   Spent with William fawden and Robart Ellet when they Leed out the maner on the mour at michelmes, 6*d*.   For the persons Hors on the bounder day, 1*s*.   Spent at Simon Lightfouts on the bounder day, 2*s*.   Given to the person in the Low (*lieu*) of his bounder diner, 2*s*. 6*d*.   Paed the drumer on the bounder day for druming, 2*s*. 6*d*.   Paed to Walter Hair on the bounder day, 1*s*.   Given to the tow Garlens, 2*s*.   Given to the fideller, 1*s*.   Paed for the sadell to William Botchabe, 8*s*. 6*d*.   Paed for a Hat for the boyes to run for, 2*s*. 8*d*.   For a pare of glufes to dans for, 1*s*. Given to the gerell that danst for the glufes and Lost her part, 6*d*.   Spent at Abraham Allensons before bounder began, 1*s*. 3*d*.   To Richard Bradle for on hespe and stapell for ye pound fould, 6*d*.   Paed to Robart Ellet for stubing 3 akers of whins, 1*l*. 1*s*. Paed to Robart Ellet for drising the 3 akers of whins and burning the rubish and scaling the asis (*ashes*) and scailing the maner 3 dayes, 6*s*. Paed to William fawden for Leading the maner out that was Lade on the mouer with 2 Carts one day and on half, 5*s*.—Rests due to us, 17*s*.

1709. Grassmen, Thomas Hugall & Nickolas Johnson.

Rec^d at y^r enterence 4*s*. 7*d*.—More to be rec^d of Wm Lasanby, 2*l*.—More to be rec^d of George Nickkelson, 12*s*.—In all, 2*l*. 16*s*. 7*d*.
No further accounts are preserved till 1717.

1717. Grassmen, Iohn Harland & Tho. Hastin.
Receipts imperfect, but including—Recaved of Saragh Longstaff For Her Fred (*freedom*) of ye moor, 12*s*. Recaved of James Ladar for His Fredom of ye moor, 12*s*. Of In^o Richardson For whins, 1*l*. Of Judeth James for Tentar Rent, 2*s*. Of ye Shumacars For an acknowledgement, 1*s*.[1] For Tinkares lane, 1*s*.
No disbursements preserved.

1718. Grassmen, Antho. Greveson & Tho. Burdon.
Receipts in all, 13*l*. 4*s*. 2*d*.—*Disbursements*, 12*l*. 11*s*. 6.
[*No disbursements specified*].

1719. Grassmen, *the same. Receipts*, 6*l*. 12*s*. 2*d*.

Disbursements include—For Dresing out gils bridge for water at severall times, 7*s*. 6*d*. Given to ye bellman for Calling ye plates,[2] 1*s*. For Dresing & stubing ye moor for ye Course, 6*s*. For bying stoops & seting them, 5*s*. 6*d*. Given to ye plates 5*s*. & for ye ten stone weights 2s., 7*s*. For takeing up young whins, 13*s*. 10*d*. Spent at severall times About scabd horses, 2*s*. 6*d*. For makeing ye blind lane hedge 2 new stoops & mending ye gate, 2*s*. 3*d*. Spent at Driveing ye moor at severall times, 5*s*. Spent at Micaell pickerings, 5*s*. ye bounder diner, 19*s*. a horse for ye person, 1*s*. P^d for ye garlans, 2*s*. Given to ye Drumer, 2*s*. 6*d*. P^d to Mr Roper for Charges against Iohn harling. Disburst in all, 8*l*. 8*s*. 8*d*.—Rec^d in all, 6*l*. 16*s*. 2*d*. Resting dew to us, 1*l*. 12*s*. 6*d*.

Seen and Alowed by us. [*Eight signatures; all but one write their own names*].

---

[1] See above, p. 99, note 1.
[2] *I.e.*, To be run for at the horse races on Bounder Day. See below.

1720. Grassmen, Peter Greveson & Wm Hare.
Receipts in all, 6l. 16s. 6d.

Disbursements include—For bricks & Lime & sand & Lead for ye well, 10s. 3d. For working ye trough & building ye well,[1] 19s. 6d. For Cuting ye new Gutter, 4s. 6d. Spent when we paid ye workmen, 1s. 6d. Spent for going for ye plate to newcastle & hors hire, 3s. 6d. Given to ye Drumer on ye bounder day, 2s. 6d. Paid to ye owld grasmen, 1l. 12s. 6d. For stubing An Aker of whins, 10s. for ye bounder diner & Drinke, 1l. 7s. 6d. paid to ye garland & ye Persons hors & his diner, 2s. 6d. for stubing ye young whins, 1l. 17s. 6d. Spent at Collecting 3d. p. gate and Cavells, 6s. 6d. given to ye bellman for calling ye plates, 1s. Spent at Letting ye young whins to stub, 2s. Spent when we paid them, 1s. 6d. for scouring gillsbridge gutter & ye Ponds, 7s. 8d. For ye Drum on St James day, 1s.[2] *Total, 11l. 7s. 0d.*

Seen these Acc^{ts} & allowed by us. [*Nine signatures; six write their own names*].

1721. Grassmen, *the same as in 1720.*
Receipts of usual kind, amounting to 13l. 13s. 3d.

Disbursements include—Spent at measuring ye ground that was stobed, 2s. Spent at severall times scabd horses, 2s. P^d for stobing young whines, 1l. 9s. 6d. Spent when we p^d them, 1s. 4d. P^d for stobing ye old whines, 2l. 0s. 6d. Spent when we bargined with them, 1s. 6d. Spent when we p^d them, 1s. 6d. Spent when we collected yt 3 pence per gaits and cavels, 4s. 6d. P^d for scouring out ye water holes, 4s. 4d. Spent when we moweded ye moore, 1s. 6d. P^d ye Garlinds, 2s. P^d ye drume and for ale, 3s. P^d for ye parson hors and spent at micel pickerene, 1s. 8d. P^d for ale and bread one ye moor one ye bunder day, 7s. 8d. P^d for ye bounder diner and for ale for ye lads, 1l. 8s. 9d. P^d for prier Stable and gilsbridge hedg, 1s. 6d. Spent when we went a bought (*about*) to get money for ye plaits, 6d. Resting due to us sins last yeare, 4l. 10s. 6d.—*Total, 13l. 11s. 7d.* Seen & allowed this Acc^t. [*Five signatures; one only makes his mark*].

1722. Grassmen, Wm Forster & Robt Ellott.
Receipts of usual kind, including Rec^d for Countrey Whins 8s. ; At 3d. p. Gates & Cavell, 2l. 14s. 10d. ; For

---

[1] Probably what is called the "Moor Well" in 1724, when a ball is set on it. It may have been where "the Pant" on the Moor formerly was. See above, p. 13, note 1.

[2] The occasion of the drumming on St. James' Day (July 25th) in this year invites enquiry.

ye blind Lane, 5*s.* ; For ye Common Lane, 6*s.* ; For ye Tenters, 3*s.*, *amount to* 11*l.* 14*s.* 6*d.*

Disbursements include—P^d for stubbing old Whins, 1*l.* 17*s.* 3*d.* Spent out of Grants money, 3*s.* Spent out of Richardsons money, 1*s.* For stubbing Young Whins, 13*s.* 6*d.* Expended at ye Bounder Dinner & drinke, 1*l.* 11*s.* 6*d.* Spent at ye same time at Mich. Pickerings, 2*s.* 6*d.* Y^e parsons horse, 1*s.* For Impounding Scabbed horses, 2*s.* Dressing Gills Briggs pond, 6*s.* Making ye hedge in ye blind Lane & opening ye watercourse, 3*s.* Spent at the breaking ye Gapps of Iohn Harling, 2*s.* given to Geo. Milburne for Warneing ye Inhabitants to dresse ye Moore, 6*d.* Given to Mich. Davison to Warne to mould ye Moore, 8*d.* p^d for 4 draughts & two men leading ye Manure out of Duck poole, 19*s.* 0½*d.* to ye drum & Garlands, 4*s.* 6*d.* Robt Ellott Stubbing two days, 2*s.*—

	9*l.*	12*s.*	9½*d.*
to Bal.	1	19	9½
	11	14	6

Seen & allowed this Acc^t. [*Nine signatures ; one only makes his mark*].

1723. Grassmen, James Finney Esqr & Iohn Simpson.

Receipts include, together with gates *at 12s. and 6s.,* Rec^d of Mr Dunsey for Whins, 1*s.* Of Wid^w Greveson for pellaleases lane, 6*s.* 6*d.* Of Iⁿ Richardson for Whins, 1*l.* Of Antho. Greveson Geo Robinson and Iohn Tilley for Whins, 15*s.* Of Gilb^t Burne an acknowledgement, 1*s.* Rec^d att 3*d.* p. gate & Cavels, 2*l.* 10*s.* 1*d.*—Rec^d in all, 21*l.* 7*s.* 4*d.*

Disbursements include—Paid for makeing holes for ye goods[1] to drink, 6*d.* For porter Close laying hedge, 6*d.* Paid Rob't Ellot for stubbing 6 Acres of Whins, 2*l.* 2*s.* 6*d.* For scailing the mannor on the Moor, 2*s.* For Driveing the Moor for Scab^d Horses, 1*s.* P^d for ale at several times when we agreed for stubbing with Valentine Allenson, 4*s.* Given to Robt Ellot at several times in Ale, 4*s.* 5*d.* Given to George Milburne for warning ye Jury, 6*d.* given to the Jury in ale, 1*s.* 3*d.* paid to Braidley & Hutchinson for their Judgm^t of the

---

[1] "The goods" here evidently means the cattle. Holes seem to have been dug in the marshy parts of the Moor to serve as drinking places.

scab^d horses, 2s. 6d. to ye Bell women, 6d. to Geo. Miburne for warning to dress ye Moor, 6d. Spent for Moulding ye Moor, 1s. Spent when ye Neighbours burnt ye Rubbish Whins, 2s. 8d. p^d Richd Tilley for warning ye people to dress ye Moor, 6d. for a Hatt, 8s. Spent att Michael Pickerings on the bounder day, 7s. 6d. p^d the Drummer, 2s. 6d. given to ye Lads that run for the hatt, 8d. paid to ye musisoners, 2s. to the garland, 1s. for driveing the Moor on hollow (*Holy* or *Hallow*) Thursday, 1s. 6d. for the Bounder dinner, 1l. 2s. 6d. Spent when we Rec^d George Browns money, 5s. 4d. Spent when we Bought ye Saddle, 8d. to the Clarke ye Drummer & ye two Musisoners in Ale on hollow Thursday, 2s. Pryors Stable & gillsbridge hedge, 2s. p^d Geo. Willson for dressing gillsbridge pond, 5s. 6d. To Thos Lough & others for stubbing 10 acres of Whins, 4l. 5s. 6d. to Robt Ellot for stubbing four Acres of Whins, 1l. 2s. gave to Robt Ellot upon Complaint of an hard bargain, 2s. 6d.—*Total*, 5l. 14s. 4d.— Rests, 5l. 13s. 0d.

Seen these Acc^{ts} & allowed by us [*ten signatures; one only makes his mark*].

1724. Grassmen, Mr Fynney & Iohn Simpson [*the same as in 1723*].

Receipts include—Enter'd James Denton at ye same time a Freeman of ye said Gillygate Moor, or stinted Pasture, in right of his Father. Rec^d then of Thom^s Young (in Right of his Wife) for his six Gates on Gillygate-Moor, or stinted Pasture, 13s. 6d. Rec^d of Iohn Richardson for Whins, 1l. Rec^d of Gilbert Burn for an Acknowledgement, 1s.—Rec^d in all, 14l. 11s. 4d.

1725, Sept. 9th. Rec^d then of Valentine Allison (in Right of his Wife) for his six Gates on Gillygate-Moor, or stinted Pasture, 13s. 6d.

1724. *Disbursements include*—Paid for Carrving the Clay of the Causey, 2s. paid for makeing holes & Scouring Pryers Stable, 1s. 6d. For Setting on the Ball of ye Moor Well, 1s. 6d. For driveing the Moor for Scab^d Horses, 3s. P^d Robt Ellot for Six Acres Stubing, 2l. 5s. given him in Ale, 2s. p^d Mr Hoppers Fee about Ralph Allenson Swine, 1s. 8d. P^d for Searching Wm Wilkinsons daughters Age, 6d. Spent when Mr Tempest seized of Iohn Tilleys Wins^t, 1s. 9d. P^d Robt

---

¹ Here we see the first step towards the suit in Chancery of John Tempest, then lord of the manor, against certain parishioners, alluded to above, p. 18, note 1. It has been seen that there had in late years been

Ellott for stubing three Acres of Whins, 1*l.* 2*s.* 6*d.* given him in Ale at several times, 2*s.* 8*d.* For three Acres more for Stubing, 1*l.* 2*s.* 6*d.* Spent when we agreed with him, 1*s.* given Robt Ellott in Drink att Ann Grevesons, 1*s.* 6*d.* p^d Robt Ellott for stubing young whins, 8*s.* and in ale, 1*s.* 3*d.* Spent when we measur^d the Stubing, 3*s.* 6*d.* given for warning ye Neighbours to mowd ye Moor, 6*d.* given the Neighbours in Ale, 2*s.* 6*d.* for Stubing a Tree

an extensive stubbing and sale of whins on the Moor, and, though in 1661 an order seems to have been obtained from the lord of the manor, his claim to payment for them had been ignored. Consequently John Tempest, of Old Durham, now lord of the manor, seized certain whins that had been gathered, and afterwards instituted a suit in the Chancery Court of Durham in vindication of this and other asserted manorial rights. See below (p. 110) for a statement of the case, and the resolution of the parishioners to contest the claim, John Tilly, whose whins had been seized, being one of the defendants.

The following appears in the Records of the Chancery Court of Durham :—

"6th Sept., 1726,
            Tempest et al.
                 v.
            Seymour et al.

"Ordered by the worshipful Dormer Parkhurst, Esq., Chancellor of the County Palatine of Durham, that the compt. Tempest shall, if he thinks fit, bring an action of trespass against the deft. Anthony Greivson, a freeholder in Gilligate, for cutting and carrying away whinns of and from the said Gilligate moor, and in which action the said defendant shall answer and plead thereunto soe as to his right of cutting and selling such whinns may be brought into issue and tried at ye next assizes to be held for this County.

"And it is further ordered that the complainants and defendants shall go to another trial at ye next assizes to be held for this County upon a figured wager to try this suit, to wit : whether ye occupyers of freehold houses in Gilligate within the complainant's manor of Gilligate or any or which of them are obliged to bake their bread pyes or other and what things by them used and spent baked in their freehold houses in Gilligate within ye said manor or by them baked for sale and by them or any of them sold, at the complainant's bakehouse in Gilligate, and upon trial of this said issue the said complainants and defendants shall make use of the depositions taken in this cause as by law they may and after trial thereof ye parties may report back to this court when such further order shall be made thereon as shall be just. In both of which actions said complainant shall declare at least three months before the said assizes.

(Signed) Dormer Parkhurst."

Many entries appear below of proceedings and expenses connected with this suit ; viz., in 1725, and in 1726, and afterwards in 1728, 1729, 1730, when the case, having presumably been tried at the Assizes, had apparently come again before the Court of Chancery. The whins continued to be stubbed by the parishioners, the stenters being taxed for the purpose, but there is no mention of money received by the Grassmen for them. On the contrary, in 1798, they themselves pay for young whins and for thorns to one William Tilley, who may have acted for the lord of the manor. (See entries in 1775, 1780, 1788 and 1798). It may be here noted that in the Act for Enclosure of the Moor, A.D. 1816, land amounting to one-sixteenth part of the whole common was assigned to the lady, or lord, of the manor as an equivalent for the soil of Gilligate Moor and other waste lands.

for Sherburn gate, 1*s*. 6*d*. Spent att Simon Lightfoots on ye bounder day, 6*s*. p^d^ for a Saddle, 12*s*. 6*d*. p^d^ the Drummer, 2*s*. 6*d*. p^d^ to the Musick, 2*s*. p^d^ to the Garland, 1*s*. Given to ye Drummer & Musick In ale, 1*s*. 6*d*. for a bounder Dinner, 1*l*. 18*s*. for Tobacco & pipes, 2*s*. 3*d*. for gathering the 3*d*. p. gate, 6*s*. 1*d*. for Makeing Accompts, 2*s*. 6*d*. Spent att Makeing our Accompts, 2*s*.—Disburst in all, 12*l*. 10*s*. 10*d*.

1725. *Grassmen not named.*

Receipts. Brought from the other Side, 13*s*. 6*d*.— *Other receipts of the usual kind for* gates, Pella-Leezes lane, Whins, tenter-rents, Cavels & 3*d*. per gate, *and* Rec^d^ of Iohn Tilly Geo Robinson & Anthony Greveson Junr towards carrying on a Lawsuit, 1*l*. 10*s*. : *amounting in all to* 10*l*. 17*s*. 11*d*.

Disbursements include—For my own Journey to Shields, 3*s*. 8*d*. Paid to Mr Smith advising with him about ye Bill in Chancery, 1*s*. 8*d*. Paid to Mr Harrison his Bill, 3*l*. 8*s*. Paid to Lawyer Hall his Fee, 1*l*. 1*s*. Paid to Mr Mowbray his Bill, 2*l*. 7*s*. 2*d*. Spent at several times when we met about putting in an Answer to ye Bill in Chancery & were sworn, 3*s*. Paid to Simon Colson for repairing Magdalene-Lane Gate, 8*d*. For Wood & Iron work for ye s^d^ Gate, 1*s*. Spent with ye four & twenty when we consulted them how to raise money to carry on ye s^d^ Lawsuit, 2*s*. Spent when we took in ye names of Stinters, 4*d*. Spent at several Meetings about ye Bill in Chancery, 2*s*. 10*d*. Paid for driving ye Moor on Easter Tuesday, 1*s*. 6*d*. Paid for driving ye Moor of scab'd Horses, 1*s*. 6*d*. Paid for getting water for ye Cattel to drink, 1*s*. For taking up young Whins, 13*s*. For letting ye Water out of ye Pit, 6*d*. gave back to Tho. Burdon his Earnest when he took Magdelene Lane, 6*d*. Paid for ye Boundary Dinner, 1*l*. 19*s*. 2*d*. Gave to ye Drummer in Drink, 1*s*. Gave to ye Drummer in Money, 2*s*. 6*d*. Paid to ye Musick, 2*s*. Spent at Simon Lightfoot's, 2*s*. 6*d*. Spent at Mich. Pickering's, 4*s*. 6*d*. Gave to ye Garland, 1*s*. Spent at ye Boundary Dinner, 1*s*. 6*d*. Paid for ye Parson's Horse, 1*s*. Spent at collecting ye 3*d*. p Gate and Cables (*cavels*), 4*s*.—Disbursed in all, 15*l*. 1*s*. 9*d*.—Rec^d^ in all, 10*l*. 17*s*. 11*d*.—Balance due to ye Grassmen, 4*l*. 3*s*. 10*d*. (*Seven signatures ; five write their own names*).

1726. *Grassmen not named.*

Receipts include Rec^d^ of Antho: Greveson for ye Winters Eating of Magdalen Lane, 2*s*. 6*d*. Rec^d^ of Iohn

Tilley in part, 10*s*. Rec^d by Iohn Simpson att 6*s*. p. house, 3*l*. 13*s*. Rec^d more att 6*s*. p. house, 18*s*.—Total, 7*l*. 9*s*. 11*d*.

Disbursements include—Paid to Edward Ridley about ye Suit of Law, 3*l*. 2*s*. for Impounding Iohn Tilleys Goods, 1*s*. 6*d*. Spent in Collecting Money for a Plate, 3*s*. 9*d*. Spent att two Meetings about ye Law Suit, 5*s*. 8*d*. Spent when Mr Mowbray sought Witnesses, 1*s*. 6*d*. Spent with Ino. Harland about an Order, 1*s*. 6*d*. Spent at ye Chancery Sitting ye first day, 1*s*. 8*d*. given to Richd Coulson, 6*d*. given to Christabell Chilton, 6*d*. for 2 Times Rideing to Haswell, 1*s*. 6*d*. for 2 Times to Croxdale, 1*s*. 4*d*. Spent more about ye Chancery Suit in seaking witnesses, 1*s*. Spent ye two last days ye Chancellor sit with D^o, 4*s*. 8*d*. Paid for Stubing young Whins, 7*s*. 1*d*. for Collecting ye six shillings p house, 6*s*. Spent at warning to a Meeting, 8*d*. Lawyer Halls Fee, 5*s*. 3 pints of Wine with Mr Mowbray, 3*s*. Driveing ye Moor on Hallow Thursday, 1*s*. 6*d*. given to ye Drummers & others in Ale, 1*s*. Spent att Mich. Pickerings, 2*s*. 6*d*., given ye garland, 2*s*., 4*s*. 6*d*. P^d to ye Drumer & Musick, 5*s*. for bread to ye boys, 1*s*. for ye Parsons horse, 1*s*. to Simon Lightfoot for going to Shearburn for Hanging two gates & nailes 14*d*., & a Stile 13*d*., 2*s*. 3*d*. Spent when we Rec^d ye 6 *sh*. p house, 2*s*.—Disburs^d in all, 10*l*. 8*s*. 6*d*.—Receiv^d, 7*l*. 9*s*. 11*d*.—Ballance due, 2*l*. 18*s*. 5*d*.

Whereas Iohn Tempest Esq. hath exhibited a Bill in ye Court of Chancery at Durham against James Fynney Iohn Simpson Anthony Greveson Geo. Robinson & Iohn Tilly thereby setting forth his Title in & to ye Moor or Common called Gillygate-Moor & ye Furzes & Whins growing thereupon as Lord of ye Mannour of Gillygate & also claims y^t all ye Inhabitants of Gillygate are obliged to bake all their Pyes & other Things at his Bakehouse & Grind at his Mill within ye said Mannour And by his Bill he also pretends y^t ye Inhabitants of Gillygate aforesaid cannot depasture their Cattel upon ye said Moor without his permission & consent And forasmuch as we look upon ye Demands of ye said Iohn Tempest to be unreasonable & unjust And as ye Tryal & Defence in this Cause will tend generally to us all & we are all as lawfully Parties as if ye said Iohn Tempest had made us Defendants We whose Names are underwritten being Grassmen & ye four & twenty & other Inhabitants of Gillygate having power by ancient Custom to make Orders & Bylaws for ye preserving their Right to ye said Gillygate Moor do hereby order yt for ye defending of ye said Suit yt we & all every ye Inhabitants of Gillygate shall pay at ye Rate of one Shilling a Stint for every Stint he or they shall (or have a Right to) put upon ye said Moor which said Money shall be paid into ye Hands of ye said James Fynney & Iohn Simpson to be applyed by them towards defending ye sd Suit & ye said one Shilling a Stint shall be as often collected as there shall be occasion. As Witness our Hands this thirtieth day of Augst 1726.

Anth. A Greveson Senr	Anthony Greaveson Junr
his mark	Tho. **X** Pierson
Geo R Robinson	his mark
his mark	James **X** Kelsy
Henry Parkinson	his mark
Iohn Simpson	Gilb. **X** Burn
Anth. Dobson	his mark
Tho : Hastings	Iohn Forster
Matt Robinson	James Ladler
Tho : Burdon	William Greeveson
J Fynne Junr	Thomas Hayes.

The Acct Continued by James Fynney Esqre and James Celsey Grassmen for the year 1727.

Receipts of the usual kind.

*Disbursements include—*For taking up whins, &c., 1*l.* 9*s.* 5*d.* By removeing of the hay from Ralph Allesons in the Palmer Close,[1] 1*s.* 6*d.* By Stoping the Carridge on Gillygate Moor, 1*s.* 6*d.* By Drink, 1*s.* 6*d.* By Makeing up 4 Gapps that Ralph Allison pull'd down, 1*s.* By Scouring the Hallywell Gutter,[2] 7*s.* By the Drummer & Waits,[3] 3*s.* By Pruans for the Boys, 1*s.* 6*d.* By Horse Hire, 1*s.* By the Garland, 1*s.* By the Bounder Dinner, 10*s.*

Disbursed, 3*l.* 17*s.* 1*d.*—Recd on ye other side, 3*l.* 1*s.* 11½.—Balance, 15*s.* 1½*d.*

Seen & Allowed this Acct by us whose names are hereto subscribed this 10th day of June 1728. [*Seven names ; two make their marks*].

---

[5] A close on the South side of the road to Sherburn just West of "Gillsbridge." See Tithe Map.

[6] The "Holy Well" remained till recently, and was still so called, a little South East from the Church below the modern cemetery, the parishioners having common access to it. Before its destruction it was protected by upright blocks of stone with another for a roof. We shall find it several times alluded to in subsequent years, as whitewashed from time to time, and in 1755 surmounted by a cross.

[7] This is the first occurrence of the term "waits" for the musicians on Bounder Day.

1728.   Grassmen, James Celsey & Anthony Dobson.

Receipts for gates, tenter-rent, &c., including—Rec^d
at 3*d*. per Gate, 2*l*. 11*s*. 3*d*.   Rec^d at 12*d*. p gate, 7*l*. 16*s*. 6*d*.
Maugham's Garth, 6*d*.   Rec^d of Smith for Harland's
Garth, 1*s*.   of Gilb^t burne for Shoemaker's Garden, 2*s*. 6*d*.
of James Kelsey for ye Common Loaning, 6*s*.   of Geo.
Stoute for ye blind Loaning, 5*s*.

Disbursements include—Spent when went to make
an Agreem^t with ye Lawyers about Mr Tempest, 15*s*.   8
Subpenas, 8*s*.   4 Subpenas more, 4*s*.   Spent in Charges
when we Sought ye Witnesses, 1*l*. 10*s*.   Spent with y^e
Witnesses on ye Green, 10*s*. 6*d*.   To Waugh for his
charges, 9*s*.   To Hutchinson, Hugill, Ovington, Thompson, Bradly, Davison, Mr Baker, Mr Shaftoe &c., 16*s*.   To
Alderson for ye Witnesses Meate & drinke 3 days,
3*l*. 10*s*.   To 3 Councellors at ye Chancery Sitting 2*l*. 12*s*. 6*d*.
Spent in attending ye Chancery, 2*s*. 6*d*.   Spent at Light-
foots & Mich. pickerings to Ale & bread, 4*s*. 8*d*.   To y^e
Garlands, 1*s*. 6*d*.   To ye Drumer, 2*s*. 6*d*.   To ye Bounder
Dinner, 1*l*. 2*s*. 6*d*.   To Simon Lightfoot for takeing care
of ye Gate, 2*s*. 6*d*.   To ye Clerke & Sexton, 1*s*.   for
Collecting ye Sesse, 2*s*. 6.

Total, 15*l*. 15*s*. 6½*d*.—Take, 15*l*. 15*s*. 1*d*.—Ballance,
5½*d*.   Seen & Allowed [*Six signatures; all but one
write their names*].

1729.   Grassmen, Geo: Brown & Anthony Greveson.

Disbursements include—For Opening of Gillsbridge
Gutter, 5*s*. 5*d*.   For Reparing ye Fencis & Hedgis
Adjoyning to Ralph Allison & Iohn Hubathorn, 1*s*. 5*d*.
Exspended when summoned to Wm Rippons Conserning
ye parrish Affair, 2*s*.   The Balifs Feess & Expencis for
Serving y^e 'po'neys (*subpoenas*), 5*s*. 6*d*.   For Opening
& Cleneing ye Strand Adjoyning to Gills Bridge, 1*s*. 1*d*.
Paid Daniell Mackjunkin for Scouring & Brushing y^e
Hedg or Fence in Elles Leesiss Adjoyning to ye Rid
House, 2*s*. 6*d*.   Spent about paing Mr Mowbery Our
Charges, 6*d*.   Paid Mr Jos. Marton Atturney at Law for
His Advise in Defence of ye parrish, 7*s*. 8*d*.   for ye Drum
& Fidler, 2*s*. 4*d*.   ye Persons Dinner Spent att pickerons
(*Pickering's*), 1*s*. 6*d*.   for ye Bounder Dinner, 1*l*. 0*s*. 3*d*.
Paid to Mr Mowbry for Charges, 1*l*. 6*s*. 4*d*.   Paid M^r
Finney as per Note appears, 10*l*.   Paid Mr Finney as per
Note, 4*l*. 9*s*.

19*l*. 19*s*. 10*d*.

Received for disbursment as above for}
   paid out our pockets for hedging} 1   3   6
   opening Gills bridge, &c. ... ...}

18 16 4

Receipts, including—Received of the Subscribers & other Inhabitants, 13*l*. 15*s*. 0*d*. *Total*—18*l*. 15*s*. 2*d*. Due from the parish to ballance, 1*s*. 2*d*.

Omitted in the disbursments for the Gar-}
   land, 1*s*. so due to the Grassmen ...}   2*s*. 2*d*.
D° Omitted in ye Disbursments for ye Jurey   1   0

3 2

Rec^d of In° Maugham after ye closing of ye Accompts, 4*s*. Due from ye Grassmen to Ballance, 10*d*. [*Twelve signatures ; nine write their own names*].

1730.   Grassmen, Wm Greveson & Mark Nichalson.

Receipts include—To ye Moor hedge at 2*s*. p. house, 2*l*. 19*s*. 6*d*. to 2*s*. p. gate for ye Reembursing of James Finey Esqr, 9*l*. 4*s*. 6*d*. to an acclowdgement for ye Showmaker garth, 2*s*. 6*d*. More towards ye gates money, 1*l*. 4*s*. More towards ye Moor Hedge, 3*s*. *Total*, 22*l*. 5*s*. 6*d*.

Disbursements include—To ye Wates & Drums, 5*s*. to ye Bounder Dinner, 1*l*. 16*s*. 7*d*. to opning Gils Brig Gutter, 5*s*. 6*d*. to Scouring ye Common Lane, 1*s*. to opining ye Water Holes, 2*s*. to Volintine Allison for Repairing ye Moor hedge, 4*l*. 10*s*. 6*d*. Spent about Trying of Wilkinson, 3*l*. Spent at Several times about Scab^d horses, 2*s*. Spent at Gathering of 2*s*. p. gate, 4*s*. 6. *Total*, 12*l*. 11*s*. 3*d*.

1731 & 1732.   Grassmen. *The same as for 1730.*

Receipts include—Recceived of Peter Greeveson for his six gats on our stented Paster, 12*l*. 6*s*. To the money for the Gates for the reimbursing of James Finney Esqre, 6*l*. 11*s*. To an acknowledgment for the Shoemakers Garth, 2*s*. 6*d*.

Disbursements include—To the Bounder Dinner, 1*l*. 14*s*. To the Drummers & Waits, 5*s*. To Simon Lightfoot, 4*s*. 6*d*. To the Wickett In the Blind lane, 6*s*.

   8

1733.   Grassmen, Iohn James & Rob. Farfax.

Disbursements include—yᵉ Bounder Diner, 6*s*. 1*d*. yᵉ Drumer, 2*s*. 6*d*. for white bread at Lodge hill, 1*s*. to Simon Lightfut for ale, 1*s*. at Mickel pickerons for ale for yᵉ lads, 1*s*. for dresing yᵉ watter holes at brines stable and gils brig, 2*s*. 6*d*. to scouring gils brig gutter, 4*s*. to Cha (?) young at yᵉ dike at owld durm (*Durham*) Cross, 10*d*. to Rob. Eliot stoping yᵉ carts of yᵉ moure, 6*d*. a Loup for Shirburngate, 10*d*. and a new hartree, 6*d*. pidington gate a crook, 8*d*. Iohn Greveson for finding 2 sheths for yᵉ pounfould and seting one yᵉ lock mending Sherburn gate pidington gate, 3*s*. 6*d*. payd to Rob. Eliot for Diken and haining, 6*s*. 6*d*. yᵉ garling, 1*s*. Driving yᵉ moure for scab'd horses at several times, 2*s*.

Disbursed in 1732, 1*l*. 16*s*. 9
        in 1733, 2   9   2
                        ——————   4   5 11
Recᵈ as apears   1   19   8
                        ——————
        due to Ballance   2   6   3
                        ——————

1734.   Grassmen, Robᵗ Fairefax & Tho. Richardson.

Received—To Pella Leazes Lane, 11*s*. To yᵉ Scabbᵈ Lane, 8*s*. 6*d*. Towards the mower hedge, 12*s*. 10*d*., *&c.*—*Total*, 1*l*. 16*s*. 8*d*.

Disbursed—To yᵉ Parson, 2*s*. 6*d*. to macking a Causway in Pella Leases, 12*s*. 6*d*. to scowring yᵉ Gilsbridge Gutter & Cleaning out yᵉ watter hole, 6*s*. to Looking after yᵉ Scabᵈ horses, 1*s*. 6*d*. to yᵉ Bounder dinner, 14*s*. to yᵉ Drum, 2*s*. 6*d*. to Simon Leightfoot, 4*s*. 2*d*. Spent at Michal Pickerons in Bread and drink to yᵉ Childer, 1*s*. to yᵉ Garlands, 2*s*. to a Loope & nales to yᵉ Gate, 4*d*. to Getting yᵉ Stones for yᵉ Leazes Causway, 1*s*., *&c.* Disbursᵈ 4*l*. 3*s*. 9*d*.—to Ballance, 2*l*. 7*s*. 1*d*.

June 7ᵗʰ 1734. Memerand. that Thomas Thompson hath agreed with yᵉ grasmen for thre gats one gilligate moure or stented pasture for thre gates paying 1*l*. 10*s*. if stenting any more to pay every gate ten Shillings as he stenteth as witness my hand, Tho. Thompson.

1735.   Grassmen, *the same as in 1734.*

Receipts include—Recᵈ towards yᵉ Moor hedges, 19*s*. 7*d*. Dᵒ Wᵐ Greveson to yᵉ Scabᵈ Lane, 6*s*.—*Total*, 4*l*. 16*s*. 7*d*.

Disbursements include—P^d to the moor hedge, &c.,
1*l.* D^o to Wm Greveson for a Tree for Stoops &c. for
Shearburn & Pitington Gate, 5*s.* D^o a Deal, 1*s.* 4*d.*
D^o holes, 7*d.* D^o Busby to Leading ye Stoop, 1*s.* 4*d.*
P^d to a new Stile, 5*s.* Scowering of Gils Bridge Gutter
& Cleaning out ye Watter hole, 6*s.* Looking after Scab^d
Horses, 2*s.* 6*d.* To ye Bounder Dinner, 11*s.* 6*d.* To y^e
Drum, 2*s.* 6*d.* To a Garland, 1*s.* Spent at Pickerons
& to Raisins, 1*s.* 8*d.* To mending ye hedge next to y^e
Sands, 2*s.* 6*d.* p^d to a new Bridge over ye Gils Bridge
Gutter, 10*s.* 6*d.*—Due to Ballance of the Last years
Account, 2*l.* 7*s.* 1*d.*—*Total, 6l. 10s. 0d.* [*Eleven signatures;
eight write their own names*].

1736. Grassmen, *the same.*
Receipts amount to 7l. 3s. 2d.
Disbursements include—To ye Bounder Dinner,
1*l.* 3*s.* 2*d.* To ye Drum & Wates, 3*s.* 6*d.* To y^e
Garland, 1*s.* Spent at Sherburn Gate ye Bounder day, 1*s.*
D^o at Robt. Thompsons, 1*s.* To bread & Spice, 1*s.* 4*d.*
To mending Pryers Stable Hedge and Gils Bridge D^o,
2*s.*—*Total, 5l. 0s. 2.*—Rests due, 2*l.* 3*s.* 0*d.* [*Eleven
signatures; all write their names*].

1737. Grassmen, Michaell Johnson & Peter Greveson.
Receipts, including Rec^d for ye Cavill money, *amount
to 5l. 19s. 5d.*
Disbursements include—For a New Saddle, 16*s.*
Spent at Attending ye four & Twenty upon takeing in y^e
Overstints, 1*s.* Spent at attending ye four & Twenty for
a New Stile, 6*s.* Spent at Abrah^m Burdons about Iohn
Tilleys affairs & expences, 6*s.* 6*d.* Spent at Hazards
about Wm Tilley given to Ripley, 6*d.* P^d to Wm Rippon
for a Distringth (*Distringas?*) upon ye account of W^m
Rowntree, 2*s.* 9*d.* Spent in goeing to ye Sherif for
asking advice, 9*d.* to ye Drum for giveing notice to
Scale ye Moor, 6*d.* Spent at Moulding ye Moor, 1*s.* 6*d.*
to ye Bell man for Dischargeing ye Carts to go cros y^e
Moor, 2*d.* Spent at Robt Thompsons for ye boys, 1*s.* 6*d.*
To ye Drum & garland, 3*s.* 6*d.* To a Saddle, 10*s.* To
a Bounder Dinner, 1*l.* 4*s.*—*Total, 6l. 10s. 6d.*

1738. Grassmen, *the same as in 1737.*
Receipts, including Resting in our hands upon y^e
Account of Tilleys Tryall, 1*l.*, *amount to 2l. 5s. 11d.*
Disbursements include—To Mending ye hedge at
Old Durham Cross, 4*d.* For Bread Spice & Ale att Robt
Thompsons, 2*s.* For ye Drum & Waites & Garland, 6*s.*

For a Bounder Dinner, 13*s*. 6*d*.   Due to Ballance upon Tilleys Account, 2*l*. 1*s*. 10*d*.—*Total*, 4*l*. 12*s*. 6*d*.

The accounts or other entries for succeeding years, 1739-1790, are contained in a second volume.   But at the end of Vol. I, the accounts for 1798, which we have transcribed in full, are entered as follows :—

Tobias Child and Thomas Clark Grasmen for the Parish of S[t] Giles from May 28th 1798 to May 13th 1799 both Inclusive.

1798.   D[r]—May 28th.   By Cash rec[d] from the preceding Grasmen, 1*l*. 1*s*. 2*d*.   By D[o] for Jerimiah Millers acknowledgement, 1*d*.   Oct. 26th By D[o] for David Martin fredom & Stints, 3*l*. 9*s*.   1799, Jan[ry] 14th By D[o] for Mary Nungs fredom, 12*s*.   By D[o] for Ino. Atkinson's acknowledgement on account of his Trespass by liveing in a House out of the Street,[1] 6*d*.   March 26th.   By D[o] for the Blind Lane, 1*l*. 5*s*.   By D[o] for 28th stints at 1 sh. per Stint, 1*l*. 8*s*.   By D[o] for Stints & Caveing,[2] 19*s*.   By D[o] for W[m] Elliot Laying his Wood upon y[e] Waste, 2*s*.   By D[o] for 8 Gates at 1 sh. per Gate, 8*s*.   By D[o] for scaling & Caveing, 2*s*. 6*d*.

1798.   Cr.

May 28th, By Cash to Go[e] Stookley for a stone Stile, 1*l*. 1*s*.   Oct[r] 16th, By D[o] fore laying down Entercommons, 2*s*. 6*d*.   Oct[r] 24th, By D[o] to W[m] Tilley for opening Bryans stable Ditch & his Wife & Daughter assisting in gathering the young Whins, 6*s*. 8*d*.   D[o] 26th, By D[o] on David Martins account for his fredom, 5*s*.—1799, Jan[y] 14th, By D[o] on Mary Nungs acc[t] for her fredom, 1*s*.   D[o] 18th, By D[o] to M[r] Tilly for Calling a Meeting Relating new Bye Laws, 1*s*. 6*d*.   D[o] 26th, By D[o] to W[m] Tilly for 4 Load of Thorns & Leading, 13*s*. 6*d*.   D[o] 28th, By D[o] to In[o] Robson for ale when y[e] Commite met, 3*s*. 6*d*.   Feb[y] 2nd, By D[o] to Mich[l] Atkinson for leading 4 Load of Thorns, 12*s*.   D[o] 6th, By D[o] to In[o] Robson for ale when y[e] Commite met, 2*s*. 6*d*.   March 26th, By D[o] to Jos[h] Potts, being y[e] Balance of his acc[t] for last year, 9*s*.   By D[o] to In[o] Robson for ale on letting Blind Lane, 1*s*.   By D[o] to Go[e] Scott for a new Wood Stile and setting, 7*s*. 6*d*.   April 1st, By D[o] for Writing Paper to Dra[t] new Bye Laws, 1*s*. 2*d*.   By D[o] for ale on satteling new Bye Law for Dra[ts], 1*s*.   D[o]

---

[1] He had probably stinted on the Moor without being qualified for the privilege by residence in Gilligate.   *Cf.* below, A.D. 1772.

[2] This word, repeated below, may be taken as referring to the "Cavels," from which a yearly revenue has long been derived.   It may represent "Cavelling."

16th, By Do to Mr Lambert for Coping new Bye Laws, 15s. 2d. May 2nd, By Do for Boundary Cake, 5s. By Do for Drums & Wates, 5s. By Do for Two Hats & Two Ribbands to Run for at Bounders, 4s. By Do for Ale, Bread, & Chease for Bounders, 11s. 6d. By Do for Bounder Dinner, 1l. 1s. By Do for Priest,[1] Clerk, Drummers, & Wates Dinner, 12s. By Do for Jingle Pot,[2] 1s. Do 6th, By Do for Ale when Commitee met for satts new Bye Laws, 1s. 3d. Do 2nd, By Do for Fruit at Bounders, 2s. 6d. Do 13th, By Do for Washing Holy Well, 2s. 6d. By Do for makeing up accounts, 2s. 6d. By Do for Two days work to Thos Cummin's Daughter for assisting in gathering ye young Whins, 1s. 4d. By Do To Jas Adamson for the Sands Hedge, 2s. 6d. ... £8 16 3

By Cash to G. Atkinson for Moor Hedge	...		17	0
By Do to Wm Tilly for ye young Whins	...		16	0
By Do to Goe Scot for a Gate &c.	...	...	11	6
		11	0	9

Pd Chrisr Robinson 2 . 6, error in the account of Holiwell.

Cash Recd from the Parish	...	..	...£11	17	3
Do Disburst'd	... ...	..	... 11	0	9
				16	6
By Do for 10 Stints at 1sh. per St.			0	10	0
By Do for Caveing &c.			0	1	4
By Do Due to Preceding Grassmen	...		1	7	10
By Do	..		0	2	0
			1	9	10
By Do on acct of Holy Well			0	2	6
By Cash Paid to ye Grassmen			1	12	4

[1] First occurrence of the term "priest" for the Curate of the Parish. It is now the common designation of the clergy in the Counties of Durham and Northumberland, and has probably always been so, though the scribes of these accounts had not used it.

[2] "*Jingle-cap*, shake-cap, a pitmen's and keelmen's game (*Sc.*, Jingle-the-bonnet). *Brockett.*"

"Jingle-the-Bonnet.—Two or more put a halfpenny or other coin each into a cap or bonnet, and after jingling or shaking them together throw them on the ground, and he who has most heads when it is his turn to jingle wins the stakes that were put into the bonnet."—*Jamieson.*

The Editor has been informed by an old inhabitant of Gilligate that there still exists somewhere in the parish a pewter pot, called the "Jingling pot," which was formerly used on Bounder Day for collecting money in from the "riders" both during the perambulation and at the dinner afterwards at the "Britannia," and that it used also to be placed on the ground for the reception of coins, which were thrown into it from a distance.

GRASSMEN'S ACCOUNTS.—Vol. II.
(1739—1790).

[The entries in this volume being for the most part of the same character with those of Vol. I, it has not been thought necessary to do more than extract from them such as invite peculiar attention. It may be observed with regard to them that sums, varying in amount according to the circumstances of each case, continue to be received for gates *or* freedom of the moor, *and for* cavells *annually; that after 1741 there is no more mention of the* common lanes *as sources of revenue, or of any lane but* the blind lane, *for which rent is still received; that after 1758 there are no entries of disbursements in detail, but that the receipts for* gates *are carefully specified, with notice of the ground in each case on which persons were admitted to* stint, *and the varying sums paid accordingly for the privilege, in accordance with the order of 1701. (See p. 96). The festivities on* Bounder Day *go on in full swing; the Holy (or Hallow) well still receives attention; and there is no diminution in the number of* scabbed horses].*

1739. *On the Bounder day*—To the Baliffs Dinner, 6d.[1]

1740. *Paid*, To ye Jury & Balif at Hugals Lane gate, 1s. 6d. Y^e Clark & Baliffs diner ye Bounder day, 1s. To Labour Lime &c. to ye pinfold, 5s. 6d.

1745. Pade for opining the halowell Guter, 2s. 6d. For Diner for the Sagerstine (*sacriston* or *sexton*) and Klark, 2s.

1748. Spent when the Wallat Dicke was vewed, 6d.

1749. To Letting the Water of at Gils Bridge, 6d. For Reparing of ye halley well and Setting up the Cross for Lime briks Sand & Laberrours, 14s. 6d.

---

[1] The Bailiff, presumably of the lord of the manor, now appears on the scene, and in this and the two following years has his dinner provided him, but not after 1741. On the contrary, the expenses charged to the parish on the Bounder Day no longer include a general dinner; from which it may perhaps be supposed that the later and modern custom of the lord of the manor providing it had then begun. The Grassmen, however, still provide dinners for the parson, clerk, and drummer, and plenty of drink, with other refreshment for the boys and others, during the day.

1750. [*On the Bounder day, in addition to 1s. for* the Parson's Dinner]. To a Bottel of Wine to the parson, 2*s*. To a Sadle Bridel Whipe and Spurres, 1*l*. 8*s*.

1752. Paid for the Grand Will, 1*l*. 3*s*. 6*d*.[1] Paid for Turney and Licar (*Attorney and Liquor?*) 1*l*. 7*s*.

1753. *The Receipts, without further details, are entered thus :*—June ye 11, 1753. Rec^d of Thos Pearson The ful Sum of Thre pounds for six Stents upon the paster Cald Gillsgate paster and all Comens and Enter Comans in the parish of Sent Gills ney the Sittey of Durham in the Ward of Easengton and in the Countey of Durham. Thos Pearson.

1753. Pinfould, Cart of lime 6 Carts of Sand 12 Carts of Stone, 12*s*. Day leading Rubish, 4*s*. leading Bricks, 8*d*. Willm Rods Day at the fould, Greafson hinging the door, 1*s*. 4*d*. In^o Forster, Poke lime and labor, 15*s*. Spent with In^o Forster, 2*s*. 6*d*. Georg Nicholson tow Hun^d Bricks, 1*s*. 8*d*. Spent when the fowld was finished, 2*s*. 6*d*.

1754. Mending and Whitning the Hallow Well, 2*s*. Sixpence for the Ale to the Boys going down the Blind Lane, 6*d*.

1755. Ap. 1st. Lett this day to In^o Newton The Blind Lane at ten Shillings for the year.

1755. To Mending the Hallow Well and Setting up the Cross and Whitning, 2*s*.

1756. To mending the Moor hedge after the Greet Wind, 5*s*. To takeing Iohn Liddles Glandert Horse, 1*s*. 6*d*. To Iohn Allison for helping to faiding the Cayleys (*Feeding the Kyloes?*), 1*s*. To Wm Rods 30 days Hedging at the Moor Dicke, 1*l*. 5*s*. To Thomas Atkinson 30 days at D^o 1*l*. 5*s*. To one Day Thos Atkinson mare Hedgin Whins, 2*s*. To James Teasdell 5 days at the Hedg, 4*s*. 2*d*. To William Rods 7 days Hedgen, 10*s*. To Thomas Atkinson 7 days D^o, 10*s*. To mending the Hedg in Jan^y, 5*s*. To James Teasdell 2 days at the Hedg, 1*s*. 8*d*. To one day Thos Atkinson Hedgin Whins, 2*s*. To Wm Rodds 20 days Hedging at the moor Dicke, 16*s*. 8*d*. To Thomas Atkinson 20 days at D^o, 16*s*. 8*d*. To Cleaning and Whitening the Hallow Well, 2*s*.

1757. To Cleaning and Whitening Hallow well, 1*s*.

---

[1] *Cf.* "To Mr. Richardson Reading the Will" (A.D. 1758). There are other allusions to it. What it was has not been discovered.

1758. *After several entries for work, partly at the* Sand Hedge :—To 4 Sledge Load of Thorns to the sand Hedge, 10*d.* Two Days a Horse Sledging Whins to the Moor Hedge, 4*s.* Wm Bates new stile att the Garth Foot, 3*s.* 6*d.* Mending Wm Bates and Robt Lambs Stiles, 6*d.* To Mr Richardson Reading the Will, 1*s.* To Mr Herrisons Fees, 3*s.* 4*d.* To Whitening the Halley Well, 1*s.* To Drising out the Halley well Gutter and Water Holles, 1*s.* 8*d.*

1769. April 11th, Rec^d of Robt Lawes the sum of twilve Shillings for the right of stenting giligate moor which right hee takes by his Wife Mary Daught. of Wm Burn.

1772. Rec^d of Robt Renny the sum of two shillings and sixpence having Impounded his mare he not living in the Street of Gilligate.

1775. Paid for Swearing into the office, 2*s.* *Among expenses on Bounder day:*—To Jingal Pott,[1] 1*s.* To Wm Rods for making a Dick and Chane for Holy Well, 5*s.* To making Peter Carter free, 5*s.* *Ditto for* Iohn Robson *and* Mr Webster. To Impounding Mr Ogle Goss (*goose?*) and Henry Atkinson Do., 1*s.* To Impounding Wm Burn Horse, 1*s.* [*The same for two other horses*]. To Gathering the Cavels in and Middins, 1*s.* 6*d.* To Impounding Iohn Wilkinson Keyle and Iohn Brokets, 2*s.* 6*d.* To Stubbing the Whins on the Moor, 2*l.*

Among receipts:—Rec^d of Iohn Wall for his hors Going on the Moor, 10*s.* Of Geo Sowler Do., 3*s.* Of Wm Burn for a tresspas, 1*s.* Of Han^ha Teasdle Do., 1*s.* Of Joseph Robinson for His filde belonging to Mr Geo. Appleby, 6*d.*

1776. To Swearing into the Office, 2*s.* To Jingle Pott (*on Bounder day*), 1*s.* To Scouring and haining the Hedge, 1*l.* 18*s.* To Rebuilding the Pinfold, 5*l.* 10*s.* To a Farrier coming to see two horse's suppos'd to be glan^t, 3*s.*

1780. January 12. Received from the Revd Mr Lambe[2] the Sum of three pounds for his six gates on Gilly-

---

[1] See p. 117, note 2.

[2] The Rev. Robert Lambe is supposed to have been a native of Durham. He was an M.A. of St. John's College, Cambridge, Minor Canon of Durham, and in 1747 was presented by the Dean and Chapter to the Vicarage of Norham, which he retained till his death during a visit to Edinburgh, 7th May, 1795. He wrote a History of Chess (1764), and a ballad called "The Laidley Worm of Spindeston," and edited Weber's Ballad of "Flodden," with a preface and miscellaneous notes, which

gate Moor in the right of his house which he is now rebuilding on the South Side of the Street in Gillygate wch said house adjoins or bounders on a garden belonging to the Blue-coat Hospital now tenanted by Joseph Robinson on the East wth ye garth or garden belonging to Mr Lambe on the South and adjoining to a house belonging to Iohn Manners on the West and adjoining on the King's high Street on the North.

Witness

Iohn Tilly	In° Manners ⎫
Geo Ovington	Robt Renny ⎭
Iohn Robinson	Grassmen.
Wm Winter	

1782. Memorandum that it is agreed at a meeting this day by us whose names are under Written to pay Sixpence for each and every Stent anny Stenter shall have on

Dr. Raine, in his "History of North Durham," describes as "teeming with discursive disquisitions." In them he gave publicity to the late story of St. Cuthbert floating down the Tweed in his stone coffin, of which Sir Walter Scott availed himself in "Marmion." Notices of him will be found in "Men of Mark 'twixt Tyne and Tweed," by Richard Welford (London, 1895), vol. iii, pp. 1—6; and in Raine's "North Durham," in connexion with Norham Church. See also "Archæologia Æliana," vol. viii, pp. 162, 256, 283, 285. One incident in his personal history is curious enough to be mentioned. After going to Norham, he bethought him of one Philadelphia Nelson, the daughter of a carrier between London and Edinburgh, with whom he had become acquainted in Durham, and invited her, by letter, to come to him and be his wife. He undertook to meet her on the pier at Berwick-on-Tweed, and, having retained apparently an imperfect recollection of her features, desired her to carry a tea-caddy under her arm whereby he might recognize her. The article selected suggests to one's mind that, like Dr. Johnson, he may have been a great tea-drinker, and had a tender memory of many cups which Philadelphia had regaled him with at Durham. She went; but he (being perhaps excusable as a scholar) forgot the appointment, and the poor young woman paced the pier for many hours, faithfully carrying her tea-caddy. There was living at Berwick an old naval officer, called Howe, whose habit was to walk to the end of the pier and back regularly three times a day before his meals. Before his dinner, and again before his tea, he had observed her with her tea-caddy, and in his third walk found her sitting on a stone, tired and disconsolate. This time he addressed her, and, having heard her story, said, "Ha! Robin Lamb is a great friend of mine. Just like him, but he'll make you a capital husband." Next morning he took her by coach to Norham, where she and Lamb were married, 11th April, 1755 (*Norham Parish Registers*). Her burial is recorded in the Giligate Register thus: "Burials 1772. Philadelphia wife of the Revd Mr Lamb, Vicar of Norham in Northumberland. Jany 13th." The story, as above given, is derived from a paper in "Archæologia Æliana," vol. viii, by the late Rev. James Raine, the historian of "North Durham," who says that he had himself got it from the widow of Lambe's successor in the Vicarage of Norham. He says also that it was to occupy his mind after the loss of his wife that Lambe prepared his "Flodden." There are several entries in the Giligate register of the name of Lambe, which go to confirm the belief of the Rev. Robert having

Gilligate moor (he or she having no more Stents then six) and the s[d] sixpence p. Stent to be expended in Stobing the whins and that the Grassmen give a Just Account to the s[d] Stenters of such his expender when called on to account. Witness our Hand this 12th day of May, 1782. [*Twenty signatures*].

1788. Memorandum that it is greed at a meeting this day by us whose names are under Written to pay sixpence for each and every Stent anny Stenter shall have on Gilligate moor (he or she having no more Stents then six) and the s[d] sixpence per Stent to be expended in Stobing the whins and that the Grassmen give a just account to the s[d] Stenters of such his expender when called on to account. Wittness our Hand this 12th day of May 1782.

Robert Salkeld 　
his 　 } Grassmen.
W[m] X Crow 　
mark 　

[*Eight other signatures; three make their marks*].

This second volume extends to the year 1790. From its commencement a number of parishioners have appended their signatures on settlement of the accounts each year, and since 1769 with some such note as the following:—"Seen and allowed by the four and twenty present"; or, "We whose names are here under written have perused the above account, and do allow the same"; or, "We the stenters of Gilligate moor present at a meeting in the parish Church of S[t] Giles have perused the within written account and believe the same to be Just."

---

been a native of Durham, viz. :—"Jane d. of Edward and Elizabeth Lamb, baptized Ap. 7, 1778"; "Elizabeth d. of Henry and Mary Lamb, bapt. Aug. 15, 1773"; "Mary Lamb of S[t] Oswalds, buried June 15, 1728"; "Mary d. of M[r] John Lamb a papist was buried March 17th, 170⅞." The Rev. Robert Lamb appears to have had or acquired property in Gilligate. The house he was rebuilding in 1780, in right of which he became entitled to gaits on the moor, has not been identified. But ten years later he purchased from John Burdon, of Hardwick, in the County of Durham, for £260, two parcels of freehold land called *Bower Banks,* containing 6 ac. 1 r. 31 p., which lie to the South of the Church, and include what is now called "Grove House." In the deed of conveyance, dated 7th April, 1790, he is described as "of the Parish of S[t] Giles, in or near the City of Durham." But his having to pay £3 for his six gaits in 1780 shows that he was not entitled to them by birthright, but from having recently come into possession of a house in the "Street," by purchase or inheritance. See "Preface," p. 2.

PARISH REGISTERS.

The Parish Registers of St. Giles date from A.D. 1584. Extracts from the first three volumes are given below, having been selected with regard to the persons and families referred to, or to anything otherwise interesting.

VOL. I. (1584—1666).

It will be observed that the entries, usually in English and sometimes ill-written and ill-spelt, begin in 1630 to be for a time in Latin, written in a clerkly hand, and evidently made by some classical scholar, not without a touch of pedantry. Now about this time "Sir John Watson" was succeeded as Curate of the parish by Mr. Elias Smith. The former is designated ("Mickleton MSS.," No. 32, "*De Canonicis Minoribus,*" p. 52) "Iohannes Watson, alias Sir Iohn Lack-Latin"; the latter is described *(Ibid.)* as "Archididascalus Scolae Gram. Dunelm post Ricardum Smelt Clericum," having been also a Minor Canon and Precentor of the Cathedral, and Librarian to the Dean and Chapter. To this learned man may perhaps be attributed the Latin entries. For, though they begin some two years before the date assigned by Surtees to his incumbency, he may even so have previously assisted good Sir John Lack-Latin in his parochial duties, including that of keeping the Register. May we not imagine him correcting Sir John as the schoolmaster Holofernes corrected the curate Sir Nathanael?—"*Sir Nath.:* Laus Deo. Intelligo bone. *Holof.:* Bone? Bone for bene. Priscian a little scratched: 'Twill serve." ("Love's Labour Lost," Act v, Sc. 1).

BAPTISMS. (*Extracted Entries*).

THE REGESTER BOOKE OF THE CHRISTNINGES, WEDDINGES AND BURYALLES OF THE PAISHE OF S. GILES IN DURHAM SINCE Y͏ᴱ YERE OF Oᴿ LORD 1584 FROM EASTER TO EASTER VIDELYCET.

A.D. 1584. 6. Cuthbert Prentisse sonne of Thomas prentisse was christined yͤ xxvjᵗʰ of December.[1]

---

[1] Entries of the name of Prentice (*al.* Prentize, Prentise, Prentisse) are included in these extracts because of a Robert Prentice having been a curate of St. Giles. His name occurs as such at Visitations under Bishop Barnes in 1577, 1578, and 1579. He was also Minor Canon of Durham from April, 1571, to 1595, and in 1583 was appointed by Henry Dethick, Prebendary of Durham and Official of the Dean and Chapter, as his Surrogate,

1588. 9. Marye prentisse daughter of Thomas prentisse was christined y[e] x[th] of November.

1591. 4. Ann murray daughter of Will'm murray Curate was christined y[e] viij[th] of Sept[r].[1]

1592. 1. Elizabeth prentisse daughter of Thomas prentisse was christined y[e] iiij[th] of June.

8. Agnes murray Daughter of Will'm murray Curate was christined the vij[th] of Januarie.

1593. 6. Jane prentisse Daughter of Thomas prentisse was christined Sept[r] xix.

1594. 9. Robert murray soune of Will'm murray Curate was christened the xij[th] of Maye.

1598. 9. Annas morlan daughter of Iohn morlan a bastert was christened the xij[th] of Maye.

1604. 7. George Carter Sonne of Iohn Carter sheriffs bayliffe was christened the xth day of June.

8. Iohn Heath Sonne of Thomas Heath of Farr Grange gent was christened at Pittington Church the last day of Sept[r]. Witnesses M[r] Iohn Heath the elder of Kepeyere Esquier And M[ris] Ann Bonney of Newland in Yorkshier.[2]

---

in which capacity he presided over the Court of the Officialty. (See Surtees Society's Publications, vol. lxxxiv, p. 22, note 1, and Appendices A. and B.). He is thus shown to have been a man of some mark. He is mentioned in the Will of John Binley (or Byndley), a Minor Canon of Durham, and Vicar of Muggleswick, given in the Surtees Society's Publications (vol. ii, p. 217). It hence appears that he was the eldest son of a Durham man called Prentise, apparently of the tradesman class, who had married Jane, the sister of the said John Binley. The testator, after several legacies, including 6s. 8d. to "the poure peapele of the parriche of Sanct Giles," leaves his residue to "Robert Prentes, William P., Thomas P., Rychart P., and Isabell P., my sister's children." To Robert, who seems to have been bred a scholar, he leaves appropriately all his books, together with the bed he lies on, and other articles. The rest appear to have occupied no high position. Provision is made for one of them, William, on being apprenticed to "John Chilton of Durham, taler." Thomas, the baptisms of whose children appear here in the Register, was a younger brother of Robert, being the third son, to whom John Bynley, the testator, had left £6 13s. 4d. and "all my stufe at Muggleswick, &c."

[1] For notice of William Murray see "Grassmen's Accounts," p. 15, note 3.

[2] Thomas Heath was a grandson of the original John Heath of Kepyer, being the second son of the John who was at this time in possession. Far (or East) Grange is what appears on the Ordnance Map as Kepyer Grange, near the present Grange Iron Works, West Grange (elsewhere mentioned) being what is now known as High Grange, nearer to Kepyer, where an old grange barn still remains. Mistress Ann Bonney was no doubt a relative of Dorothy, the wife of the abovesaid Thomas Heath, who was a daughter of Richard Bonney, of Newland, in Yorkshire. This baptism is entered in

10. Ann Heath daughter of M[r] Iohn Heath of Ramsyde[1] was Christened the iii[th] day of March in the yeare Abovesaid.

A.D. 1606. 5. Margarett Colson daughter of Iohn Colsen cooke was christened the first day of June.

6. Elizabeth heath daughter of M[r] Iohn heath of Ramsyde was christened the 13 day of July in the yeare Abovesaid.

17. Edward smyth sonne of Iohn smyth challan weaver was christined the xxij[th] day of marche in the yeare Abovesaid.

A.D. 1607. 7. Jane Crofton daughter of Anthoney crofton yonger A bastard was christined the xviij[th] day of october.

9. Thomas Hethe Sonne of M[r] Thomas heath of Fargrange was christined the Firste day of November in the yere Abovesaid. Godfathers—M[r] Thomas Chator of Butterbie And M[r] Iohn Kinge of Durham; Godmother M[ris] Margarett Heath.

11. Edward heath Sonne of M[r] Iohn heath of Ramsyde was christined the vi[th] day of december in the yeare Abovesaid.

A.D. 1608. 18. Dorothy heth daughter of M[r] Iohn heth of Ramsyde was christined y[e] 29 daye of Januarie.

19. Elizabeth heth Daughter of M[r] Thomas heth was christined the vth day of feabruarie in the yere Abovesaid.

A.D. 1609. 4. Henry heth Sonne of M[r] Thomas heth was christined the xii[th] day of Feabruarie in the yeare Abovesaid.

the register of the parish of Pittington as follows:—"Anno 1604. Iohn Heth sonne of Mr Thomas Heth of Powden grange within St Gyles parishe was xpistened here att Pittington Churche the xxvth of September. Godfathers Mr Iohn Heth of Keepyere the elder and Iohn Heth of Ramside. Godmother Maris An Bunny of Newlands." It thus appears that "Far Grange" was also known as "Powden Grange." The Bunnys of Newland, in the parish of Normanton, were a family of some importance. Their burial-place was the chapel on the South side of the chancel of Normanton Church, where there are brasses dated from 1547 to 1586. ("Banks's Walks in Yorkshire," 1871, pp. 229, 233).

[1] Ramside Grange was close on the Eastern boundary of the Kepyer estate, being where now stands the mansion bearing the modern fancy name of Belmont, from which the new parish of Belmont has been named. The name Ramside is now obsolete; but in Forster's Map of the County, dedicated to Bishop Butler, and to be seen in the Dean and Chapter Library, the place is still so designated. Ramside was devised in the Will of the first John Heth of Kepyer to his youngest son Edward and his heirs male, of whom this John was the son and heir.

A.D. 1610. 1. Barbarie Lever daughter of M[r] Thomas Lever gentleman nowe dwellinge at Kepeyere was christined the 29 day of marche.

15. Thomazine hethe daughter of M[r] Thomas heth of Farr Graunge[1] was christined the third day of feabruarie.

A.D. 1612. 1. Marye heth daughter of M[r] Thomas heth was christined the xiij[th] day of Aprill in the yere Abovesaid.

A.D. 1613. 10. Perker heth Sonne of M[r] Thomas heth of Far Graunge was christined the xxvij[th] day of december.

A.D. 1614. 1. Marye prentice daughter of Cuthbert prentice carpinter was christined y[e] 27 of Marche.

5. Ann hall daughter of William hall of Ramsyde was christined at Ramsyde by Rayson of weaknes the ix[th] day of october.

7. Nycholas heth Sonne of M[r] Topp heth gent[2] was christined the xviij[th] day of december.

A.D. 1615. 11. Edwarde Heth Sonne of M[r] Thomas Heth was christined the vth day of Nov[r].

13. Willyam Heth Sonne of M[r] Topp heth was christined the xth day of december.

1616. 11. Ann heth daughter of M[r] Thomas heth gent was christined the 24 of November.

13. Robert prentice sonne of Cuthbert prentice carpinter was christined the 20 day of Januarij.

1619. 5. Will'm Blaxton sonne of M[r] Iohn Blaxton gent was xp'ined the 17 day of August.

1620. 1. Margarett Crawdocke daughter of Richard Crawdocke gent was christined y[e] xxvj[th] day of Marche in the yere Abovesaid.

1621. 8. Robert Watson sonne of S[r] Iohn Watson curate of S[t] Gilles was christined y[e] xvj[th] day of December.[3]

1625. 7. Jean Fresse the daughter of Henrie Fresse Souderer (*i.e.*, *solderer*) Christined the ix daye of october.

---

[1] See above, p. 124, note 2.

[2] Nicholas, the second son of the original John Heath of Kepyer, had married Ann, daughter of Mr. John Topp, of London, and had purchased Little Eden in the parish of Easington. The Mr. Topp Heath of this entry was his eldest son. (See Surtees' History of Durham, vol. i, p. 38, and vol. iv, pt. ii, p. 71).

[3] For notice of Sir John Watson see "Grassmen's Accounts," p. 19, note 2, also p. 123 above.

1627. Chrestenings from Easter to Ester 1627.

3. Francies Helyard daughter to Mr Crestofer Helyard of Keper was crisned the 10 day of May, 1627.

4. An Heeth daughter to Iohn Heeth of Ramside was Crisned the 13 day of May, 1627.

1628. Christenyngs twext Ester & Ester in Anno 1628 (*six entries*).

1629. Chrisnings from Ester to Ester in Anno 1629 (*ten entries*).

1630. *The entries now begin to be in Latin. See above, p. 123.*

Elizabeth filia Ægidii Atchison baptizata fuit quarto die Aprilis. Georgius Jackson & Thomas Jackson gemini & filii Gualteri Jackson Baptizati erant decimo tertio die Septembris. Elizabetha filia Jacobi Hodshon pistoris baptizata erat septimo die Novembris. Iohannes filius Mri Edwardi Smurthwaite Clerici baptizatus erat vicesimo tertio die Decembris.

1631. Anna filia Francisci Pearson sutoris baptizata fuit decimo nono die Maij die Ascentionis. Jacobus filius Johannis Bambridge generosi baptizatus fuit secundo die Junij. Margereta filia Abrahami Bambrick molitoris baptizabatur octavo die Januarij. Johannes filius Mathaei Burrow sartoris baptizabatur quinto die Februarij.

1632. Thomas filius Johannis Colson Carbonarij baptizabatur vicesimo quinto die Junij. Gulielmus Filius Roberti Barker sartoris baptizabatur vicesimo sexto die Junij. Elizebetha filia Richardi Corneforth Restionis baptizabatur vicesimo octavo die Octobris. Robertus filius Richardi Corneforth stragulorum textoris baptizabatur vicesimo septimo die Januarij. Isabella White notha [1] baptizabatur decimo septimo die Martij.

1633. Anna Stott filia illegitima Johannis Stott baptizabatur decimo die Junij. Anthonius filius supposititius Iohannis Ducket baptizabatur secundo die Martij.

1634. Elizabetha Filia Simonis Arnot Londinensis baptizabatur duodecimo die Octobris.

---

[1] It may be observed that illegitimate births, which about this period are less unfrequent than might have been wished, are denoted in English by "basterd," and in Latin by "spurius," "nothus," "fil-illegit.," or "fil-suppositit.," and that, when (as is usual) the name of one parent only is given, it is always that of the father.

1636. Thomas filius Nicolai Cole[1] de Keypere generosi baptizabatur primo die Septembris. Henricus filius Henrici Iohnson fullonis baptizabatur vicesimo nono die Octobris. Gulielmus filius Gulielmi Buston spurius Baptizabatur secundo die Januarij. Robertus filius Thomae Heath generosi baptizabatur vigesimo primo die Februarij.

1637. Elizabetha filia Roberti Barker operarii Bapt. 31 Maij. Robertus filius Roberti Colson coqui Baptiz. 21 Septemb. Iohannes filius Christopheri Barker mercatoris baptizabatur 24 Septembris. Margareta filia Iohannis Gray piscatoris Bapt. 28 Janu.

1638. Thomas filius Iohannis Peele carbonarii. Elizabetha filia Roberti Dobson piscatoris Baptizabatur 25º die Septembris. Richardus filius Simonis Martin agricolae baptizabatur primo die Novembris. Dorothea filia Thomae Heath Generosi baptiz. 2º die Decembris. Margareta filia Henrici Johnson fullonis baptiz. 16 die Decembris. Tobias filius Johannis Wilkinson vitratrij baptiz. 22º die Januarij. Robertus filius Roberti Heighington Pellionis baptiz. 15º die Martij.

1639. Margareta Spuria Nicolai Carre & Franciscae Bayly bapt. 23º Februarij.

1641. Iohannes filius Gulielmi Heath[2] generosi baptiz. 20º die Martij.

1642. Anna filia Roberti Richardson tibicinis baptiz. 4º die Maij.

---

[1] The Cole family came into possession of Kepyer as follows. The main estate, exclusive of such parts of it as had been devised to younger sons by the first John Heath, passed after his death to his eldest son John, and from him to a third John, the son of the latter. On the death of Thomas, the only son of this third John, in 1594 (see Register of Burials), it passed to Thomas Heath, of Far Grange, who was brother to the said third John. He, after coming into possession, sold the mansion house and appendages of Kepyer to Ralph Cole, of Gateshead, A.D. 1630. (See Surtees' History of Durham, vol. iv, pt. 2, p. 66). Consequently Kepyer itself became the residence of the Coles, the Heaths being thenceforth described as not of Kepyer, but of Old Durham, which they owned as impropriators of the Rectory of St. Nicholas, of which Old Durham had been glebe. Sir Nicholas and Sir Ralph Cole in the entry before us were the son and the grandson of the Ralph of Gateshead, to whom Kepyer had been sold. Kepyer remained in the possession of the Cole family till about 1674, when Sir Ralph Cole, of Brancepeth, sold it to Sir Christopher Musgrave, of Carlisle, Bart., to whose descendants it now belongs.

[2] This William may have been the son of Mr. Topp Heath of Little Eden whose baptism appears above in 1615.

Baptismata 1643.

[A blank page follows, and no more entries till 1651, nor any for 1652; nor again any in this book, except two for 1667 and 1668 respectively, which are on a blank page at the end of the book in English. For reasons see above, p. 68, note 2].

1651. Edmondus Cole filius Radolphi Cole Armigeri filii maximi natu Nicolai Cole de Keeper Equitis et Baronetti baptizabatur undecimo die Septembris Anno Domini 1651. Iohannes filius Iohannis Tempest Armigeri baptizabatur 22° die Decembris 1651. Thomas filius Thomae Moore generosi baptizabatur vicesimo septimo die Januarij 1652. Lancelotus filius Lanceloti Taylor Stannarii baptizabatur Julij 28, 1651. Carolus filius Caroli Wren Armigeri baptizabatur Augusti 3° 1652.

1653. Thomas filius Roberti Grey Generosi baptizabatur Octobris 4° 1653. Gulielmus filius Iohannis Tempest Armigeri baptizabatur Januarij 31° 1653. Nicolays filius Radulphi Cole Armigeri baptizabatur vicesimo octavo die Februarij 1653. Maria filia Thomae Foster Armigeri baptizabatur Vicesimo Octavo die Februarij, 1653.

The following are entered separately after the rest :—

Baptismata in parochiâ Magdalenensi.

[Eight baptisms, entered in Latin, viz., one for 1636, one for 1637, two for 1638, and two without mention of the year. Then one in English for 1666, one in 1667, and lastly, Abraham Alleson sune of Abraham Allison was Baptysed the 5th day of february Anno Dom. 1668].

MARRIAGES (1584—1642) (*Extracted Entries*).

WEDDINGS SENCE THE YERE OF OR LORDE GOD 1584, YERELY AS FOLLOWETH :—

1. Robert Johnson was marryed with Isabell Birkett the xxijth day of November in ye yere Abovesaid.

1590. 7. Mr Thomas Lever was maryed with mistres Thomazin heth[1] att Kepeyere the ixth day of November.

1591. 1. William murray Curate of St Gyles was maryed with Elizabeth Orde the xxtie day of aprill.

---

[1] This Thomazin was a daughter of the second John Heath of Kepyer. See *Heath Pedigree.*

9

1613. 1. Cuthbert prentisse carpinter was maryed wth Margarett Hurdman the xix^th day of January.

1614. Thomas patteson And Jane deanam was maryed in the parishe churche of St Andrewes in the wardrobe in london as by a certifecat derected by ye minister of the saide parishe unto the curate of St Giles parishe in durham by vertue of a lysene procured from my Lords grace of canterbar the said Jane beinge heare a parishioner Was mared the sixt day of September 1614.

1628. George Middleton Gentleman was married with Elizabeth[1] ye daughter of Thomas Heath Esquire ye 30 day of December 1628.

1629. Edwardus Smaithwait clericus in Artibus Baccalaureus uxorem duxit Elizabetham Simson 22° die Decembris 1629.

[*N.B.—Here begin the Latin entries. See p. 123*].

1630. Christopherus Barker Generosus Eboracensis uxorem duxit Thomasinam filiam Iohannis Heath de Ramside generosi decimo octavo die Aprilis.

1630. Iohannes Smith viduus vxorem duxit Margeretam Watson relictam Iohannis Watson ecclesiae Cath. Dunelm. minoris canonici et huius ecclesiae capellani vicessimo octavo die Septembris.

Richardus Kidney saltator & Elizabetha Coussons conubiali vinculo juncti erant die decimo sexto februarij.

1631. Lanceletus Scrafton generosus cives Eboracensis uxorem duxit Thomasin filiam secundam Thomae Heath Armigeri decimo die Augusti.

Thomas Easterbeus (*Easterby?*) uxorem duxit &c.

Richardus Hicks magister in artibus & clericus uxorem duxit Dorotheam filiam Johannis Heath generosi de Ramside decimo quinto die Decembris 1631.

1634. Richardus Bell Generosus uxorem duxit Annam filiam minimam natu Thomae Heath Armigeri decimo octavo die Augusti.

1636. 15. Nicolavs Hobson Cantor Laicus ecclesiae Cathedralis Dunelmensis aetatis suae Anno 82° vxorem duxit Annam Ramsdon viduam decimo nono Januarii.

---

[1] See A.D. 1608 for the baptism of this Elizabeth.

16. Thomas Emerson mercator pannarius vxorem duxit Graciam Walton filiam Nicolai Walton Artium Magistri vigesimo quarto die Januarii.

1637. Gulielmus Rumford operarius uxorem duxit Annam Morley gravidam 4° die Februarij.

1638. Iohannes Elves Generosus parochiae de Bedlington uxorem duxit Annam Ingleby viduam aetate provectam 29° Novembris.

1639. Iohannes Rowell Latomus uxorem duxit Elizabetham Ellison. 2° die Novembris.

1642. Iohannes Tempest Armiger uxorem duxit Elizabetham filiam unicam Iohannis Heath armigeri 27° die Octobris.[1]

1643. Gulielmus Orde de Houghton in Le Spring vxorem duxit Margaretam Bailey. 8° die Maii.

1648. Thomas Wilson musicis professor uxorem duxit Margaretam Colpots. Maii 25, 1648.

1649. Carolus Wren Armiger uxorem Duxit Peregrinam Fetherstonhalgh. Decemb. 28, 1649.

Radulphus Bowes Armiger uxorem duxit Margaretam Cradock. Januarii 29° 1649.

1650. Robertus Gray generosus uxorem duxit Annam filiam primogenitam Gulielmi James Ecclae. Cath. Dunelm. prebendarii. Aprill 25, 1650.

1653. Henricus Nettleton de Leeds uxorem duxit Franciscam filiam Richardi Mar. August 8, 1653.[2]

---

[1] This was the marriage by which the Tempests came into possession of Old Durham and the Manor of St. Giles. The John Heath, whose heiress his daughter Elizabeth was, had been himself the only son and heir of Thomas Heath, originally of East Grange, who had succeeded his brother, the third John Heath of Kepyer, as possessor of the estates on the death of Thomas, the only son of the latter, in 1594. (See above, p. 128, note 1). It was the said Thomas who, with his wife Dorothy, and John, their son and heir, alienated Kepyer to the Coles.

[2] It is significant of the state of things during the Parliamentary war and the Commonwealth that from 1643 to 1653 inclusive only 14 marriages are recorded, and all these of persons of superior position, described in most cases as armiger, generosus, clericus, musicis professor, &c. ; and that from 1653 to the Restoration there are none, the civil marriages that would take place during the Commonwealth not having been recorded in the Parish Register. On a later page in this volume (after the Terrier given below) there are 23 marriages, after the Restoration, in the years 1664-66, with one in 1662 out of place ; also one of 1637 " in Ecclesia Sanctae Mariae Magdalenae," and 7 baptisms, 1636-66, in the same parish.

BURIALS (*Extracted Entries*).

BURYALLS SINCE THE YEAR OF Oᴿ LORD 1584 YERELY AS FOLLOWETH.

1584.   Francis Heath infant was buryed the xxj[th] day of november.

1.   Phillis yonger was buryed yᵉ xix[th] of July.

1589.   Christopher Booth infant sonne of Mr. Booth of old Durham[1] was buryed the vth day of July.

1589.   (42).   A child of Thomas Prentisse buryed November 7.

1589.   *After entry 2 (August 8th) is this note,* Plague began the first tyme in gelegait; *after entry 44 (Nov. 19th),* Plauge ceased.

1590.   1.   Jane Prentice was buryed the xxv[th] of Aprill.

8.   The right Worshipfull Mr Iohn Hethe of Kepeyere Esquire was buried the xi[th] day of August in the yere abovesaid. [2]

---

[1] Old Durham had been glebe of the Rectory of St. Nicholas, which was appropriated to Kepyer Hospital by Bishop Neville A.D. 1443. Ralph Booth, Master of Kepyer, leased it A.D. 1479 on a lease of 99 years to his brother Richard Booth. The lease would expire in 1578, when it reverted to John Heath as the then impropriator. It appears from this entry that the Booths had continued to reside there for some time afterwards.

[2] This was the original John Heath of Kepyer, who had purchased the estates of the dissolved Hospital from John Cockburn, lord of Ormeston, in 1568. There is a recumbent effigy, supposed to be his, in the chancel of St. Giles, in the South East corner within the Altar-rails. It is a painted wooden figure, with head uncovered, resting on a helmet, on which is the crest, a cock's head attached by a wreath. The body is clothed in a complete suit of plate armour ; hands in gauntlets, placed with palms together over the breast, as in prayer. Around the neck, appearing from beneath the armour, is a red collar with slits all round, also a small laced frill or linen ruff. The face is represented with a moustache and short pointed beard ; the eyes are open. A sheathed sword is slung around the body by a red strap. The breast-plate, of the sixteenth century, extends from the neck to the pubes. Around the lower edge of the breastplate is a gilt edging (or strap ?). Many of the joints, pins and fastenings of the armour are gilt. Spurs with rowells are attached by red straps. The feet, which are not crossed, rest upon a support, on which are carved representations of two death's heads. On the upper part of the support, the words "*Hodie michi*"; below, "*cras tibi.*" The effigy now rests upon a sort of high tomb of oak, substituted in 1894 for a very mean one of painted deal. Below the head is a shield with a guige. This shield, as appeared from a date on its inner surface (seen when it was taken off the deal box in 1894), was put on about 40 years ago, probably when the deal box aforesaid was made. The arms on the shield are :—Party per chev. or and sa., in chief 2 mullets, in base a heath-cock wattled gu., countercharged. Crest on helmet :— On a wreath, a heath-cock's head erased sa., wattled gu

1594. 3. Thomas heath sonne of Mr Iohn heath the yonger [1] was buryed the 39 of June.

1597. *After entry 14 is this note:* Plague began the Second tyme; *after entry 126,* Plague ceases.

[*N.B.—There are 134 burials in this year, the largest number in any former year having been 47, viz., in 1589, the first year of the plague. The average number in ordinary years is not more than 20*].

1599. 5. Edward Heath of Ramsyde gent. was buryed the xxivth day of Sept.

1603 to 4. 6. Alice Prentisse wedowe was buryed the vth day of January.

A° Dom 1604.

1. Robert Prentisse bachler was buryed the xvij day of aprill in the yere abovsaid.

5. Annas Frissell wyfe of Rychard Frisell Fuller was Buryed ye vth day of September. Dyed of the plauge.

7. Grace Handlawe daughter of Mr Handlaw deceased was buryed the viijth day of Septr dyed of the plauge. *Opposite this entry*, plauge began. [*After No. 16 of the 26 entries in this year "plauge" or "pla'" is appended; and after entry No. 20 (Nov. 8th) "pla' ceased." But four more entries after this have again "pla'" appended, till the last, viz., No. 26, which see below*].

8. Cuthbert Huegeson apprentice to Rychard Frissell Fuller was buryed the xvjth day of September.—pla'.

10. Elizabeth watson daughter of Iohn Watson clarke and curate of St Giles was buryed the 18 of Sept^r.—pla'.

11. Rychard frissell fuller dyed the 23 day of September and was buryed at magdlens the same day & yere Abovesaid.—pla'.

12. Annas Helcott daughter of Iohn helcote labourer dyed at Kepeyere the xxvth day of Sept^r & was buryed at magdlens the same day and yere Abovesaid.—pla'.

19. Nell mewer servant to Mr Watson Curaite of St Giles was buryed the vjth day of November.—pla'.

22. Xpofer ourde Labourer was buryed the iiijth day of Jan. in ye yere Abovesaid.—pla'.

23. A child of ye said Xpofer ourde was buryed ye xixth day of Januarie.—pla'.

[1] This John Heath the younger was the third John of Kepyer, grandson of the original possessor, *i.e.*, of "the Right Worshipfull Mr. John" of the last entry. It was by the early death of his son Thomas, here recorded, that the Kepyer estate passed to his brother Thomas. See above, p. 128, note 1, and p. 131, note 1.

24. Another child of yᶜ foresaid Xpofer—was buryed the xxij^th day of Januarie.—pla'.

25. Dorotie ourde daughter of yᶜ said Xpofer ourde was buryed yᶜ 24 day of Januarie.—pla'.

26. Ann Orde wyffe of the foresaid Christofor Ourde was Buried the xxv^th day of Januarij so all the hole housholde dyed in the visitacion at this tyme and so yᶜ plauge ceased.

1609. 4. Ann Heath wyfe of Mr Iohn Heath of Ramsyde was Buryed the 23 day of July in the yeare aforesaid.

9. Henry heth infant sonne of Mr Thomas heth of yᵉ Far Grange was Buryed the xth day of march.

1612. 8. The Worshopfull Mistrice Elizabeth heth wyfe of the Right Wor Mr Iohn heth the elder of Kepeyere Esquer [1] was Buryed the 21 day of october in the yere Abovesaid.

1613. 4. Iohn Trotter An informer was Buryed the second day of June.

15. A poore woman was buryed the vj^th day of Januarie found dead on gelegait moore perished upon a tempesteous night of snowe which was the xviij^th day of december.

1615. 5. Iohn peerson aged [2] was buryed at Madglens the xij^th day of June in the yere Abovesaid.

1617. 15. The Right Worshopfull Master Iohn Heth of Kepeyere Esquire was Buried the xxviij^th day of Januarij in the yere Abovesaid.

1618. 2. Margarett Heth daughter of Mr Thomas heth of yᵉ East grange infant was xp'ined & buryed both upon the 12th day of Aprill 1618.

1621. 7. Ann heth daughter of Iohn heth of Ramsyde gent was buryed yᶜ 22 of Nov.

1622. 6. Margaret hall wedowe was burred the fift of Januarie. [3]

---

[1] Viz., the second John Heath of Kepyer, son of the original possessor. His own burial is recorded below, A.D. 1617.

[2] In ordinary cases of persons far advanced in life the age is not given, being probably seldom known. They are usually described, as here, as "aged," or, when the entries are in Latin, as "provecta aetate."

[3] Surtees (*History of Durham*, vol. iv), in his extracts from the Registers of St. Giles, gives erroneously 1632 as the year of Margaret Hall's death, and £30 as her bequest instead of 30s.

Md that the foresaid Margarett hall wedow laite wyf of Edwarde hall deceased did give to this parishe for a standinge stock the some of xxxs and the increase of the same to be bestowed in repairinge of the cawsie from Giles brigge to the cawsie foot[1] betwext the therde daye of Maye and the fower and twentye daye June or itt to returne to the executors.

1627. 4. The worll Mr Nicholas heth[2] who died in the south baily in Durham of the age of 72 yeres was buryed att St Gyles here the xiij day of July 1627.

1630. [*The entries now begin to be in Latin. See p. 129*].

Roger Richardson tibicen sepultus fuit quinto die Aprilis. Francisca filia Nicolai Heath generosi sepulta fuit decimo quinto die Martij.

1631. Dorothea uxor Iohannis Heath Armigeri[3] matrona pia et casta totum totius vitae suae terminum postquam annum septuagesimum attigisset in domino decessit decimo nono die Octobris.

Georgius Taylor Corarius sepeliebatur vicesimo quinto die Decembris, i.e. die nativitatis Xti.

1632. Filius Grangeri Chater infans & non baptizatus sepeliebatur decimo secundo die Junii.

Robertus Baker piscium venditor . . . .
Iohannes Colson coquus . . . .
Edvardus Corneforth Restio . . . .
Gulielmus Bainbridge mellitor . . . .
Edmundus Smyth aedituus . . . .

Sybilla Tomson malae famae vetula in ergastulo mortua hoc in Coemeterio sepeliebatur decimo secundo die Februarij.

1635. Richardus Robinson κοσκινοποιὸς[4] . . . .

1636. Jana filia Richardi Corneforth scoenoploci[5] . .

---

[1] For the locality of " Giles brigge " (or Gillsbridge), see p. 10, note 2.

[2] No doubt Nicholas, second son of the first John Heath of Kepyer, and ancestor of the Heaths of Little Eden. See above. His will, proved at Durham, is dated 28th June, 1627. (Surtees' History of Durham, vol. iv, pt. ii, p. 70).

[3] This was the third John Heath of Kepyer. (See above, p. 132, note 3). His wife, Dorothy, whose burial is here recorded, was a daughter of John Blakiston, of Blakiston, Esq. See Surtees' History of Durham, vol. iv, pt. ii, p. 70, in *Heath Pedigree*.

[4] The Greek word denotes a *sieve-maker*, and may be meant as an equivalent for *searer*, which occurs elsewhere in the English entries.

[5] Evidently meaning the Greek σχοινοπλόκος, presumably for *roper*. *Cf.* above " Edwardus Cornforth, *Restio*." The Cornforth family seems to have been engaged in the rope-making industry, which has continued in the parish.

1638. Anna King matrona pia et devota aetatis suae anno nonagisimo naturae concessit et sepulta est vigesimo tertio die Septembris. Gulielmus Inops mendicus vagabundus sepeliebatur ultimo die Januarij.

1639. Iohannes Heath de Keepeyr Armiger[1] vir pius, pauperum pater, et hujus Ecclesiae benefactor, Poculum enim Argenteum (quo Sanguis Christi preciosissimus populo potandus exhibetur) cum operculo Huic Ecclesiae dono dedit, naturae concessit sexto die Januarij (Anno Aetatis suae 71º) et sepeliebatur die sequente circa quartam horam matutinam.

1642. Dorothea Heath uxor Thomae Heath Armigeri[2] matrona pia ac multis virtutibus ornata sepeliebatur 17º die Maij.

Sepulturae 1643. [*Followed by two blank pages, and no further entries of burials till September, 1661, when they are resumed illiterately in English, not consecutively, and only seven till 1665. They include*

1664. Iohn Heath Esqre of ould Durham[3] was buried the 7th of March 1664.

---

[1] See above, p. 132, note 3. The reason of his burial by night, immediately after his death, does not appear. The cup and cover, intended, as was usual, to serve as a paten, are of the usual Elizabethan shape, without any ornament. The Hall-marks denote the years 1637-1638. Round the base of the cup there is this inscription :— "Remember Iohn Hethe Esqr the third and last of Keepeire (*the i altered to y*) : 1638." On the foot of the cover, underneath, "Desember the : 25th : 1638."

[2] The Thomas, originally of Far Grange, who succeeded his brother John as possessor of Kepyer, and who (with the concurrence of his wife Dorothy, and his son John) sold Kepyer to the Coles. See above, p. 128, note 1. Thenceforth, as abovesaid, the Heaths were described as of Old Durham.

[3] This was the son of Thomas and Dorothy, referred to in the last note, whose daughter and heiress, Elizabeth, married John Tempest of the Isle. The wife of this John Heath of Old Durham was Margaret, daughter of William Smith, of Durham, Counsellor-at-Law. They were married at St. Mary-le-Bow, 27th October, 1623. She is memorable as having been one of the three "gentlewomen" whom Cosin was accused of having insulted in the Cathedral for not standing up when the Nicene Creed was being sung.
The following account of what took place on that occasion will be found in the Volume for 1868 of the Surtees Society's Publications :
" Articles to be exhibited by His Majestie's Heigh Commissioners against Mr. John Cosin, &c. And another tyme you, John Cosin, sayd to some gentlewomen, sitting quietly when the others stood when the Nicene creed is song, you, I say, goinge to theire pue, sayd in the audience of many, ' I pray you stand, I pray you stand '; and catching a gentlewoman by the sleeve, you tare her sleeve, with these reprochfull words, ' Can ye not stand, ye lazie sowes ? '

After the last entry of a baptism (1668) in this volume there is inserted the following Terrier:—

A register or terrier of all ye Burgages & tenements which belong to ye Church of St Giles for ye reparation thereof. 1637.

1. Imprimis a Burgage or tenement & garth on ye North side of Gilligate between A tenement belonging to ye Deane & Chapter of Durham in ye tenure of Toby Hudspeth on ye East & a tene- 10s. 0d. ment belonging to ye Church of St Giles & in ye occupation of Richard Robinson on ye west. Let to W^{ll} Hubbock.

2. It. one tenement & garth on ye North side of Gilligate between a tenement belonging to ye Church of St Giles in ye Occupation of W^{ll} Hubbock on ye East & another tenement belonging to ye 8s. 0d. sayd Church in ye tenure of W^{ll} Bambrick on ye West. Let to Ric. Robinson.

3. It. one tenement & Garth on ye North side of Gilligate between a tenement belonging to ye Church of St Giles & in ye tenure of Ric. Robin- son on ye East and another tenement belonging to 5s. 6d. Francis Pearson which is is free Land on ye West. Let to W^{ll} Bambrick.

4. It. one tenement & garth on ye North side of Gilligate in ye occupation of Iohn Busby, lying between a tenement belonging to Margaret 10s. 0d. Chilton on ye East & a tenement belonging to Thomas Busby on ye West.

5. Item a tenement & Garth (in ye Occupa- tion of Sissely Renton boundering on a tenement belonging to George Man on ye west, & another

---

Again, from Smart's Common-Place Book :—

"*Question.*—With whom did Mr. Cosin brawle and fight in the time of divine service for the observation of ceremonies ?

"*Answer.*—(1) He brawled in the church with the Dean himself about the gentlewomen which would not stand when he bade them ; whose pew he locked up, and afterwards nailed, because they would not stand, &c.

"(2) He called the same gentlewomen lazie sows, and tare their sleaves, because they refused to stand, Mrs. Smith, and her daughter Heath, and her son Mr. Baker's wife of Newcastle."

Mrs. Smith, the mother of Mrs. Heath, was, when married to Smith, the widow of Oswald Baker, of the city of Durham. Thus the three gentle-women were (1) Mrs. Smith, of Durham, (2) her daughter by her second marriage, who was the wife of John Heath, of Old Durham, (3) the wife of her son by her first marriage, viz., Mrs. Baker, of Newcastle.

tenement belonging in to ye Church of St Giles in ye Occupation of Iohn Ducket on ye East) with a parcell of ground in ye broad close butting upon ye sayd tenement & garth, on ye north side of Gilligate.

6. Item a tenement & Garth (in ye Occupation of Iohn Ducket) on ye North side of Gilligate betwixt two tenements belonging to ye Church of St Giles viz. ye one in ye Occupation of Sissely Renton on ye West & another in ye Occupation of Rowland Robson on ye East.

7. Item, one tenement & garth on ye North side of Gilligate in ye Occupation of Rowland Robson boundering on a tenement Belonging to ye Church of St Giles in ye occupation of Iohn Ducket on ye west, & a waist or parcell of ground belonging to George Man on ye East.

8. Item, a tenement & Garth on ye North side of Gilligate neare ye Duck poole in ye occupation of George Rowel, boundering on a waist or parcell of Ground belonging to George man on ye west & A parcell of Ground belonging to Edward Burdisse on ye East.

9. Item, one tenement & garth on ye South side of Gilligate in ye tenure of Mr Hugh Walton boundering on a tenement belonging to ———— on ye East & belonging to ———— on ye West. The sayd Tenement hath five riggs of Land belonging unto it, two riggs where of doe bounder on ye Garth of ye sayd tenement on ye North, & on Pellay wood on ye South, and a parcell of ground belonging to Iohn Smith on ye West, & a rigg of land belonging to the sayd Mr Hugh Walton on ye East. The other three riggs lye in ye broade close & doe bounder on ye Dean & Chapters Land on ye East, & on ye West, & on ye North, & upon Gilligate Common on ye South.

10. Item one tenement & garth on ye South side of Gilligate in ye Occupation of Cutbert Swinburne boundering on a tenement belonging to ———— on ye East, & another tenement belonging to Peter Booth on ye West.

11. It. A parcell of land on ye North side of Gilligate (where on there stood a Burgage) boundering upon a Close belonging to ye Deane & Chapter & in the tenure of W^{lt} Mawer on ye West, & a tenement belonging to Iohn Shipherd-son of Bp. Warmouth & in ye Occupation of of Iohn Wilkinson on ye East, & butting on Gilligate Street on ye South and on Magdalenes lane on ye North.   Let to George Greeveson.   5*s*. o*d*.

12. Item one Parcell of ground in ye Ellesse Leazes on ye North side of Gilligate called the Common Rigge (in ye occupation of W^{lt} Watson) boundering on a parcell of ground belonging to ye sayd W^{lt} Watson on ye West, & a Parcell of Ground belonging to ye Church of St Giles in ye uper end, & in ye Occupation of Timothy Hubbock on ye East & an other parcell of ground in ye lower end belonging to Mr Thomas Wanles like-wise on ye East, & butting at ye end of a waist belonging to ye Deane & Chapter & in ye tenure of Toby Hudspeth on ye South & extending downe-ward to a place of Common called ye Sands on ye North.   3*s*. 4*d*.

After this Terrier are entered the Marriages and Baptisms referred to above, p. 131, note 2: also five Burials from 1661 to 1664.

On another page, as follows :—

1636. Memorandum that Ralph Young gave ten pounds to ye Parish of St Giles in Durham for ye use of ye Poore : viz. That the Churchwardens chosen every yeare shall enter in bond before ye Minister & ye foure & twenty upon ye account day, that they shall deliver in ye sayd ten pound to the Churchwardens which shall succeed them yearly upon ye account day ; & pay interest for the sayd mony according to ye Kings rate allowed by statute, which interest mony shall be devided to ye poore, ye one halfe at Christmas & ye other halfe at Easter, According to ye discretion of ye Churchwardens, According to ye true intent & meaning of ye will.

(*Alia manu*) Memorand. that this Legacy was laid out on a parcel of ground for the use of the poore in Gylligate.

On the last page of the volume is the following list of books belonging to the church :—

Catalogus librorum qui pertinent ad ecclesiam Sancti Ægidii Dunelmensis.

Imprimis opera Juelli Episcopi Sari.

2. Paraphrasis Erasmi [1] in 4 Evangelia & acta apostolorum.

3. Tomus primus & secundus Homiliarum.

4. Canones ecclesiastici.

5. liber continens gratiarum actionem pro inauguratione regiae Majestatis.

6. liber continens gratiarum actionem pro liberatione regis et nobilium a pulvere sulphureo.

7. lib. continens Gratiarum actionem pro liberatione regis Jacobi a conspiratione Gouriana. [2]

8. Duo libri continentes formam jejunii ut deus a nobis avertat pestem & alia judicia.

9. Duo libri continentes deprecationes ut liberemur e manu Hostium ferocium.

10. Liber continens gratiarum actionem pro liberatione nostra a peste.

11. Injunctiones Reginae Elizabethae.

12. Biblia.

13. Duo libri precum communium.

---

[1] Ordered by Edward the Sixth's Injunctions to be set up in some convenient place within each parish church (Strype's "Cranmer," 1848, ii, 447). The first English edition was issued in two volumes by Edw. Whytchurch, 1548. About half-a-dozen English translators were employed upon it; among these, it is said, was the Princess Mary, afterwards Queen. (J. H. Blunt, "Hist. Ref.," ii, 51; Lowndes, and reff. there). Hence we find:—"1549. Una cum empcione diversorum librorum vocatorum paraphracez Erasmi" ("Memorials of Ripon," iii, 41); "1549. For a boke calld ye parafases" ("Leverton Accounts," in *Archæologia* xli, 358). The Paraphrases occur in several lists of books belonging to churches in Durham and the neighbourhood ("Parish Books," Surtees Society, vol. lxxxiv, Index *s.v.* Erasmus).

[2] The "Gowrie Conspiracy," alleged by James I to have been one against his own life by John, Earl of Gowrie, and his brother, at Perth, on 5th August A.D. 1600; for an account of which see Surtees Society's Publications, vol. lxxxiv, p. 137, note 3.

PARISH REGISTERS, Vol. II. (1667—1695).[1]

This booke was bouth (*bought*) by us Curchwardens of the parish of S[t] Gilles Robert Fairfax and Georg Robinson the 18 tenth (*eighteenth*)[2] year of our Soverine Lord the King Charles the second by the Grace of God King of England Scotland Franc and Ireland defender of the faith.

Elias Smith minister of this parish 1667.[3]

Clarke, Thomas Alleson of the parish of S[t] Gyles.

MARRIAGES (*Extracted Entries*).

1. Thomas Martten and Elizabeth Fell was maryed 4 day of May 1667.

There are six entries on what remains of the page, of which the bottom is torn off. The entries of marriages which follow are at the other end of the volume.

1669. Edward Coke and Ellener Heeth was maryed the 6th day of May.

1671. M[r] Thomas Cradock and M[rs] Doryty Heath was maryed the 21 of December.

After 2nd February, 1686, Delivered a Catalogue into y[e] Bishop's office.

1691. Alexander Davison Esq. and M[rs] Thomasine Nicholson were married upon Thursday y[e] 21th of May being Ascension day.

[1] These are the extreme dates of the entries in this volume. But there are omissions in some of the later years, which are partially supplied in Vol. III. Thus the Baptisms after 1680, the Burials from 5th July, 1678, to 16th October, 1680, and the Marriages for 1694, are found in Vol. III. The third volume, begun in 1678, appears to have been procured in the first place for the entry of duly attested burials in woollen, in pursuance of the Act 30 Car. II, which will be hereafter referred to, and to have been further utilized for supplying deficiences in Vol. II, and then for continuing the general register.

[2] *I.e.*, dating from the death of Charles I in 1649.

[3] For an account of him, see above, p. 3, and p. 62, note 2.

1692. Mr Wm Done Minister of St Gyles and Mrs Elizabeth Davies of West Chester [1] were married July ye seventeenth Anno D'ni 1692.[2]

1692. Walter Hair and Katherine Nixon were married December the 20th And was made the Parish clerk the year following.

CONJUGIA IN ANNO 1693, GULIELMO DONE CURATO.

Thomas Thompson de Parochia S'cti Oswaldi uxorem duxit Elizabetham Reed hujus parochiae primo die Maij, bannis pub.

Johannes Davison jun^r pellio duxit uxorem Elizabetham Brath in Ecclesia Cathedrali Dunelm. sexto die Junii.

Richardus Hall de Pittington duxit uxorem Izabellam Richardson de Parochia Easington 24° die Junij facultate datâ eodem die.

Will^s Salkeld de Aukland S^ti Andrei & Frances Hutchinson Capellaniae S'ctae Margaretae Dunelm. Conjugium inierunt connubiale 17° die August f. datâ.

Iohannes Hull Chirothecarius uxorem duxit Margaretam Starfield de parochia S'ctae Margaretae Dunelm. 16° die Novembris.

[The following entries, for 1694, are found in Vol. III].

MARRIAGES 1694.

Mark Haswell & Elizabeth Hutchinson both of Old Durham in ye Parish of St Oswalds were married at St Gyles's Durham ye first day of July 1694. Per Wm Done Curate. Memorand. it was ye first stampt Licence.

Mr Thomas Wilson & Mrs Ann Rodes were married ye last day of July 1694. Both of Elvett parish.

Mr Iohn Conyers & Margaret Baily Spinster both of Chester le Street were married Saturday the 22^d of September 1694.

Abraham Allenson of this Parish and Margaret Fisher of Elvett parish were married on St Luke's day being the 18th day of 8^ber 1694.

---

[1] Chester on the Dee was sometimes so called, and may be supposed to be intended here, to distinguish it from Chester-le-Street.

[2] William Done (al. Dun) was minister of the parish from 1691 to 1706, as appears from other entries in the register. See also List of Curates of St. Giles.

Thomas Heaviside of Keepyer and Jane Snowdon of ye Chappelry of Sadberge were married ye fourth day of March 1694.

[Entries of Marriages are continued in Vol. II to 25th May, 1895].

BAPTISMS AND BURIALS (*Extracted Entries*).

1668. 7. Wedow Chilton of Poullton Greinges[1] was Buryed the 4 day of May.

1669. Sir Nicholas Cooll Knight and Barrenet was Buryed the 17 day of Desember.

(No. 3). Anne Hepleton doughter of Robert Hepleton of West Grainge Bastard was Baptized the 20 day of July.

10. Mayry Bastter Doughter of Iohn Bastter Est Gra(*nge*) Bastard was Baptized the 4 day of November.

1670. Thomas Sun and Bastter of Jann Skages was Baptized the 9 day of October.

1671. tow Childeren of one Louders A pour man was buryed the 16 day of May. Ann Nellson wif of Iohn Nellson fouller (*fuller*) was Buryed the 18 day of June.

1673. A pour man that Lay at Thomas Readhead that dead one the Casse (*died on the Causeway*) was buryed the 30 day of March.

1674. Nicholas Coull sune of Sr Nicholas Coull was buryed the 29 of Aprill.

1675. A Child that Came from Line was buryed Aprill 14.

1676. A soulger that Lived in the Backhous was buryed the 19th day of August.

1678. William Houlden sun of Ihon Houlden of Marllen (*Magdalen*) parish was Baptized 3th day of november.

---

[1] The same with East (or Far) Grange on the old Kepyer estate. See above, p. 124, note 2.

*Subsequent entries of Burials till 16th October, 1680,
are found in Vol. III, being headed thus* [1] *:—*

August first 1678.

A true Regester of all such persons who were Buried
Att the parish Church of St Gyles since ye Act of parlament
came out For Buryeing in Sheeps Wooll onely is as
follows.

William Adam Reg^r

Tho : Allinson
     et   }Churchwardens.
Rich : Mawgham

———

Iohn Corby was buryed the 12th day of September (78)
Wittnes

Mr Major {Io^n Stothard
         {Cath. Sharpe

Ann Corby was Buryed first of Octtober 1678
Wittnes

Mr Major {Ann Beals
         {Isabell Foster

Cuthbart Wattson was Buryed 20th day of October
Wittnes

Mr Morlen {Dorothe Nickholson
         {Urseley Leper

---

[1] The reason why Burials at this date began to be entered in a new
volume has been shown above (p. 141, note 1). The entries are now signed by
the Mayor of Durham, or some person other than the Minister of the parish,
with the addition of the names of two witnesses. This, as has already been
intimated, was in pursuance of the Act 30 Car. II, which provided that, for
the encouragement of the woollen manufactures, no corpse should be buried
except in woollen ; requiring that within eight days after every burial one
of the relations of the party deceased, or other credible person, should bring
to the minister or parson an affidavit under the hands and seals of two or
more witnesses, and under the hand of the magistrate or officer before
whom the same was sworn, that the said person was not put in, wrapt, or
wound up in any material but sheeps' wool only ; the said affidavit to be
made before a Justice of the Peace, or Master in Chancery, Mayor, or other
chief officer of the County, borough, Corporation, or market town where the
party was buried. Afterwards (32 Car. II, A.D. 1681) it was further provided that in the absence of any Justice of the Peace resident in any
parish where a person had been interred the parsons, vicars or curates
within the County (except only those of the parish or chapel of ease where
the party is interred) might administer the said oaths or affidavits.

Forty-seven similar entries follow, in each case attested by " Mr. Major," " Mr. Hutchison, Mayor," " Mr. Morland," or " Mr. Davison," with the names of two witnesses ; the last being—

Mary Wade was Buried 27th November (1680).

Wittness
Mr Morland { Margery Maugham
{ Jane Howeet

BURIALS (*continued in Vol. II*) (*Extracted Entries*).

1680. Thomas Baells was burred 9th of October 1680

Mr Iohn Davison   Wittnes
                    Ann Hilton
                    Elizeb. Denton

Grace Burdus was buried 7th of December 1680

Iohn Duck Maior [1]   Wittnes
                    Alles Daveson
                    Ann Blaklock

Richard Tailer was buried 23rd of December 1680

Mr Iohn Morland   Wittnes
                    Ann Tiller
                    Alis Heirison

1681. Ann Tyller was buried 30th of October 1681

Mr Iohn Duck   Wittnes
                    Ann Tyller
                    Ellen Ramforth

Thomas Miller was buried ye 12th of Feb.

Sam : martten Minister of St nich.   Wittnes
                    Ambros Miller
                    Margrett Miller

1682. Abraham Allinson was buried ye 8th of September 1682

Mr Hutchinson, Maior   Wittnes
                    Jno. Allinson
                    John Gebson

---

[1] The well-known Sir John Duck. See Surtees' History of Durham, vol. iv.

Mr Cam Rect^r of Gyllegate was Buryed 26th of September 1682.[1]

1685. Mr Richard Beell minister of St Gyles was buried at London May ye 12, 1685.[2]

Mr Anthon Emerson was buried 9 of November in Lining 1685.

[*At the end of December, 1686*] A Catologue into the B'pps Court.

1688. Bridget Catherine Tempest doughter of Mr Tempest was buried 15th of febr. 1688.

Mr Antho Kirton　　　　Wittnes
Marjery Kirton
Mary Robinson

1691. Michaelmas 1691. Mr Will'm Dunn Minister of this parish.

Nathaniel ye son of Mr Manlove Presbyterian Minister was buryed october ye 14th 1691. affidavit brought to me. Jane Dent made oath.

Willm Greeveson, Major.　　Witnesses
Jane Hutchinson
Wm Roper

Jane Wildon was buryed October ye 17th 1691. No affidavit brought. Memorand. y^t I certifyd ye Church wardens Thomas Gelson & Walter Hair on Sunday ye 25th &c.[3]

[*N.B.—After this attestations are only occasional*].

Elizabeth ye wife of Iohn Hall Glover was buried the 26th day of Februay 169¾.

Ann the Daughter of William Tempest Esq. of Old Durham was buried the 21 of March 169⅔ her father and mother being then at London.

Burials in the year 1693. Wm Done Curate.

Mrs Hannah Drury died on Easter munday and was buried the 18th of April being Easter tuesday.

---

[1] See List of Curates of St. Giles, and Introduction under "Church and Living."

[2] See List of Curates.

[3] The Act of 30 Car. II above cited provided further that, in case of the required affidavit not being brought to the minister where the party was buried within eight days, such minister was to give notice thereof under his hand to the churchwardens or overseers of the parish, who were to take proceedings against the defaulters.

Jane filia Josephi Done & Margaretae uxoris de Clapeth in Parochia S^{ti} Nicholai Dunelm. sepulta est duodecimo die Maij.

Elizabetha filia gemella Michaelis Thompson & Janae uxoris de Keepyer wood sepulta fuit sexto die Junii.

Thomas Bell (?) Challenge weaver sepultus fuit 17 die Augusti. papist.

1694. Willielmus Selbey Papist sepultus fuitt die quarto.

[*After this the few remaining entries in the book are again in English*].

1694. Jane Dobson a beggar was buried ye 19th of Sept^r /94.

An old man was buried without fees—17th of October.

On the back, in stamped and gilded letters,
Registrum Ecclesiae Sancti Egidii Dunelm.

BAPTISMS (*Extracted Entries*).

Richard son of William Cam Rector of this parish was Baptiz'd the 18th of March in the yeare of Our Lord God 1680-1.

Ann Coulson and Merrell Coulson daughters of Iohn Coulson was baptized ye 9th of Aprill bouth Basterds, 1682.

Simond Sampson Sun of Simond Sampson basterd was baptized ye 30th of November (1682).

Nebuchadnezar Bastard Son of Tho. Bell & Margaret Scage was baptized ye 14th of December 1684.

(*After 10th April, 1687*) Delivered a Catologue into ye Bpp's Court.

Anne .   .   .   . A Child of Traveller was baptized y^e 3 of March—1688.

George Pearson sun of Necholas Pearson was baptized y^e 9th of Auguast 1692.   Note that Nich. Pearson had another son named George who died in the yeare before this was borne.

George the Son of Robert Macklend was baptized Feb. 12th 169$\frac{2}{3}$.   this Macklend was a Scotch Beggar that came from Edinborough.

Iohn & Thomas y^e Sons of Willm Hunter Fuller vulgo dict. Salter Will were baptized y^e first of January 1692.

From 8th February 169$\frac{2}{3}$, to 9th June, 1695, the entries are in Latin. Those for 1693 (beginning according to old style) are headed :

Baptizmata in Anno 1693 Gulielmo Dunneo S'cti Ægidii Curato.

The entries which follow include :—

Martha et Elizabetha filiae Gemellae Michaelis Thompsoni & Janae uxoris de Keepyer baptizabantur octavo die Aprilis 1693.

Margery filia Walteri Barker & Annae uxoris nata & baptizata fuit vigesimo primo die Maij.   private Bap.

Izabella filiola Jacobi Alderson Carbonarii & Barbarae uxoris baptizata fuit eodem die [*25th May*].

Iohannes filius Gulielmi Dobson pellionis & Sarae Uxoris baptizabatur quinto die Junij.   [Private bap.].

Martha filia Gulielmi et Elizabetae Done S^{ti} Ægidii Curati baptizata fuit decimo Septimo die Julii 1693.

After 10th September there is this note :

Thus far the book kept by myself the rest of this page kept by Walter Hare. [1]

Edwardus fillius Abrahami & Anne Brantingham Baptizatus fuitt vicissimo primo die Octob^r: 93.

James the Son of Thomas & Elizabeth Hutchinson weaver (as we are informed) was baptized at a Conventicle October the 18 : 1693°.

Maria filia Georgii Baker de Elm Park in Parochiâ off Wolsingham annos nata circiter viginti quinque Baptizabatur vicesimô quarto die Februarii 1693.

Johannes filius Edwardi Richardson pistoris baptizabatur Circiter finem Decembris & Sepeliebatur Circiter 2^{dum} vel tertium Januarii.

Walter Hare's neglect. [2]

1694.

Baptismata in Anno 1694to Gulielmo Doneo Curato.

2. Elizabetha filia Roberti & Elizabethae Welsh Lapicidae baptizabatur vigesimo secundo die Aprilis 1694°.

3. Gulielmus filius Gulielmi & Margaretae Gregson Agricolae de Ramside baptizabatur die Veneris videlicet quarto die Maii : & Pater ejus sepeliebatur eodem die. 1694.

4. Cuthbertus filius Richardi & Mariae Hutchinson textoris baptizabatur tertio die Junii 1694°.

5. Thomas filius Gulielmi & Joannae Wheatly yeoman baptizabatur tertio die Junii 1694°.

7. Barnabas filius Gulielmi & Barbarae Baker operarii baptizabatur vicesimo quarto die Junii.

---

[1] Having been a Churchwarden in 1691, Walter Hare (*al.* Hair) was appointed Parish Clerk in 1692. See under Marriages of the latter date.

[2] This appears to be Mr. Done's remark, the Parish Clerk, to whom he had left the keeping of the Register, having neglected to make the last entry in its proper place.

8.   Margery filia Thomae & Alice Lowther pellionis baptizabatur vicesimo tertio Julii 1694.

15.   Alice filia Johannis & Susannae Hall Calceamentarii baptizabatur Januarii vicesimo tertio die. 94.

16.   Simon⁵ filius Simoni & Margaretae Richardson Fullonis baptizabatur vicesimo septimo die Januarii Annoque D'ni 1694. a great snow.

Baptismata in Anno 1695ie. Will. Done Curato.

1.   Gulielmus filius Radulphi & Izabellae Robinson [Hortulani] baptizabatur tertio die Maij. 95.

2.   Elizabetha filia Supposititia Georgii Holden baptizabater Aprilis vicesimo octavo die. 95.

3.   Elizabetha Filia Thomae & Elizabethae Hutchinson [Lanii] baptizabatur tertio die Aprilis. 1695.

19.   Marth ye daughter of Jonas Ryley a Passenger was baptized ye 18th day of February. 95.

Teste Gulielmo Done Curato

Gulielm Hill
Radulpho Richardson }Guardianis

Baptismata Anno D'ni 1696.

9.   William ye Son of Ralph and Ann Herrison of Lampton in ye Parish of Chester Le Street was baptized the 16 day August 96. The mother being deliverd as she was going home from ye market.

1697.

7.   Iohn Son of Roberto & Elizabeth Welch was baptized June ye 8th 97 : private Baptism, pub : Cert. (*i.e.*, *publicly certified*) July ye 4th.

Memorandm. That on Monday The One & Thirtyeth day of May Ao D'ni 1697 The Honble Robert Boothe Archdeacon of the Archdeaconry of Durham with the Revd Hamond Beaumont Officiall visited this Church personally & then admonished the Churchwardens to recommend the repaire of the Chancell to the Impropriator, & that they Whiten the Church & remove the Seates at the low End of the Church to the End it may be flagged.[1] The doeing of which they are to Certifye at the next Michaelmas Visitation.

Posth. Smith,
Register.

---

[1] For evidence of churches having been commonly unflagged, the bare earth of the floor being covered with straw or rushes, *cf.* "Churchwardens' Accounts," Surtees Society's Publications, vol. lxxxiv (See Index to that

1698.

3. Izabell daughter of James Waller of Keepyer a Collier was baptized yᵉ 22ᵗʰ of May 1698.

5. Ambrose Son of Anthony Grievson Skinner was baptized June the 26ᵗʰ 1698.

8. Richard Son of Rowland & Ann Brown Fuller was baptized yᵉ last day of July 1698.

18. Martha of Walter Haire Parish Clerk was Cert' for her baptism¹ April yᵉ 2ⁿᵈ 1699.

1699.

Cuthbert the Son of William and Elizabeth Hunter Fuller (vulgò dict. Salter Will) was baptized yᵉ 20ᵗʰ day of September 1699.

1700.

Issable of David Hall a poor Blind man was Baptized yᵉ 18ᵗʰ day of August 1700.

1. Wᵐ Son of Richᵈ Hall of west Grange baptized yᵉ 16ᵗʰ Day of November, 1700 Aetatis Suae Anno 19° and 5 months.

2. Richard Son of Richard Hall of west Grange was baptized yᵉ same day being in the 13ᵗʰ year of his age.

3. Izabell daughter of Richard & Izabell Hall of West Grange was baptized yᵉ 26ᵗʰ of November being then 5 years & about 6 moneth old.

4. George son of yᵉ sᵈ Richard & Izabell Hall was borne yᵉ 21 of Febʸ, 96, and baptizᵈ yᵉ 26 of Novʳ 1700.

5. Iohn Son of yᵉ sᵈ Richard & Izabell Hall borne Janʸ yᵉ 12, 98, & baptized Novʳ 26ᵗʰ 1700.

6. Ralph Son of yᵉ sᵈ Richᵈ & Izabell Hall borne yᵉ 27ᵗʰ of 8ber 1700 and baptized November the 26ᵗʰ 1700.

Baptismata post 25 Martii 1701.

Iohn Sone of Walter & Catherine Haire was Certified for yᵉ 21ᵗʰ of Septʳ 1701.

1703.

Thomas Son of Ralph Smith of Woodwell house yeoman had private baptizm : but was Certified for publickly August 31 1703.

Volume under "Flagging of Churches"). It thence appears that the church of Houghton-le-Spring was flagged for the first time in 1604, that of St. Oswald's, Durham, in 1607-8, and of Pittington in 1634. It may be worth noting that, previously to the last restoration of the church of St. Giles, one of the flags near the west end had the letters of the alphabet cut on it in deep and distinct characters. Were they intended for the instruction of children, or merely to exhibit and advertise the skill of the stone-cutter?

¹ *I.e.*, as appears from other preceding and succeeding entries, her private baptism was certified publicly in the church.

Robt Son of Robt Mackland a beggar baptized 8ber ye 10th 1703.

Thomas Heaviside of Keepyer and Jane Snowdon of ye Chappelry of Sadberge were married ye fourth day of March 1694.

Durham 1693. A Note of Lands paying Tyth to ye Church of St Gyles and taken out of a Copy found in ye Study at Old Durham writ by Mr Elias Smyth once Curate there.

	Acres	Roods
Pello Leas.		
Robert Chambers	oo	2
Midlam Poor Land	oo	3
Mr Robt Smyth	o1	o
Mr Emerson	oo	2
Dr Brewin's Corps	o2	o
Mr Marshall	o2	o
Bull rigge	oo	2
Bridge Land...	o2	o
Mr William Suretys	3	o
Dr Gray's Corps		
Broad Close.		
Prebends Corps	12	o
Wm Midleton		
Mr Emerson		
Willm Hutchinson		
Bridge Land Tho. Brown ...	2	1
Iohn Atkinson		
Anth. Dobson for his Church Land	o	1
Broad Close in all	20	1
Bakehouse Leas.		
Nich. Ladler closes	1	2
Common rigge. q^y how much		
Poors Land	1	o
Nich. Paxton	2	o
Iohn Atkinson	o	2
Porter Close Gilbert Snawdon	3	o
Bricks Garth G. Snawdon	1	o
Almner Leas Gilbert Snawdon	3	o
Robt Cornford's Closes	3	o
Ralph Nicholson a litle Close next to Tinker's Lane	o	1
Mr Wm Suretys a litle close near Tedbury hall	1	o
Henry Frizel a Close near ye Ashgates ...	3	o

The Closes called 5 Acres & 7 Acres		12	0
besides these viz.			
Abraham Allenson		0	1
Tho. Forster		0	2
Mr Beaumont		5	0
Eliz. Ladler		1	0
Doct. ———— Corps per Anthon.			
Dobson tent		7	0
Palmer Close		4	2
Mr Emerson a litle Close near Bower banks			
Widow Halls litle Close adjoyning to ye Street not an acre... ...		1	

taken out of a Copy drawn by Mr Elias Smyth Anno 1655. Wm Done.

Michælmas 1693.

Recd of John Brown a Tyth goose
    John Coulson for ½ a goose ————6
    Tho. Hughill for ½ a goose ————6
Abr'am Allenson a goose & eat her at his own house.
    Widdow Maltby for ½ a goose ————6

          1s. 6d. and 2 geese
            at 2s.

       2 0

Tyth goose Anno D'ni 1694   3 6d.
    John Brown —1
    Rob't Baker —1

      in all   2

Recd Anno 1692 at New brewhouses and ye street of St. Gyles's about 18 tyth piggs.

[Here follow the five Marriages in 1694 which have appeared above, including that of Abraham Allenson (whose tithe goose was eaten at his own house) on St. Luke's Day, 1694].

Easter 1696. Mem. that Whereas there was a little Close formerly called Thomas Snawdon's Close and (of late) ye Brick Garth or Gilbert Snawdon's Close situate on ye North Side of Gilligate and boundering upon ye Causey on ye South, a Tenement of Robt Johnsons on ye West, and a tenement of ye Church of St. Giles on ye East. the said litle Close being converted to a Brickyard yeilded no tyth to ye Minister for several years last past, therefore for incouraging Willm Hill Gardiner to improve ye same, I have agreed with ye said William for ye tyth of ye said Close to pay me yearly at Easter two shillings & sixpence so long as I am Minister of St. Giles's & he the said Willm is Tenant of ye said Close of which Gilbert Snawdon is Landlord, but if in ye time that I am Minister &c. the said William cease to be Tennant, then this contract to be void. witness my hand.   Wm Dunn.

A true Register of all the Orchards, Gardens or yards that pay a Modus to ye Rector or his Curate at Easter with the several summes as they have been paid time out of mind in lieu of the tyth of hay, herbs or fruit growing in ye same Orchards or yards &c. yearly.—And received Anno 1693 per Wm Done Curate.

Yards on the South Side in order as they lie.   (1) Thomas Hughill pays 2*d.* ; (2) Jane Dobson, 4*d.* ; Will. Brown bought of Will. Hills, 3*d. And so on ; fourteen names in all, ending with,* Gilbert Snawdon per tennant, 3*d. ; followed by* From the town's head to ye Church Lane, 3*s.* 1*d. Then*—Now from the Church yard to ye Tinkler's Lane which divides this parish from St Nicholas's are these that follow. *Forty-two names follow, including these, which are here given as specimens :*—(1) Robt Errington, 1*d.* ; (3) Mr Dury per Wm Baker, 2*d.* ; (4) Robt Errington for a waste, 3*d.* ; (10) Willm Hills for Snawdon's yard 6*d.* ; (11) Wm Hills for Pant Close, 12*d.* ; (19) Iohn Coulson with Wood-Leggs, 1*d.* ; (21) Nich. Sparke a tennant, 2*d.* ; (26) Wm Hills for his orchard, 10*d.*   Mr Suretys per tenant adjoyning to Tinkers Lane, 2*d.*

Then follows :
Mem'd. y^t Robt Cornford did ever pay 4*d.* for ye narrow yard but only bargaind Anno 1694 to pay 6*d.* for the square garden which when in corn paid tyth in kind. the Tennant's obliged to pay it ; but if it want a tennant seek it on the Landlord.

North Side in order as they lie. *Fifty-eight names follow, including :*—Imprimis, The Bakehouse yard, 3*d.* ; (5) Robt Maugham for Iohn Robinson's Children, 3*d.* ; (6) Abraham Eden a waste, 3*d.* ; (13, 14) Wm Suretys & Robt Suretys two wastes per tenants, 6*d.*

Church Land :—(16) Mary Crooks, 2*d*. ; (17) Turbutt per Walter Hair, 3*d*. ; (18) Geo. Easterly per ten[ts] 3*d*. ; (34) Will[m] Wilson : a waste church land, 2*d*. ; (35) Tedbury hall per R. Williamson, 2*d*. ; (48) Widow Hall y[e] waste pays tyth in kinde, but y[e] litle garden 2*d*. ; (53) Anthony Dobson Church land waste, 2*d*. ; &c.

North side, 13*s*.——South side, 16*s*. 1*d*.——in all, 1*l*. 9*s*. 1*d*.

Finis.

Every housholder is to pay 2*d*., bread & wine
Every plow in the parish ... ... 2*d*.
Every Cow in the street 1½
Man & wife 6*d*. thus

as Communicants	...	3*d*.	look the Register for
bread and wine	...	2	the young persons &
Reekpenny[1]	...	1	take a Copy of all
		6	betwixt 16 & 20, or we shall be cheated.

Every widow or young person keeping house 4½*d*.
   thus, as a Communicant 1½*d*.
   Bread and wine ... 2
   Reekpenny 1
          4½

[*Name erased*][2] elected Clark of the Parish Church of S[t] Gyles one Easter Tuesday 1693 and was to have y[e] fees from y[t] time.

Memorandum that Walter Haire was discharged from officiating as parish clark on Candlemas day 1709, & Richard Martin had orders to officiate from John Perkin Minister of S[t] Gyles, Durham.

Walter Haire was Elected parish Clark for y[e] parish of S[t] Gyles y[e] 23[d] of Febb' 1694 & undertooke y[e] management of all y[e] parish Conferences & Kings Assesments having for y[e] same 1*l*. Sallery & for making poor Sc'edals 3 : 6 : for y[e] Kings Conference as it will allow.

---

[1] *I.e.*, *Smoke* or *hearth* money ; a due payable by householders who had fire-places. It has been collected among Easter dues in some parishes within living memory, and may possibly in some be continued still.

[2] Obviously "Walter Haire," which can be partially read.

April ye 2^d 1705.

Memorand. That on Tuesday ye 27th of March last when Dr. Murton and Dr. Finney put up a new gate in the Pello Leases they also in Charity to widow Hunter put up a new stile adjoying (*sic*) to it which she (being Tenant to Mr. Marshall's Land there) ought to make and maintain.   Test   Wm Dunn
                                                                    Curate.

Marriage Fees for a Parishioner with Licence, 8*s.* 6*d.*

viz. to ye Curate   ...   5*s.*   0 ⎞ If strangers, then it was
     to his Clerk   ...   2*s.*   6 ⎟ (as we are inform'd)
     to ye Seggerston   ...   1   0 ⎟ usual to take 13*s.* 4*d.*
                             ———————   ⎟ which is equal to y^e
                               8   6 ⎠ price of ye Licence.

Bannis matrimonialibus publicatis, 5*s.* 6*d.*
        Curate   ...   ...   3*s.*   6*d.*
        Clerke   2   0
        Seggerston   ...   0   6
                                 ———————
                                   5   6

Memorandum that Mr Wm Done (*altered to* Dunn) Curate of St Gyles entred at Michaelmass 1691
                    Thomas Gelson & ⎫ Church Wardens.
                    Walter Hair   ⎭

———————

Easter Reckonings

                                    ⎛ as Communicants   ...   3*d.*
                                    ⎟ Bread & wine   ...   2
Every man & wife at Easter ⎟ for Reek   1
pays 6*d.* thus   ⎜   ———
                                    ⎝   6*d.*

Every housekeeper pays for all ye Children, Servants or Strangers (above sixteen years of age) that have been resident in his or her family forty days before Easter two pence a piece for bread and wine whether they communicate or not.   Take a Copy of the Register book for all borne in the Parish that are above sixteen and under twenty years old, for some will never be 16 (at Easter) till they be two & twenty.

Every plow in the Parish—2*d.* Every Cow in y*e* Street Lands, 1½*d.* Every widower, widow, or single person keeping house is to pay 4½*d.* as followeth—

as a Communicant	...	1½*d.*
Bread & wine ...	...	2
Reekpeny	...	... 1
		4½

Collected Easter 1692 : Will' Done Curate.

For a Churching 7*d.* to the Minister & 4*d.* to y*e* Clerk & 2*d.* to y*e* Seggerston. Churching is in all 1*s.* 1*d.*

Burial fees in y*e* Churchyard by a Parishioner, 1*s.* 1*d.* ; seven pence to y*e* Parson & 6*d.* to y*e* Clarke.

For a Stranger double fees, as also a Papist or other Recusant.

For Burial fees & Larestall in the Quire to ye Curate ... ... £0 13*s.* 4*d.*
to the Parish Clarke ... 0 3 4

16 8

A Stranger or dissenter double.

---

[1] Note that Mortuaries have been paid in this Parish time out of mind according to Statute. . . . . 21—H : 8 Cap : 6.

3*s.* 4*d.* a Larestall in the Church quere *to be paid to y*r* Churchwardens* (these words written over an erasure).

Burial fees in the Church { to y*e* Curate 2*s.* 6
{ to y*e* Clark 1 3

For a stranger of another Parish double fees ut in ceteris.

[1] This note is on flyleaf one-third size of folio at the end of the volume.

Though it has not been thought necessary to continue our extracts throughout this more recent volume, yet the following entries in its earlier part appear worth producing.

On paper fly leaf at the beginning of the book.
William Hill & Ralph Richardson, Churchwardens.

Will. Done
Curate of
St Giles's Parish.

This Book belongs to the Parish of St Giles in Durham and was Bought June ye 7th 95 of Abraham Ashworth for 12*s*., Containing 12 sheets of parchment at 9*d*. a sheet 9*s*., & ye binding 3*s*.

In pursuance of an Act of Parliament Anno sexto et septimo Gulielmi 3 Regis Intitled an Act for Granting to his Majesty certain Rates & duties upon Marriages, Births and Burials, and upon Batchelours and Widowers, for the Term of five years, for Carrying on the warr against France with vigour.

Every Burial to pay 4*s*. ; a Gent, his wife or child, to pay 1*l*. 4*s*. ; An Esq. 5*l*. 4*s*. Every Birth 2*s*. ; A Gent for his Child 1*l*. 2*s*. A Marriage 2*s*. 6*d*. ; A Gent 1*l*. 2*s*. 6*d*.

In the book itself on the parchment folios.
1695. Isabell the Daughter of Richard & Izabell Hall was born May the 5th, 1695 ; A Quaker. Iohn ye son of William & Elizabeth Harrison Papist was born July the 17th, 1695. Grosier son of Richard Smith of Ramside Gent was buried November the first, 95. Margaret Harrison widow aged about 100 years was buried November the first, 95. Matthew Meaborne & Elizabeth Coltman married clandestinely at Newcastle March ye 9th 1695 ; Non-Conform'. Martha ye Daughter of Jonas Ryley a passenger that came with a Brief & is gone was borne & baptized.

1696. Ursila the daughter of Nicholas Pearson being on the ye poors scroll was borne. Cuthbert Selby & Jane Hutchinson both of Brancepeth parish were married ye 30th day of March 96 & his Majesties duty p^d then to Iohn Brown, Coll^r.

1697. Katherine yᵉ wife of William Hunter Vulgo Corby's Will. was buried.

1698. Iohn Rogers, who had in his lifetime attended nine ministers successively as Seggerston of this Church, was buried yᵉ 11ᵗʰ of December, 1698, Anno Ætatis suae 85°.

1699. Iohn Falkner a stranger that came here to get his Legg cutt off (his parents being poor & settled in no Parish) was buryed July yᵉ 24ᵗʰ. Anthony Claxton of yᵉ parish of Hurworth weaver marryed Ann Stephenson of the same Aug. 1 : 99. King's duty pᵈ to Abᵗ Allenson. Ann wife of William Pattison yᵉ Windmiller of Gillegate was buryed. Mr William Tempest of Old Durham Patron of our church was buried on yᵉ 15 day of March $\frac{1699}{1700}$

1700. Thomas Hastings of Keepyer Wood, an honest labourer, was buryed. Thomas Nicholson and Merill Orton Papists . . . . . are said to be married.

1701. Robert Young, Mercer & Grocer, a Prisoner in his Majᵗⁱᵉˢ Gaol at Durham & Ann Richardson . . . were married. William yᵉ son of Thomas Hugill & Searcher to yᵉ Company of Glovers was buryed yᵉ 9ᵗʰ of September 1701. He was murthered on Sunday yᵉ last of August at 12 at night by Iⁿ Luckenby & Thom. Dixon.

1702. George Liddell of Hawthorne in yᵉ Parish of Easington Labourer who died by a suddain fall & departed about 30 hours after (being speechless all that time) was buried.

1703. Thomas Lowther of Giligate Skinner (a man of great estimation amongst his neighbours) was buryed. William Hunter, fuller (vulgo dict. Salter Will.).

1704. Frances yᵉ daughter of Wᵐ Dunn Minister of this Parish was buryed on good friday yᵉ 14ᵗʰ day of April, 1704. She was his second of that name. Mary Walton a Quaker died at Wᵐ Brown & was buried at yᵉ Quakers meeting yᵉ 8ᵗʰ day of May, 1704. No notice was given.

1705. Iohn Coulson Miln-wright & milner of Keepyer Corn-milns dying suddenly by a fall on yᵉ causeway over against his own house early in yᵉ morning (being on foot and leading a Horse to water) was buried. Margaret A bastard child of Elizabeth Sharp & supposed of James Denton was baptized yᵉ 18ᵗʰ day of 7ᵇᵉʳ, 1705.

A.D. 1707. Memorand. that James Denton & Elizabeth Sharpp dreed penance ye 2nd day of octob^r 1707.[1]

A.D. 1708. Henry Parkinson senior did penance July ye 11th 1708. [for committing fornication with the above named Elizabeth Sharpp (*alia manu*)].

A.D. 1711. Elizabith the daughter of Mr Dunn formerly minister of this parish was buried May ye 23rd, 1711.

A.D. 1756. William Sugden a Quaker thirtyfive years of age was baptized Feb. 21.

A leaf, apparently comprising baptisms between the dates November 21, 1736, and May 15, 1737, has been cut out of the book ; and on the narrow slip of parchment remaining is written in pencil, Is there a leaf cut out here ? *There is a distinct mark of a knife having cut into the following pages.*

---

[1] For notice of penance in churches or market-places, *cf.* "Churchwarden's Accounts" (Surtees Society's Publications, vol. lxxxiv, p. 49, note). The latest instance known to the editor was told him by a native of Pittington, apparently about the year 1770, when a girl had done penance, clothed in a white sheet, in the church of that parish. He was also told many years ago by an old woman of Melsonby in Yorkshire of her own recollection (about the same date) of having seen, as she went into church among the school children, a girl, whom she described as "a bonny lass," standing in the porch in a white sheet, bare-foot and with her hair hanging down, and having seen her in the same plight, crying, when the congregation left the church. The same informant spoke also of a young woman having stood up in church, at Melsonby, before the assembled congregation, to name the father of her child—which was an evidence of paternity formerly accepted as sufficient—and of the two culprits having afterwards repeated a form of words after the minister, standing before the reading-desk, after which the woman had gone up to the altar to be churched.

"LIBER SANCTI EGIDII, DUNELM."

This is a bound Volume, lettered as above, and kept in the Vestry of the Church, in which the following ancient documents have been pasted for preservation.

LIST OF DOCUMENTS.

(1). A.D. 1373. Charter of Cunstancia Taillour to Thomas de Kyrkland, granting a burgage in Gilligate.

(2). A.D. 1449. Indenture between Richard Mur and John Padingham, concerning a burgage in Sadlergate.

(3). A.D. 1504. Copy of Court Roll, concerning a burgage in Gilligate.

(4). A.D. 1505. Copy of Court Roll, *ditto*. (John Boerius, Master of Kepyer).

(5). A.D. 1522. Copy of Court Roll, *ditto*. (William Frankleyn, Master).

(6). A.D. 1523. Copy of Court Roll, *ditto*. (William Frankleyn, Master).

(7). A.D. 1525. Copy of Court Roll, *ditto*. (William Frankleyn, Master).

(8). A.D. 1542. Copy of Court Roll, *ditto*. (William Frankleyn, Master).

(9). A.D. 1542. Copy of Court Roll, *ditto*. (William Frankleyn, Master).

(10). A.D. 1555. Copy of Court Roll, *ditto*. (John Heath, Lord of the Manor).

(11). A.D. 1558. Copy of Court Roll, *ditto*. (John Heath, Lord of the Manor).

(12). A.D. 1563. Lease by the Churchwardens (with consent of the Steward of the Manor and the parishioners) of a tenement in Gilligate.

(13). A.D. 1564. Lease by the Churchwardens (no consent of others mentioned) of a tenement in Gilligate (*imperfect*).

(14). A.D. 1565. Copy of Court Roll. (John Heath, Lord of the Manor).

(15). A.D. 1594. Lease by the Churchwardens (no consent of others mentioned) of a tenement in Gilligate.

(16). A.D. 1594. Counterpart of the above.

(17). A.D. 1584. Lease by the Churchwardens (no consent of others mentioned) of a tenement in Gilligate.

(18). A.D. 1584. Counterpart of the above.

(19). A.D. 1584. Lease by the Churchwardens (with consent of the Lord of the Manor and the parishioners) of a tenement in Gilligate (*imperfect*).

(20). A.D. 1584. Lease by the Churchwardens (with consent of the Lord of the Manor and the parishioners) of a tenement in Gilligate (*imperfect*).

(21). A.D. 1590. Lease by the Churchwardens (with consent of the rest of the parishioners) of a tenement in Gilligate.

(22). A.D. 1600. Copy of Court Roll, concerning four burgages in Gilligate.

(23). A.D. 1617. Copy of Court Roll, concerning four burgages in Gilligate.

(24). A.D. 1618. Bond of Margaret Hall to Churchwardens for fulfilment of conditions of a Covenant.

(25). A.D. 1619. Bond of Robert Carr and Richard Tripp (*as above*).

---

(1). A.D. 1373. *Charter of Cunstancia Taillour, granting a burgage to Thomas de Kyrkland.*

Sciant praesentes et futuri quod ego Cunstancia filia Walteri Taillour de vico Sancti Egidii in Dunelm. in mea pura virginitate dedi concessi et praesenti carta mea confirmavi Thomae de Kyrkland Taillour unum burgagium jacens in vico Sancti Egidii inter burgagium Johannis Warker ex parte una et domum de Kypier vocatam le Curthous ex alia, quod quidem burgagium michi jure hereditario post decessum Marjoriae sororis meae decendebat, habendum et tenendum predictum burgagium cum omnibus libertatibus et libris consuetudinibus ac omnibus aliis pertinentiis suis prefato Thomae heredibus et assignatis suis libere quiete integre bene et in pace imperpetuum de capitalibus dominis feodi illius per servicia inde debita & de jure consueta. Et ego antedicta Cunstancia et heredes mei totum praedictum burgagium cum pertinentiis suis universis praefato Thomae heredibus et assignatis suis contra omnes gentes warrantizabimus et imperpetuum defendemus. In cujus rei testimonium huic praesenti cartae meae sigillum meum apposui. Hiis testibus, domino Johanne Lambe capellano, Adam Spurcottes, Johanne de Ruston, Hugone Sclacter, Thoma Goldsmyth, Roberto Taillour, Roberto de Corbrygges, et aliis. Datum in vico Sancti Egidii in Dunelm die Lunae prox. post festum Sancti Hilarii Anno Domini millesimo trecentesimo septuagesimo tertio.

Seal gone.   *Endorsed*, Carta Thomae Kirkland.

---

(2). A.D. 1449. *Indenture between Richard Mur and John Padingham concerning a Burgage in Sadlergate.*

Haec indentura facta inter Ricardum Mur ex parte una & Iohannem Padyngam in Dunelm. fullator ex parte altera testatur quod praedictus Ricardus dedi concescit et hac praesenti carta confirmavit praedicto Iohanni unum burgagium sicut jacet in Sadlargate inter burgagium Willelmi Chesman ex parte una & burgagium Thomae Trate capellano ex parte altera, habendum et tenendum praedictum burgagium cum omnibus suis pertinentiis libertatibus et aisiamentis suis praedicto Iohanni pro toto tempore vitae suae libere quiete & pacifice de capitalibus dominis feodi illius per servicia inde jure consueta. Reddend. inde annuatim praedicto Ricardo heredibus et assignatis suis decem solidos argenti ad duos anni terminos, viz. ad festa Pentecostes & Sancti Martini in yeme per aequales porciones. Et si contigerit praedictum redditum decem solidorum a retro fore in parte vel in toto non solutum post aliquem terminum praedictum per spatium dimidii unius anni, quod tunc bene liceat praedicto Ricardo heredibus et assignatis suis in praedicto burgagio cum omnibus suis pertinentiis reintrare et in pristino statu possidere. Et praedictus Ricardus et heredes sui praedictum burgagium cum omnibus suis pertinentiis praedicto Iohanni pro toto tempore vitae suae in forma praedicta contra omnes gentes warrantizabunt et defendent. In cujus rei testimonium partes praedictae hiis indenturis sigilla sua alternatim apposuerunt hiis testibus, Thoma Maldeson, Thoma Hauxwell, Willelmo Brune, et aliis. Dat. apud Dunelm prima die mensis Januarii anno domini millesimo quadragentesimo quadragesimo nono.

Seal gone.

(3). 1504. *Copy of Court Roll.*

Burgus de Gelygate { Curia capitalis tenta apud Gelygate Tercio die Octobris Anno Domini millesimo D^{mo} quarto.

Dimissio

Robertus Kay cepit de dominis quatuor burgagia simul jacentia unde unum eorum est aedificatum cum suis pertinentiis prout jacent in Gelygate inter burgagium Wyllelmi Wylson ex parte orientali ex (*et?*) burgagium Magistri Hospitalis de Kepyere ex parte occidentali, habendum et tenendum eidem Roberto heredibus et assignatis suis a festo Pentecostes ultimo praeterito usque finem termini nonaginta et novem annorum ex tunc proxime sequentium et plenarie complendorum. Redend. domino curiae per annum ad festa Sancti Martini et Pentecostes quinque solidos et tres precarias [1] in Autumpno. Et dictus Robertus heredes et assignati sui dictum tenementum cum burgagiis praedictis sufficienter reparabunt et sustentabunt sumptibus suis propriis durante termino praedicto dicto termino. Et in fine termini praedicti sufficienter reparatum dimittent Et facta domino et vicario quae &c. Per plegium Ricardi Huchenson & Wyllelmi Robynson. Et dominus inveniet eis cum opus fuerit grossum mariemium.[2] Et dat. pro fine xx*d*.

(4). 1505. *Copy of Court Roll.*

Burgus de Gelygate

Curia Capital Magistri Johannis Boerius tenta ibidem die Jovis vicesimo nono die maii Anno domini millesimo D[imo] quinto.

Sursum

Robertus Kay venit ad hanc curiam et sursum reddidit totum jus titulum et terminum quae habet in iiij[or] burgagiis simul jacentibus cum suis pertinentiis in Gelygate in Dunelm. de quibus burgagiis unum eorum edificatum est ad opus Iohannis Thoroby. Et super hoc venit dictus Iohannes Thoroby et fecit fidelitatem suam domino pro dictis iiij[or] burgagiis cum suis pertinentiis habendis et tenendis dictis iiij[or] burgagiis cum omnibus libertatibus et aliis suis pertinentiis dicto Iohanni heredibus et assignatis suis secundum vim formam et effectum dimissionis copiae predicto Roberto Kay factae et durante termino in eadem specificatione.

---

[1] *I.e.*, Boon-days.

[2] For *Meremium*, which means timber for building purposes. "Grossum" may be taken to mean *large* timber, such as would serve for beams and posts of half-timbered buildings.

fidelit^e

Et fecit finem cum domino de ij*s*. Et admissus est & juratus. Et facta domino & vicinis quae incumbunt. Per plegium Antonii Wylkynson & Iohannis Throp.

---

(5). 1522. *Copy of Court Roll.*

Burgus de Gelygate

Curia Capitalis Magistri Willelmi Frank-leyn Clerici Magistri hospitalis de Kepyere tenta ibidem die Jovis xxvj die Junii Anno domini millesimo D^{mo} xxij^{do}.

Dimissio

Iohannes Thoroby venit ad hanc curiam et sursum reddidit in manus domini totum Jus & terminum quem [*habet in*] iiij^{or} burgagiis simul jacentibus in Gelygate in Dunelm. quorum unum eorum est edificatum ad opus Henrici Orrey. Et super haec venit dictus Henricus Orrey et cepit de domino dicta iiij^{or} burgagia cum omnibus lebertatibus eis perti-nentibus et suis pertinentiis habenda et tenenda dicta iiij^{or} burgagia cum suis pertinentiis praedicto Henrico heredibus et assignatis suis A Festo Pentecostes ultimo preterito usque finem termini nonaginta et novem annorum extunc proxime sequentium & plenarie com-pletorum. Reddend. inde annuatim domino ad Festa Martini & pentecostes ————. Et dictus Henricus heredes et assignati sui dictum burgagium edificatum reparabunt et sustentabunt sumptibus suis propriis & expensis durante termino praedicto, et in fine termini sui suffienter reparatum dimittent. Per plegium Iohannis Wylkynson & Iohannis ————. Et dat. domino pro fine ij*s*. Et juratus.

---

(6). 1523. *Copy of Court Roll.*

Burgus de Gelygate

Curia Capitalis Magistri Willelmi Frank-ley Clerici Magistri Hospitalis de Kepyere tenta ibidem die Jovis xxi^{mo} die Januarii.

Fidelitas

Willelmus Cotysfurth filius et heres Rogeri de Cotysfurth venit ad hanc Curiam et fecit fidelitatem suam domino pro uno burgagio cum suis pertinentiis jacente ex parte australi Vici de Gelygate inter burgagium Roberti

Huddyspeth ex parte orientali et burgagium
Thomae Spraghen ex parte occidentali, quod
quidem burgagium dictus Willelmus habet
jure hereditatis durante termino annorum per
Magistrum Hospitalis de Kepyere Johanni
Aygett & assignatis suis concessum, reddend.
ut predictus Johannes prius reddidit per annum
et faciend. domino & vicario suo quae &c.
Per plegium Johannis Thorp & Ricardi Carn-
furth. Et fecit finem de ij*s*.

(7). 1525. *Copy of Court Roll.*

Burgus de
Gelygate
{ Curia Magistri Frankeley Clerici Magistri
Hospitalis de Kepyere tenta ibidem die Jovis
xiiij die Decembris anno Domini millesimo
D^mo xxv^to.

dimissio
{ Ad hanc Curiam venit Ricardus Orrey et
sursum reddidit in manus domini totum jus
et terminum quae habet in quatuor burgagiis
simul jacentibus in Gelygate in Dunelm.
quorum unum eorum est edificatum ad opus
Rogeri Bothe. Et super hoc venit dictus
Rogerus Bothe et cepit de domino dicta
quatuor burgagia cum omnibus libertatibus
eis pertinentibus et ceteris suis pertinentiis
habenda et tenenda dicta quatuor burgagia
cum suis pertinentiis predicto Rogero heredibus et assignatis suis a festo Sancti Martini
ultimo preterito usque finem termini nonaginta
et novem annorum extunc proxime sequentium
et plenarie completarum. Reddend. inde Annuatim domino curiae ad festa Pentecostes &
Sancti Martini in yeme v*s*. et tres precarias in
Autumpno. Et dictus Rogerus heredes et
assignati sui dictum burgagium edificatum
reparabunt et sustentabunt sumptibus suis
propriis & exspensis durante termino predicto,
et in fine termini sui sufficienter reparatum
dimittent. Per plegium Petri Trued (?) et
Johannis Thorpp. Et dat. domino pro fine—
ij*s*. ij*d*. Et Juratus.

(8). 1542. *Copy of Court Roll.*

Curia Willelmi Frankeleyn Clerici Magistri Hospitalis
de Kepyer tenta ibidem die Jovis xix° die Januarii Anno

Regni Henrici octavi Dei gratia Angliae. ——— domini
Hiberniae et in terra supremi capitis Anglicanae ecclesiae
tricesimo tertio coram Johanne Frankeleyn Senescallo
ejusdem Hospitalis et Jacobo ———— Ad hanc curiam
venit Ricardus Corneforth de Dunelm. Tanner & cepit de
domino totum illud burgagium situatum & jacens in vico
de Geligate ex parte ———— inter burgagium Roberti
Hudspath ex parte orientali et burgagium Thomae
Spraghen ex parte occidentali. Habendum & tenendum
predictum burgagium cum suis pertinentiis sibi et assignatis suis ———— Reddend. inde per annum domino curiae
sicut prius redditum est. Quod quidem burgagium cum
suis pertinentiis predictus Ricardus Corneforth habet et
———— sibi et assignatis suis ex dono et concessione
Willelmi Cottisforth sibi et heredibus Rogeri Cottisforth
defuncti, prout patet per cartam ejusdem Willelmi prefato
Ricardo et assignatis suis ———— dat. xjᵒ die Novembris
anno regni Henrici octavi &c. tricesimo tercio hic in curia
ostensum. Et facta domino et vicinis quae incumbunt.
Per plegium Johannis Thorpe & Petri Grenewell. Et dat.
domino pro fine. Et ingressu ———.

---

(9). 1542. *Copy of Court Roll.*

Burgus de Gelygate

Curia capitalis magistri Willelmi Frankeleyn Clerici magistri Hospitalis de Kepyere
tenta ibidem die Jovis xvᵒ die Junii Anno
Domini millesimo quingentesimo quadragesimo secundo Coram Willelmo Bulmer
senescallo dicti hospitalis et Jacobo Parkynson.

Dimissio

Ad hanc curiam venit Rogerus Bothe de
———— generosus (?) et Sursum reddidit in
manus domini totum jus et terminum quae
habet in quatuor burgagiis simul jacentibus in
Geligate in Dunelm. quorum unum est
edificatum ad opus Johannis Coltman. Et
super hoc venit idem Johannes Coltman et
cepit de domino dicta iiijᵒʳ burgagia cum
omnibus libertatibus eis pertinentibus &
ceteris suis pertinentiis habenda et tenenda
dicta iiijᵒʳ burgagia cum suis pertinentiis
prefato Johanni heredibus & assignatis suis
a Festo Pentecostes ultimo preterito ante
datum presencium usque finem termini nonaginta et novem annorum ex tunc proxime
sequentium et plenarie complendorum, Red-

dend. inde annuatim domino hujus curiae ad Festa Sancti Martini et Pentecostes vs. et tres precarias in Autumpno. Et dictus Johannes heredes et assignati sui dictum burgagium edificatum reparabunt et sustentabunt sumptibus suis propriis et expensis durante termino predicto et illud in fine termini sui sufficienter reparatum dimittent. Per plegium Ricardi Cornforth et Roberti Coltman. Et dat. domino 17s. 11d. Et juratus est.

----

(10). 1555. *Copy of Court Roll.*

Burgus de Gelygatt
{
Curia capitalis Johannis Heithe ibidem tenta vicesimo die Junii Annis Regnorum Philippi et Marae Dei gratia Regis & Reginae Angliae Franciae Neapolis Jerusalem & Hiberniae fidei defensorum principum Hispaniorum et Siciliae Archducum Austriae Ducum Mediolani Burgundiae et Brabanciae Comitum Harpurgi Flandriae & Tirolis primo et secundo Coram Antonio Middilton generoso senescallo ibidem.
}

Ad hanc curiam venit Robertus Cornfurthe filius et heres Ricardi Cornfurthe defuncti Et cepit de domino totum illud burgagium Scituatum et jacens in vico de Geligatt in suburbiis civitatis Dunelmi ex parte australi vici inter burgagium Roberti Huddespethe ex parte orientali et burgagium Thomae Spraghen ex parte occidentali, in quibus Isabella Cornfurthe vidua nuper uxor dicti Ricardi Cornfurthe inde pretendens here[*ditarium?*] jus vid[*uitatis?*] hic in plena curia coram senescallo totum jus suam viduitatis sursum reddidit in manus domini & inde finire *consensit* (?) ad opus dicti Roberti Cornfurthe, habendum eidem Roberto Cornfurthe et assignatis suis a festo Pentecostes ultimo preterito ante datum presentium usque finem Termini nonaginta et novem annorum ex tunc proxime sequentium et plenarie complendorum. Reddend. inde annuatim domino Curiae ad festa Pentecostes et Sancti Martini in yeme aequis porcionibus xijd. et unam precariam in autumpno. Et faciend. domino & vicinis quae incumbunt. Per plegium Gerrardi Cooke et Ingrami Tailior. Et dat. domino pro fine et ingressu ijs. Et Juratus &c.

(11). 1558. *Copy of Court Roll.*

Burgus de Gelygatt.

Curia capitalis Johannis Hethe Armigeri ibidem tenta xvij" die Januarij Anno Regnorum Philippi et Mariae dei gratia Regis et Reginae Angliae Hispaniorum Franciae utriusque Siciliae Jerusalem et Hiberniae, fidei defensorum, Archiducum Austriae, Ducum Burgundiae Mediolani et Brabantiae comitum Hapspurg Flandriae et (*Tirolis?*) quarto et quinto coram Anthonio Middilton generoso senescallo.

Ad hanc curiam venit Agnes Coltman nuper uxor Johannis Coltman defuncti. Et cepit de domino quatuor burgagagia simul jacentia in Giligate in Dunelm. cum omnibus suis pertinenciis quae praedictus Johannes Coltman ———— dum vixit ———— . [*the rest illegible*].

(12). 1563. *Lease by Churchwardens.*[1]

THIS INDENTURE mayde the xix^th day of Maii in the fyfte yeare of the Reigne of oure Soveraigne Ladye Elizabethe by the grace of God quene of Englande France & Irelande Defender of the faythe &c. BETWIXE Thomas Robson John Gayre Umfray Smythe and Richarde Smythe Churche Wardens nowe of the parishe Churche of Saynte gyles in Durham one the one partye and Richarde Carter of gyllegait in the parishe one that other partye WITNESSYTHE that the saide Churche Wardens for theym and there Successors withe the assent consent And agrement of Anthonye myddleton of Keapyere gentleman and the parishioners of the holle parishinge have demysed granted and to ferme letten and by these presents doythe demyse grante and to ferme lett unto the saide Richarde Carter all that there Tenement and garthe sett lyenge and beynge in gelligate Aforesaide betweene a tenement of James Colsons of the east And A tenement of Cuthbert Andersons of the west To HAVE and to holde the saide tenement withe the garthe to the saide Richarde Carter And his Assignes from the feast of penthecost next insuinge the dayte herof unto the full ende and terme of twentye and one years thence next ensuyinge fullye to be complett and

---

[1] This lease, and those below numbered 13, 15, 17, 19, 20, 21, would be of tenements included in the "Church Estate," which was held by the Churchwardens for the Parish. See "Introduction" under "Parish Church and Living."

ended YEILDINGE And payenge therfore yearlye durynge
the said terme unto the saide Thomas Robson John gayre
Umfraye Smythe and Richard Smythe Churche Wardens
nowe of the said parishe Churche And theyre Successors
for tyme beynge the somme of vj^s of lawfull money of
Englande at the feast of saynte Martin in Winter and
penthecost by even proportions AND if yt happen the sayd
Rentt of vj^s or anye parte or parcell therof to be behynde
& unpaide in parte or in all by the space of xiiij dayes ——
after anye of the saide feastes at whiche yt ought to be paid
at That then yt shalbe lawfull to and for the saide
Churche Wardens and there Successors for the tyme beynge
in and upon the saide Tenement ———— and everye parte
and parcell therof to enter and dystrene And the dystresse
then and ther so taken to leade beare dryve & carye
awaye and the same to hold untyll suche tyme the saide
Rent withe the arreares yf anye suche be be unto the saide
Churche Wardens & ther Successors fully ———— AND
the sayde Richarde Carter for hym and his assygnes
covenantithe grauntithe and agreethe by these presents to
and withe the sayde Churche Wardens and ther Successors
That he the sayde Richarde Carter and his Assygnes shall
well and suffycyentlye upholde mayntayne and repaire the
sayd tenement withe the appurtenances belongynge unto yt
durynge all the sayde terme at his proper costes and
charges and shall at the ende of the sayde terme of xxj yeres
leave the sayde tenement well and suffycyentlye repared at
the syght of foure neyghbours within the sayde parishynge
wherof the sayde Churche Wardens to taike Twoo And
the sayde Richarde Carter to taike other twoo to vewe &
judge the saym. IN WITNESS wherof the partyes abovesaid
to these present Indentures interchangeablye have putt
their scalles the daye and yeare abovesaid.

Seals gone.

---

(13).   1564.   *Lease by Churchwardens.*   (*Imperfect*).

THIS INDENTURE maid the xxxiiijth day of marche in the
sext yeare of the Reign of oure sovereigne ladye Elizabeth
by the grace of God quene of englande france and Irelande
defender of the fayth &c. BETWENE Thomas Robson
Richard Smyth John Gayre and Humfray Smyth churchwardens of the parish of S^t gyles within the suburbes of
the cytie of Durham on the one partie And John pereson
of the cytie of Durham in the countie of Durham ————
of the other partie WITNESSETH that the saide Church

wardens for them and there Successors with the assent
consent and agreement as well of Anthonie mydleton of
Kepeyere gent. as the parishyoners of the said parish
Haythe dimised granted and to ferme letten and by these
presents dimiseth granteth and to ferme letteth unto the
saide John Pereson one tenemente with the appurtenances
Set lyinge and beynge in gyllygate aforesaide betwene a
tenemente —— —— tenure of Richard carter of theast
partie And a tenemente nowe in tenure of thomas amerye
———— and to hold the said tenemente with all and
singular the appurtenances to the said John pereson ——
his assignes ———— penthecost next ensuynge the dayt
hereof unto thende and terme of twentie and one yeares
then and from the ———— to be complet and ended
Yeldinge and payng therefore yerelye duringe the said
terme unto the said Church Wardens ———— successors
for the tyme beynge iij.s. iiijd. of lawfull ynglish money at
the feaste of S^t. Martyn in winter and penthecost ———————
And yf yt happen the said Rent of iiij.s. iiijd. or anye part
thereof too be behind and unpaid in part or in all at anye
———— by the space of —— dayes and lawfully demaunded
that then yt shalbe lawfull to the said Church wardens
and their successors ———— the said tenement with the
appurtenances to enter and distreyne and the distresse so
taken to lede dryve ———— to deteane and hold unto
suche tyme the said Rent with the arreares thereof yf anye
suche ———— be fully ———— pereson for him and his
assignes covenants and grants by these presents to and
with the said ———— the tyme beynge That he the said
John pereson and his assignes shall sufficiently ————
with the appurtenances in all manner of necessarye repara-
tions ————. And the same so sufficientlye repaired at
thende of the said terme shall then ———— persons of
bothe the said parties to be electe and chosen. And the
said Church wardens for them and ———— to and with
the said John pereson and his assignes that they the said
Church wardens ———— with the appurtenances to the
said John pereson and his assignes agenst all men shall
————. In Wytnesse whereof the parties abovesaid to
the present Indenture severallye have putt ————.

———————

(14). 1565. *Copy of Court Roll.*

Curia capitalis Johannis Heathe armigeri ibidem
tenta xviij° die Januarij Anno Regni Elizabethae Dei
gratia Anglie Franciae et Hiberniae Reginae fidei

defensoris &c. Septimo, coram Anthonio Midleton generoso Senescallo.

Ad hanc curiam venit Thomas Cornefourthe et cepit de domino totum illud Burgagium situatum et jacens in vico de Geligait in suburbiis civitatis Dunelm. ex parte australi vici inter burgagium Roberti Huddespethe ex parte orientali et burgagium Thomae Spragen ex parte occidentali; In quibus Robertus Huddespeathe inde habens jus hic in plena curia coram Senescallo totum jus titulum et statum suum sursum reddidit in manus domini ad opus predicti Thomae Cornefourthe habendum et tenendum prefato Thomae Cornefourthe executoribus et assignatis suis a festo Sancti Martini in yeme ultimo preterito ante datum presentium usque finem termini nonaginta et novem annorum ex tunc proxime sequendorum et plenarie complendorum. Reddendo inde annuatim Domino curiae ad festa pentecostes et Sancti Martini in yeme aequis portionibus xij*d.*, Et unam precariam in autumpno, Et faciendo Domino et vicario quae incumbunt. Per plegium Ingrami tailyer et Johannis taylyer. Et dat. Domino pro fine. Et Juratus &c.

---

(15). 1594. *Lease by Churchwardens.*

THIS INDENTURE made the first Daye of Marche In the xxxvj^tie yere of the Reigne our Sovereigne Ladie Elizabeth by the grace of God Quene of England Fraunce and Ireland Defendour of the faith &c. BETWENE Cuthbart Martinn Richard Storye Richard Glover and Thomas Cornforth Churchwardonns of the parrish of St Gyles in gilligate on the one partye And William Homble of gilligate within the Countie of Durham Carpenter on the other partye WITNESSETH that the saide Cuthbert Martin Richard Storye Richard Glover and Thomas Cornforth (togither with the assent consent and agreement of the rest of all the parishioners of the saide Parrishe of St Gyles) for Dyvers good causes and consideracions them movinge have Demysed graunted and to ferme letten and by thes presents Doe Demise graunt and to ferme lett unto the saide William Homble all that theire tennament or burgage & garth with all and singuler the appurten-naunces thereunto belonginge scytuate lyinge and beinge in gilligate aforesaide on the southside of the saide street, betwene A tennament or burgage belonginge to Thomas Hudspith on the east side and A little garthe belonginge to Mr Raiph Billingham on the west side which said

Tennament or burgage is nowe in the tenure & occupacyon of Iohn Wardell milner To HAVE and to hold the saide tennament or burgage and garth with all and singuler the appurtenaunces thereunto belonginge unto the saide William Homble his heires executours Administratours and Assignes frome the feast of Pentecost next ensewinge the Date hereof unto the full end and terme of Twentie and one yeres then next followinge & fullye to be complett ended and runn. YEILDINGE and payinge therefore therefore yerely Duringe the saide terme unto the saide Cuthbart Martinn Richard Glover Richard Storye and Thomas Cornforth Churchwardons, and to their Successours for the tyme beinge the sum of Tenn shillings of lawfull monney of England, att twoe tearmes in the yere, that is to say att the feast of St Martin the Bushopp in Winter and Pentecost by evenn poreyons and also iiij*d.* or one bone daye to Keepyere yerelye. AND yt it happenn the saide yerelye [*rent*] of x*s.* or any part or parcell thereof to be behinde and unpayed att any of the Feastes aforesaide att which it ought to be payed or within xx^{tie} Dayes after any of the said Feastes beinge lawfully Demanded that thenn and frome thensforth it shall and may be lawfull unto the said churchwardonns and their Successours for the tyme beinge unto the saide tennament or burgage with all and singuler the appurtenaunces thereunto belonginge to reenter and the same to have againe as in their former estate this Indenture or any thinge therein conteyned to the contrarye notwithstandinge AND yt is also agreed betwene the said Cuthbert Martin Richard Storye Richard Glover and Thomas Cornforth churchwardons And the saide William Homble, that hee the saide William Homble his Executours Administratours and assignes shall sufficyenlye repare uphold and maintein all the said tennament or burgage with the appurtennaunces in all manner of necessarye reparacions so oftenn as need shall require Duringe all the saide terme of xxj^{tie} yeres, And att the end of the saide terme shall leave the same so sufficyentlye repared att the sight of fower honest men to be indifferently chosen betwene the saide partyes. AND FURTHER it is agreed betwene the said Churchwardons and the said William Homble, that he the said William Homble and his assignes shall builde and sett upp one round (?) roofe with tymber and slate and all things necessarye thereunto belonginge betwene the forehouse and backhouse of the said tennament within one yere after the Date of thes presentes. IN WITNESSE whereof the partyes abovesaide to thes present Indentures interchaungeably have sett theire hands and sealles the day and yere first above wryttenn

Will'm Homble   X————

Seal gone.

Endorsed: Sealed and delyvered in the presence of thes witnesses ·

John Bourdess
Symond Smith
James Hodshon
[*with others*].

---

(16). *Counterpart of the above Indenture, with two seals (both gone), and signed by the Churchwardens.*

---

(17). 1584. *Lease by the Churchwardens.*

THIS INDENTURE maid the First daye of marche in the Sex and Twentie yeare of the Reigne of our Soveryne ladie Elizabeth by the grace of God quene of England France and Ireland defender of the faith &c. BETWENE Symond Alderley Christofer Sherroton Railphe Gaire and Richard Hunter Churchewardens of the parishe Churche of St Gielles in the Suburbes of the Cittie of Durham on the one partie and James Colteman of the said parishe wever on the other partie WITNESSETH That the said Churchewardens haith Demised Granted and to ferme letten and by these presentes demiseth granteth and to ferme letteth unto the said James Colteman one Tennement or burgaige with the appurtennances and one garthe thereunto belonginge lyinge and beinge in Gilligaite in the parishe aforesaid adjoinynge to one tennement nowe in the tenure of Humfry Smythe on the East and one tenemente of Richard Carter on the West the quenes street on the Southe and one Close called Elleseleases on the Northe laite in the tenure of wedow Colsonne or hir assignes To HAVE and to holde the said tenemente or burgaige and garthe with the appurtenances to the said James Colteman his executors administrators and assignes Frome the Feast of Pentecost next comynge unto the Full ende and tearme of Twentie and one yeares then next Ensuynge fullie to be compleat and ended YEILDING and payinge therefore yearlie duringe the said Tearme of Twenty and one yeares to the said Churchwardens and their Successours the Some of six shillinges of good and lawfull Englishe money at the Feaste of St Martyn the bushopp in winter and Pentecost by even porcions And yf it fortune the said yearlie rente of six shillinges or anie parte or parcell thereof to be behinde and unpaied in parte or in all after anye of the Feastes aforesaid at which it ought to be paied by the space of Twentie dayes That then it shalbe lawfull to the said Churchwardens and their successours into the said tenemente or burgaige with the appurtenances [*to*] Enter and dystreyne and the distresse so taiken to lead drive and carrie Awaye and the sayme to detayne and holde unto the said yearlie Rente With tharrearages of the sayme yf anye suche be fullie and whollie Contented and payed. AND also the said James Colteman covenantes and grantes by these presentes for hym his executors administrators and assignes That they shall sufficientlie Repaire upholde mainteyn and kepe up of their proper Costes and Charges all the said Tenemente or burgaige and all other howses nowe builded — — — — upon the said Tenement or burgaige duringe all the said terme and the sayme so sufficientlie Repaired at the ende of the said tearme shall leave. AND the said James Coltman Covenantes and grantes by these presentes to and with the said Churchwardens that it shall and maye be lawfull to the said Churchwardens and theire successoures once or twise in the yeare in the Sommer season yearlie duringe the said tearme to enter into the sayme Tenemente or burgaige and to vew and se the sayme and everie parte and parcell thereof and wheir they finde anye decaye in or upon anye the said howses belonginge to the premisses the said James covenantes and grantes for hym his executors and administrators to Amend build and Repaire the sayme before Winter then next followinge of his and their proper Costes and Charges or elles it shalbe lawfull to the said Churchwardens and theire successours into all and everie the premisses Abovesaid to Reenter and the sayme to have again in theire former estaite, and the said James Coltman his executors administrators and assignes Clearelie to expell and put out, this Indenture or anye thinge herein Conteyned to the Contrarie notwithstanding. IN WITNESSE whereof the parties Abovesaid to these Indentures interchangeablie have put to theire handes and seale the daye and yeare Abovesaid.

One seal (gone) and signature (obliterated).

Endorsed: Sealed and delivered in the presence of thes witnesses   Richard Conyers
John Cooke
Thomas Browne
Will'm Deanam.
Anthony Cooke.

(18). *Counterpart of the last.*

Four seals (all gone), and signatures, viz., Symond alderlie, Xpofer Sheraton, Raphe Gayre, H.R.

Endorsed with names of the same witnesses.

———

(19). 1584. *Lease by Churchwardens. (Imperfect).*

THIS INDENTURE maied the xx^{tie} daye of June in the xxvi yere of the ——— Irelande defendour of the faith etc. BETWENE William Deanam Richard ——— Suburbes of the Cytye of Durham on the one partye And Rychard Carter of Gillygate in the same ——— and theire Successours with the assent consent and agremente aswell of Mr John Heth [*of*] Kepeyere ——— letten and by thes presentes demiseth graunteth and to ferme letteth unto the ——— A tenemente nowe in the tenure of James Cotman of the east parte and A tenemente *theire* in the tenure of ——— the garth with all and singuler thappurtenances to the saide Rychard [*Carter*] ——— next ensuyinge the daite hereof unto the full end and terme of twentye and one yeres ——— yerely durynge the said terme unto the said Churchwardens and their *Successours* ——— St Martine in Winter and Pentecoste by even porcyons AND yf it ——— at any the feastes aforesaide by the space of twenty daies and ——— to the said Churchwardens and theire Successours for the tyme beinge ——— to enter ——— carrye awaye and the same to Deteyne and holde unto such tyme ——— fortune that a Distresse shalbe founde within the saide house ——— theire successours to reenter into all and singuler the premises ——— or any thinge therein conteyned to the contrarye notwithsandinge And ——— with the said Churchwardens and theire Successours that he the said ——— with the appurtenaunces in all manere of necessary reparacion ——— said terme shall leave and quietly depart frome at the syght ——— And that all and everie the promises of the partyes ———.

Four seals, all gone.

———

(20). 1584. *Lease by the Churchwardens. (Imperfect).*

THIS INDENTURE maide the xv^{te} daye of June in the six and twenteth yere of the reigne of our sovereigne ladye Elizabeth by the grace ——— of Englande Fraunce and Irelaunde defendour of the Faith &c. BETWENE William Deanam Richard Frizell George ——— and Anthony Co——— of the parishe of St Giles within the suburbes

of the Cyty of Durhame on the one partye and Symond
Awderley of the Cyty of Durham in the County of ————
of thother partye WITNESSETH that the said churchwardens for them and theire successours with the
assent consent & agreement aswell of Mr John [*Hethe of*]
Kepeyere Esquire as the parishioners of the said parishe
haith Demysed graunted and to ferme letten And by these
presentes demyseth graunteth and to ferme letteth unto
the said Symonde Awderley one tenemente with the
appurtenances &c. lyinge and beinge in Gillygate aforesaid
betwene A tenement belonginge to ————— nowe in the
tenure of Rychard Chaitor of theaste parte And a tenemente
nowe in the tenure of George Surtise of the west parte
To HAVE ———— tenemente with all and singuler the
appurtenaunces to the saide Symonde Awderley and his
assignes frome the Feaste of the nativitie of ————
commonly called Mydsommer daye nexte after the daite
hereof unto the end and terme of twenty and one yeres then
and frome thenceforthe ——— to be complete and ended
YELDINGE and payinge therefore yerelie Duringe the said
terme unto the saide Churchwardons and theire successours
[*for the tyme*] beinge five shillinges & six pence of lawfull
English money at the Feastes of St Martine in winter and
Penticoste by even poreyons ———— Rente of v*s*. vj*d*.
or any parte thereof to be behinde and unpayed in parte or
[*in*] all att any the Feastes aforesaide by the space of
twenty Daies and ———— nowe Dwellinge house of the
saide Symonde that then it shalbe lawfull to the said
Churchwardons and theire successours for the tyme beinge
into ———— the appurtenaunces to enter and Distreaine
and the Distresse so taken to leyde drive and carrye awaye
and the same to Deteine and holde unto suche tyme the said
Rent with the arrerages thereof if any suche be lawfully
contented and payed. And if it shall fortune that no
distresse shalbe founde within the said house ———— to
be taken for the none pament of the saide Rente then it
shalbe lawfull for the saide Churchwardons and theire
successours to reenter into all and singuler the premises
and then and there to have againe in as large and ample
manere as heretofore they have had, this Indenture or any
thinge herein conteyned to the contrary notwithstanding.
AND the saide Symonde Awderley for him and his Assignes
covenantes and grauntes by these presentes to and with
the saide Churchwardens and theire successours for the
tyme beinge that he the said Symonde Awderley and his

Assignes shall sufficientlye repaire uphold and mainteine all the said tenemente with the appurtenaunces in all manere of necessary reparacions so ofte as neade shall require duringe all the saide terme, and the same so sufficiently repairede at thende of the saide terme shall leave and quietly departe frome at the sight and vewe of fower honest men of both the said parties to be elected and chosen [*three lines erased here*] AND that all and every the promises (?) of the part of the saide Symond Awderley shalbe surely performed fulfilled and kepte, George Surtisse and William Selbye yeomen of the City of Durham within the County of Durham Doe binde them and eyther of them in the sume of fower poundes of lawfull Englishe moneye to be paid to the said Churchwardons and theire successours for the tyme beinge if yt happen the said Symond to faile in the promises or in any of them. IN WYTNESSE whereof aswell the surties aforesaid as the parties abovesaid to thes present Indentures have put to theire Scalles the Daye and yere abovewritten ————

[*The rest obliterated. Six seals, all gone*].

[*Signed*] Wylliam Denham ; George ————

Endorsed : Scaled signed and delivered in the presence of thes witnesses ;

> Richard Smith
> Umfray Smith
> James Dow
> Thomas
> John Hubbeke

———

(21).   1590.   *Lease by the Churchwardens.*

THIS INDENTURE made the fowertenth Day of Februarye In the xxxij^ue yere of the reigne of our Sovereigne ladye Elizabeth by the grace of God Quene of Englande Fraunce and Irelande Defender of the Faith &c. Betwene John Bourdesse Thomas Marshell William Coltman & Arche Cunnyngham nowe Churchwardons of the Parrishe of St Gyles in Durham on the one partye And Edward Brantingham of Gylligate within the Countye of Durham laborer on the other partye WITNESSETH that the said Churchwardons for them and theire successours with the assent consent and agreement of the rest of the parishioners of the said Parrishe have Demysed graunted and to ferme lettenn and by thes presentes Demyseth graunteth and to ferme letteth unto the saide Edward Brantingham all that

one tennament or burgage and garth with all and singuler
the appurtennances thereunto belonginge scituate lyinge
and beinge within the saide streett of Gilligate neere Duke
poole late in the tenure & occupacion of one wyddowe
Howe deceased To HAVE and to holde the saide tennament and garth will all and singuler the appurtennances
thereunto belonginge unto the said Edward Brantingham
his heires Administratours and assignes frome the Feast of
Pentecost next ensewinge the date hereof unto the full end
and tearme of Twenty and one yeres then next followinge
fullye to complett ended and Run YEILDINGE and payinge
therefore yerely Duringe the saide tearme of xxj{tie} yeres
unto the said Churchwardons & theire successours for the
tyme beinge the sum of syxe shillinges of good and lawfull
English monney att two tearmes in the yere, viz. att the
Feast of St Martin the Bushopp in winter & Pentecost.
———— if it happen the said yerely rent of vjs. or any
part or parcell thereof to be behind and unpayed att any of
the saide Feastes or within xx{tie} dayes after beinge lawfully
demaunded that then it shalbe lawfull to the saide Churchwardons and their successours into the said tennament and
garth with all and singuler the appurtennances to reenter
and the same to have againe ———— in theire former
right, thes Indentures or any thinge herein conteyned
to the contrary notwithstandinge. AND the said Edward
for him his executours and assignes covenaunteth and
graunteth by thes presentes to and with the said Churchwardons and theire successours that he the said Edward
Brantingham his executours and assignes shall sufficiently
repare uphold and mainteyne all the said tennament in all
manner of necessary reparacons so often as need shall
require Duringe all the said tearme and the same so
sufficiently repared att the end of the said tearme shall
peaceably leave and quietly depart from. In witnesse
whereof the partyes abovesaid to thes present Indentures
interchaungably have put theire handes & scalles the
Day and yere first above written.

One seal (gone). Signed, Edward Brantingham.

---

(22). 1600. *Copy of Court Roll.*

Curia Capitalis Iohannis Heathe Armigeri tenta ibidem
nono die Aprilis Anno Regni Elizabethae Dei gratia
Angliae Franciae et Hiberniae Reginae fidei defensoris &c.
Quadragesimo secundo Coram Michaell Calverley generoso
Senescallo.

Ad hanc curiam venit Mergaret Smithe nuper Relicta Ricardi Smithe defuncti et cepit de domino quatuor Burgagia jacentia in Geligate in Dunelm. cum pertinentiis habenda eidem Mergaret et assignatis suis a festo Sancti Martini in hyeme proxime futuro usque finem Termini Nonaginta et Novem Annorum ex tunc proxime sequentium et plenarie complendorum. Reddendo inde annuatim domino curiae vs. ad festa Pentecostes et Sancti Martini in hyeme aequis porcionibus et tres precarias in Autumpno nec non Molere granem suam ad molendinum domini Et pinsere panem suum ad Communem pistrinam domini, nec non Reddendo Annuatim domino curiae ad festum Nativitatis domini unam gallinam et faciendo domino et vicinis quae incumbunt et dat. domino pro fine.   Et jurata est et admissa est burgensis.

Michaell Calverley.

———————

(23).   1617.   *Copy of Court Roll.*

<table>
<tr><td>Burgus
de Giligate</td><td>Curia Capitalis Johannis heeth senioris Armigeri domini hujus manerii Die Martis nono Die Julii Anno Regni Regis Jacobi nunc Angliae &c. decimo quarto et Scotiae quadragesimo nono Coram Johanne Richardson Armigeri Senescallo ibidem.</td></tr>
</table>

Ad hanc curiam venit Willelmus Sheraton et cepit de domino quatuor burgagia jacentia in Giligate in Dunelm. cum pertinentiis ex dono et concessione Georgii Smith, Habenda dicto Willelmo Sheraton et assignatis suis a festo Sancti Martini in hyeme proxime futuro usque finem termini Nonaginta et Novem Annorum ex tunc proxime sequentium et plenarie complendorum.   Reddendo inde annuatim dicto domino curiae vs. ad festa Sancti Martini in hyeme et Pentecostes per aequales porciones et inveniendo tres precarias in Autumpno annuatim, Et faciendo Domino et vicinis quae incumbunt. Et dat. Domino pro fine iij^ti. Et Juratus est.   Et admissus est inde burgensis

Per me Johannem Richardson Sen. Armi-
gerum Senescallum ibidem.

———————

(24).   1618.   *Bond of Margaret Hall with Church-wardens.*

Noverint universi per praesentes nos Margratam Hall de Giligate in Civitate Dunelmae widdowe et Hugonem Walton de Civitate Dunelm. Draper et Christoferum

S——— de gilligate in Civitate Dunelmae taner teneri
et firmiter obligari Tho. Corneforth Thomas Wan Robt
Baker and Tho. Dauson Iocomiis [1] parochiae Sti Egidii
in Civitate Dunelm, praedict. in octo libris bonae et legalis
monetae Angliae Solvend. eidem Tho. Corneforth Tho.
Wann Robt. Baker et Thomas Dauson Icomiis pro
tempore existante parochiae praedictae aut certo atturnato,
ad quam quidem solutionem bene et fideliter faciendam
obligamus nos et utrumque nostrum per se pro toto et in
solidum heredes executores et administratores nostros
firmiter per praesentes Sigillis nostris Sigillatas. Dat.
decimo tertio die Septembris Anno domini nostri Jacobi
Dei gratia Angliae Scotiae Franciae et hiberni Regis fedie
defensoris vicessimo sexto : Anno Domini 1618.

Signum
Georgii **G** Cradgs

Signum
Margret **X** Hall

Hugh Walton

Sealed Signed and
Delivered in the presents of us ——— Swallow
Edward Cornfor
Signum Xpori **C** Simpson.

Endorsement.

The Condition of this obligation is—That if the said
withinboundent Magrett Hall her heires executores administratores and assignes and everie of them doe well
and trewly performe fullfill and kepe all and singuler
articules covenants grants and agrements which on hir
part and behalfes are to be performed fullfilled and kept
set downe and declared in one paire of indentures of
divise (?) bering date heareof maid betwene the said Tho.
Corneforth Tho. Wann Robt. Baker and Tho. Dauson
of the one partie and the withinboundent Magrett Hall
one the other partie according to the trew meaning of the
said indenters that then this present obligation to be void
and of none effect or else to stand and be in full force poure
and vertue.

———

(25). 1619. *Bond to fulfil conditions.*

Noverint universi per praesentes nos Robertum Carr
de gilligate in suburbis civitatis Dunelm. lauborer et
Richardum Tripp de Gilligate in suburbis praedictae

---

[1] Meaning "Iconomis" (for "œconomis"), *i.e.*, churchwardens.

civitatis Dunelm. yeoman teneri et firmiter obligari Thomae Cornfurth Roberto Baker Thomae Wann et Thomae Dawson gardianis parochiae de S^{ti} Egidii in suburbis praedictae civitatis Dunelm. in decem libris bonae et legalis monetae Angliae solvendis eidem Thomae Cornfurthe Roberto Baker Thomae Wann et Thomae Dawson et successoribus suis, ad quam quidem solutionem bene et fideliter faciendam obligamus nos et utrumque nostrum per se & pro toto executores et administratores nostros firmiter per praesentes sigillis nostris sigillatum. Datum octavo die Maii Anno Regni domini nostri Jacobi dei gratia Angliae Scotiae Franciae et Hiberniae Regis fidei defensoris &c. Angliae Franciae et Hiberniae decimo septimo, et Scotiae Anno Domini 1619.

The condicion of this obligacion is suche that yf the above bounden Robt. Carr his executors administrators and assignes do well and trewly observe performe fulfill and keap all and everie covenant article clause and agreement which on his partie ar to be observed performed fulfilled and kept specified and declared in one paire of Indentures of lease maid betwene the above named Thomas Cornfurth Robt. Baker Thomas Wan and Thomas Dawson on the one partie and the above bounden Robt Carr on the other that then this present obligacion to be voyde and of none effect or elles to stand remane and be in full power strength and vertue.

Robert Carr his   Richard Tripp
Mark X   his X mark

Endorsed as follows :

Sealed signed and delivered in the presence of John Watson, Robert Barwicke, Christopher ———————, Robert Wan.

BONDS.

There are also preserved in the Vestry, on separate sheets, 21 sealed Bonds, bearing dates from 1629 to 1718 inclusive, for guarding against certain persons becoming chargeable to the parish.

The following are here given as specimens :—

I.   Noverint universi per praesentes me Wm Bainbrige de Gyllygate juxta Civitat. Dunelm. in Com. Dunelm. milner teneri et firmiter obligari Georgio Tayler de eadem in eodem Com. tanner et Roberto Heighington de eadem in eodem Com. roper in tres libris & quatuor solidis bonae et legalis monetae solvend. eisdem Georgio & Roberto aut suis certis in hac parte Attornatis executoribus administratoribus vel assignatis.   Ad quam quidem solucionem bene et fideliter faciendam Obligo me heredes executores et Administratores meos firmiter per praesentes sigillo meo sigillatas.   Dat. ultimo die mensis Augusti Anno regni domini nostri Caroli dei gratia regis Angliae Scotiae Franciae & hiberniae fidei defensoris, &c., quinto Annoque domini 1629.

The Condicon of this obligacon is such that whereas Richard Garthfote hath by the consent of the abovenamed George Tayler and Robert Heighington (being over seers for the poore of the parish of St Gyles nere the said Cittie of Durham) hath put himselfe to be an Apprentice for and during the tearme of seaven years from henceforth and that the said W^m shall during the said tearme finde for the said Richard meate drinke and clothes and also sufficiently to instruct him in the milner's craft so that the said parish shall not from henceforth during the said tearme be charged with any further trouble or releaveing of the said Richard.   If therefore the said Wm Bainbrige doe well hold performe fulfill and keepe all & everie particler of this present condicon, That then this obligacon to be void and of none effect, or else the same to stand remaine and be in full force strength and vertue.

Sealed and delivered in the   Signed
       presence of   wilm **X** Bainbrige
          marke   [*Seal, with impression*]
Katherine   **X**   Maland   IHS.
Rob't Maland
      Notarie publiqe.

II. Noverint universi per praesentes me Elizabeth Edon de Gilligate in suburbiis civitatis Dunlm. et Comitat. Dunlm. vediam teneri et firmiter obligari Radulp Richardson et Richard Hutchinson de Gilligate in suburbiis civitatis Dunelm. praed. et Comitat. Dunlm. praed. Churchwardings in Viginti libris bonae et legalis monetae Angliae solvendis eidem Ralph Richardson et Richard Hutchinson aut suo Certo Attornato suessecitoribus (*successoribus*) Churchwardings vel Assegnatis suis. Ad quam quidem solutionem bene et fideliter faciendam obligo me heredes executores et Administratores meos firmiter per praesentes Sigillatas meo sigillo. Dat. vicessimo die Febuaris Anno Regni Domini nostri Carroli secundi dei gratia Angliae Scotiae Francae et hebernae Regis fedei Defensor. Vicesimo Quinto, Annoque Domini 1672.

The Condition of this obligation is such that Whereas one William Thompson & dority his Wife hath taken a Roume or house of the above bounden Elizabeth Edon in Gilligate aforesaid in ye parish of St Gilles, Whereas the said Ralph Richardson & Richard Hutchinson now Churchwardings would not their unto Alow of the said William Tompson & his wife or Children to be troublesom or burdinsom to ye said parish of St Gilles, now ye said Elizabeth Edon doth bind herself her heires executors & Administrators that the said Tompson nor his wife or Children shall not at Any tyme or tymes hereafter trouble but shall fully and Clearly Aquit discharge & save harmlesse as well Ralph Richardson & Richard Hutchinson now Churchwardings of the said parish of Gilligat & Church of St. Giles & their successiors wardens for ye tyme being & every of them as also all the Inhabitance of ye said parish dureing ye tyme they doth remaine her tennants or in ye said parish of St Gilles, That then this present obligation to be voyd & of none effect, or else the same to stand Abide remaine & be in full force strength & vertue.

Sigillat. et deliberat. in
    praesentia nostri   Mark X & seale

(Seal.)   his mark
     John I M Mastin Elizabeth (Seal.) Edon.
     his make
     Will' M Weames
     Martin Harbotle.

III.   Noverint universi per praesentes nos Matthew Denten & Jacobus Denton Teneri & firmiter obligari Johanno Martin Anthonio Dobson Richardo Coulson Johanno Busbey Matthio Denton Thomae Hastans officiores parochiae sancti egedii & successoribus eorum in Quadragintis Libris bonae et Legalis monetae Anglae solvendum eisdem officiores predictis vell successoribus suis; ad quam quidem solutionem bone & fideliter faciendam obligamus noss heredess executores et administratores nostros firmiter per praesentes sigillis nostris. Datt. vicessimo octavo die Augusti Annoque Dom. 1705.

The Condicon of this obligation is such that if ye abound [*above bounden ?*] matthew Denton & James Denton both of this parish do well and truly save harmles as well the above named John Martin Antho. Dobson Richard Coulson John Busby Tho Hastans Matthew Denton officers of ye parish of St Gyles from all manner of Charge or Charges that now is or hearafter may happen to them or any of ye parish from the time being & from time to time to their successor officers of ye said parish & parishioners of Elizabeth Sharpe & Margret Sanderson of ye said parish, both of which are by information of them before John Tempest Esqre sworn to be ye Basterd Children of James Denton aforesaid when born ; if therfor ye said James & Matthew Denton do from time to time & at all times hearafter save harmles as well ye officers above said as their successors from year to year from all & all manner of Charge that may be imposed upon any officers or parishioners by reason of ye said Elizabeth Sharpe Mary Sanderson or their bastards now sworn ; that then this obligation to be voyd, otherwise to stand in full force effect & vertue.   Given under our hands this 28 August 1705.

<table>
<tr><td>Signat. Sigillat.
Deliberat. in
praesentia nostri</td><td>his
George X Maugham
mark
Henry Parkinson
Walter Howie.</td></tr>
</table>

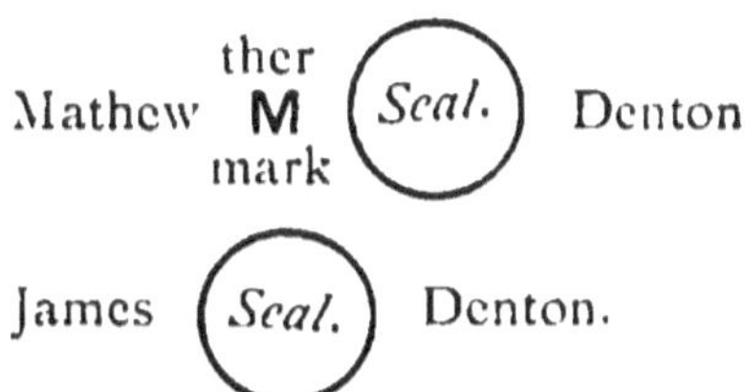

EXTRACTS FROM THE ACCOUNTS OF THE CHURCHWARDENS OF THE PARISH OF ST. GILES, DURHAM.[1]

DISBURSEMENTS.

A.D. 1664. To John Rogers for his wages (sexton). To John Fawell for filling up a hole in the Cawse. For this New Book. For Spyles & Wood for the Cawsee, 3s. Item for our labour & charges when we gathered the sess for the Church & going about the Church business. Paid for ringers the 5th of November. Paid to Mr. Heath for half a years rent due at Martinmas last. Disburst to the poor at Easter, £1 14s. 0d. Paid to Robert Brantingham for the Turnpike, 1s. 4d. Paid to Mr Tempest for half a years rent, 8s.

1665. Paid at Elvet Church to the Archdeekon, 3s. 4d. For Wood & Spyles for the Cawsee, 3s. For mending the Turnpike. Disburst to the Poor at Christmas. Disburst to the Poor at Easter. For counter pens & in charges when we sealled the Leeses, 5s. To Mr Tempest for a years rent, 16s.

1666. To Wm Hall for a Pate's head, 6d. Nicholas Dotchon for his rent at Pentecost, 5s. Spent when Nicholas Dotchon renewed his leese by us four Churchwardens, 2s. 6d. Nicholas Dotchon for his Lease, 9s. Paid Mr Tempest for a years rent, 16s. For sweeping the Church lane.

1667. P^d to Colonel Tempest for a years rent, 16s.

1668. Paid at the Bishops visitation. Paid to Robert Brantingham for mending the pulpit, 4d. To Thomas Hayne for mending the Church porches. Given to the Power now at Whitsontide. To John Brown for a fox head.

1669. For Counterpens of the leeses. Disburst to the poore.

---

[1] The Churchwardens' Accounts of the Parish of St. Giles date from A.D. 1664, according to a Schedule of Books and Documents made by order of Vestry, December 26th, 1843, and entered in the Vestry Book, during the incumbency of the Rev. Francis Thompson. These extracts, found among his papers relating to the parish, appear to have been made by him as being representative specimens, or otherwise interesting. The three volumes from which they have been made, specified in the above-mentioned Schedule, are now said to be missing, but it is to be hoped that they will be found.

1670. For Carrowinge of Stones for the Cawsey. Mr John Tempest for his rent.

1671. To the Kings receiver for rent.

1672. Paid to Mr John Tempest.

1673. To the collectors for a sesse for the royall aide. To John Rodgers for laying 2 layer stalls. To Cornell Tempest for his years rent. Paid to the Poore.

1674. For lead for the queare dore & for the mans work. For the Kings rent. For watenng [*waiting?*] of the Dean & Chapr about the peticion all day. Paid to the Poore.

1675. Wood & Spiles for the Cawsees. To the Poor at Christmas. To John Rodgers for laying a layerstall. To Mr Tempest for a years rent. For making a grave for a poor woman. Item bestowed upon this minester at several times. For getting a warrant for removing Mrs Booth.

1676. Disburst to the minester, 3s. 6d. Bestowed upon the minester, 1s. Mow at another time, 6d. Mow spent upon the minester, 1s. 4d. Mow at six times spent upon the minester, 1s. 2d. Mow spent upon the Parson, 2s. 4d. For two years church rent. For a fox head. Bestowed upon a Stranger that preached, 1s. To Captain Tempest for a years rent. To the Poore the Church rent & other Gifts in all.

1677. For 3 days work at the Cawssee. To Captain Tempest for rent. Paid to the Poore. Recd of John Cosbell for his leese, 2s. 6d.

1678. A poor Lankeshire man. Spent for Keeper & Grange sess. A Peats head. Washing ye church stalls. Paid for the Cawsees. For attending Midsumr Sesshons for taking of ye £20 fyne. Item for gathering Keepr & Grange sess, 1s.

1679. A kye to ye quire doore.

1682. Paid to Mr Cam for buring Nell Roumfouts two children. For mending the pue for the parson. Paid for Mr. Cam larstawle [*lairstall*]. For Cornwell Tempest rent. Spent when John Maston went to Hexhom aboute the man that gatt the childe with Hesse Leepers daughter.

1683. For paving the Cawsy beyond Gills bridge. For ringing ye 4th Augt when ye Judges came in. For 2 years rent to ye Kings receivers. Spent with Mr Smith when he preached. Spent with Mr Gilpin at two times. Spent with Mr Martin. Spent with Mr Blakeston. Spent with Mr Knaggs. For repairing the Cawsy. For dressing the poors land. To Thos Allenson for colouring ye Litany Desk. For bread & wine for communicants. For Colonell Tempest rent.

1684. Spent with Mr Gilpin when he preached. Spent with Mich. Corby when we let his Lease. Spent with Mr Thompson when he preached. P^d ye Kings rent. P^d for ringing of ye coronation day.

1685. Spent with person Teasdall at Thos Allinsons. Spent with person Tompson when he preatched. Paid the Kings rent. For laying Mr Emmerson Layer stall. Spent with person Teasdale & the rest of the Churchwardens. Paid to Margery Allinson for Ale given to person Martin.

1686. Spent with Mr Forster. Spent when Mr Beamond preached. Spent when Mr Blackston preached. Given to John Bee in his sicknesse. To Nicho Dixon & Thos Watson for ye Cawses in renton loning. Paid the Kings rent. For laying Thos Hunters layer stall. Spent wⁿ let Mr Wilsons lease. Spent with Mr Deane & Mr Martin. Spent at several times at Thos Allisons by ye person wⁿ we were not present. Paid for mending 2 stalls in ye church.

1687. Spent wⁿ ye person went to Cambridge. Paid wⁿ Mr Lyell preached. Spent wⁿ we let David Torburn his Lease. For lending ye chancery office two days. For Mrs Hubbuck laire stall. For ye causees in renton Loning & all ye other cawsays.

1688. For making a new battlement upon the church, £10 0^s. 0^d. Spent when we got our sess laid. Spent upon the pavers. Paid ye Kings rent, 3^s. 4^d. Spent when Mr Kirton preached. Given to a poore woman in labor at Ed. Dentons. To ye ringers when King William was proclamed, 3^s. 6^d. When Mr Neele preached. Wⁿ the Bishops was set at liberty, 3^s. For one fox head. For a warrant for removing incomers. For repairing the causes. For church garth dieke.

1689. Receipt wanting. For the Kings rent. For treating ye persons w^h preached ye whole yeare. Spent wⁿ we were forced to attend the justises 2 times when Eden & Paxton petitioned for a redress of ye poore sess.

1690. For laying the church porch. Given person Martin in ale when he preached. For ye Kings rent, 3s. 6d. For church rent, 16s. Walter Haires Sellery. John Rogers his wages. For ye church hedge.

1691. Two years church rent, £1 12s. 0d. Kings rent and acquittance, 3s. 4d. Given Mr Gamwell & other persons in drink.

1692. For changing [cleynyng?] ye church plate. For ye causees, sand & stones. Rec^d for Anthony Dobson's lease, 2s. 6d. Anthony Dobson Churchwarden. For ye Kings rents. P^d ye Painter for ye sentances. For Jane Browns Grave. Spent when we gathered in ye out rents and street rentals in ye street to give Mr Newhouse. P^d Margery Allinson for drink given to persons. P^d for 2 years church rent, 18s. 6d., being in arrears of Polton Grange assesment to make it up, £1 12s. 0d.

1694. Spent at ye summons of Mr Dobson maior for ye returning ye list of our poore, at the Bishop of Durham's request, who promised to send moneys into ye parish that the poore might not come to his gates. Spent at Gattey Whites with ye parson. P^d to ye minister & clark for 3 funerals. P^d for ringing at ye Queens funeral. For treating parson Newhouse several times. P^d Walter Haire his 94 Sallery. P^d for Stones, &c., for ye church causeyes. For the church Hedge.

1695. At the taking of Namure, 4s. 3d. Stones & Slates & pointing the South porch. 3 years arrear of the Kings rent. Thanksgiving for delivery from ye late plott. P^d Mr Done by Sir Christopher Musgrave, Sir Ralph Carr and W. Tempest Esqre order for cassing up ye old poor scrowles & coppying ye new one, 2s. 6d. Spent upon Mr Forster when he preached several times.

1696. Y^e Kings rent. Two fox heads. Spent when Mr Martin Mr Forster & other persons preached. For labour & drink at the causey.

1697. Given Mr Forster in ale when he preached, 2s. 0d. For mending the pulpit. Spent when Sir George Whealer preached, 2s. 0d. For Births & Burials. Allowed Colonel Tempest for Church rent.

1698. Paid for whitening ye church. Spent when Sir Geo. Wheeler preached (twice this year). Paid Colonel Tempest for Church rent, 16s. Given to bury Geo. Taylor. Paid for King's rents, 10s. For a bottle of wine for the sicke. Spent when Mr Sanderson preached.

1699.   Paid for person y^t preached charged us by Abram Allinson.   For mending ye Ducke Poole.   Paid Robt Richardson in his sickness.   Paid Walter Haire. Paid John Davinson for his Salary.   For Kings rents.

1700.   For Kings rents, 10s. 4d.   P^d ye Lord rent, 16s. 4d.   P^d for burials.   For part of a Coffin for Littlefairs child.   P^d for treating the person.   Mowe church hedge & turnpike.

1701.   Kings rent, 3s. 4d.   For ringing when Queen Anne was proclaimed.   P^d Mr Tempest his out rent.   For treating of ministers the whole yeare, 17s. 6d.   For one paite head.   Given Mary Cooks in her sickness.

1702.   Rec^d for Bankes' Larestall, 3s. 4d.   For mending the church Bible.   For a rope for ye font.   To a woman in child bed y^t was delivered in the field.   Kings rent, 3s. 4d.   Mr Jno Tempest for his out rent, 16s.   P^d for John Bankes lare stall, 1s.   For wine & bread at Christmas.   Spent about persons preaching.

1703.   For Flaging ye church, £4 9s. 6d.   Spent when Mr Parkin preached.

1704.   P^d John Tempest Esqre 2 years rent, £1 12s. 0d. P^d ye Queens rent, 3s. 4d.   For ale when Sir George Chap^n preached, 2s. 3d.   John Forster for setting the grave stone.   Spent w^n we set ye Lad in ye stocks.

1705.   P^d for Queens rent.   P^d ye Lord's rent.   Given in ale to ye Scotch person.

1706.   Spent upon preaching ministers in Mr Dunn's sickness.   P^d ye Lords rent 1705.   Clarks wages.   Saxons wages.   Queens rent.   (Signed by John Perkins, Curate). Given Mr Dunn in sickness, 5s.

1721.   P^d to the Kings receiver, 3s. 4d.   P^d John Tempest Esqre, 16s.

1722.   To John Tempest Esqre, 8s.

1724.   Treat parson Rimer when preacht.   To John Tempest Esqre, 8s.

1725.   Kings rent, 3s. 4d.

1728.   By the Kings rents & attending, 4s.   By 3 several meetings of the 24 ab^t Mr Tempest.

1729.   For the Kings rent.   Spent in treating parsons at several times.

1730.   Spent in going to Mr Tempest at several times. To a warrant & trouble to carry Frank Thompson and his fammaly to Bpp Auckland.   To 1 fox head, 5 fooment heads & 1 owl.

1754.   Spent on a parson (3 times this year).

1756.   Spent with parson Robson.

1778.   Short paid in the out rents. John Tempest Esqre, 4s. 4d.

APPENDIX A.

DOCUMENTS RELATING TO KEPYER HOSPITAL.

I. Bishop Nevill's Confirmation of Charters, and Impropriation of St. Nicholas.[1]

[Durham Cursitor's Roll, 43, M. 6, No. 31, in Public Record Office].

Robertus[2] Dei gratia etc. Omnibus ad quos etc. Salutem. Inspeximus literas patentes venerabilis patris Johannis[3] nuper Episcopi Dunelmensis praedecessoris nostri factas in haec verba, Universis Sanctae matris ecclesiae filiis ad quorum noticiam praesentes literae pervenerint Johannes permissione divina Dunelmensis Episcopus salutem in Domino sempiternam. Noveritis nos inspexisse cartam concessionis et confirmacionis quam bonae memoriae Thomas[4] dudum Dunelmensis Episcopus praedecessor nostri immediatus fecit magistro et fratribus hospitalis Sancti Egidii de Kypier juxta Dunolm. in haec verba ; Universis Sanctae matris ecclesiae filiis ad quorum noticiam praesentes literae pervenerint Thomas permissione divina Dunolmensis Episcopus salutem in Domino sempiternam. Noveritis nos inspexisse cartam concessionis et confirmacionis quam bonae memoriae Ricardus[5] dudum Dunolmensis Episcopus Lodovici[6] quandam Dunelmensis Episcopi mediatus praedecessor fecit magistro & fratribus hospitalis Sancti Egidii de Kypier juxta Dunolm. in haec verba ; Ricardus permissione divina Episcopus Dunolmensis Omnibus ad quos praesentes literae pervenerint salutem. Inspeximus quandam inquisicionem quam per dilectos & fideles nostros Thomam de Fysscheburn & Willelmum de Denum nuper fieri fecimus in hec verba ; Inquisicio capta apud Dunolm. die Martis in festo Sancti

---

[1] This is the confirmation by Bishop Robert Neville in 1445 of the old Charters of Kepyer, which had been destroyed by the fire in 1309, as verified by a commission issued by Bishop Kellaw in 1380. In it previous confirmations by bishops after Kellaw are cited ; the constitution and procedure of Kellaw's commission are described ; the Charters themselves, numbered I—XIX, are recited ; and annexed is the Impropriation by Bishop Neville of the Rectory of St. Nicholas to the Hospital. The same Charters, as exhibited in the Patent Rolls of Richard II, are printed in Dugdale's *Monasticon* under " Kepyer Hospital." The edition of them here given is from the Close Rolls of Bishop Neville, now preserved in the Record Office, London.

[2] Robert Neville (1437-57).   [5] Richard Kellaw (1311–18).

[3] John Fordham (1382–88).   [6] Lewis Beaumont (1317–33).

[4] Thomas Hatfield (1345–87).

Thomae Apostoli anno Pontificatus domini Ricardi
Dunolmensis Episcopi primo coram Thoma de Fysscheburn & Willelmo de Denum per Willelmum Hiberne
Johannem de Aldewode Willelmum dominum de Medmesley
Henricum de Lumley Thomam de Graystanes Robertum
de Bespole Ricardum de Moreton Willelmum dominum de
Neuton Willelmum Postel Petrum de Trillesden Ricardum
Stere de Wlmston & Johannem de Wheteley per breve
ipsius domini episcopi in haec verba, Ricardus Dei gratia
episcopus Dunolmensis dilectis & fidelibus suis Thomae
de Fysscheburn & Willelmo de Denom salutem. Quia
ex querela dilectorum nobis in Christo magistri & fratrum
hospitalis Sancti Egidii de Kypier accepimus quod
quaedam cartae & munimenta sua per quae ipsi & praedecessores sui terras redditus & tenementa hospitalis praedicti
tenuerunt nuper per incendium in quandam domum infra
idem hospitale in qua cartae & munimenta illa reposita
fuerunt subito superveniens combusta fuerunt & consumpta,
per quod eisdem magistro & fratribus & successoribus suis
hospitalique praedicto poterit exheredacionis periculum
de facili minere, Nos statim eorundem magistri & fratrum
ac hospitalis sui praedicti pie compacientes & eisdem
providere volentes in hac parte assignavimus vos ad
inquirendum per sacramentum proborum & legalium
hominum de comitatu Dunelm. et Sadberg. per quos rei
veritas melius sciri poterit quas terras quos redditus et
quae tenementa iidem magistri et fratres vel praedecessores
sui tenuerunt tempore combustionis praedictae et a quo
tempore et de quibus et per quae servicia et quas terras
et quos redditus et quae tenementa tenuerunt tempore
praedicto per cartis et munimenta, et per quas cartas et
quae munimenta, et quas terras et quos redditus et quae
tenementa tenuerunt sine cartis et munimentis, et qualiter
et quo modo et in quibus locis terrae illae redditus et
tenementa existunt, et per quos terrae redditus et tenementa
eidem Hospitali collata fuerunt, et a quo tempore et qualiter
et quo modo. Et ideo vobis mandamus quod ad certos dies
et loca quos ad hoc provideritis inquisicionem illam faciatis
et eam distincte et aperte factam nobis sub sigillis vestris et
sigillis eorum per quos facta fuerit sine dilatione mittatis et
hoc breve. Mandamus enim Vicecomiti nostro comitatuum
praedictorum quod ad certos dies et loca quos ei scire
faciemus venire faciat coram vobis tot et tales probos et
legales homines de comitatibus praedictis per quos rei
veritas in praemissis melius sciri poterit et inquiri. In
cuius rei testimonium has literas nostras fieri fecimus

patentes. Dat. Dunelm. per manus Willelmi Denum
Clerici nostri sexto die Decembris Anno Pontificatûs nostri
primo. Qui dicunt super Sacramentum suum quod tempore
domini Petri de Thoresby nuper Magistri Hospitalis
praedicti per incendium in quandam domum infra idem
Hospitale subito superveniens die Martis in Crastino Sancti
Brandani Abbatis, Anno Domini Millesimo CCC^{mo} sexto
in qua cartae et quaedam munimenta per dominum Petrum
tunc Magistrum dicti Hospitalis fuerunt posita combusta
fuerunt. Et dicunt quod iidem Magister & fratres habuerunt
cartas et munimenta de terris tenementis et redditibus
infrascriptis die combustionis praedicti Hospitalis quae
eidem Hospitali a diversis dantur et conceduntur imperpetuum, videlicet carta domini Ranulphi quondam Episcopi
Dunolm. in hec verba :—

HOSPITALE DE KYPIER, IN COM. PALAT. DUNELMENSI.

Num. i.   [*Bishop Flambard's original Foundation*].

In nomine sanctae et individuae Trinitatis notum sit
omnibus sanctae matris ecclesiae filiis, tam praesentibus
quam futuris, quod ego Ranulphus, licet peccator et
indignus, tamen Dei gratia Dunelmensis episcopus, hanc
ecclesiam in honorem Dei et sancti Egidii feci fieri, quam
etiam tertio idus Junii dedicamus, anno ab incarnatione
Domini MCXII°, qui est tertius decimus annus mei episcopatus ; in qua dedicatione eidem ecclesiae, ad subsidium
clerici qui inibi serviturus est, et ad sustentationem
pauperum qui ibidem in hospitali domo quam feci con-
versaturi sunt, res inferius subscriptas in liberam et
perpetuam elemosinam dono ; et volo et praecipio, et
auctoritate Dei et ista mea donatione, et praesentis cartulae
attestatione confirmo, ut firma maneat et perpetua pro
salute animae meae, et pro redemptione animarum illorum
qui me nutriverunt ; scilicet Willielmi regis qui Angliam
conquisivit, et Matildae reginae ; pro anima quoque
Willielmi regis qui me in episcopatus honorem sublimavit,
et pro salute animae regis Henrici qui me in eodem honore
confirmavit ; necnon pro animabus illorum qui aliqua dona
vel quamcunque elemosinam Ecclesiae S. Cuthberti con-
tulerunt vel collaturi sunt. Haec autem quae dono, villam
meam nomine Caldecotes cum omnibus quae ad eam
pertinent, in planis et pascuis, in pratis et sylvis, in aquis,
terris cultis et incultis, et exitibus, et omnibus consuetudinibus et libertatibus, tam ecclesiasticis quam saecculari-
bus ; et unum molendinum de Milneburn et duas garbas

de meis dominicis de hiis villis ; scilicet de Newbotel,
Hoghton, Wermuth, Refhope, Esingtone, Seggefelde,
Schireburne, Qwerington, Neutone, Cestre, Wessingtone,
Boldone, Clyvedone, Qwicham, et Ryton : quae omnia
quieta et libera ab omnibus consuetudinibus praedictae
ecclesiae Sancti Egidii et hospitali ad opus pauperum
Christi dono. Quicunque autem ex hiis minuere inquietare
vel auferre, vel ablata retinere, vel aliquibus vexationibus
fatigare temere praesumpserit, noverit se illud Christo et
Sancto Egidio auferre, et idcirco divino judicio cum
sacrilegiis reus existere, atque districtae ultioni in extremo
examine subjacere, et cum damnatis aeternaliter perire.

Et dicunt quod magister et fratres habent unam garbam
de decimis dominicis, et de alia garba penitus ignorant.

Item cartam domini Hugonis quondam Dunelmensis
episcopi in haec verba :—

Num ii. [*Bishop Pudsey's first Charter*].

Carta Hugonis Dunelmensis Episcopi.

Hugo Dei gratia episcopus Dunelm. omnibus Christi
fidelibus praesentem cartam inspecturis salutem in Domino.
Notum facimus universitati vestrae nos dedisse, et hac
carta nostra confirmasse, omnes donationes quae Ranulphus
bonae memoriae praedecessor noster hospitali S. Egidii
de Kypier dedit et confirmavit. Concedimus etiam eisdem
magistro et fratribus liberum burgagium, et omnibus
hominibus eorum quibus illi concesserunt libertatem in vico
S. Egidii Dunelmo : et quieti erunt de exercitu et omnibus
auxiliis, et in-tol et u-tol, et operationibus et consuetudinibus
et vexationibus et exactionibus. Concedimus etiam eisdem
pasturam ad averia sua infra hayam et extra ; focale et
maeremium et clausturam ubi eis sit magis ad aisiamentum
habebunt sine vasto ; et quieti erunt per totam forestam
nostram de pannagio. Damus etiam eisdem quandam
partem de peterio nostro de Neutone per illas divisas
quibus Willielmus de Howedone et Philippus Forestarius
eis seisivit ex parte nostra. Damus etiam eisdem et
confirmamus unum toftum in qualibet villa ubi habent
decimas de dominico nostro ; viz., in Hoghtone, Refhope,
Esingtone, Derlyngtone, Seggefelde, Boldon, et Qwick-
ham. Quare volo et firmiter praecipio ne aliquis
ministrorum nostrorum nec clericus nec laicus namium
fratrum accipiat, nec infra burgum nec extra, nisi in curia
eorundem jure deficiant, et tunc per licentiam nostram vel

justiciariorum nostrorum. Haec omnia damus eisdem in puram et perpetuam elemosinam.

Item cartam dicti Hugonis in haec verba :—

Num. iii. [*Bishop Pudsey's second Charter*].

Alia carta dicti Hugonis.

Hugo Dei gratia, ut supra. Notum facimus vobis nos dedisse et concessisse dictis magistro et fratribus S. Egidii, ad suscipiendos et sustentandos pauperes ibidem, villam de Clyftone, cum omnibus pertinentiis suis, in terris, aquis, molendinis, et piscariis, et omnibus quae ad eam pertinere noscuntur, cum omnibus consuetudinibus et libertatibus tam ecclesiasticis quam secularibus ad ipsam pertinentibus in liberam et perpetuam elemosinam. Dedimus etiam eisdem de unaquaque caruca de dominicis nostris in episcopatu nostro unam travam bladi sicut datur hospitali S. Petri in Eboracshire. Damus etiam eisdem decimas de omnibus novalibus nostris; id est de terris quae ante tempora nostra cultae non erant, quas de paludibus, et de frutectis in terram arabilem traximus, tam in Eborum provincia quam in nostra dioecesi, et in parochia de Hovedene ; ipsam quoque ecclesiam S. Egidii volumus et auctoritate Dei et nostra decrevimus liberam et quietam existere imperpetuum a synodabilus et omnibus aliis consuetudinibus quae per archidiaconum, sive per decanum, sive per aliquem officiarium eorum exigi solent. Haec omnia eisdem in liberam et perpetuam elemosinam, cum travis quae barones et alii nostrae dioecesis eis concesserunt et Deo auctore concedent, concedimus et praesenti carta confirmamus.[1]

---

[1] The following *Ordinatio* of Bishop Pudsey for the regulation of the hospital, not included among the verified Charters, has been taken from "Collectanea," by Allan and Hutchinson, which will be found in the Durham University Library (*Routh Collection*, LVI, c. 1, p. 574) :—

" *Ordinatio Hospitalis de Kypier.*—PROVISUM est per Venerabilem Dominum HUGONEM Episcopum Dunelmensis Ecclesiae, quod sint in Domo de *Kepyer* tresdecim Conversi, qui Professionem faciant Domui et Priori Domus more consueto, et tenebuntur ad Castitatem et ad renunciationem Proprietatis, et ad obedientiam Magistri quem Dominus Episcopus praeposuerit ; et erunt de numero Fratrum sex Capellani celebrantes pro animabus ejusdem *Hugonis* Episcopi, et venerabilis memoriae Domini *Ranulphi* Episcopi Dunelmensis primi Fundatoris de *Kypier*. Qui quidem Capellani ministrabunt in Capella in eadem, et unus eorundem Capellanorum quem Magister Hospitalis Priorem voluerit assignari una cum consensu Fratrum audiet Confessiones Fratrum Conversorum et Infirmorum infra Cunam [*cuvam = crypt-chapel* ?] et faciet Correctiones de ordine. Septimus Conversus erit Dispensator et Lardarius. Octavus erit Custos Tannariae. Nonus erit Pistor Hospitalis. Decimus erit Custos Molendini. Undecimus erit Graunger et Custos Carucarum. Duodecimus erit Custos Instauri in

Item carta Radulphi de Epplingden in haec verba :—

Num. iv. *Carta Radulphi de Epplyndone.*

Sciant praesentes et futuri quod ego Radulphus de Epplyndone dedi concessi et hac praesenti carta mea confirmavi magistro et fratribus S. Egidii de Kypier ad feodi fermam unam carucatam terrae cum suis pertinentiis in Epplyndone, cujus singulae bovatae sunt quindecim acrarum terrae, cum incremento xx bovatarum terrae de dominico meo, cum duobus toftis quae fuerunt Radulphi de Ponte et Normanni filii Sprowe ; quam quidem carucatam et viginti acras terrae cum toftis et aliis pertinentiis Robertus de Clivedon aliquando de me tenuit, et postea mihi reddidit in plena curia Dunelmi, et per chartam quietam mihi clamavit. Tenendum et habendum cum omnibus aysiamentis in pratis pascuis aquis stagnis et molendinis cum liberis introitibus et exitibus in viis et semitis in moris et mariscis et omnibus rebus et locis libertatibus et consuetudinibus infra villam de Epplyngdon et extra pertinentibus. Reddendo inde annuatim domino feodi illius quatuor solidos. Concedo etiam quod averia praedictorum magistri et fratrum pascantur ubique cum averiis meis et haeredum meorum, et habebunt duodecies viginti oves et xx porcos, ubi oves meae et porci mei vadunt in pastura ejusdem villae. Et praedicti magister et fratres capient omnimoda focalia ubique ubi ego et haeredes mei capiemus vel capere debemus in communi pastura

diversis locis ubicunque habent Instaurum. Tertius decimus erit Receptor et Generalis Procurator omnium Negotiorum Hospitalis interius et exterius, quem Magister cum assensu Prioris et Fratrum ad hoc praeficere voluerit. Et sciendum quod licebit Magistro Hospitalis per consensum Prioris illius loci et fratrum singulos istorum successive in officiis suis mutare secundum quod providerit utilitati Domus magis expedire. Si autem plures Fratres fuerint in eadem Domo quam supra dicti tresdecem, variis officiis ejusdem Domus pro dispositione Magistri, Prioris, et Fratrum intendant. Fratribus autem numerum tresdecem excedentibus successive decedentibus, in loco illorum alios substituere nullus praesumat nisi Magister cum consensu Prioris et Fratrum ejusdem loci.

"Si aliquis conversus ceciderit in languorem continuum, erit in Infirmitorio, et habebit necessaria in Victualibus sicut unus Frater percepit in Aula. Et sicut Magister habebit mensam suam in Aula nisi fuerit infirmus vel minutus, ita et Conversi mensam suam in eadem Aula habeant, nisi Magister pro necessitate Hospitum vel alia causa honesta aliquo tempore aliter judicaverit de necessitate faciendum. Et omnes Conversi simul jacebunt in Dormitorio, et omnes Fratres erunt vestiti decenti habitu et honesto, sicut decet Religiosos semel in anno. Et erunt calciati Fratres Capellani cum Botis bis in anno ; caeteri Conversi qui plus laborant quotiens necesse fuerit per annum Socularibus cum Coreis ligatis. Caetera autem necessaria, scilicet de Staminis Pannis lineis, et de Pannis ad Lectos Fratrum pertinentibus de Custuma Domus per visum Prioris illius Domus quotiens necesse fuerit sine contradictione aliqua obtinebunt."

ejusdem villae. Praedicti vero magister et fratres dabunt
multuram ad vicesimum vasculum quando et quamdiu ad
molendinum meum molere voluerint et molent proximiores
post me et haeredes meos. Et ego Radulphus et haeredes
mei praedictam terram cum omnibus pertinentiis suis ut
praedicitur praedictis magistro et fratribus per praedictum
servicium contra omnes homines warrantizabimus et
defendemus imperpetuum &c.

Item cartam Gilberti Haunsard in haec verba :—

Num. v. *Carta Gilberti de Haunsard.*

Universis Christi fidelibus ad quos praesens scriptum
pervenerit Gilbertus de Haunsard Salutem. Noverit
universitas vestra me concessisse et hac praesenti mea
carta confirmasse Deo et sanctae Mariae et hospitali S.
Egidii extra Dunelmum quod vocatur Kypier totam
terram meam de Aymuneston cum pertinentiis suis in villa
et extra, et redditum x sol. quos mihi reddidit Willielmus
de Boultone in eadem villa annuatim, et quinque bovatas
terrae in villa de Hurtheworth, scil. illas quas bovatas
terrae quas tenuit Edwardus de Clevedon cum toftis croftis
ad quatuor praedictas bovatas terrae pertinentibus, et
quintam bovatam terrae de dominico meo in tribus
partibus, sicut jacet per campos, cum omnibus aisiamentis
et libertatibus et liberis consuetudinibus, in liberam puram
et perpetuam elemosinam, ad sustentationem unius
capellani qui in perpetuum in dicto Hospitali divina
celebrabit pro anima mea, patris, et matris meae, et omnium
parentum meorum. Habenda et tenenda de me et
haeredibus meis imperpetuum ita libere et quiete sicut
aliqua elemosina liberius et quietius habetur et tenetur in
episcopatu Dunelmense. Et ego vero Gilbertus et heredes
mei praedictas terras et dictum redditum contra omnes
homines imperpetuum warrantizabimus. Hiis testibus, &c.

Item cartam Walteri de Witton in haec verba :—

Num. vi. *Carta Walteri de Witton.*

Omnibus Christi fidelibus ad quos praesens scriptum
pervenerit Walterus de Witton miles salutem. Sciatis me
dedisse et praesenti carta mea confirmasse Deo et Hospitali
S. Egidii de Dunelmo et magistro et fratribus ibidem Deo
servientibus pro salute animae meae et haeredum meorum
in liberam et perpetuam elemosinam totam terram meam de
Frosterley sine aliquo retenemento cum omnibus pertinentiis
et libertatibus in pratis et pascuis molendinis et aquis et

omnibus escaetis quae jure contingunt vel imperpetuum
contingere poterunt. Hanc terram concedo praedicto
hospitali magistro et fratribus quietam et solutam de me et
heredibus meis imperpetuum. Reddendo michi et heredibus
meis unam libram cimini ad festum sancti Cuthberti in
Septembre et faciendo domino episcopo debitum servicium
quod ad dictam terram pertinet pro omni alio servicio. Et
ego Walterus et heredes mei praedictam terram cum
omnibus pertinenciis suis praedicto hospitali magistro et
fratribus contra omnes homines imperpetuum waran-
tizabimus. Hiis testibus, &c. Et istas donacionem et
concessionem quas praedictus Walterus de Witton fecit
deo et Hospitali S. Egidii et Magistro et fratribus ibidem
deo servientibus de tota terra de Frosterley Nicholaus
quondam Episcopus Dunelmensis confirmavit in omnibus
sicut carta praedicta testatur.

Item cartam Hugonis quondam Episcopi Dunelmensis
in haec verba :—

Num. vii. [*Bishop Pudsey's third Charter*].

Alia carta Hugonis Episcopi Dunelmensis.

Hugo Dei gratia Dunelm. episcopus priori et conventu
S. Cuthberti et archidiaconis et omnibus sanctae matris
Ecclesiae filiis salutem. Notum facimus universitati
vestrae nos dedisse et praesenti carta nostra confirmasse
Deo et hospitali S. Egidii de Dunelmo Quitteleys et
Swyneleys per istas divisas, a sursa Knokedenburne usque
ad sursam de Ayelshopburne ; Deinde recta linia usque ad
Darewent, quae est divisa inter eos et archiepisc. Ebor. et
Walterum de Bollebec, sicut Derewent decurrit usque
dum Ayelshopburne descendit in eam, et quicquid
continetur infra istas divisas sit imperpetuum ad suscipien-
dum et sustentandum pauperes Christi. Minerum quoque
plumbae ad cooperiendum ecclesiae S. Mariae et Omnium
Sanctorum et infirmatorium hospitalis praedicti ; et
minerum ferri infra Rokehope ad carucas et alias
necessitates faciendas : Et pasturam ad omnimoda averia
sua habebunt undique in eadem. Et pedes canum eorum
non sint ibi, neque ad wacheriam de Werdale truncati ; set
pastores ducant eos ligatos pro feris ad averia sua servanda
pro lupis. Et unum toftum quod dedimus eis per
procurationem fratris Ranulphi ad opus dicti hospitalis ;
scilicet praedictum toftum de la Laundene. Pasturam etiam
in foresta nostra ad averia sua habebunt. Damus etiam
praedicto hospitali et confirmamus decimam de tota terra
quae pertinet ad Bradewode, et totam decimam de Besan-

kelde usque ad Witheles, et unam travam bladi de
unaquaque caruca de Werdale. Decimas quoque de
omnibus novalibus nostris ; id est de terris quae ante
tempora nostra cultae non erant, quas de paludibus et de
frutectis in terram arabilem traximus per nummos nostros
vel per kirsete.[1] Omnia ista praedicta praedicto hospitali
damus damus concedimus et confirmamus in puram et
quietam liberam et perpetuam elemosinam existere, &c.

Item cartam Johannis de Romeseye in haec verba :—

Num. viii. *Carta Johannis de Romeseye.*

Sciant praesentes et futuri quod ego Johannes de
Romesheye dedi concessi et hac praesenti carta mea
confirmavi Deo et S. Egidio et custodi hospitalis de
Kypier et fratribus ejusdem loci ibidem Deo servientibus
et in perpetuum servituris, in subsidium sustentationis
pauperum ibidem confluentium, redditum sexaginta et
quinque solidorum, quem Leonius filius Willielmi de
Herz et Gregorius de Levingthorth Waltero de Monasteriis
reddere consueverunt, et homagia et servicia, relevia,
wardas, et escaetas de tota medietate villae de Claxtone,
quam de me tenuit : Et quicquid juris habui vel habere
potui in eadam medietate villae praedictae sine aliquo
retenemento affectu pietatis ; petens quod fiat in singulis
missis celebrandis in capella de Kypier per unam collectam
commemoratio, et in canone missae pro anima piae
recordationis Ricardi Dunelmensis episcopi secundi, et pro
anima venerabilis patris et domini mei Nicholai Dunelmensis episcopi ; habenda et tenenda praedictis magistro
et fratribus et eorum successoribus de Willielmo de
Monasteriis capitali domino dictae medietatis villae, et
heredibus suis, in liberam et perpetuam elemosinam
imperpetuum. Reddendo eidem Willielmo et heredibus
suis xij*d.* per annum ; scilicet sex denarios ad festum
Pentecostes et sex denarios ad festum S. Martini, et
faciendo forinsecum servicium debitum, sicut continetur
in carta Walteri de Monasteriis patris praedicti Willielmi
de Monasteriis inde confecta et dictis custodi et fratribus
liberata. Nicholaus quondam episcopus Dunelmensis
donationem et concessionem praedictam sicut in praedicta
carta continetur confirmavit.

---

[1] Meaning apparently the same as Kirkscot, or Church-Scot, thus
defined in Jacob's Law Dictionary, 1762 :—"Customary oblations paid
to the Parish Priest ; from which duty the Religious sometimes purchased
an exemption for themselves and their tenants."

Item cartam Roberti de Corbech et Sibillae filiae ejus in haec verba : –

Num. ix. *Carta Roberti Corbech et Sibillae filiae ejus de villa de Hunstanworth.*

Notum sit omnibus tam praesentibus quam futuris quod ego Robertus Corbech et Sibilla filia mea et omnes heredes nostri dedimus et concessimus et fide praestita quietum clamavimus domui S. Egidii de Dunelmo villam de Hunstanworth et omnem terram ad eam pertinentem, divisis apertis divisam, de Boltisburne usque Boltislawe, et de Boltislawe usque ad Evelshopheved, et Evelshopheved usque ad Derewentam, et de Derewenta usque ad Boltisburne pro amore et fraternitate domus, et propter decem marcas quas magister de Argentaneo et fratres praenotatae domus nobis in caritate dederunt, honorifice et pacifice possidendam cum omnibus libertatibus ad illam terram pertinentibus, quas libertates carta domini Hugonis episcopi memoratur et confirmat ; Faciendo episcopo Dunelm. servicium duodecimae partis cujusdam militis, de omnibus aliis serviciis pacificam et quietam.   Quam conventionem ut ipsa rata permaneat ego Robertus assensu filiae meae Sibillae et omnium heredum meorum sigilli mei munimine roboravi.

Item cartam Roberti de Corbech et Sibillae filiae ejus in haec verba :—

Num. x.   *Alia carta ejusdem Roberti.*

ROBERTUS CORBECH omnibus videntibus vel audientibus istas literas salutem. Sciatis me calumpniam quam habui de terra illa quae est inter Knokendenburne et Derewentam quietam clamasse, et communem pasturam in Hunstanworth dedisse et hac praesenti carta mea confirmasse Deo et hospitali S. Egidii de Dunelmo et fratribus ibidem Deo servientibus, pro salute mea et uxoris meae et heredum et parentum meorum, et pro anima mea et antecessorum meorum, &c.

Item cartam Roberti quondam episcopi Dunelm. in haec verba :—

Num. xi.   *Carta Roberti Dunelmensis Episcopi.*

Universis sanctae matris Ecclesiae filiis ad quos praesens scriptura pervenerit Robertus Dei gratia Dunelm. episcopus salutem in Domino.   Noveritis nos divinae

miserationis intuitu dedisse concessisse et hac praesenti
carta nostra confirmasse Deo et ecclesiae S. Egidii de
Kypier, magistro et fratribus ibidem Deo servientibus et
servituris totum tenementum nostrum cum suis pertinentiis
quae habuimus in villa de Crawcrok ; quod quidem
tenementum habuimus de dono Thomae de Holynside et
Isoldae uxoris ejus, cum molendino et tota secta ejusdem
villae sicut nos liberius tenuimus ; et redditum Daniel et
Johannis Loty cum terra sua et cum tota sequela sua.
Et terram quam Adam de Rytone quondam tenuit ; et
quendam boscum qui vocatur le Frith cum toto alio bosco
ad dominicum pertinente ; et totum Altunside a molendino
descendendo usque le Frith ; et omnes operationes ejusdem
villae cum piscaria aquae de Tyne, una cum tofto,
tenemento, et suis pertinentiis quod habuimus de dono
Laurentii de Lyntz in eadem villa de Crawcrok.   Dedimus
etiam Deo et dictis ecclesiae S. Egidii magistro et fratribus
ibidem Deo servientibus totam villam de Inestan cum suis
pertinentiis, quam quidem villam habuimus de dono Jacobi
Birun sicut plenius testatur in cartis dictorum Thomae
Isoldae Laurentii et Jacobi : habenda et tenenda dictae
ecclesiae S. Egidii magistro et fratribus ibidem servientibus
Deo et servituris bene et in pace, libere et quiete, in
liberam et perpetuam elemosinam cum omnibus pertinentiis
ad dicta tenementa et villam spectantibus ; faciendo tamen
pro praedictis tenementis de Crawcroke et dicta villa de
Inestane et suis pertinentiis nobis et successoribus nostris
Episcopis Dunelmensibus servicium debitum et consuetum,
&c.

Item cartam Radulphi de Mundavill in haec verba :—

Num xii.   *Carta Radulfi de Mundavill.*

Universis Christi fidelibus ad quas praesens scriptum
pervenerit Radulfus de Mundavill salutem in Domino.
Noverit universitas vestra me caritatis intuitu concessisse
et hac praesenti carta mea confirmasse Deo et hospitali
S. Egidii de Kypier, pro salute animae meae et antecessorum et successorum meorum, unam travam bladi
de singulis carucis villae meae de Stotfold, tam in dominicis
meis quam de aliis, ad sustentationem pauperum ibidem
undecunque confluentium, &c.

Item cartam Gilberti camerarii in haec verba :—

Num. xiii.   *Carta Gilberti Camerarii.*

Omnibus sanctae matris ecclesiae filiis tam praesentibus quam futuris Gilbertus camerarius salutem.   Noverit

universitas vestra me dedisse concessisse et hac praesenti
carta mea confirmasse Deo et hospitali S. Egidii et fratribus
in domo sua servientibus figere stagnum molendini sui de
Kypier super terram meam quando utilius facere poterint
in liberam et quietam et perpetuam elemosinam, pro salute
domini mei Hugonis Dunelmensis episcopi, et pro salute
animae Theobaldi fratris mei ; et pro salute animae meae
et uxoris meae Julianae Papedy, et pro salute heredum
meorum, ut elemosinarum et omnium beneficiorum Hospitalis Sancti Egidii participes efficiamur, &c.

Item carta Willelmi de Herz in haec verba :—

Num. xiv. *Carta Willielmi de Herz (Heriz).*

Omnibus has literas videntibus vel audientibus
Willielm de Herz salutem. Sciatis me dedisse concessisse
et hacc praesenti carta mea confirmasse Deo et hospitali
S. Egidii de Kypier et fratribus ibidem Deo servientibus
in liberam puram et perpetuam elemosinam, pro salute
animarum patris et matris meae et omnium parentum
meorum, duas bovatas terrae in villa de Claxtone cum
omnibus pertinentiis suis quae fuerunt Henrici de Herz,
scilicet viginti et quatuor acras terrae et unam acram prati,
et unam rodam in le Holme versus Cretterton cum tofto
propinquiori Waltero Bernard versus orientem continentes
in longitudine quinque perticatas et in latitudine quinque
perticatas. Habenda et tenenda de me et haeredibus meis
praedicto hospitali et dictis fratribus et eorum successoribus
imperpetuum libere quiete et integre et ab omni seculari
servicio exactione et demandis in pratis et pascuis in moris
mariscis aquis stagnis molendinis in introitibus et exitibus
et omnibus communibus libertatibus et aysiamentis praedictae terrae pertinentibus infra villam et extra. Et ego
Willelmus et heredes mei warrantizabimus imperpetuum
contra omnes homines praedictam terram cum omnibus
pertinentiis suis praedictis Hospitali et fratribus et eorum
successoribus. Hiis testibus, &c.

Item cartam Quenilldae uxoris Ricardi de Lockes in
haec verba :—

Num. xv. *Carta Quenildae uxoris Ricardi de Lokes.*

Notum sit omnibus sanctae matris ecclesiae filiis tam
clericis quam laicis literas istas audientibus vel videntibus
quod ego Quenilda uxor Ricardi de Lokes, consensu et
voluntate heredis mei Willelmi, et Ricardus de Lockes
maritus meus ex parte mea damus et concedimus et [*per*]

praesentem cartam nostram confirmamus xij acras terrae in Medomesley Deo et S. Mariae et omnibus sanctis, et hospitali S. Egidii in Dunelmo in puram et perpetuam elemosinam liberam quietam et solutam ab omnibus terrenis serviciis pro amore Dei et pro salute animarum nostrarum et et antecessorum nostrorum et successorum.

Item cartam decimae de Clifton in haec verba :—

Num. xvi. *Compositio inter Pr. et Conv. Dunelmensis Ecclesiae et Procuratorem dicti Hospitalis.*[1]

Anno ab incarnatione dominicae MCXCVII.[2] septimo kal. Augusti, scilicet in crastino Beati Jacobi, Pontificatus domini Hugonis Dunelmensis episcopi anno tricesimo sexto, facta est haec compositio inter Germanum priorem et coventum Dunelmi ecclesiae, et Adam canonicum procuratorem hospitalis S. Egidii, et fratres ejusdem hospitalis, ex voluntate et consensu domini Hugonis Dunelmi episcopi ; scilicet quod prior et monachi quietam clamaverunt imperpetuum decimam bladi di Cliftone domui S. Oswaldi de Elveta ; ita quod fratres dicti hospitalis nullo unquam tempore aliquam decimam de praedicta terra reddent ; sed tota decima bladi terrae illius, sicut aliae obventiones, sine omni diminutione et retractione praefato hospitali quieta remanebit imperpetuum. Fratres autem dicti hospitalis, in recompensationem singulis annis in perpetuum reddent super altare S. Oswaldi de Elveta in die ejusdem Sancti unum bisantium vel duos solidos. Et insuper duas garbas de decima dominii de Newtone quietas clamaverunt imperpetuum praedictae ecclesiae S. Oswaldi quae a tempore Ranulphi episcopi, sicut in ejusdem cartâ continetur, usque ad illud tempus reddi solebant praefato hospitali ; ita quod nullo unquam tempore aliquam decimam occasione cartarum suarum vel privilegiorum exigent infra divisas villae de Newtone, set tota decima bladi infra divisas ejusdem villae, sicut et aliae obventiones, sine omni diminutione et retractione quieta remanebunt imperpetuum ecclesiae S. Oswaldi de Elveta ; et, ne alterutra pars ab hac compositione resilere possit, in praesentia domini Hugonis

---

[1] This Composition, together with Bishop Pudsey's confirmation of it, still exists in the Durham Treasury (*4ᵃ, 16, Spec., No. 45*). From the copy of the Composition there preserved, Kellaw's Commissioners may be supposed to have verified it.

[2] Apparently an error for MCLXXXIX, as it is in the original document preserved in the Durham Treasury. This, and not 1197, was the 36th year of Hugh Pudsey's pontificate.

Episcopi huic inde in verbo veritatis promiserunt se etiam bona fide imperpetuum servituros, et ipse Episcopus eam carta sua confirmavit imperpetuum et confirmandam statuit, &c.

Item cartam Henrici Lyghfot in haec verba :--

Num. xvii. *Carta Henrici Lyghfot.*

Omnibus hoc scriptum visuris vel audituris Henricus Lyghfot salutem. Noveritis me dedisse concessisse et hac presenti carta mea confirmasse in puram et perpetuam elemosinam magistro et fratribus domus de Kypier in subsidium sustentationis elemosinae ibidem faciendae totam terram meam quam habui apud Dernecrok, tam terram quam habui ex emptione quam terram quam tenui de domino episcopo Dunelm., quietam et solutam de me et haeredibus meis imperpetuum tenendam et habendam de dominis feodi illius cum omnibus libertatibus liberis consuetudinibus et aisiamentis dictis terris pertinentibus faciendo servicium debitum in cartis feodacionis meae contentum libere, &c. Quam quidem donationem Robertus quondam episcopus Dunelmensis in omnibus confirmavit et concessit dictis Magistro et fratribus et successoribus suis hanc clausulam. Nos autem eisdem concedimus housbote et haybote in boscis nostris et successorum nostrorum, per visum et liberationem forestariorum nostrorum, et quieti erunt de sectis curiarum nostrarum et molendinorum et de pannagio porcorum, videlicet de porcis propriis, &c.

Item cartam de Bedlyngtonshire in haec verba :—

Num. xviii. *De novem Solidis pro Travis Carucarum de Bedelyngtonshire dicto Hospitali datis per Inhabitantes ejusdem.*

Omnibus Christi fidelibus ad quos praesens scriptum pervenerit Willielmus Halchor, Robertus Cnowald, Willielmus Birilot, Thomas filius Rogeri de Bedlyngton, Walterus et Robertus filii Roberti de Nedderton, Adam et Elyas frater ejus de Chapyngton, Thomas et Johannes de Slyburne, Alanus, Adam et Walterus Caritas de Camhuse, Edmundus filius Rogeri, et Laurentius filius Odardi, et Adam Serviens, et Ranulphus filius Petri, Robertus filius Henrici, et Robertus Palnure de parva Slykburne, salutem in Domino. Cum antiqua constitutione venerabilium patrum et dominorum nostrorum Dunelm. episcoporum constitueretur ut de singulis carucis omnium dominiorum

eorum daretur una trava bladi hospitali S. Egidii extra
Dunelmum caritatis intuitu ad sustentationem pauperum
et peregrinorum ibidem undecunque confluentium,
Nos eorum constitutionem approbantes et devote acceptantes
dedimus et concessimus et hac praesenti carta nostra
confirmavimus, pro salute animarum nostrarum patrum
et matrum et omnium parentum nostrorum, Deo et dicto
hospitali S. Egidii extra Dunelmum spontanea voluntate
nostra, in puram et perpetuam elemosinam, novem solidos
pro travis carucarum nostrarum de Bedelyngton-shire ; ita
quod tam nos quam haeredes nostri ad hanc elimosinam
praestandam imperpetuum teneamur ad festum S.
Michaelis solvendam ; ita quod nisi infra xv. dies proxime
post festum Michaelis solvantur, nos et haeredes nostri
elapsis illis xv. diebus, pro novem solidis nomine poenae
solvemus decem solidos. Et ut haec nostra donatio rata
et inconcussa futuris temporibus permaneat, praesens
scriptum sigillorum nostrorum appositione roboravimus
hiis testibus, etc.

Item cartam Stephani Capellani in hac verba :—

Num. xix. *Carta Stephani Capellani.*

Omnibus Christi fidelibus ad quos praesens scriptum
pervenerit Stephanus capellanus salutem. Noveritis me,
caritatis intuitu et pro salute animae meae dedisse concessisse et praesenti carta mea confirmasse Deo et domui
S. Egidii extra Dunelm. totam terram quam habui
in vico S. Egidii de Southcrofte, cum aedificiis et
omnibus pertinentiis suis, Tenendum et habendum libere
quiete pacifice et honorifice in liberam puram et perpetuam
elemosinam reddendo inde annuatim Adae de Lumesdene
et haeredibus suis xii*d.* per annum, et haeredibus de
Kelnelawe unum denarium per annum, et faciendo burgo
omnia servicia debita et consueta. Et ut haec mea donatio,
&c.

———————

Nos autem praemissa testificari et veritati volentes
testimonium perhibere, ne Magister et fratres aut successores
sui seu dictum Hospitale Sancti Egidii per defectionem
cartarum et munimentorum suorum praedictorum sic
combustorum dampnum aut exheredacionis periculum
futuris temporibus incurrant, inquisicionem praedictam
duximus exemplandam. Et volumus et concedimus pro
nobis et successoribus nostris quod praedicti magister et
fratres omnes terras redditus decimas et tenementa

supradicta de quibus scisiti fuerunt die confectionis
praesencium habeant et teneant sibi et successoribus suis
imperpetuum, Et quod ipsi omnibus libertatibus et liberis
consuetudinibus quibus ipsi vel praedecessores sui
temporibus retroactis usi sunt vel gavisi decetero gaudeant
et utantur prout eis uti et gaudere consueverant sine
contradictione nostri vel successorum nostrorum, donaciones
concessiones et confirmaciones praedictas Magistro et
fratribus factas prout in dicta inquisitione continetur ratas
habentes, et grantatas eas pro nobis et successoribus nostris
sibi et successoribus suis ut praedictum est tenore
praesencium confirmamus. Et in testimonium praemissorum sigillum nostrum praesentibus duximus
apponendum. Datum apud Kypier undecimo die Marcii
Anno Domini Millesimo ccc. xj et Pontificatus nostri
primo ; Nolentes quod praedicti Magister et fratres vel
successores sui quicquam de terris tenementis aut redditibus
supradictis decetero vendant aut alienent sine nostra vel
successorum nostrorum licencia speciali : Set eis omnem
potestatem ad hoc totaliter interdicimus per praesentes.
Et si contrafecerint factum suum in hujusmodi decernimus
non valere nec roburis firmitatem aliqualiter optinere.
Nos autem omnia praemissa et singula in honorem Dei et
beatae Mariae et Sancti Egidij et pro salute animae nostrae
praedecessorum et successorum nostrorum tenore praesencium pro nobis et successoribus nostris praedictis Magistro
et fratribus et successoribus suis concedimus et confirmamus
imperpetuum. Quare volumus et concedimus pro nobis et
successoribus nostris quod praedicti Magister et fratres
hospitalis praedicti et eorum successores habeant et teneant
omnes terras possessiones et tenementa sua in omnibus
cum omnibus libertatibus liberis consuetudinibus et
quietanciis de exceritu [sic] et omnibus auxiliis in tol et utol
operacionibus consuetudinibus vexacionibus exaccionibus
Muragiis pickagiis et panagiis tam temporibus nundinarum
et Marcati quam omnibus aliis temporibus anni pro se et
hominibus suis de vico Sancti Egidii et pro ipsis Magistro
et fratribus et eorum successoribus de serviciis et servagiis
et quibuscumque demandarum secularium, ac eciam omnes
terras et tenementa sua libertates et quietancias ac omnia
et singula in ista confirmacione et in aliis cartis et
confirmacionibus contenta eisdem Magistro et fratribus aut
praedecessoribus suis per quemcunque datis et concessis
eisdem Magistro et fratribus et eorum successoribus tam
pro se quam pro hominibus suis de vico Sancti Egidii
concedimus ratificamus et confirmamus pro nobis et

successoribus nostris imperpetuum. Et ad haec volumus et
concedimus pro nobis et successoribus nostris, si ministri
praedecessorum nostrorum vel nostri de praedictis Magistro
et fratribus aut eorum tenentibus aliquid contra tenorem
praesencium usurpaverint seu levaverint temporibus
retroactis, quod amodo non trahatur in consequenciam nec
quicquam de eis levetur in futurum, set volumus et
concedimus pro nobis et successoribus nostris quod ipsi
Magister et fratres et eorum successores omnibus libertatibus
et liberis consuetudinibus praescriptis libere et quiete in
omnibus decetero gaudeant et utantur sine contradictione
nostri vel successorum nostrorum imperpetuum. Et in
testimonium omnium praemissorum sigillum nostrum
praesentibus duximus apponendum. Datum in Castro
nostro de Aukland viij die mensis Marcii Anno Domini
Millesimo cccxlv^{to}, et pontificatus nostri primo. Nos
igitur Johannes Episcopus memoratus ob specialem
affeccionem quam ad Sanctum Egidium et dictum Hospitale
gerimus et habemus, Volentesque dictorum Magistri et
fratrum eorumque successorum quieti providere, praedictas
concessiones ratificaciones et approbaciones ratas habentes
pariter et acceptas eas quantum in nobis est pro nobis et
successoribus nostris juxta formam et tenorem earundem
ratificamus approbamus et tenore praesencium imperpetuum
confirmamus. In cuius rei testimonium sigillum nostrum
praesentibus duximus apponendum. Datum in Manerio
nostro de Stokton ultimo die Mensis Maij Anno Domini
Millesimo ccclxxxiiij^{to} et pontificatus nostri tercio.

[Impropriation of the Rectory of St. Nicholas.[1]]

Inspeximus eciam quasdam literas nostras sub sigillo
nostro ad causas Johanni Lound in utroque jure Bacallau-
reo nunc Magistro sive Custodi Hospitalis praedicti et
fratribus ejusdem de annexione unione et incorporacione
ecclesiae parochialis Sancti Nicholai Dunelmensis factas et
per Priorem et Capitulum Dunelm. confirmatas in hec verba:
Universis Sanctae Matris ecclesiae filiis praesentes literas
inspecturis vel audituris Robertus permissione divina
Dunelmensis Episcopus salutem in Domino sempiternam.
Ex pastoralis officii debito nobis incumbit paternae

---

[1] There is a copy of this Deed of Impropriation in the Dean and Chapter
Treasury, *Register* III, folio 291. The variations therein are given in the
notes. The Deed is here given almost in full, notwithstanding its intolerable
verbiage, which often obscures the sense. It may serve as a specimen of
the ancient art, not yet obsolete, of spinning out legal documents with a
view to payment for them.

consideracionis intuitum [1] diligenter ad ea dirigere [2] quae ad
ecclesiarum statum et utilitatem ac subditorum nostrorum
quietem tendere videantur. Significato nobis nuper per
partem Magistri Johannis Lounds [3] in utroque Jure Bacallarii
Magistri sive Custodis Hospitalis de Kepier nostrarum
collacionis et diocesis quod, licet ipsum Hospitale de
Kepyer ex sua prima fundacione sufficienter fundatum
extiterat sieque per nonnulla tempora retroacta in fructibus
redditibus et proventibus ad sustentionem Magistri sive
custodis et ceterorum in eodem degencium competenter
dotatum permanserat, Jamque [4] temporis cursu indeterius
dilabente fructus redditus et proventus ejusdem Hospitalis
ita tenues et exiles existunt in praesenti quod ad
exhibicionem dictorum Magistri sive custodis et aliorum
ut praefertur inibi degencium, edificacionem reparacionem
et construccionem domorum eidem Hospitali pertinencium,
ac ad Hospitalitatem pro qua principalius fuerat fundatum
aliaque omnia eidem incumbencia debita [5] supportanda non
suppetant ejusdem Hospitalis facultates nisi ei de alicujus
subvencionis remedio succurratur ; Presertim cum idem
Hospitale juxta civitatem nostram Dunelm. et viam
publicam sit notorie constitutum et ex adventu et recepcione
Hospitum pauperum et egenorum ad illud indies confluencium multipliciter oneratur, dictumque Hospitale
propter causas praemissas et alias legitimas pro parte dicti
Magistri sive custodis ejusdem coram nobis allegatas tanto
onere pregravatur et adeo notorie indegens existat,
Presertim propter subtraccionem et detencionem travarum
bladi [6] quas de unaquaque carucata terrae de dominicis
nostris in Episcopatu nostro et eciam diocesi de tenentibus
percipere deberet de consuetudine et eciam de jure, quod
annexio unio et incorporacio ecclesiae parochialis Nicholai [7]
Dunelmensis nostrarum eciam collacionis et diocesis
ecclesiae et domui Hospitalis Sancti Egidii de Kepier
antedictis ejusdem Magistro sive Custodi et fratribus
facienda tam Juri quam pietati consonae merito censerentur,
propter quae ex parte dicti Magistri sive custodis nobis
humiliter extitit supplicatum et instanter petitum quod
propter praemissa specialiter expressata et alias causas
veras justas et legitimas coram nobis pro parte ejusdem
sufficienter expositas dictam ecclesiam Sancti Nicholai cum
suis libertatibus juribus et pertinenciis universis ecclesiae

[1] Intuitu.
[2] Erigere.
[3] Lounde.
[4] Jam tamen.
[5] Debite.
[6] " Travae Egidi " in margin.
[7] Sancti Nicholai.

14

et domui Hospitalis antedicti ejusque [1] Magistro sive
Custodi et fratribus ac eorum successoribus quibuscumque
unire annectere et incorporare in usus suos proprios
perpetuo possidendam et alia de quibus et prout inferius
continetur ac de et super supra et infrascriptis pronunciare
declarare ordinare statuere et decernere in hac parte quod
justum fuerit et consonum pietati auctoritate nostra
ordinaria dignaremur intuitu caritatis. Nos igitur, qui
piorum locorum ecclesiasticorum et praecipue Hospitalium
relevacionem et conservacionem appetimus cultumque
divinum ubique cupimus adaugeri, precibus et peticionibus
dicti Magistri sive custodis super causam appropriacionis
et unionis huiusmodi superius expressatam quantum de
jure possimus favorabiliter annuentes, ad diligentem
prosecucionem ejusdem Magistri sive custodis de et super
ipsa causa unionis annexionis incorporacionis et appropriacionis antedictam, &c., &c., in forma juris
inquisivimus et inquiri fecimus diligenter, ac subsequenter
super unione annexione incorporacione sive appropriacione
hujusmodi facienda et aliis cum dilectis filiis Priore et
capitulo ecclesiae nostrae Cathedralis Dunelm deliberacio-
nem habuimus diligentem et tractatum : Et quia, tam per
deciciones[2] testium in inquisicione de qua supra fit mencio
productorum juratorum et diligenter examinatorum tam
per ea quae coram nobis Priore et capitulo ecclesiae nostrae
praedictae sunt allegata proposita et probata, nobis constat
manifeste pro evidente utilitate et urgente necessitate
unionem annexionem, &c., fore rationabiliter faciendam ;
Nos Robertus Episcopus antedictus Invocata Sancti Spiri-
tus gratia una cum consilio et consensu Prioris et capituli
ecclesiae nostrae Cathedralis Dunelm. supradictae aliorumque Juris peritorum nobis assidencium causas appropriacionis hujusmodi in dicta peticione nobis expositas, &c.,
veras legitimas et sufficienter et rite ac recte propates[3] fuisse
et esse pronunciavimus decrevimus et declaravimus, ac
ipsam ecclesiam Sancti Nicholai Dunelm. predictam cum
suis libertatibus juribus et pertinenciis universis ex causis
praedictis et propter eas praedictam ecclesiam domui
Hospitalis memorati Magistro sive custodi et fratribus
ejusdem ac eorum successoribus omnibus et singulis de
voluntate et expresso consensu dicti Prioris et capituli
ecclesiae nostrae antedictae, jure cujuscumque semper salvo,
auctoritate nostra ordinaria annexuimus[4] univimus incor-

---

[1] Ejusdemque.

[2] Depositiones.

[3] Probatas.

[4] Annexuimus.

poravimus et appropriavimus, sicque annectimus unimus
incorporamus et appropriamus in usus suos proprios
perpetuo possidendam per praesentes : Ita quod liceat
praefato Magistro sive custodi qui pro tempore fuerit
cedente decedente resignante vel amoto Rectore dictae
ecclesiae Sancti Nicholai qui nunc est seu ea quomodolibet
vacante ipsius ecclesiae possessionem auctoritate propria
apprehendere et licite retinere in usus suos proprios
perpetuo possidendam nostri vel successorum nostrorum
Dunelmensium Episcoporum auctoritate voluntate seu consensu nullatenus requisita. Et, ne dictae [1] unionis annexionis incorporacionis sive appropriacionis negocium
ultra debitum prorogetur aut nostra in ea parte intencio
quovis modo frustretur, Rectori dictae ecclesie Sancti
Nicholai moderno facultatem permutandi eandem interdicimus et ipsam ecclesiam ad eundem effectum reser-
vandam decernimus et afficimus per decretum. Per hanc
autem unionem annexionem incorporacionem sive appropriacionem nostram praedictam nolumus nec intendimus
quod onera ipsius ecclesiae Sancti Nicholai ordinaria vel
extraordinaria imposterum quovis modo subtrahantur
cultusve divinus in aliquo diminuatur aut cura animarum
parochiae ejusdem neeligatur in eadem : Set volumus et
tenore praesencium statuimus et decernimus quod status
ejusdem ecclesiae et onera quaecumque de jure vel consuetudine eidem incumbencia debito modo supportentur
ipsique ecclesiae deserviatur laudabiliter in divinis, et
cura ejusdem per bonos ministros et ydoneos debite
supportetur ; In quibus conscienciam Magistri sive custodis
dicti Hospitalis de Kepier pro futuris temporibus existentis
oneramus et onerandam [2] esse decernimus per praesentes.
Juribus nostris Episcopalibus et ecclesiae nostrae Cathedralis
Dunelm. libertatibus privilegiis et dignitate, Juribus eciam
et privilegiis alterius cujuscumque semper salvis. In
quorum omnium et singulorum testimonium atque fidem
sigillum nostrum ad causas praesentibus est appensum.
Datum in Manerio nostro de Aukland quinto die Mensis
Junij Anno Domini Millesimo CCCCXLIIJ° [3] et nostrae
Translacionis Anno sexto. Et nos Prior et capitulum
supradicti, in fidem et testimonium huiusmodi diligentis
tractatus per praefatum Reverendum patrem dominum
Robertum Dunelm. Episcopum nobiscum super praemissis
unione annexione incorporacione appropriacione ecclesiae

---

[1] Dictum.   [3] Quadringentesimo tertio.
[2] Oneratam.

praedictae et causis ejusdem in domo capitulari praedicta, et aliis solempnitatibus quae in hujusmodi
concessionibus unionibus annexionibus incorporacionibus
et appropriacionibus requiruntur, habiti,[1] ac consensus
nostri supradicti ad praemissa praestiti, sigillum nostrum
commune praesentibus apposuimus. Datum in domo
nostra capitulari supradicta quoad apposicionem sigilli
nostri antedicti sexto die dicti mensis Junij Anno Domini, et
eciam Anno Translacionis dicti Reverendi patris Episcopi
Dunelmensis supradictis. Nos autem ob internam
affeccionem quam erga Sanctum Egidium et Hospitalis
saepedicti nunc Magistrum gerimus et habemus, volentesque dictorum Magistri ac fratrum eorumque successoribus
securitati et quieti generose providere, donaciones concessiones, &c. (praedictis concessionibus, &c., travarum
bladi de unaquaque carucata terrae de dominicis nostris
in Episcopatu nostro Dunelm. ac eciam Diocesi de
tenentibus nostris per praedecessores nostros praefatis
Magistro et fratribus concessarum, et ante unionem
annexionem appropriacionem et incorporacionem dictae
ecclesiae Sancti Nicholai per nos ecclesiae et domui
hospitalis memorati, &c., factam perceptis, solomodo
exceptis) ratas habentes, pariter accepta et approbata ea,
necnon unionem annexionem, &c., ecclesiae Sancti
Nicholai praedictae pro nobis et successoribus nostris
quantum in nobis est praefatis nunc Magistro et fratribus
Hospitalis praedicti et eorum successoribus juxta formam
et effectum eorundem acceptamus approbamus ratificamus
ac tenore praesencium concedimus et imperpetuum
confirmamus. In cuius, &c. Dat. Dunelm., &c., octavo
die Aprilis Anno Pontificatus nostri septimo.

Raket.

per breve de privato sigillo.

II. A.D. 1189. COMPOSITION BETWEEN THE CONVENT OF
DURHAM AND KEPYER HOSPITAL WITH RESPECT
TO THE TITHES OF CLIFTON.

[*Durham Treasury, 4ᵃ 16ᵐᵃᵉ Specialium, L. 3, No. 45*].

Anno Incarnacionis Dominicae Mᵒ Cᵒ LXXXIXᵒ, VIIᵒ
Kal. August., scilicet in crastino Sancti Jacobi, &c.

The rest is as in Charter xvi (*See p. 204*), *down
to* confirmandum statuit, *after which as follows :—*

---

[1] Habere.

Quarum alteram praedicto Priori et alteram Adae Canonico et fratribus Hospitalis tradidit, Hiis testibus ; Domino Hugone Dunelm. Episcopo, Burchardo et Willelmo Archidiaconis, Simone camerario, Magistro Ricardo de Coldingham, Magistro Willelmo Blesensi, Magistro Stephano Lincolnensi, Willelmo de Houedon, Rad. dapifero, Ricardo et Germano notariis domini episcopi, et aliis multis.

[*Seal of Kepyer Hospital, in green wax*].

Endorsed, Dupplicatur praeter datam. *Indented through the word* CYROGRAPHVM.

A.D. 1199. *There is another copy, thus dated, of the above Composition, with some omissions of technical terms, under the same reference.*

It has a different seal of Kepyer Hospital in white wax, and is endorsed, Dupplicatur praeter datam. *Indented through the word* CYROGRAPHVM.

III. A.D. 1189. CONFIRMATION OF THE SAME BY BISHOP PUDSEY.

[*Durham Treasury, 2228, 4ᵃ 16ᵐᵃʳ Specialium, No. 45*].

Hugo Dei gracia Dunelmen. Episcopus Priori Dunelmen. et Archidiaconis et universo clero totius Episcopatus sui salutem. Sciatis nos concessisse et hac praesenti carta confirmasse composicionem illam quae inter Germanum Priorem Dunelmen. et Conventum et Adam Canonicum procuratorem hospitalis Sancti Egidii et fratres ejusdem hospitalis ex voluntate nostra et consensu factam, scilicet quod Prior et monachi quietam clamaverunt in perpetuum decimam bladi de Cliftona Domui Sancti Egidii, quae usque ad illud tempus reddi solebat ecclesiae Sancti Oswaldi de Elueta ; Ita quod fratres Hospitalis nullo unquam tempore aliquam decimam de praedicta terra reddent. Sed tota decima bladi illius terrae sicut aliae obventiones sine omni diminutione et retractatione praefato hospitali quieta remanebit in perpetuum. Fratres autem hospitalis in recompensationem reddent singulis annis in perpetuum super altare ecclesiae Sancti Oswaldi de Elueta in die ejusdem Sancti unum bisantium vel duos solidos, et insuper duas garbas de decima dominii de Neutona quietas clamaverunt in perpetuum ecclesiae Sancti Oswaldi, quae a tempore Ranulfi Episcopi sicut in ejus carta continetur usque ad illud tempus reddi solebant praedicto Hospitali ;

Ita quod nullo unquam tempore aliquam decimam occasione cartarum suarum vel privelegiorum exigent infra divisas villae de Neutona. Sed tota decima bladi infra divisas ejusdem villae sicut et aliae obventiones sine omni diminutione et retractatione quieta remanebit ecclesiae Sancti Oswaldi de Elueta in perpetuum. Et ne alterutra pars ab hac compositione resilire posset, in praesentia nostra hinc inde in verbo veritatis promiserunt se eam bona fide in perpetuum servaturos. Hanc quidem composicionem cartis nostris, quarum unam praedicto Priori et alteram memorato canonico tradidimus, corroboravimus et in perpetuum conservandam statuimus. Hiis testibus, Burchardo et Willelmo Archidiaconis, Simone camerario, Magistro Ricardo de Coldingham, Magistro Willelmo Blesensi, Magistro Stephano Lincolnensi, Willelmo de Houeden, Rad. dapifero, Ricardo et Germano notariis domini episcopi, et aliis multis.

[Episcopal seal of Bishop Pudsey in green wax].

Endorsed, Confirmatio Hugonis Episcopi super compositione facta inter nos et fratres Hospitalis Sancti Egidii de decimis de Clifton et de Neuton ecclesiae Sancti Oswaldi cum pertin. Reddend. per annum 2*s*. Clifton & Kypiyer Graunge.

IV. A.D. 1243. EXCHANGE OF LANDS BETWEEN KEPYER AND FINCHALE.

[Durham Treasury, Cartul. IV, fo. 108—3ᵃ 6ᵗᵃᶜ Specialium, K. 1, No. 10].

Anno gratiae millesimo cc°™° xliij°. Convenit inter priorem et monachos de ffinchall ex una parte et magistrum et fratres de Kippeyare ex alia utilitatibus utriusque domus per earum custodes diligenter et provide consideratis, viz. quod dicti prior et monachi de ffinchall de consensu et voluntate prioris et conventus Dunelm. concesserunt dimiserunt et quietam clamaverunt domui de Kippeyare in perpetuum dimidiam carucatam terrae cum pertinenciis in villa de Aimundeston quam habuerunt de Johanne de Rudys. Et pro hac concessione dimissione et quieta clamacione concesserunt dimiserunt et quietam clamaverunt magister et fratres hospitalis de Kippeyare priori et monachis de ffinchall in perpetuum totam terram quae dicitur Sanctae Mariae leya cum omnibus suis pertinenciis sine aliquo retinemento quae fuit quondam fratris Roberti Manche cum aedificiis et bosco et omnibus aliis dictae terrae pertinenciis. Ita scilicet quod illa pars quae dictum escambium non warrantizaverit solvat alteri parti nomine poenae quinque marcas argenti quam cito cessaverit warrantizacio, et fiat sine dilacione mutua restitucio praedictarum terrarum domibus praedictis, viz., dictae terrae de Aimundeston sine aliquo retinemento domui de ffinchall et dictae terrae Sanctae Mariae leya cum pertinenciis praedictae domui de Kypeyare. Ad cujus pecuniae solucionem et dictarum terrarum restitucionem, si poena fuerit commissa prout praemissum est, fideliter et sine dolo faciendam partes ad invicem fide media se obligaverunt subjacentes se jurisdictioni archidiaconi Dunelm. qui pro tempore fuerit renunciando omni fori privelegio et omni juris remedio tam canonici quam civilis et etiam regia et episcopali prohibitione, ut omni contra-dictione cavillacione et appellacione remotis possit partem illam quae praedictum escambium non warrantizaverit per censuram ecclesiasticam compellere ad praedictam poenam quinque marcarum solvendam, et ad dictarum terrarum mutuam restitucionem partibus sine dilacione faciendam. Et in hujus rei testimonium parti hujus scripti cirographati residenti penes priorem et monachos de ffinchall appositum est commune sigillum magistri et fratrum de Kypeyare una cum sigillo archidiaconi Dunelm., et parti residenti penes magistrum et fratres de Kypeyare appositum est sigillum capituli Dunelm. una cum sigillo ejusdem archidiaconi. Testibus mutuis sigillis, scilicet capituli Dunelm. et praedictorum fratrum de Kyppeyare.

V. A.D. 1331. LICENCE BY BISHOP BEAUMONT FOR THE GRANT OF THE ADVOWSON OF HUNSTANWORTH BY THE CONVENT TO THE HOSPITAL IN EXCHANGE FOR A RENT-CHARGE OF 60s. ON THE MANORS OF CALDECOTS AND CLIFTON.[1]

[*Durham Treasury*, 1ma 3^{ciae} *Pont.*, *No. 1.*—2da 7^{mae} *Spec.*, *No. 7*].

Ludouicus permissione diuina Dunolm. Episcopus omnibus balliuis, ministris et fidelibus nostris salutem. Noveritis quod nos de gracia nostra speciali quantum in nobis est concedimus et licenciam damus specialem dilectis

---

[1] This and the following documents, VI, VII, VIII, IX, X, XI, have reference to the transference, in the fourteenth century, from the Convent to the Hospital, of the advowson of Hunstanworth with certain lands in the parish. The Hospital already held the Vill of Hunstanworth. See Appendix A (*Verified Charters*, ix).

filiis Willelmo Priori ecclesiae nostrae Dunolm. et eiusdem
loci Conuentui quod ijdem Prior et Conuentus possint dare
et concedere Deo et beato Egidio ac hospitali eiusdem
beati Egidii de Kypier prope Dunolm., et fratri Hugoni de
Monte alto magistro dicti hospitalis et fratribus eiusdem
ibidem Deo et beato Egidio imperpetuum servituris, omnes
terras et omnia tenementa sua, redditus et seruicia qua
habent in villa et territorio de Hunstanworth, vna cum
aduocacione ecclesiae eiusdem villae, cum omnibus suis
pertinenciis sine vllo retinemento.   Habenda et tenenda
dictis magistro et fratribus hospitalis praedicti et eorum
successoribus quibuscumque, de nobis et successoribus
nostris imperpetuum, Et eciam eisdem Magistro et fratribus
eiusdem hospitalis quod ipsi terras et tenementa, redditus
et seruicia praedicta, cum aduocacione ecclesiae praedictae
cum omnibus suis pertinenciis recipere possint et habere in
forma supradicta.   Praeterea concedimus pro nobis et
successoribus nostris et licenciam damus specialem eisdem
Magistro et fratribus hospitalis de Kypier supradictis, quod
ijdem Magister et fratres hospitalis praedicti in escambio
pro praedictis terris tenementis et aduocacione concedere et
dare possint Deo et beato Cuthberto, et Priori et monachis
Dunolm. Deo et praedicto Sancto in maiori ecclesia
Dunolm. imperpetuum seruituris, quemdam annuum
redditum sexaginta solidorum annuatim percipiendorum
de maneriis suis de Caldecots et de Clyftone ex parte
orientali hospitalis de Kypier, quae nunc uocantur grangiae
ad quorumcumque manus dicta maneria qualitercumque
deuenerint, videlicet, medietatem ad festum Pentecostes et
aliam medietatem ad festum Sancti Martini in hyeme,
termino primae solucionis incipiente in festo Pentecostes
anno domini m⁰ ccc^mo tricesimo tercio, et sic de anno in
annum et termino in terminum imperpetuum, quodque
ijdem Magister et fratres possint obligare se et successores
eorum ad solucionem dicti annui redditus suis terminis ut
praemittitur imperpetuum annuatim faciendam, ac concedere
pro se et successoribus suis quod dicti Willelmus Prior
Dunolm. et eiusdem loci Conuentus et eorum successores
quicumque licite distringere valeant in dictis maneriis de
Caldecots et Clyftone, et in quacumque parte eorundem
quocienscumque contigerit dictum redditum annuum sexaginta solidorum a retro esse in parte vel in toto ad aliquem
terminum praenotatum, et quod obligare possint maneria
praedicta de Caldecots et Clyftone ad praemissa facienda
districcioni dictorum Prioris et Conuentus ad quorumcumque manus deuenerint imperpetuum.   Concedimus eciam

eisdem religiosis Priori et Conuentui, et licenciam damus
specialem, quod ipsi annuum redditum praedictum de
maneriis de Caldecots et Clyftone supradictis recipere
possint et habere ac districcionem facere in forma supradicta, statuto de terris et tenementis ad manum mortuam
non ponendis edito non obstante : Nolentes quod praedicti
Prior et Conuentus, magister et fratres vel eorum
successores occasione praemissorum per nos vel successores nostros, vicecomites, exactores vel alios ministros
nostros, contra iusticiam in aliquo molestentur seu
grauentur imperpetuum. In cuius rei testimonium duas
fieri fecimus literas indentatas sigillo nostro maiori
munitas, quarum vnam penes dictos Priorem et Conuentum
Dunolm. remanere volumus, altera penes praefatos
magistrum et fratres hospitalis praedicti imperpetuum
remansura. Datum in manerio nostro de Midelham secundo
die Nouembris Anno Domini millesimo ccc° tricesimo
primo et consecracionis nostrae quarto decimo.

[*Seal of Bishop Lewis Beaumont*].

VI. A.D. 1335. BISHOP BURY'S LICENCE FOR EXCHANGE
BETWEEN THE CONVENT AND THE HOSPITAL OF
CERTAIN LANDS AT HUNSTANWORTH WITH THE
ADVOWSON OF THE LIVING FOR TITHES IN THE
PARISH OF PITTINGTON.

[*Cart. secundum, fol. 116, recto. Original wanting*].

Nouerint vniuersi praesentes literas inspecturi quod
dilectis filiis Priore Dunelm. pro se et Conuentu Dunelm.
ex parte vna, ac Magistro hospitalis de Kyppier nostra
dioceseos pro se et fratribus eiusdem ex altera, coram nobis
Ricardo permissione diuina Dunelm. Episcopo personaliter constitutis dictus Magister pro se et dictis
fratribus dedit et concessit praefatis Priori et Conuentui
Dunelm omnes decimas quas percipiunt et ab antiquo
percipere consueuerunt infra parochiam ecclesiae de
Pydyngdon de quibuscumque locis prouenientes, habendas
et percipiendas imperpetuum, sine contradiccione quacumque, saluis dumtaxat dictis Magistro et fratribus garbis
Sancti Egidii, quas consueuerunt percipere infra parochiam
memoratam. Idemque Prior, pro se et Conventu praedicto, dedit et concessit memoratis Magistro et fratribus de
Kyppier aduocacionem seu patronatum ecclesiae de Hunstanword nostrae dioceseos in permutacionem dictarum
decimarum possidendam imperpetuum et habendam,

quibus omnibus nostrum inpendi consensum humiliter supplicarunt. Vnde nos considerantes quod ex praemissis donacionibus concessionibus et permutacionibus vtilitati tam monasterii Dunolm. (presertim cum dictae decimae percipiantur de locis infra parochiam ecclesiae de Pitting-done quam ijdem religiosi in proprios vsus optinent notorie situatis) quam dicti hospitalis de Kyppier (maxime cum dicta ecclesiae de Hunstanword vicina sit loco de Knoke-dene, quam prefati Magister et fratres habent infra parochiam eiusdem ecclesiae) consulitur et indempnitatibus praecauetur ad instanciam dictorum religiosorum, quos quanto affectu sinceriori complectimus et fauoris gracia prosequimur plenioris tanto libencius suis peticionibus quas digne nobis porrigunt exaudicionis graciam aperimus, dictas donaciones concessiones et permutaciones appro-bamus ratificamus ac auctoritate pontificali tenore praesencium confirmamus. In cuius rei testimonium tria instrumenta in modum indenturae sunt confecta, quorum vni parti penes praedictos Priorem et Conuentum reman-surae sigillum nostrum vna cum sigillo magistri et fratrum hospitalis de Kyppier est appensum, alteri vero penes Magis-trum et fratres de Kyppier remanenti sigillum nostrum vna cum sigillo communi Capituli Dunelm. est appensum, terciae vero parti quam in archiuis nostris perpetuo volumus residere sigilla dictorum Prioris et Conuentus Dunelm. ac Magistri et fratrum de Kyppier apponuntur. Datum per Priorem et Conuentum praedictos in capitulo Dunolm. xij° die mensis Februarii, ac per Magistrum et fratres de Kyppier eodem die apud Kyppier. Et per nos Episcopum memoratum in castro nostro Dunolm. eodem die, videlicet, xij° mensis praedicti Anno Domini m° ccc^{mo} xxx° v°, et Consecracionis nostrae tertio.

Heading of Document.

Conuencio permutacionis ecclesiae de Hunstanworth cum decimis in parochia de Pitingdone inter nos et domum de Kypyere.

VII. A.D. 1335. BISHOP BURY'S SIMILAR LICENCE FOR EXCHANGE OF THE HOSPITAL'S TITHES AT SOUTH SHERBURN FOR ADVOWSON, &c., OF HUNSTAN-WORTH.

[*Durham Treasury,* 2da 7^{mae} *Spec., No. 12*].

Nouerint vniuersi presentes literas inspecturi quod dilecto filio Domino Priore Dunolm. pro se et Conuentu Dunolm. ex parte vna ac magistro hospitalis de Kypier nostrae dioceseos pro se et fratribus eiusdem ex altera, coram nobis Ricardo permissione diuina Dunolm. Episcopo personaliter constitutis, dictus magister pro se et dictis fratribus dedit et concessit praefatis Priori et Conuentui Dunolm. omnes decimas medietatis de dominicis terris manerii de South shirburne cum pertinenciis, quas percipiunt et ab antiquo percipere consueuerunt infra parochiam ecclesiae de Pytingdone de dictis terris prouenientibus, Habendas et percipiendas imperpetuum sive contradiccione cuiuscumque. Idemque Prior pro se et Conuentu praedicto dedit et concessit memoratis magistro et fratribus de Kypier omnes terras et tenementa sua cum suis pertinenciis, quae habuerunt in villa et territorio de Hunstanworthe, vna cum aduocacione ecclesiae Sancti Jacoby in eadem villa, quae ecclesia est nostrae dioceseos, in permutacionem dictarum decimarum possidendas imperpetuum et habendas, quibus omnibus nostrum impendi consensum humiliter supplicarunt. Vnde nos considerantes quod ex praemissis donacionibus concessionibus et permutacionibus vtilitati tam monasterii Dunolm. (presertim cum dictae decimae percipiantur de locis infra parochiam ecclesiae de Pytingdone, quam ijdem religiosi in proprios vsus optinent notorie situatis) quam dicti hospitalis de Kypier (maxime cum dicta ecclesia de Hunstanworthe vicina sit loco de Knokedene, quam praefati Magister et fratres de Kypier habent infra parochiam eiusdem ecclesiae) consulitur et indempnitatibus praecauetur ad instanciam dictorum religiosorum, quos quanto affectu sinceriori complectimur et fauoris gracia prosequimur plenioris tanto libencius suis peticionibus quas nobis digne porrigunt exaudicionis graciam apperimus, vnde dictas donaciones, concessiones et permutaciones approbamus ratificamus ac auctoritate pontificali tenore praesencium confirmamus. In cuius rei testimonium tria instrumenta in modum indenturae sunt confecta, quorum vni parti penes praedictos Priorem et Conventum remansurae sigillum nostrum vna cum sigillo Magistri et fratrum hospitalis de Kypier est appensum, alteri vero penes Magistrum et fratres de Kypier remanenti sigillum nostrum vna cum sigillo communi Capituli Dunolm. est appositum, tercia vero quod in archiuis nostris perpetuo volumus residere sigilla dictorum Prioris et capituli Dunolm. ac Magistri et fratrum de Kypier apponuntur. Datum apud Gatesheved septimo Idus Februarii Anno Domini millesimo tricentesimo tricesimo quinto, et pontificatus nostri secundo.

Endorsed : Confirmacio Ricardi Dunolm. Episcopo super permutacionem decimarum de medietate terrarum dominicarum manerii de South shyrburne infra parochiam de Pytingdone pro terris et tenementis cum patronatu ecclesiae de Hunstanworthe.

Non registratur quia non emanarunt.

[*Conventual Seal of Durham and the Seal of Kepyer (very fine) attached*].

VIII. A.D. 1352. CONCESSION BY THE HOSPITAL TO THE CONVENT OF AN ANNUAL RENT OF 13*s.* 4*d.* ON THE GRANGE OF CALDECOTS.

[*Durham Treasury, 2da 7ma Spec., No. 4*].

Vniuersis pateat per praesentes quod nos Will's Legate magister hospitalis de Kepier et fratres eiusdem loci attornauimus et loco nostro posuimus Johannem de Elvete ad liberandam Johanni Priori ecclesiae Dunelm. et eiusdem loci conventui scisinam de quodam annuo redditu tresdecim solidorum et quatuor denariorum annuatim percipiendorum de grangia nostra de Caldcote. In cuius rei testimonium sigillum commune hospitalis praedicti praesentibus est appensum. Datum apud Kepiere die dominica in Octavis Epiphaniae Domini, Anno Domini mccc^{mo}, quinquagesimo secundo.

[*Imperfect seal of white wax. St. Giles standing*].

Endorsed : Litera attornatorum magistri hospitalis de Kypier ad liberandam scisinam Priori et Conventui Dunolm. in quodam annuo redditu xiij*s.* 4*d.* in grangia de Caldecote percipiendorum ad . . . . . .

IX. A.D. 1352. GRANT BY CONVENT OF THE ADVOWSON OF HUNSTANWORTH TO KEPYER HOSPITAL IN EXCHANGE FOR A RENT-CHARGE ON CALDECOT GRANGE.

[*Durham Treasury, Cartul. IV, fo. 112.—2da 7^{mae} Specialium, No. 5*].

Praesens indentura facta inter religiosos viros dominos priorem et conventum Dunelm. ex parte una et magistrum et fratres de Kepeyere ex alia testatur quod dicti prior et conventus dederunt et concesserunt praefatis magistro et fratribus et eorum successoribus advocationem ecclesiae de Hunstanworth cum gleba et suis pertinenciis universis

habendam et tenendam sibi et successoribus suis imperpetuum de capitalibus dominis feodi. Et pro hac donacione
et concessione iidem magister et fratres concesserunt praefatis priori et conventui et eorum successoribus quendam
annuum redditum tresdecem solidorum et quatuor
denariorum capiendorum annuatim de grangia dictorum
magistri et fratrum de Caldecots ad festa Pentecostes et
Sancti Martini per aequales porciones. Ita quod quotiens-
cunque contigerit dictum redditum post aliquem terminum
a retro esse tunc licebit praedictis priori et conventui et
eorum successoribus in dicta grangia et terris ad dictam
grangiam pertinentibus distringere et eciam in omnibus
aliis terris et tenementis dictorum magistri et fratrum et
successorum infra libertatem Dunelm. et districtiones
retinere quousque de arreragiis plenarie eisdem priori et
conventui et eorum successoribus fuerit satisfactum. In
cujus rei testimonium partes praedictae sigilla sua coram
alternatim praesentibus apposuerunt. Dat. Dunelm. die
Domini in oct. Epiph. Anno Domini Mº CCCº LIIº.

X. A.D. 1352. LICENCE OF BISHOP HATFIELD TO THE
MASTER AND BRETHREN OF KEPYER FOR THE
APPOINTMENT OF A STIPENDIARY CHAPLAIN TO
RECEIVE THE REVENUES OF HUNSTANWORTH AND
SERVE THE CURE.

[Registrum Hatfield, fo. 28].

Licentia concessa Magistro et Fratribus de Kypier ad
constituendum Iconomium in Ecclesia de Honstanworth.

Thomas, &c., dilectis filiis magistro et fratribus hospitalis S. Egidii de Kypier nostri patronatus et dioeceseos
salutem gratiam et benedictionem. Cum personam ydoneam
ad ecclesiam de Honstanworthe nostrae Dunelm. dioeceseos
vestrique patronatus vacantem per vos nobis presentandam
quae eandam velit admittere et per nos canonice rector
institui in eadem, tum propter fructuum et proventuum
ipsius ecclesiae exilitatem cumque propter grandem et
necessariam reparacionem et refeccionem defectuum in
cancello et ornamentis ac manso rectoriae ejusdem ecclesiae
jam notorie existentium, reperire minime valeatis, ne cura
ipsius ecclesiae totaliter deseratur et praetextu dictorum
defectuum, non apposito celeriori reparationis remedio,
dicta rectoria ad dampnum irreparabile exiguo tempore
deducatur, vos magistrum antedictum ad deputandum et
deponendum aliquem capellanum ydoneum stipendarium
ad divina obsequia in dicta ecclesia celebrandum et curam

parochianorum in eadem exercendam, necnon ad colligendum et percipiendum per vos vel deputatos vestros fructus et proventus quoscumque ad eandem ecclesiam pertinentes et defectus supra dictos reparandos de proventibus memoratis, et si quid residuum fuerit futuro rectori fideliter reservandum, vobis potestatem specialem, donec ecclesia praedicta ad fortunam pervenerit pinguiorem, concedimus per praesentes. In cujus, &c. Datum apud Aukland in manerio nostro xxiii die Mensis Januarii Anno Domini supra et Consecrationis domini Episcopi supra dictis.

———

XI. A.D. 1379. BISHOP HATFIELD'S CONFIRMATION OF BISHOP BEAUMONT'S LICENCE (v).

[Durham Treasury, 2ᵃ 3ᵗⁱᵃᵉ Pont., No. 5.—2ᵈᵃ 7ᵐᵃᵉ Spec., No. 8].

Thomas Dei gracia Episcopus Dunolm. Omnibus ad quos praesentes literae pervenerint salutem. Inspeximus quandam cartam licentiae indentatam Priori et Conventui ecclesiae nostrae Dunelm. per Ludouicum nuper episcopum Dunelm. praedecessorem nostrum concessam, cuius quidem cartae tenor talis est.

[Beaumont's charter recited].

Nos autem tenorem cartae licentiae praedictae per praesentes duximus exemplificandam. In cuius rei testimonium has literas nostra fieri fecimus patentes. Datum Dunelm. per manum Willelmi de Elmedens cancellarii nostri xxiiij die Januarii Anno pontificatus nostri tricesimo quarto.

[Hatfield's seal in Chancery affixed].

———

XII. A.D. 1341. GRANT OF A TOFT IN CROSSGATE BY EDMUND HOWARD, MASTER OF KEPYER, TO EMMA DE TODHOWE.

[4ᵗᵃ 2ᵈᵃᵉ Elemos., No. 15 (Misc. Cart. 2283)].

Anno Domino millesimo cccᵐᵒ xljᵒ ad festum Sancti Martini in hyeme convenit inter Edmundum Howard magistrum hospitalis Sancti Egidii de Kypier et fratres ejusdem loci ex parte una et Emmam relictam Johannis de Todhowe manentem in Dunolm. ex altera, videlicet, quod iidem Magister et fratres concesserunt et ad firmam dimiserunt praedictae Emmae unum toftum edificatum cum crofto adjacente in Crossegate in Dunolm. illud scilicet quod habuerunt ex concessione et dono Nicholai del Gerner in Crossegate, Tenenda et habenda praedicta tenementa cum pertinenciis praefatae Emmae ad terminum vitae suae de praedictis magistro et fratribus et eorum successoribus libere quiete integre bene et in pace cum omnibus libertatibus liberis consuetudinibus proficuis et avsiamentis praedicto tenemento pertinentibus. Reddendo inde annuatim praedictis magistro et fratribus et eorum successoribus sex solidos argenti ad duos anni terminos scilicet medietatem ad festum Pentecostes et aliam medietatem ad festum Sancti Martini in hyeme et faciendo burgo de Crossegate omnia servicia inde debita et consueta. Et, si ita contingat quod dicta firma sex solidorum in toto vel in parte a retro fuerit, quod absit, bene licebit praedictis magistro et fratribus et eorum successoribus dicta tenementa intrare et distringere et districcionem retinere quousque praedictis magistro et fratribus et eorum successoribus de praefata firma plenarie fuerit satisfactum. Et praedicta Emma domos edificatas, terram in crofto, et clausturam circa croftum sustentabit per visum fidedignorum et in adeo bono statu dimittet sicut eadem tenementa recepit. Dicti vero magister et fratres omnia tenementa praedicta praefatae Emmae usque ad terminum vitae suae contra omnes gentes warantizabunt pro servicio supradicto et defendent. In cujus rei testimonium partes praedictae atternatim sigilla sua apposuerunt. Hiis testibus, Roberto de Cokside, Johanne Mody, Roberto Schakelok, Johanne de Egisclyf, Johanne Aurifabro, Willelmo de Chiltone, et aliis.

Endorsed : Dimissio Magistri de Kypyerhouse, Anno Domini mcccxlj ad terminum vitae. Jacet cum Crossegate. Scriptum Emmae de Todhow de tenemento in Crossegate.

Indented through CYROGRAFUM.

[*Two seals gone*].

XIII. A.D. 1355. INDULGENCE OF 40 DAYS BY BISHOP HATFIELD FOR THE BENEFIT OF KEPYER HOSPITAL.
[*Registrum Hatfield, fo. 20*].

Indulgentia concessa omnibus bona facientibus hospitali de Kypiere. Thomas permissione divina Dunolmensis episcopus dilectis filiis ecclesiarum Rectoribus Vicariis et eorum capellanis parochialibus omnibus et singulis in nostris Civitate et diocesi constitutis Salutem gratiam et benedictionem. Cum bona redditus et proventus magistri et fratrum hospitalis Beati Egidii de Kypiere nostrae dioceseos, tam per pestem tenentium suorum nuper contingentem quam etiam per sterilitatem terrarum suarum quae anno praesenti blada ad seminandum sufficientia minime produxerunt, necnon per morinam sexcentarum bidentium suarum contingentem anno proxime revoluto, et insuper quod dolenter referunt, per graves sumptus et intollerabiles expensas circa recuperacionem bonorum rerum et jurium ad dictum hospitale expectantium ipsis perperam et indebite hactenus subtractorum factas, adeo paupertate notoria sunt depressi quod ad supportanda onera caritativa eidem hospitali incumbencia, necnon ad manutenendum dictum hospitale, maneria seu grangias ad dictum hospitale pertinentes et refectionibus maximis et sumptuosis indigentes, non sufficiunt hiis diebus, quum potius ad dampnum irreparabile et desolationem perpetuam idem hospitale verisimiliter in proximo deducetur nisi ex devotione et elemosinarum largicione fidelium eidem celerius succurratur :—Nos, calamitatem et indigentiam dicti hospitalis magistri et fratrum ejusdem considerantes, omnes et singulos subditos et parochianos nostros monemus et exhortamur in Domino quatenus de bonis sibi adeo collatis necessitatibus dictorum magistri et fratrum velint benignius subvenire ut percipere mereantur quadraginta dierum indulgentiam per nos hujusmodi benefactoribus concessam, Et Trescentos dies indulgentiae quos predecessores nostri dudum episcopi Dunolmenses suis temporibus indulserunt. Vobis etiam praecipiendo mandamus quatenus procuratores dictorum magistri et fratrum, cum ad vos hac de causa declinaverint, negocia praedicta horis congruis in ecclesiis vestris prae caeteris aliis negociis exponere permittatis, vel eadem negocia promovere et dilucide exponere velitis intuitu caritatis, Et quid in hac parte collectum fuerit praefatis magistro et fratribus sine mora restitui faciatis. Valete.

In cujus rei, &c. Datum in manerio nostro de Aukland in crastino Annunciationis dominicae, Anno Domini millesimo ccc^mo Quinquagesimo quinto, et consecrationis nostrae decimo.

XIV. A.D. 1437. BISHOP LANGLEY'S VISITATION OF KEPYER.

[*Registrum Langley, fo. 248*].
Commissio ad Visitandum hospitale de Kepyer.

Thomas episcopus dilectis in Christo filiis magistro Johanni Bonour decretorum doctori cancellario nostro,

Johanni Lythom utriusque juris Bacallario sequestratori nostro in archidiaconatu Dunelm., domino Nicholao Hulme canonico ecclesiae praebend(al)is de Derlyngton nostrae dioceseos, et Willelmo Raket clerico cancellario nostro, Salutem. Volentes certis ex causis racionabilibus et legittimis nos moventibus Hospitale Sancti Egidii de Kypier prope Dunelm. nostrorum patronatus et dioc. infra breve annuente Domino actualiter visitare, ac non volentes propter alia diversa negocia quibus aliunde sumus occupati in ipsius visitationis officio personaliter interesse, ad visitandum Hospitale praedictum ac magistrum sive custodem singulosque probros clericos servientes et ministros ejusdem ac alios quoscunque degentes in eodem ; necnon de et super statu regimine et administracione hospitalis praedicti et bonorum ad id pertinencium vitaque et conversacione et moribus omniumque et singulorum praedictorum inquirendum, defectus crimina et excessus eorundem corrigendum et reformandum, compotum etiam et raciocinium magistri sive custodis praedicti de quibus-cumque bonis ipsius Hospitalis pro suo tempore receptis et administratis audiendum et recipiendum, ac ipsum magis-trum sive custodem ut fidelem compotum et racionem administracionis suae bonorum praedictorum plenumque et verum inventarium quorumcumque bonorum mobilium et immobilium dicti hospitalis faciat exhibeat et producat juxta juris communis exigenciam et praedicto hospitalis fundacionem compellendum et cohercendum, parcellas sumptuum et expensarum racionabilium et necessariorum in hospitali praedicto et ad commodum et utilitatem ejusdem factorum allocandum, et alias si quae fuerint disallocandum ; necnon fundacionem et ordinacionem dicti Hospitalis et alia munimenta quaecumque ad id pertinencia exhiberi faciendum, ac caetera omnia et singula facienda et exercenda quae hujusmodi visitacionis officium exigit et requirit,—Vobis de quorum fidelitate industria et conscientiae puritate plenam in Domino fiduciam obtinemus tribus et duobus vestrum tenore praesencium committimus vices nostras cum cujuslibet cohercionis canonicae potestate, Volentes quod nos de omni eo quod feceritis in praemissis finito ipso visitacionis negocio distincte et aperte vel personaliter certificetis vel per literas vestras auctentice consignatas. Dat. sub sigillo nostro in manerio nostro de Aukland xii° die mensis Julii anno Domini, &c.

XV. A.D. 1437. BISHOP LANGLEY'S ACQUITTANCE OF RICHARD BUKLEY AFTER THE VISITATION.

[*Registrum Langley, fo. 249 v.*].

Acquietancia facta Ricardo Bukley custodi Hospitalis de Kepyer super compotum administracionis suae bonorum ejusdem, ac commissio custodiae ejusdem facta eidem Ricardo ad vitam.

Thomae, &c., dilecto in Christo filio domino Ricardo Bukley presbytero, magistro sive custodi domus sive Hospitalis Sancti Egidii de Kepyer prope Dunelm. nostrorum patronatus et dioces. Salutem, &c. Cum nuper auditis ac visis et intellectis per certos commissarios nostros ad hoc sufficienter et legitime deputatos in quadam visitacione nostra domus sive hospitalis praedicti per eosdem ibidem auctoritate nostra actualiter exercita diversis compotis et raciociniis tuis de et super disposicione et administracione omnium et singulorum bonorum ejusdem hospitalis de toto tempore quo tu magister sive custos ejusdem exstitisti, Nedum per compota et raciocinia praedicta verum eciam et per quoddam inventarium plenum et fidele omnium et singulorum bonorum mobilium ipsius hospitalis ac per alia in praedicta visitacione nostra coram commissariis nostris praedictis capta exhibita et comperta et nobis legitime certificata ac penes officium nostrum remanentia invenerimus te omnia et singula bona dictae domus sive hospitalis ad divini cultus augmentum pauperumque in ipso hospitali degencium et aliorum ad idem confluencium indies sustentacionem, ac aliorum onerum eidem hospitali incumbencium supportacionem, necnon predicti hospitalis instauracionem ad commodum et utilitatem ejusdem bene et fideliter ac utiliter disposuisse et administrasse, hinc est quod te praedictum dominum Ricardum ab ulteriori compoto sive raciocinio administracionis tuae praedictae nobis vel successoribus reddendo a primo die incumbenciae tuae in hospitali praedicto usque in diem dat. praesencium quantum in nobis est seu ad nostrum spectat officium, salvo jure alterius cujuscumque, liberamus exoneramus et per praesentes te dimittimus penitus absolutum. Volentesque insuper ex praedictis et aliis causis racionabilibus nos moventibus non solum tibi praemissorum meritorum tuorum intuitu graciam liberiorem in hac parte facere, verum eciam eidem hospitali de utili et fructuoso gubernatore quantum cum Deo possumus providere, te dominum Ricardum Bukley praedictum in magistrum sive custodem domus sive hospitalis praedicti

pro toto tempore vitae tuae praeficimus et tenore praesencium deputamus, ac instituimus canonice in eadem cum
suis juribus et pertinenciis universis, Regimen custodiam et
administracionem ejusdem domus sive hospitalis ac jurium
et pertinencium suorum praedictorum tibi quamdiu vives
plenarie committendo. Proviso semper quod tu, quamdiu
custodiam habueris antedictam, plenum et fidelem ad-
ministrationis tuae bonorum hospitalis praedicti compotum
et raciocinium annuatim reddas cum per nos vel
successores nostros ad hoc legitime fueris evocatus.
Nolumus tamen quod per hanc nostram praefectionem
deputacionem seu commissionem quam tuorum meritorum
praedictorum intuitu ipsius hospitalis utilitate pensata in
persona tua jam duximus faciendam ipsum hospitale
erigatur seu beneficium ecclesiasticum censeatur, vel quod
ejus natura seu fundatio in aliquo immutetur ; sed cedente
vel decedente seu alias quomodolibet illud dimittente,
volumus quod idem hospitale in natura et forma juris
communis remaneat et prout in fundacione ejusdem est
antiquitus ordinatum, hac nostra commissione praefectione
vel deputacione in aliquo non obstante. In quorum
omnium et singulorum testimonium sigillum nostrum
praesentibus duximus apponendum. Dat. in manerio
nostro de Aukland xxv° die mensis Augusti Anno Domini
M° CCCCXXXVII^{mo}, et nostrae consecracionis xxxij°.

XVI. A.D. 1437. CONFIRMATION BY THE PRIOR AND
  CHAPTER OF BISHOP LANGLEY'S ACQUITTANCE OF
  RICHARD BUKLEY.

  [*Durham Treasury, Reg. III, fo. 208 v.*].

Confirmatio Domini Ricardi Bukley presbiteri in
Magistrum seu custodem Hospitalis de Kepier prope
Dunelm. ad terminum vitae suae.

Omnibus Christi fidelibus praesentes literas inspecturis
Johannes permissione divina Prior Ecclesiae Cathedralis
Dunelm. et ejusdem loci capitulum Salutem in omnium
Salvatore. Noveritis nos literas Reverendi in Christo
patris et domini domini Thomae Dei gratia Dunelm.
episcopi sub tenore qui sequitur inspexisse. Thomas
permissione divina Dunelm. episcopus dilecto in Christo
filio domino Ricardo Bukley presbitero, magistro sive
custodi domus sive hospitalis Sancti Egidii de Kepyer
prope Dunelm. nostrorum patronatus et dioceseos, Salutem
gratiam et benedictionem. Cum nuper auditis ac visis et
intellectis per certos, &c. (*Ut supra*).

Dat. Dunelm. 28 Aug. 1437.

XVII. A.D. 1439. CONFIRMATION BY PRIOR AND
CHAPTER OF BISHOP NEVILL'S SIMILAR ACQUITTANCE
OF RICHARD BUKLEY.

[*Durham Treasury, Reg. III, fo. 242*].

Confirmatio acquietanciae seu dimissionis factae
Ricardo Bukley pro custodia hospitalis de Kepyer per
Dominum Robertum episcopum Dunelm.

Universis sanctae Matris ecclesiae filiis ad quos
praesentes literae pervenerint Johannes permissione
divina Prior ecclesiae cathedralis Dunelm. et ejusdem loci
capitulum Salutem in omnium Salvatore. Noveritis nos
literas Reverendissimi in Christo patris et domini domini
Roberti Dei gratia Dunelm. episcopi sub tenore qui
sequitur inspexisse. Pateat universis per praesentes quod
cum nos Robertus permissione divina Dunelm. episcopus,
audito et intellecto compoto seu ratiocinio dilecti nobis in
Christo domini Ricardi Bukley nuper magistri sive custodis
hospitalis de Kepyer nostrarum collacionis et diocesos in
scaccario nostro Dunelm. in praesentia venerabilium et
discretorum virorum magistri Johannis Norton decretorum doctoris, Willelmi Chauncelere, ac Willelmi
Rakett, per ipsum dominum Ricardum nuper facto de et
super custodia regimine et administratione bonorum
omnium et singulorum ad idem hospitale quomodolibet
pertinencium, invenerimus dictum dominum Ricardum
ipsum hospitale laudabiliter gubernasse et rexisse ac bona
omnia et singula ad id pertinencia circa statum et utilitatem
ejusdem hospitalis bene et fideliter disposuisse et administrasse, eundem dominum Ricardum Bukley praemissorum
praetextu ab ulteriori compoto seu raciocinio nobis in ea
parte faciendo seu reddendo totaliter dimisimus sicque
dimittimus per praesentes. In cujus rei testimonium
sigillum nostrum ad causas praesentibus duximus apponendum. Dat. decimo sexto die mensis Octobris Anno
Domini millesimo Quadringentesimo tricesimo nono et
nostrae translacionis anno secundo. Nos vero praefati
Prior et Capitulum omnia et singula supradicta prout
superius continentur in forma concessionis praedictae rata
habentes pariter et accepta, ea quantum in nobis est sub
modo et forma praenotatatis pro nobis et successoribus
nostris ratificamus approbamus et tenore praesencium
confirmamus, juribus et libertatibus ecclesiae nostrae
Dunelm. in omnibus semper salvis. In cujus rei testi-
omnium sigillum capituli nostri praesentibus est appensum.
Dat. Dunelm. in domo nostra capitulari vicesimo tertio die
mensis Octobris Anno Domini supradicto.

XVIII. A.D. 1439. APPOINTMENT OF JOHN LOUNDE BY BISHOP NEVILL TO BE MASTER OF KEPYER.

[Durham Treasury, Reg. III, fo. 241].

Omnibus Christi fidelibus praesentes literas inspecturis Johannes permissione divina Prior ecclesiae Cath. Dunelm. et ejusdem loci capitulum Salutem in omnium Salvatore. Noveritis nos literas Reverendissimi in Christo patris et domini domini Roberti dei gratia Dunelm. episcopi sub tenore qui sequitur inspexisse. Robertus permissione divina Dunelm. episcopus dilecto nobis in Christo Magistro Johanni Lounde in utroque Jure Baccalario Salutem gratiam et benedictionem. De tuis meritis et circumspeccionis industria quae hactenus experti sumus plenam in domino fiduciam reportantes, hospitale de Kepyer nostrarum collacionis et dioeces. per liberam resignacionem domini Ricardi Bukley ultimi magistri sive custodis ejusdem in manus nostras factam et per nos admissam vacans tibi conferimus teque magistrum sive custodem, &c.

XIX. A.D. 1439. CONFIRMATION BY PRIOR AND CHAPTER OF PENSION GRANTED BY BISHOP NEVILL TO RICHARD BUKLEY.

[Durham Treasury, Reg. III, fo. 241 v.].

Confirmatio concessionis cujusdam annuae pensionis exeuntis de hospitali de Kepyer factae Ricardo Bukley ad terminum vitae per Robertum episcopum Dunelm.

Omnibus Christi fidelibus praesentes literas inspecturis Johannes permissione divina Prior ecclesiae cathedralis Dunelm. et ejusdem loci capitulum Salutem in omnium Salvatore. Noveritis nos literas Reverendi in Christi patris et domini domini Roberti Dei gratia Dunelm. episcopi sub tenore quod sequitur inspexisse. Universis sanctae matris ecclesiae filiis praesentes literas inspecturis seu audituris, Robertus permissione divina Dunelm. episcopus Salutem in amplexibus Salvatoris. Cum dilectus nobis in Christo dominus Ricardus Bukley presbyter, nuper Magister sive Custos hospitalis de Kepyer nostrarum collacionis et dioeceseos, per tantum tempus custodiam et regimen ejusdem hospitalis laudabiliter gubernavit habuit et occupavit quod ad actuale exercicium ejusdem in praesenti et pro futuro propter senectutem et corporis sui debilitatem quibus dinoscitur laborare impotens et inhabilis sit effectus, ipseque dominus Ricardus volens et affectans ab hujusmodi

custodia et regimine, ex causis praemissis et aliis veris et
legitimis coram nobis pro parte sua expositis ipsum ad hoc
moventibus, totaliter exonerari, hospitale suum hujusmodi
cum suis juribus et pertinenciis universis in manus nostras
non coactus nec vi aut metu ductus sed propria sponte
simpliciter et absolute resignavit et ipsum hospitale re et
verbo totaliter dimisit tenore praesencium, vobis innotesci-
mus quod nos, consideratis magnis laboribus & laudabili
regimine ipsius domini Ricardi Bukley quae circa
custodiam ac utilitatem ipsius hospitalis dum potuit
hactenus impendit et procuravit et in futurum Domino
duce per se et suos poterit procurare, Attendentes eciam
quod dignum sit ut qui laboravit aliquid mercedis accipiat
pro labore et ne idem Dominus Ricardus, dudum ut
praefertur magister sive custos hospitalis praedicti, in
opprobrium ordinis presbyteralis et ministerii nostri vitu-
perium victum mendicitus adquirere dinoscatur, eidem
domino Ricardo de fructibus & proventibus hospitalis
supradicti pensionem annuam quadraginta marcarum
legalis monetae Anglicanae pro sustentacione victus sui
durante vita sua ad duos anni terminos, viz., Paschae et
Sancti Michaelis Archangeli, prima solucione incipiente ad
festum Paschae proximum post datum praesentium
proxime futurum, aequis porcionibus per magistrum sive
custodem dicti hospitalis qui pro tempore fuerit fideliter
persolvendam de consensu & voluntate omnium et
singulorum quorum interest, auctoritate nostra ordinaria
decernimus assignamus & ordinamus. Volumus insuper
decernimus & statuimus quod, si contingat dictam pensionem
quadraginta marcarum per mensis spatium post aliquem
terminum solucionis supradictae in parte vel in toto a retro
fore non soluta ut praefertur, quod exeuntes fructus
redditus et proventus dicti hospitalis sint & maneant ipso
facto sequestrati, quos nos etiam exnunc prout extunc et
extunc prout exnunc tenore praesentium sequestramus,
custodiam eorundem officiali consistorii nostri Dunelm.
pro tempore existenti committentes quousque praefato
Domino Ricardo Bukley una cum dampnis et expensis
plenarie fuerit satisfactum in praemissis ; Attendente ad
hanc nostram ordinacionem seu decretum consensu et
voluntate magistri Johannis Lounde in utroque jure
Baccalaurei, in magistrum sive custodem ejusdem hospitalis
praefecti et ordinati. Quam quidem ordinationem seu
decretum hujusmodi idem magister Johannes Lounde
pro persona sua fideliter et integre in omnibus observare
tactis sacrosanctis juramentum praestitit corporale. Volu-

mus eciam et tenore praesentium decernimus quod
successores ejusdem magistri Johannis Lounde omnes et
singuli, si qui fuerint in dicto hospitale durante vita
praefati domini Ricardi Bukley, pro temporibus suis in
praesentacionibus et admissionibus eorundem ad dictum
hospitale consimile praestent juramentum. In quorum
omnium et singulorum praemissorum testimonium atque
fidem sigillum nostrum ad causas praesentibus duximus
apponendum. Datum decimo sexto die mensis Octobris
millesimo quadragentesimo tricesimo nono, et nostrae
translationis anno secundo. Quas quidem literas in
omnibus suis clausulis nos Prior et capitulum memorati
ratas habentes et gratas, eas pro nobis & successoribus
nostris ratificamus approbamus & tenore praesentium
confirmamus, juribus et libertatibus ecclesiae nostrae
Dunelm. in omnibus semper salvis. In cujus rei testimonium sigillum commune capituli nostri praesentibus est
appensum. Datum Dunelm. in domo nostra capitulari
vicesimo tertio die mensis Octobris Anno Domini supradicto.

XX. A.D. 1497. APPOINTMENT BY BISHOP FOX OF
THOMAS COLSTON TO BE MASTER OF KEPYER.

[Fox's Register, fo. 13, in Dioc. Registry].

Ricardus, &c., dilecto nobis in Christo magistro
Thomae Colston clerico Salutem, &c. Custodiam et
regimen hospitalis Sancti Egidii de Kepyer nostrae
dioceseos per mortem magistri Radulphi Both ultimi
magistri sive custodis ejusdem vacantis et ad nostram
disposicionem spectantis tibi committimus, teque custodem
sive dispensatorem ejusdem praeficimus, et deputamus per
praesentes ad nostrum bene placitum duraturum. Dat.
&c., mense et anno praedicto.

XXI. A.D. 1532. VISITATION OF KEPYER HOSPITAL BY
BISHOP TUNSTALL.

[Tunstall's Register, fo. 5, in Dioc. Registry].

Citacio pro Visitacione Domus seu Hospitalis de Kepyer.

CUTHBERTUS permissione divina Dunelmensis Episcopus dilecto filio magistro Willielmo Frankeleyn Custodi
domus nostrae de Kepyer nostrae dioceseos Salutem
gratiam et benedictionem. Inter caeteras solicitudines
humeris nostris ex debito suscepti regiminis incumbentes
non minima est intencio atque cura ut piorum praesertim

locorum dispendia nequaquam absque remedio debitae reformacionis relinquamus. Cum igitur fama publica referente nobis insinuatum sit quod et bona praedictae domus multipliciter hactenus temere consumpta sint in subversionem status ejusdem et in cultus divini diminucionem et sustentacionis pauperum aliorumque caritatis operum quae ibidem vigere solebant subtractionem, super quorum veritate volentes plenius informari ac visitacionis officium tam in personis quam in rebus domus ipsius prout convenit exercere, vos tenore presentium peremptorie citamus, ac fratres sorores capellanos ac alios quoscumque ejusdem domus ministros per quos praemissorum veritas erui melius poterit atque sciri per vos citari volumus, et mandamus quod compareatis et compareant personaliter coram nobis vel commissariis nostris in capella domus praedictae die Jovis, viz., decimo octavo die mensis Julii proximefuturo post datum praesentium cum continuacione et prorogacione dierum subsequentium visitacionem nostram hujusmodi actualiter susceptam et subitam ; Ac fundacionem seu ordinacionem domus praedictae una cum inventariis et compoto calculo sive raciocinio ejusdem secundum sanctiones canonicas exhibituri ulterius prout acceptum et factum in praemissis et ea tangentibus quod fuerit et consonum racioni. Et, ut liberius ac devotius capellani et fratres domus ejusdem obsequiis valeant vacare divinis, eosdem omnes et singulos ab officiis et administracionibus rerum temporalium praedictae domus per vos interim decrevimus et praecipimus amovendos. De die vero receptionis praesentium et quid in praemissis feceritis nos dictis die et loco definite et aperte certificetis per literas vestras patentes harum seriem continentes, ac sigillo auctentice sigillatas. Dat. sub sigillo nostro apud manerium nostrum de Stockton vicesimo octavo die mensis Junii Anno Domini millesimo quingentesimo tricesimo secundo Et nostrae Translacionis anno tercio.

APPENDIX B.

DOCUMENTS RELATING TO S. MARY MAGDALEN HOSPITAL.

I. COMPOSITION BETWEEN THE CONVENT OF DURHAM
AND KEPYER HOSPITAL.[1]

[*Durham Treasury, 6ta 4^{tae} Elemos., No. 12*].

Hospitale S. Mariae Magd. juxta Kipyer.

Radulfus de Elvet monacus procurator hospitalis
Sancti Egidii de Kipyer et fratres ejusdem loci
omnibus Christi fidelibus ad quos praesens scriptum
pervenerit aeternam in Domino salutem. Noverit universitas vestra quod cum aliqua esset contencio inter
Priorem et Conventum Dunelmensis ecclesiae et nos
de terra nostra de Aymundestun et de Hurtheworthe
quam Gilbertus Haunsard nobis dedit ad sustentacionem
unius capellani qui pro defunctis imperpetuum divina
celebraret in excambium medietatis villae de Chyrtun
in Nortumbria quae quondam fuit Johannis de Hameldun
et quam idem Johannes cum quibusdam aliis terris
dedit Priori et Conventui Dunelmensis ecclesiae ad
sustentacionem trium sacerdotum qui divina celebrarent
imperpetuum, Ita tamen quod Henricus et Walterus fratres
ejus et eorum heredes dictarum terrarum firmarii essent
feudarii et dictis Priori et Conventui Dunelmensis Ecclesiae
redderent novem marcas annuas inde ad dictum servicium
faciendum, et idem Prior et Conventus Dunelmensis
ecclesiae illud servicium recusarent faciendum, et sic ad
nos verteretur excambium medietatis villae de Chyrton,
scilicet terra de Aymundeston et de Hurtheworthe per
Radulfum de Elvet monacum procuratorem nostrum. [*Illico
autem ?*] per G. Haunsard et Walterum de Hameldun
tandem inter nos amicabilis intervenit composicio in hunc
modum, scilicet quod nos unanimi voluntate et consensu
concessimus et dedimus Priori et Conventui Dunelmensis
ecclesiae redditum annuum trium marcarum convertendum
in pios usus per manum elemosinarii sui pro anima dicti

Johannis de Hameldun et omnium defunctorum in certo loco. Unde eisdem concessimus et dedimus et in saysinam posuimus de terra nostra de Hurthewurthe quae reddit annuatim xxiiij solidos et de xij acris terrae in crofto nostro australi [1] sub vico Sancti Egidii versus Wer a sole remotioribus scilicet versus occidentem pro xvj solidis annuis ; Salva burgensibus nostris firma sua perpetua de eadem terra. Sed, si burgenses illas xii acras tenentes a solucione firmae cessaverint, liceat dictis Priori et Conventui dictarum xii acrarum possessionem ingredi et illas tam diu tenere donec eis plenarie satisfiat de firma. Dictas autem terras saepe dicto Priori et Conventui Dunelmensis ecclesiae concessimus et dedimus habendas et tenendas in puram et perpetuam elemosinam, sicut eas tenuimus, de nobis et successoribus nostris. Ita tamen quod ocasione hujus concessionis nichil a nobis aut a terris nostris aut hominibus nostris exigant praeter firmam dictarum xij acrarum, vel xij acras si dicti firmarii a dictae firmae solucione cessaverint, et has dictas terras de Hurthewurthe et de crofto Australi dictis Priori et Conventui warrantizabimus secundum quod G. Haunsard et heredes sui nobis warrantizaverunt terram de Aymundestun. Et ut haec nostra composicio concessio et donacio rata stabilis et firma. futuris temporibus permaneat praesens scriptum sigillo Sancti Egidii et nostro roboravimus. Hiis testibus, Willelmo et Alano capellanis nostris in capitulo nostro, Waltero Blunde, Ric. Fabro, Helya de Kazop, Radulfo Forestario, Waltero de Fonte, et curia nostra.

Endorsed : Compositio inter Priorem et Conventum et domum de Kypyare in qua conceduntur xij acrae terrae elemosinario juxta hospitale Sanctae Mariae Magdalenae.

II. [*Temp. Ran. Kernech, Prior of Durham 1219— 1233*]. RESIGNATION OF LAND AT AMERSTON AND HURWORTH BY THE HOSPITAL TO THE CONVENT.[2]

[*Durham Treasury, 2da 7^mae Spec., No. 1—Cart. ii, 115 recto*].

Viris venerabilibus Dominis et amicis karissimis R. Priori et Conventui Dunelm. ecclesiae universi fratres

---

[1] "Stephanus Capellanus" gave to Kepyer Hospital his land and buildings at Southcrofte in Gilligate. (See above, Charter xix, p. 207).

[2] This, and the following documents, III, IV, appear to refer to the negociations between the Convent and the Hospital, with respect to which there had been "aliqua contencio," before the Composition given above. See "Introduction," as referred to in the last note.

domus Sancti Egidii de Kippeyere salutem in Domino.
Notum vobis facimus nos et domum nostram de Kippeyere
multum gravari et magnam jacturam incurrisse occasione
firmae terrae de Amundistun et de Hurtheworthe quam de
vobis tenemus.   Unde communi consilio capituli nostri
providimus eam vobis resignandam et quietam clamandam.
Unde ad hoc faciendum mittimus ad vos dilectos R.
rectorem nostrum et fratres Albertum et Walterum et ad
hoc eos procuratores nostros constituimus, ratum et gratum
habituri quicquid super hoc una vobiscum egerint.   Et in
hujus rei testimonium has literas nostras patentes sigillo
nostro signatas vobis transmittimus.

Endorsed :—Resignacio terrae de Amundesley et
Hurtheworthe per Magistrum et fratres de Kypeyere.

[*Fragmentary seal of Kepyer, St. Giles standing*].

III.　[*Temp. Ran. Kernech Prioris*].   UNDERTAKING BY
THE CONVENT TO MAINTAIN A CHAPLAIN FOR THE
SOULS OF THE HANSARD FAMILY, AND TO PAY 30s.
A YEAR TO THE HOSPITAL BY THE HANDS OF THE
PRIOR OF FINCHALE, IN RETURN FOR THE LANDS
AT AMERSTON AND HURWORTH, WHICH HAD BEEN
GIVEN TO THE HOSPITAL BY GILBERT HANSARD,
AND WERE NOW CEDED TO THE CONVENT.

[*Printed in* " Priory of Finchale," *Surtees Society*,
1837, p. 126, with Reference to Reg. I, *p. 48*].

IV.　[*Temp. Tho. Melsonby, Prior of Durham*, 1233—
1244].   QUIT-CLAIM BY THE CONVENT TO THE
HOSPITAL OF REVENUES IN VARIOUS PLACES IN
RETURN FOR THE CESSION BY THE HOSPITAL TO
THE CONVENT OF THEIR LANDS AT AMERSTON
ON CONDITION OF THE HOSPITAL PROVIDING A
CHAPLAIN AT KEPYER TO SING FOR THE SOULS OF
THE HAMELDON AND HANSARD FAMILIES, &c.

[*Printed in* " Priory of Finchale," *Surtees Society*,
*1837, p. 127. The document is in the Durham Treasury,
2da 7^{mae} Spec., No. 2, being an indented Charter, with seal
of Convent of Durham, and endorsed*, Carta Thomae
Prioris et Conventus Dunelm. de redditibus datis domui de
Kypyer. *Then, in a much later hand*, pro sustentacione j
capellani apud Kypyer, et pro terra in Aimundistun.
Mem. de resignacione terrae de Amundesley et Hurworth
facta Priori et Conventui Dunelm. post istam cartam.
Non ostendatur.   Non registratur].

V. A Complaint (*circa temp. Edw. II, 1309—1327*) CONCERNING ALLEGED ABSTRACTION OF ALMS FROM S. MARY MAGDALEN HOSPITAL, WITH AN ACCOUNT OF ITS SUPPOSED ORIGINAL FOUNDATION AND CONSTITUTION.[1]

[*Durham Treasury, Cart. Elemos., 6ta 4ar, No. 16*].

Certayne choses est que un chevaler a noum Sir John le Fitz Alisaundre funda le Hospital de la Maudeleyn en Durem et fit une chapelle et plusours autre mesouns en cel hospital en perpetuele aumoin pour les almes touz Xtiens de ses terres et de ses Rentys de mene en quel hospitale il establit pour touz jours un chapelleyn et xiij freris et sores cest asaver hommes et femes que avaynt estee bones gentz et en bon poynt en lur juvent et lur biens avayt falye tiele gent deyt estre rescu en cel Hospital saunz rien doner pour lur entree.

Et pour aver certayne sustenauncz pour un chapeleyn et xiij freres et sores avant nomes pour touz jours assignat il dona terres le quez gysont pres de cel hospital et devant le porte de Schirburn et pour aver certeyne sustenauncz pour touz jours il dona al Aumerye de Durem la ville de Rylley od le molyne et tute le mayte de la ville de Chilton pour aver chescun ane certeyne sustenauncz a cel hospital par assent du Prior et du Convent de Durem la quele fut grante et conferme pour touz jours cest a saver pour le chapeleyn illok demorand chescun jour la livere de un moigne et chescun ane un garnement pris de un mark et les xiij freres et sores chescun semayne xxiij paynes et demy partye de blaunke payne de mayne et tray jours en le semayne pulment cest a saver chescun jour deux galouns et demy et chescun ane a chescun frere et sore pour say tres aunes de russet et tres autres de cannevas et iiij*d.* a soulers.   Et en quele sustenauncz et livere cel hospital fut seisy annz et jours jesques au temps un moygne dan John de Bulford Aumoner de Durem qui pria par fraude a un Thomas de Heworth un de les freres qui fut com gardayne que il luy prestayt lur paynes de un semayne pour overours qu il avoit a Wytton et il luy granta et de autres iij semayns prochayn ensuans et il luy pour cco que le mesoun fut a dunk en bon point et pus vient celuy Thomas et demande lur paynes quils furent prestes et pour luy cesses de sa demande et pour aver veu de lur monumenz quils furent en la garde le dit Thomas le dit dan John dona

---

[1] Concerning this document see "Introduction" under "Hospital of S. Mary Magdalen."

a le dit Thomas une surcote furee de Ray que fut a une William son serjaunt qui mort fut et le dit Thomas rescut cele surcote et luy porta touz lur monumenz pour garder et le dit dan John le rescut et par luy furent detenouz et uncorsunt ovee lur paynes et lur dras et lur argent et lur pulment dune Sir les almes tous Xtiens vos priunt de remedy et de amendment.

Endorsed : Querela de Elemos. pro Hospitali de Mawdelayns sed sciendum quod ista querela non continet veritatem pro majori parte. Jacet 6a quartae.

The above may be rendered in English and explained as follows :—

It is a certain thing that a knight, by name Sir John le Fitz Alisaundre, founded Magdalen Hospital in Durham, and made a chapel and several other buildings in this Hospital, in perpetual alms, for the souls of all Christians, out of his lands and of his demesne rents ; in which hospital he established for ever a chaplain and xiij brethren and sisters, that is to say, men and women who had been good people and in good case in their youth, and whose goods had failed ; such people were to be received in this Hospital without giving anything for their entry.

And for having certain sustenance for a chaplain and for the xiij brethren and sisters above-mentioned for ever assigned, he gave lands which lie near this hospital and before the gate of Sherburn ; and for having certain sustenance for ever he gave to the Almonry of Durham the vill of Rilley together with the mill and all the *mayte* [1] of the mill of Chilton in order to have certain sustenance every year to this hospital with the assent of the Prior and of the Convent of Durham, the which was granted and confirmed for ever ; to wit for the chaplain abiding there the *livere* [2] of a monk every day, and every year a garnement [3] of the price of one mark ; and for the xiij brethren and sisters every week xxiij loaves, and the half-part [*thereof*] of white bread *de mayne*,[4] and on three days

---

[1] Probably the right of the tenants of the estate to grind their corn at the mill. *Mais* or *mail* means a sort of coffer into which the flour falls as the corn is ground. See Ducange, *sub voce* MAITA.

[2] *I.e.*, a monk's usual daily sustenance ; probably from Low Latin *liverare*, or *liberare*, meaning to deliver, or remit. See Ducange. In Old French, *livraison* means something given or delivered in kind.

[3] A long coat, or kind of mantle.

[4] The word *mayne* should come from Low Latin *maina*, a mansion, or house. It may have been the usual term for such bread as was used in good households—household-bread.

in the week *pulment* [1]—to wit, on each day two gallons and a half ; and every year to each brother and sister for themselves three ells of russet and three others of canvas and iiij*d.* for shoes.   And of such sustenances and *livere* this hospital was seized by years and days until the time of a monk, dan John of Bulford, Almoner of Durham, who begged by fraud of one Thomas de Heworth (one of the brethren who acted as guardian) that he would lend him the loaves of one week for workmen that he had at Witton ; and he (*i.e.*, *Thomas de Heworth*) granted them to him, and also others for other three weeks next ensuing, for that the house was at that time in good case ; and then went this Thomas and asked for the loaves, which were ready, and given up to him at his request.   And in order to get sight of the muniments which were in the keeping of the said Thomas, the said dan John gave the said Thomas a surcoat *furee de Ray* [2] which had belonged to one William, his sergeant, who was dead ; and the said Thomas received this surcoat, and brought him all their muniments to keep ; and the said dan John took them, and they were by him detained, and are so still, [3] together with their loaves, and their clothes [*draps*], and their money, and their *pulment.* Wherefore, Sir, all Christian souls pray you for remedy and amendment.

Endorsed on the part of the Prior and Convent after they had received the document :—

Complaint concerning alms for the Magdalen Hospital. But be it known that this complaint does not contain truth for the most part.

VI.   A.D. 1391.   BISHOP SKIRLAW'S INDULGENCE IN BEHALF OF S. MARY MAGDALEN HOSPITAL.

[Durham Treasury, 2264—6ta 4^{tae} Elemos., No. 15].

Universis Sanctae Matris Ecclesiae filiis ad quos praesentes literae pervenerint Walterus permissione divina Dunolmensis Episcopus Salutem in Domino sempiternam.

---

[1] PULMENTUM.—Vox veteribus cognita, sed sequiori aetati maxime in regulis monasticis usurpata, ubi pro quovis obsonio accipitur.—D'Arnis.

[2] *Furee* for *fourrée*, *i.e.*, furred. *Ray* may be the English word that occurs in Ray-cloth, meaning " cloth that was never coloured or dyed." (Bailey).

[3] *Uncorsunt* in the original seems to be meant for *encore sont.*

Gratum obsequium ac Deo placitum tociens impendere opinamur quociens mentes fidelium ad caritativae devocionis opera propensius excitamus. De Dei igitur omnipotentis misericordia, piissimaeque Virginis Matris ejus ac beatorum Petri et Pauli apostolorum necnon beati confessoris Cuthberti patroni nostri gloriosi omniumque Sanctorum meritis et precibus confidentes, omnibus parochianis nostris, ac aliis quorum diocesani hanc nostram indulgentiam ratam habuerint pariter et acceptam, de peccatis suis vere contritis et confessis, qui ad hospitale beatae Mariae Magdalenae in strata vulgariter nuncupata Saintgiligate in civitate nostra Dunolmen. situatum in festis ejusdem futuris temporibus causa devocionis accesserint et ad ipsius Hospitalis et pauperum sustentacionem ibidem degencium quicquam de bonis a Deo sibi collatis obtulerint contulerint aut alio quovis modo caritatis intuitu assignaverint, seu devote verbum Dei audierint propositum in eodem, quadraginta dies indulgenciae concedimus per praesentes. In cujus rei testimonium sigillum fecimus hiis apponi. Datum in manerio nostro de Aukeland secundo die mensis Maii Anno Domini millesimo ccc° nonagesimo primo et nostrae translacionis quarto.

[*Episcopal seal in red wax*].

Endorsed: Litera Walteri Episcopi in qua concedit xl^a dies indulgenciae omnibus bona facientibus ad ecclesiam Magdalenae seu audientibus verbum Domini ibidem praedicari.

VII. A.D. 1449. BISHOP NEVILL'S LICENSE, WITH INDULGENCE, FOR REMOVAL OF THE CHURCH OF S. MARY MAGDALEN HOSPITAL.

[*Durham Treasury, 2265*].

Licencia R. Nevill, Episcopi.

Robertus permissione divina Dunelm. episcopus praedilectis nobis in Christo Priori et Capitulo ecclesiae nostrae Cathedralis Dunelm. Salutem graciam et benediccionem. Exhibita nobis nuper ex parte vestra peticio continebat quod, licet ecclesia parochialis infra hospitale beatae Mariae Magdalenae juxta vicum vulgariter nuncupatum Seyntgyligate nostrae dioceseos officio Elimosinariae ecclesiae nostrae Cathedralis Dunelm. praedictae annexa ad honorem ejusdem Sanctae in terra aquosa et minus tuta ex antiquis temporibus fundata fuerat et erecta, ipsa tamen ecclesia propter debilitatem sui fundamenti et negligenciam artificum humiditatesque subterraneas eidem quotidie ingruentes tantam et notoriam patitur ruinam in praesenti quod presbiteris et pauperibus caeterisque peregrinis ipsam visitare volentibus tutus non patet accessus, divinaque ut decet vix valent celebrari in eadem, unde nobis pro parte vestra praedicta humiliter extitit supplicatum quatenus non solum pro translacione verum eciam nova construccione ecclesiae praedictae nostram licenciam specialem vobis concedere dignaremur, Nos igitur, hujusmodi piis et devotis supplicacionibus tanquam justis favorabiliter annuentes, arbitrantesque justum fore et consonum quod petitur in praemissis ad transferendam et removendam ecclesiam hujusmodi ruinosam a loco praedicto et eam in quocumque alio loco tutiori et magis ydoneo infra territorium dicti hospitalis ad divini cultus augmentum et honorem dictae Sanctae cum omnibus suis juribus parochialibus eidem et antiquo debitis et consuetis fundandam erigendam et de novo construendam, absque praejudicio juris alieni, vobis ex causis praemissis et aliis nos ad hoc moventibus licenciam tenore praesencium concedimus, specialem potestatem tamen ipsam ecclesiam cum translata fundata erecta et constructa fuerit dedicandi sanctificandi et benedicendi nobis specialiter reservantes. Universis insuper et singulis subditis nostris, et aliis quorum diocesani hanc nostram indulgenciam ratam habuerint pariter et acceptam, de peccatis suis vere poenitentibus confessis et contritis, qui dictam ecclesiam in festo dictae sanctae peregrinacionis causa devote visitaverint, aut de bonis sibi a Deo collatis in supportacionem ejusdem contulerint legaverint seu quovis modo assignaverint subsidio caritatis, tociens quociens id fecerint quadraginta dies de injunctis sibi poenitentiis misericorditer in Domino relaxamus. Ac omnes et omnimodas indulgencias eidem hospitali et benefactoribus ejusdem a quibuscumque sanctis patribus antea concessas quantum in nobis est ratificamus et confirmamus per praesentes sigillo nostro ad causas roboratas. Dat. apud Aukelaunde die mensis Februarii secundo Anno Domini Millesimo cccc^{mo} quadragesimo nono.

[Seal of Bishop Nevill in red wax].

VIII. A.D. 1451. LICENCE TO SUFFRAGAN TO CONSECRATE.

[*Durham Treasury, 2266*].

Licentia suffraganeo data ad dedicandam Ecclesiam &c., S. M. Magd.

Venerabili in Christo patri domino Roberto Dei gratia Holen. episcopo[1] Johannes Norton decretorum doctor, Reverendi in Christo patris et domini domini Roberti Dei gratia Dunelm. Episcopi in remotis agentis vicarius in spiritualibus generalis, omnimodo reverencia debita cum honore. Intimarunt nobis nuper venerabiles et religiosi viri Prior et Capitulum Ecclesiae Cathedralis Dunelm. quod ipsi quamdam capellam infra hospitale beatae Mariae Magdalenae inter hospitale de Kepyer et vicum Sancti Egidii situatam ex speciali licencia dicti Reverendi patris Dunelm. primitus petita et obtenta ab uno loco in alium transtulerunt erexerunt construxerunt ac de novo edificarunt, nobis humiliter supplicantes quatenus pro dedicatione consecratione et benediccione ejusdem altariumque omnium et singulorum in eadem existencium, necnon coemiterii eidem adjacentis et contigui, vestrae reverendae fraternitati scribere et plenariam potestatem ad hoc tribuere dignaremur. Nos igitur eorum supplicacionibus tamquam justis et racioni consonis quantum ad nos attinet attenta benevolentia dicti Reverendi patris cujus vices gerimus de qua nobis favorabiliter annuentes ad consecrandam dedicandam et in forma canonica benedicendam capellam hujusmodi una cum altaribus et coemiterio praedictis, salvo jure cujuscumque, vestrae paternitati reverendae supradictae auctoritate nobis commissa licenciam concedimus et plenam in Domino committimus potestatem per praesentes sigillo quo in hoc officio utimur roboratas. Dat. sexto die mensis Maii Anno Domini millesimo cccc° quinquagesimo primo.

[*Oval seal of Vicar General in red wax*].

IX. BENEFACTION BY THE VICAR OF BILLINGHAM.

[*Durham Treasury, 2273, 4ta 2^{dae} Elemos. 2 A*].

Dilectis sibi in Christo burgensibus Domini Prioris Dunelm. Dominus Ricardus Vicarius de Bilingham Salutem in Domino. Noveritis me pro salute animae

---

[1] Perhaps Bishop of *Hola* in Iceland, acting for the Bishop of Durham There was a small see so called under the Archbishop of Lund.

16

meae dedisse imperpetuum elemosinario Dunelm. ad sustentacionem et recreacionem pauperum in hospitali Sanctae Mariae Magdal. iij solidos annui redditus quos percepi de domibus ex opposito ecclesiae Sanctae Margaretae quas Willelmus de Wytewel in feodo de me tenuit, unde quia super varias et necessarias ocupaciones placitis nostris interesse ad praesens personaliter non possum, dominum Ricardum Capellanum filium meum certum attornatum et procuratorem coram nobis ad instituendum et insaysandum dictum elenosinarium in dictum redditum constituo, Ratum habiturus et gratum quicquid dictus Ricardus nomine meo super praemissis duxerit faciendum. In cujus rei testimonium sigillum meum huic scripto est appensum. (*Seal gone*).

Endorsed:—De redditu iij solidorum de domo in Crossegate ex opposito ecclesiae Sanctae Margaretae.

X. NOTICES OF S. MARY MAGDALEN HOSPITAL IN MICKLETON MSS. AND HUNTER MSS. (*Cosin's and Dean and Chapter Libraries*).

De Capella Stae Mariae Magdalenae prope Dunelm. in Warda de Easington.

Luminare fuit beatae Mariae in capella juxta Kepyer Aº 1303. Vicus fuit nuncupatus Vicus Bne Mariae Magdalenae. Vide in cart. Tho : Dec. et Cap. D. In hac capella olim Magister Scholae Farmariae [Farmary Schoole] (Quae fuit extra januas Abbathiae Dunelm., ac fundata per Priores praedictae Abbathiae seu Cathedralis Ecclesiae D., ac ejusdem Domus seu Abbathiae sumptibus) obligatus fuit Missam bis in septimana dicere, ac semel in septimana in Capella apud Kimblesworth. Nomen ultimi magistri praefatae scholae fuit Robertus [dictus Sr Robert] Hartburne. Qui ita magister continuavit usque suppressionem Domus seu Abbathiae praedictae. Vide de Hospitali Bae Mariae Magdalenae juxta vicum vulgariter dictum Seynt Gyligate officio Elemosunariae connexo inter cartas Tho : praedicti. Haec capella nunc totaliter disperta, ac in magno decasu est, et nullus usus inde factus (*Mickleton MSS., No. 32, p. 110*). *Cf. "Rites of Durham," p. 77.*

Also, to the same effect, p. 37, "de Scholis Dunelm."

The following notices are from Hunter MSS., No. 37:—

(1) St. Magdalen's gate was a Passage or Lane leading from Gilligate to St Mary Magdalen Hospital its

beginning only now remaining namely a vacant narrow piece of ground open to ye street behind some Cottages on ye left hand at ye bottom of the hill in going up to ye Church.

Assisa capta pro semita in vico Magdalenae.

Memorand. quod die Lunae prox° post Fest. Ascensionis D^ni Anno Pontific. D^ni Ricardi de Bury episcopi Dunelm. septimo et A° Domini 1349 Will^s de Hextildesham attach. fuit ad respondend. D^no Episcopo de eo quod injuste obstruxit semitam in le Maudeleynggs in Seint gilygats in Dunelm. quae quidem semita se extenderat a Regia Via ibidem usque quendam fontem qui vocatur Hexham Well & ab inde usque Domum Hospitalis de Kyppier quae quidem semita erat communis ad homines de Seint gilgat, prout praesentatum fuit coram Johanne de Menvill tunc Vic. Dunelm. in Turno suo ibidem capto ad grave damnum totius Populi tam de Seint gilygat quam aliorum et contra pacem etc. Et praedictus Will^s venit et dixit quod non est inde culp. Et hoc petit quod inquiratur per Patriam. Et Johannes de Egglscluff qui sequitur pro D^no Episcopo similiter etc. Jura—etc. Juratores tam de hominibus de Seintgilygat quam de forinc. electi dicunt super Sacramentum suum quod nullam Semitam idem Will^s obstruxit ibidem eo quod nulla Semita de Jure esse debet in loco praedicto, quia dicunt quod illa semita quam homines praedicti clamant ibidem iidem homines fecerunt in loco praedicto post tempus quo quaedam Domus plantata ibidem, prout nunc est, destructa fuit per Inimicos Scotiae, & illa Placea Domus integra inclusa fuit per quendam Murum, ultra quem Murum iidem homines de Injuria eorum et non de Jure ultra Murum praedictum fecerunt Semitam praedictam &c. Ideo cons. est quod praedictus Will^s teneat Domum suam integram sine Semita.

Cartuar. Elemosinariae Dunelm., *page 125.*

(ii) TENEMENTA ELEMOSINARII *in Parochia S. Mariae Magdalenae.*

De primo, Tenementorum trium cum Tectura⎫
   straminea   ⎭ 2*s.* 6*d.*

De secundo, Tenemento Elemos. ibidem cum⎫
   Tectura straminea   ⎭ 11*s.*

De Tertio, Tenemento ibidem cum diversis
 Ædificiis et una Acra & iij Rod. Prati infra
unum Clausum ad finem Gardini ejusdem
Tenementi & cum Decima foeni dicti Prati ·xvj*s.* viij*d.*
& cum Decima Foeni unius Acrae Prati
Haeredum Comitis Westmerlandiae jacentis
infra praedictum clausum

De Haeredibus Comitis Westmerlandiae pro
libero Redditu unius acrae Prati jacent. infra
quoddam Clausum Elemosinariae pertinens ·vij*d.*
ad Tenem. proxime praedictum

Et in expens. pro una Pietanc. annuatim in
Festo S. Mariae Magdalenae dari consueta }xxx*s.*

Pro cera & vino ac factura Cerae pro Coena
Dⁿⁱ capellis Hospitalis B. Mariae Magda- ·xviij*d.*
lenae & Infirmariae

(iii) *S. Magdalen's Hospital.*

Jam Seges ubi Troja fuit. No remains even of any
Foundations of this Reservatory of indigent Persons of
both Sexes appear, even upon a diligent Search. And yᵉ
Chapell, which was erected at first with the Hospital,
proved to be situate on too moist a Soil, & became subject
to fall down. Application was made to Bp. Nevill who
granted his Licence to demolish that faulty one & to
rebuild another upon a more promising Foundation, &
afterwards gave his Mandate to his Suffragan to Consecrate
yᵉ same in his Absence out of his Diocess. The Walls
hereof without any Covering Doors or Windowes yet
remain ; yᵉ Revᵈ yᵉ Dean & Chapter nominate a Chaplain
to yᵉ same & regularly pay his Stipend yearly.

Land belonging to the Hospital.

(1) in two Inclosures with yᵉ Chapell Yard, upon
each Side of the Hospital four Acres & half of
Land.

(2) in yᵉ East field near Kypier Inclosure, in a
certain Corner—four Acres of Land.

(3) in one spacious Close in a Corner
adjoyning upon Kypier extend- } twelve Acres of Land.
ing to yᵉ River Were

(4) in one piece of Land on yᵉ west side
of the said close } One Acre of Land.

(5) One yᵉ west side of yᵉ said Acre
lies another Acre of Land which } one Acre of Land.
pays Tyth for Hay

(6) In one Inclosure in ye Corner by ye two ways leading from St Giles Gate to ye said Hospital } three Acres of Land.

(7) In one large Close called Maudeleynleys before ye Gate of Shirburn Hospital } 60 Acres of Land.

In ye year 1534 I find ye following Persons entertained in ye said Hospital. Their yearly Salary was 24*s.* 1. Mater Dⁿⁱ Roberti Benet, 1st Prebendary in ye 11th Stall A° 1542 ; 2. Agnes Davison, Daughter of George Davison ; 3. Robert Benet ; 4. Robert Kyrn ; 5. Thomas Wright.

(iv) *Carta Petri fil. Eliae Russell de Dunelm. de Tofto et Crofto ad Sustentationem Pauperum commorantium in Domo S. Mariae Magdalenae.*

Omnibus Fidelibus ad quorum Notitiam praesens Scriptum pervenerit Petrus fil. Eliae Russell de Dunelm. Salutem. Noveritis Me tactis Sacrosanctis & de mea bona Voluntate remisisse, concessisse, & praesenti Scripto meo confirmasse, ac de Me et Haeredibus meis & assignatis imperpetuum quietum clamasse Domui B. Mariae Magdalenae in Dunelm. & Fratribus infirmis ibidem commorantibus totum Jus & Clameum quod habeo vel habere potero in uno Tofto et Crofto cum pertinentiis in Vico S. Mariae Magdalenae in Dunelm. quae fuerunt Thomae Emre haereditar. Ita quod nec Ego nec aliquis alius Mortalis Nomine meo in praedicto Tofto & Crofto aliquod Jus vel Clamium de caetero erigere vel vendicare poterimus. In cujus Rei Testimonium praesenti Scripto Sigillum meum apposui his Testibus, Johanne de Malton, tunc Seneseallo Prioris Dunelm., Will° de Tremdon, Johanne de Castro, cum multis aliis.

Cartuar. Elemosinar. Dunelm., *page 126.*

(v) *Quieta Clamatio Matildis filiae Ricardi de Tenem^{to} in Vico B. Mariae Magdalenae facta Domui B. Mariae Magdalenae.*

Omnibus Christi Fidelibus ad quos praesens Scriptum pervenerit Matildis filia Ricardi de Vico S. Mariae Magdalenae Salutem in D^{no}. Noverit Universitas vestra Me tactis Sacrosanctis, & de bona Voluntate mea et in mera Viduitate & Potestate mea remisisse, concessisse, & hoc praesenti Scripto meo confirmasse de Me et Haeredibus meis omnino quietum clamasse Domui Beatae Mariae

Magdalenae in Dunelm. totam Terram et Tenementum
cum omnibus Pertinentiis suis quam habui & tenui in Vico
B. Mariae supradictae sine aliquo Retenimento ; Ita quod
nec Ego nec aliquis seu aliqua Nomine meo in praedicta
Terra vel Tenem[to] vel aliqua parte Terrae praenominatae
aliquod Jus vel Clameum de caetero exigere poterimus vel
aliquo modo vendicare. In cujus Rei Testimonium
praesenti Scripto Sigillum meum apposui his Testibus,
Will[o] de Wedawe, Hugone de Publicis, Ricardo Dante,
Waltero Fabro, Elya Pistore, Johanne fil. Bertrami, cum
aliis.

(vi) *Blada assignata per Priorem & Capitulum ad
Sustentationem Pauperum in Hospitali S. Mariae
Magdalenae Dunelm. ex Maneriis suis sequentibus.*

Wallesend - - - ij*s.* ij*d.*	Renton Est	
Willington - - - ij*s.* ij*d.*	West	
Heworth nether - xij*d.*	Moresley	
over -iiij*s.*	Pityngton North	
Hedworthe - - - x*d.*	South	
Hebburn - - - iiij*d.*	Billingham - - iij*s.* iiij*d.*	
Monkton - - - xij*d.*	Cowpen - - - iij*s.* iiij*d.*	
Jarow - - - - ij*d.*	Wolveston - - iij*s.* iiij*d.*	
Simondside - - xij*d.*	Burdon - - - viij*d.*	
Harton - - - - iij*s.* iiij*d.*	Acly - - - - xij*d.*	
Westow - - - - ij*s.*	Bermton	
Fulwell - - - - viij*d.*	Skirnyngham	
Wermouthe - - xviij*d.*	Ketton	
Southwyk - - - xx*d.*	Chilton	
Dalton	Merrington Est ⎱	
Heselden - - - xvj*d.*	Skelowe ⎰ xviij*d.*	

(vii) *Fratres & Sorores in Hosp[li] S. Mariae Magdalenae*
1532 B.

1. Mater D[ni] Roberti Benett qui est constitutus⎱
   primus canonicus in undecima Stallo⎰ xxiiij*s.*
   A° 1542

2. Agnes filia Georgij Davison - - - xxiiij*s.*

3. Robertus Kerven - - - - - xxiiij*s.*

4. Katerina Midilton - - - - - xxiiij*s.*

5. Johannes Brown - - - - - xxiiij*s.*

XI. Rev. F. Thompson's Notes, &c.

Interesting extracts made by the late Rev. Francis
Thompson from the Almoner's Rolls in the Durham
Treasury, relating to the rebuilding of the Church of the

Hospital under the authority of Bishop Nevill, and repairs both of the old and the new one in successive years, with notes about the present remains, will be found in "Transactions of Architectural and Archaeological Society of Durham and Northumberland, MDCCCLXIX—MDCCCLXXV." To these may here be added the following account of repairs as late as A.D. 1554 :—

Durham Treasury, No. 3007.

Magdaleyn Chapell.

xviij^mo die Decembris anno regni regis Edwardi Sexti etc. Septimo.

Item paid to Cuthbert Wilkinson for workinge and thiking with selat worke, upon the Magdeleyn Chauncell for three dayes at vij*d*. on the day, xxj*d*.

Item to Wiiliam Wilkinson and Thomas Wilkinson working on the same worke the space of foure days at xij*d*. betwixt theyme on the daye—iiij*s*.

Item to the said Cuthbert for two fother off sklates at x*d*. a fother—xx*d*.

Item for cariage of the sam to William Ayre and William Selbie, xvj*d*.

Item for caring of Sand and lyme to the same worke from Eluett bridge—vj*d*.

Summa—ix*s*. iij*d*. Exam. per Robertum Benett Vicedecanum.

APPENDIX C.

RELATING TO THE PARISH CHURCH AND GUILD OF ST. GILES.

The following information and extracts have been supplied to the Editor by Mr Henry Grove, of London, after search in the Record Office.

Grant of the Rectory of St. Giles, Durham.

By letters Patent dated 23rd May in the 7th year of Edward VI (1553) the King sold to Lord Ormeston, with other property, the Rectory and Church of St. Giles, Durham, part of the possessions of the late Hospital of Kepyer, to which it had been appropriated. The grant includes all tithes, oblations, obventions, pastures, rents, pensions, and portions of tithes, Court Lets, frankpledges, commodies, emoluments, and hereditaments spiritual and temporal.

There is no special mention of the right to the advowson of the Vicarage ; but it doubtless passed with the tithes under the words " Rectory and Church " of St. Giles.[1]

The Grant is enrolled on the Patent Roll of 6th Edw. VI, Part 7, No. 24.

The Guild in the Church of St. Giles.

[*Chantry Certificates, Durham. Roll 18, No. 65*].

Commission dated 14 Feb., 27 Hen. VIII (1545-6).

The Countye of Northumberlande and the Bisshopricke of Durham.

65. Com " Dunelmen."

The Guylde of Seynt Giles in the parishe churche of Seynt Gyles in the Citie of Durham.

---

[1] This is the remark of Mr. Grove. The more probable explanation is that there was no endowment of a Vicarage, the brethren of Kepyer, being an ecclesiastical Corporation, having served the church themselves. See " Introduction," under " The Parish Church and Living."

The said Guylde was founded to fynde A priest for ever for the mayntenance of Goddis servyce by the devocion of good people inhabytyng in the Citie of Durham by Reporte, but there is no Dede of any Foundacion therof to be shewed. [yearly value according to Book of First Fruits and Tenths]. lvijs. id. ob'.

What followes is thus headed.

[The verely valewe of the same according to this Survey with the verely Resolucions and Deduccions goyng out of every of theym and in what Sorte the Revenues and profittis of the same be expended and employed].

The verely valewe, vjl. xvs. xd., as appereth by a Rentall. Wherof is paid owt for Rentis resolute xxxviijs. iiijd. ob' and for the Kinges maiesties tenthes vs. viijd. ob' qa. as Doth appere by the same Rentall— xliiijs. jd. qa. And Remayneth clerely iiijl. xjs. viij ob' qa. which bene employed to the sustentacion and Relief of Richard Mydleton prieste Incumbent of the same.

The said Guylde is founded in the parishe churche of Saynt Gyles aforsaid.

[The valewe of the Ornamentis &c.] xxxviijs. xd. as appereth by A perticuler Inventory of the same.

Ther wer no other landes nor verely profittes apperteynyng or belongyng to the said Guylde syth the iiij^th day of February in the xxvij^th yere of the Kingis maiesties Reigne more than is before meneyoned.

Exchequer Q.R. Church Goods $\frac{2}{1 \text{ to } 24}$ Derby, Devon, Dorset and Durham.

No. $\frac{2}{23}$. This Inventory Indentyd made the viij^th daie of Aprill Anno H. viij^i xxxviij^oo Witnesseth that I Sr Ric. Mydleton clerk Incumbent of the chauntry or guilde of Saint Giles in the parishe of Saint Giles in the citie of Durham have had received and taken into my charge and custody by the deliverie of the King's Majesties commissioners in this behalf apointed thes particular parcells of plate ornaments and goods thereof ensving, the same savely to kepe and preserve to the King's Majesties use And untill his Majesties plesure in this behalf be further knowen.

Inprimis one chalice silver parcell gilt waing ix ounces at iiij*s.* ij*d.* the ounce } xxxvij*s.* vj*d.*

Item ij Masseboks - - - - - xvj*d.*

Sum of this Inventory xxxviij*s.* x*d.*

S*r* Ric. Medilton.

Ibid. $\frac{2}{21}$ 7 *Edward VI*[th]

Seint Gyles Churche in Duresme.

One Challice with a paton of sylver weying xiiij unces. Thre Bells in the Stepell, a lyttell Sance bell, a sacring bell, and a hand bell.

A.D. 1548.   *Chantry Certificate, Durham. Roll 17, No. 6.*

Commission dated 14 Feb., 2 Edw. 6 (1547–8).

The Busshopprycke off Duresme

The Parishe Churche of Sainte Giles having of howsling people ccccxx

The Guylde of Saincte Giles in the said churche

[Incumbent]   Richarde Middleton of the age of lj yeres

The yerelie valewe - - -	vij*l.* vij*s.* ij*d.*
Reprises - - - - -	xxxiij*s. ob'.*
Remayne - - - - -	cxiiij*s.* j*d. ob'.*
Stocke - - - - -	None
Plate one challies Gylte Wayeing	ix ownce
Ornamentes - - - - -	Not praised
Leade - - - - - -	none
Bells - - - - - -	none

The Obitt of John Smithe withein the said parishe.[1]

The yerelie valewe - - -	iiij*s.*
Reprises - - - -	xij*d.*—opus j[us] Diei.
Remayne - - - - -	iij*s.*
Stocke of money - - - -	None
Plate - - - - - -	None
Ornamentes - - - - -	none
Leade and Bells - - - -	none

---

[1] There is a Grant of this Obit in the 6th of James to Morrice and Phelips, together with a free Chapel in Kingsgate, valued at 8*s.* But there is nothing to show that this Chapel belonged to either the Guild or to the Obit in St. Giles' Church. The grant is enrolled on the Patent of 6 James part 30, M. 8.

GRANTS OF THE PROPERTY OF THE GUILD.

The houses that were comprised in the leases were all subsequently granted in fee by James I. The first Grantees were Ward & Morgan in the 6th year of James, of several houses named in the leases. The second Grant was to Morris & Phelips in the 7th of James, which comprised the residue of the houses.

Beyond stating that the houses were once the property of the Guild of St. Giles in the city of Durham, the Grants do not give any particulars of interest. One is enrolled on the Patent of 6 James, part 21, & the other on the 6th James, part 30.

APPENDIX D.

I.—MASTERS OF KEPYER HOSPITAL.

The following list with annotations and references, with the exception of the names printed in italics, is what is given in the "Mickleton MSS.," No. 32. The meaning of some of the abbreviated references has not been discovered by the present Editor. The names in italics have been supplied, as will appear, from other authentic sources. Further notices of what is known of the successive rulers are given in the foot-notes. In documents referring to them their official title varies, "Magister sive Custos" being the most usual expression, and the word "Gubernator" being sometimes used. But in Bishop Pudsey's original "ordinatio" of the Hospital the title "Magister" alone occurs. It is obvious that their position was one of dignity, and often occupied in conjunction with other honourable and important offices. The bishops, having the appointment in their hands, appear to have usually conferred it on men whom they delighted to honour, and whom they continued to employ in other ways.

Extracts from "Mickleton MSS.," No. 32, fo. 71 v., et seq.

De Procuratoribus, Magistris, Custodibus, Gubernatoribus Hospitalis de Kypier.

	Bishops.	Kings
ADAMUS Canonicus Procurator Hospitalis praedicti.[1] (M.D., 133).	*Temp.* Hugonis.	H. 2.
RADULFUS Rector Hospitalis de Kypier.[2] (MS., Gowland, fo. 8).	*Temp.* Ric. [Pauper].	H. 3.

[1] There seems to be nothing to show positively that this Adam was Master of the Hospital. All that appears is that he acted as proctor for the house, being also designated "Canonicus" in its Composition in the year 1189 with Germanus the Prior and the Convent of Durham with regard to the tithes of Clifton (See above, p. 204).

[2] In a Composition between the Convent and the Hospital in the earlier part of the thirteenth century *Radulfus de Elvet*, there described as *monacus*, acts as *procurator* for the Hospital (See Appendix B, I). In another document of the time of Prior Kernech (1219—1233) we find also *R. rectorem nostrum* (presumably the same Radulfus) among the *procuratores* for the Hospital (See Appendix B, II).

	Bishops.	Kings
MAGISTER DE ARGENTINO,[1] Magister Hospitalis praedicti in cart.	*Temp.* Nich. [de Farnham].	H. 3.
John de Lundoniis.[2]		
PETRUS DE TYLYNSBY,[3] Magister Hospitalis A° 1300.	3 Reg., fo. 83 *b.* Anthonii *cp.*	
PETRUS DE THORESBY,[4] presbyter, Magister Hospitalis praedicti. In quo quidem Petri tempore incendium in quandam domum infra idem Hospitale subito supervenit A° 1306. In qua domo Chartae & quaedam Munimenta Hospitalis praedicti combusta fuerunt.	Anth. Bek.	E. 2.

[1] His name occurs in the form of "De Argentaneo" in No. IX of the Verified Charters (See above, p. 201), in which Robert and Sibilla Corbech quit-claim to the Hospital certain lands at Hunstanworth in return for ten marks, "quas Magister de Argentaneo et fratres praenotatae domus nobis in caritate dederunt."

[2] His name is omitted altogether in the Mickleton MSS. In the list of Masters given in the Hunter MSS. he comes first, thus : —"1254—Johan. de London." He is said by Surtees to have been Chaplain to Bishop Walter de Kirkham (1249—1260). He was commissioned with W. de Meru by Bishop Kirkham to receive the resignation of Bertram, Prior of Durham, A.D. 1258 ("*Tres Scriptores*," cap. vi, p. 43), but he is not there designated as Master of Kepyer.

[3] Omitted in the Hunter MSS., and ignored by Hutchinson and Surtees. But see "*Registrum III Prioris et Convent. Dunelm.*" in the Durham Treasury, fo. 83 *v.*, where in a pronouncement of contumacy by the Bishop (Anthony Bek) against the Prior and Convent (13 Kal. Jun., 1300), "dominus Pet. de Tyleynsby Magr Hospitalis de Kepeyere" is among the witnesses. Other witnesses are the Master of Sherburn and the Rector of Brancepeth.

[4] Thus, according to the Mickleton MSS., he was Master of the Hospital at least as early as 1306, when the Scots burnt the muniment room. In 1311 he was cited as "Custos de Kepiyere" in a visitation to be held by the Bishop (Ric. Kellaw) concerning his acts of dilapidation at Kepyer (Kellaw's "*Reg. Palat.*," Rolls Edition, vol. i, p. 34). In 1312 (*4 Kal. Nov.*) he was witness, with his "capellanis," to a confirmation of a grant to the Chapel of St. James on New Bridge at Durham (*Ibid.*, vol. ii, p. 1176). In the same year (*7 Id. Mar.*) he was witness to royal confirmation of grants made by Bishop Bek to Roger de Esse ; and (*4 Id. Nov.*) to Inspeximus of the same. In 1315 his name occurs as having been one of the receivers of Bishop Bek, in a King's writ in favour of the executors of that bishop (*Ibid.*, vol. ii, p. 1097).

The following previous notices of him are also found in the same "*Registrum Palatinum*" of Bishop Kellaw :—

A.D. 1295. — There is the record of a fine levied in the Bishop's Court at Durham (*23 Edw. I : 12 Ant. Bek.*) "coram Guychardo de Charron et Petro de Thoresby, justiciariis assignatis" (vol. iii, p. 69). In the same volume, p. 236, there is also the copy of a grant by Anthony, Bishop of Durham (not dated), in which "dominus Petrus de Thoresby" is one of the witnesses.

A.D. 1305.—It is recorded that Bishop Bek, having seized the Priorate of Durham, "custodes et ballivos suos in eadem prioratu apponit, scilicet Petrum de Thoresby," &c. (vol. iv, p. 17). In the same year the deprived Prior "nunciavit Petro de Thoresby custodi prioratus tunc quod pax inter dominum Episcopum et ipsum coram domino Rege pacta fuit, et idem Petrus custos in hoc gavisus," &c. (*Ibid.*, p. 47).

	Bishops.	Kings
Vide Cart. Aº 1311, Aº 4 E. 2, in M.D. Qui Petrus etiam fuit tempore Roberti [Stichell 17] Epi D. Unus ejus Justiciarius. Ac Constab. castri D. Ac Cancellarius temporalis ejusdem Anthonii Ep'i et unus ejus Justic. Vide de isto Petro Wh. fo. 746, Aº 1312.		
Hugo de Monte Alto,[1] Unus Monachorum Monasterii D., Magister anno 1311. 2 Reg. fo. 1, 81. Ac lis orta inter hunc Hugonem Magistrum Hospitalis praedicti & fratres ejusdem loci	Ricardi [Kellaw]	E. 2.

It was probably he who assisted in rescuing the Archbishop of York (Tho. Grimston) from the mob, when the latter, A.D. 1283, had visited Durham, *sede vacante*, had been refused entrance into the Cathedral, and had proceeded to the Church of St. Nicholas, where he was about to excommunicate the Prior and Convent, when a tumult arose, and he had to escape by the waterside to Kepyer, having had one of his palfrey's ears cut off, and might have been killed, "si Wycardus de Charrons et Petrus de Thorsbi non impedissent" (" *Tres Scriptores*," 65). It will be observed that we have found him associated with the same "Guychardo de Charron" in the record of 1295 above referred to, both being there described as "justiciarii."

[1] He had been among the monks of Durham excommunicated, A.D. 1308, by Bishop Anthony Bec for not receiving Henry de Luceby as Prior in place of Richard Hotoun, and, when the latter had been dragged out of his stall by one of the monks, and imprisoned by the Bishop, Hugo Montalto, with another monk, John de Castro, had been imprisoned with him (" *Tres Scriptores*," cap. xxiii, and Appendix lxxxv). He is named also, with other monks of Durham, in a letter of Pope Clement V with reference to this excommunication (*Ibid.*, p. ciii, No. lxxxv). He was also the entertainer of Isabella, Queen of Edward II, when on the 21st of April, 1311-12, she was lodged at Kepyer, the Master being paid £18 17s. 9d. for her expenses. "Item domino Hugoni de Monte Alto per unam literam, vjl. ijs. viijd.—Item in solucione facta pro expensis Reginae apud Kypyer xxj die mensis Aprilis xviijl. xvijs. ixd. Item in liberacione facta Domino Roberto de Dunelm. in partem debiti in quo Dominus ei tenetur, viijl. xs. iiijd. per dominum H. de Monte Alto" (" *Tres Scriptores*," Appendix lxxxvi, pp. cv, cvi). His name occurs as Master of Kepyer in a grant by the Hospital to Robert de Epplynden, A.D. 1311. See "Introduction," p. xxiv. It was during his incumbency (A.D. 1311) that Bishop Kellaw issued his commission for verifying the Charters of the Hospital, which had been destroyed by the fire of 1306 (See above, Appendix A, p. 192). It was during his incumbency too (A.D. 1315) that Kellow established a fourteenth prebend, to be attached to the Mastership of Kepyer, in the Collegiate Church of St. Andrew Auckland ("*Registr. Palat.*," ii, p. 1272). In 1312 the Prior of Durham, having been summoned to a Parliament to be holden at Lincoln, sent two proctors to represent him, one of whom was Hugo de Monte Alto (" *Tres Scriptores*," p. cx). He had previously (A.D. 1306), while still a monk of Durham, been appointed by the Prior, along with William De l'Escheker, to transact his business in any court of England (*Ibid.*, p. cii). In 1317, during his incumbency, a pension was granted by the Hospital to one Symon de Wycot, which was confirmed by the Prior (Galfrid) and the Convent, 1st Feb., 1319 (*Durham Treasury, Reg.* ii, fo. 67 v.). He is named as Master of Kepyer in Bishop Beaumont's licence with respect to the advowson of Hunstanworth (See Appendix A, V).

	Bishops.	Kings

et Thomam de Hessewell clericum Rectorem ecclesiae parochialis de Seggefield super jure et possessione percipiendi Decimam Garbarum de Hardwicke loco Medietatis Decimarum de Seggefield provenientium de Dominiis Ep. Dun. olim de consensu partium praedictarum tunc existentium dicto Hospitali assignatarum, &c. Et Ricardus (Kellow 20) episcopus Dun. A° 1314 arbitrator electus ad ordinationem circa praemissa faciendam Ordinavit quod Magister et fratres Hospitalis praedicti & successores sui imperpetuum percipiant decimam de Hardwicke sicut ipsi Magister et praedecessores sui percipere consueverunt, Quodque persolvant Rectoribus de Seg' 20*s.* annuatim in Festo Natalis Johannis Baptistae. Vide hanc Ordinationem seu transcriptum inde inter cartas Scholae Keperiensis de Houghton in le Spring.

Vide Erectionem et Collationem unius prebendae in Ecclesia de Aukland ad Hospitale de Kypyer A° 1315. 2 Reg., fo. 11 *a.*

Vide cartam Willelmi [Cowton 20] Prioris & Capituli D. super varia munimenta facta ratione combustionis de K. 3 Reg., fo. 9, 10, initio.

Vide cartam Magistri et Fratrum Hospitalis praedicti A° 1336, 2 Reg., fo. 107 *a.*

EDMUNDUS HOWARD,[1] Magister Hospitalis S[ti] Egidii de Kypier A° 1341.	Ricardi [de Bury].	E. 3.

[1] In 1341 he granted a lease of a toft in Crossgate to Emma, relict of John de Todhowe (See Appendix A, XII). In 1343 he occurs as Archdeacon of Northumberland. In 1345, during his incumbency, Bishop Hatfield confirmed the evidences of the Hospital. In his time, too, was probably built the gateway of the Hospital which still remains, and on which are two shields, one of which bears three crowns, and the other a bend between what may have been crosses crosslet fitchy, much defaced by weather. The latter correspond with the arms of Howard, which are:— *Gu.,* a bend between 6 crosses crosslet fitchy *arg.* The three crowns on the other shield were borne by the Abbey of Bury St. Edmund's, and by Tynemouth Priory. Why they appear on the gateway has not been discovered. Richard de Bury was the contemporary bishop; but he is not known to have adopted these arms.

	Bishops.	Kings
Vide inter cartas in Thes. Dec. et Capituli Dunelm.		
WILLELMUS LEGAT,[1] Custos seu Magister Hospitalis praedicti. 2 Reg., fo. 139 *b*.		
Iste Willelmus & Fratres Hospitalis &c. A° 1351 dederunt Thomae de Lomeley Capellano burgagium in vico S^ti Egidii [Gyley strete]. 1 Cart., fo. 292 *b*.	Tho. [Hatfield].	E. 3.
Et vide in dicto 1 cart. separales concessiones in Gilestrete dict. Thomae episcopi inter praefatum Willelmum et Willelmum de Dalton, Rectorem ecclesiae de Hoghton A° 1350. Vide Ordinationem confirmatam per Johannem Priorem, &c., D. A° 1351. 2 Reg., fo. 139 *b*.		
N.B.—Johannes [Fossour 21] Prior et Capitulum D. A° 1352 concesserunt Magistro et Fratribus dicti hospitalis Sancti Egidii de Kypier et successoribus suis Advocationem eorundem Prioris & D. ecclesiae parochialis de Hunstanword. 1 Cart., fo. 116 *b*, et 4 Cart., fo. 108 *a*.		
Richard Rot', 1362.[2]		
Hugo Herle, 1388 (*Hunter MSS.*).		
Robertus Wycliff, ob. 1423 (*Hunter MSS.*).[3]		

---

[1] What is said in the Mickleton MSS. shows him to have been Master as early as 1350. He is mentioned by name as Master in a document of 1352 (See Appendix A, VIII). He was Bishop Hatfield's Spiritual Chancellor in 1351 ("*Reg. Hatf.*," fo. 2 *v*.; also fo. 3, fo. 3 *v*.). In 1353 he was Rector of Brancepeth ("*Reg. Hatf.*," fo. 13).

[2] This name occurs in none of the lists of Masters. But we find in Bishop Hatfield's Register, A.D. 1362, mention of the induction as Master of "dominus Ricardus Rot'" (*Roter* or *Rutter*?) ("*Reg. Hatf.*," fo. 57).

[3] It is curious that this notable personage should have been omitted from the list of Masters in the Mickleton MSS. The following notices of him, before and during his incumbency, are from notes on the Masters of Kepyer left by the late Rev. Francis Thompson :—

"In 1399 the Archdeacon of Durham issued a mandate (in the absence of Bishop Skirlawe) to the Prior of Durham and others (of whom Robert Wycliffe was one) for a general array of the county, which seems to have taken place on the 24th of March, 1400, on Gilesgatemoor. At this time Wycliffe was constable of Durham" (See "*Tres Scriptores*," clxxxiii, clxxxv).

	Bishops.	Kings
RICARDUS BUKLEY,[1] Clericus, nuper Parsona ecclesiae Beati Nicholai in Dunelm. Magister hospitalis praedicti. Qui Ricardus etiam Receptor Generalis Episcopi D. Vide Commissionem Thomae [Langley 26] Episcopi D. ad visitandum Hospitale de Kepyer, Dat. 17 Julii A° 1437, A° 31 consecracionis suae, directam Johanni Bonour Decretorum Doctori Cancellario Episcopi, Johanni Lythom utriusque juris Bac-	{ Thoᵉ [Langley] { Robⁱ [Nevill].	H. 6.

In a note, p. 66, on the "Durham Wills" of the Surtees Society, it is said that this Robert Wycliffe was of the family of Wycliffe of Wycliffe, and a near relation, probably a nephew, of Wycliffe the reformer. Rector of Wycliffe, 1362, res. 1363. Rector of Hutton Rudby in Cleveland from 1377 to his death. Rector of Kirby Ravensworth in 1379, res. 1382. Rector of St. Crux in York, res. 1391. Appointed by the King as guardian of the heir of Lord Fitz-Hugh, res. 1391. Master of Kepyer before 1405. Temporal Chancellor and Receiver General of the Bishopric, and Constable of Durham Castle from 1390 to 1405. One of the executors of Bishop Skirlawe. One of the executors of Sir Philip D'Arcy in 1399. One of the executors of Margery, widow of William de Aldeburgh, once wife of Peter de Mauley, 1391. His armorial bearings (*arg.*, a chevron sable between 3 cross crosslets *gules*) occur in the cloister of Durham begun by Bishop Skirlawe. In his will he leaves "cuilibet capellano et cuilibet fratri Hospitalis de Kepier vjs. viijd. Item lego cuilibet pauperi scholari sedenti ad skepham infra aulam praedicti Hospitali ijs." His will dated at Kepyer 8th Sept., 1423. It is in the Durham series, and contains the following clause, "corpusque meum sepeliendum ubi contigerit me decedere ab hac vita, vel ubi executores mei disposuerint illud sepeliri." His inventory is in the York series (*Test. Ebor.* I, 403), and contains, "Item datur Hospitali de Kepier ciphus coopertus cum nodo aliquantulum perforato. Item datur j duodena coclearium Hospitali de Kepier.—*Legata lectorum apud Kepier*; Datur Roberto Toppyng j lectus rubeus cum certis (sertis) intextis; Datur Willielmo Semar j coopertorium rubeum cum armis Walteri nuper Episcopi. *Legata librorum*; Datur Hospitali de Kepier liber dictus Catholicon; Dantur eidem Hospitali j liber Evangelii & j Psalterium. Datur Johanni de Midelton" (one of the executors) "parvum portiphorium & j missale pro tempore vitae, et post vitam ejus redditur ad praedictum Hospitale de Kepier. Item datur Alano de Shirborn & Roberto Toppyng j magnum Portiphorium cum claspis argenti." In 1398 a hundred shillings were lent to the Priory of Finchale by Robert Wycliff. An indulgence was granted by Bishop Langley, 5th April, 1414, for the repair of the Church of St. Giles.

No record of this alleged indulgence has been discovered by the present editor.

[1] He appears to have succeeded Wycliff in 1423, having been also Rector of St. Nicholas in Durham. So in Mickleton MSS., and so described in Bishop Langley's Will, dated 1436, proved 1439. In 1435 Bishop Langley gave licence to him and others to form the Guild of Corpus Christi in the Church of St. Nicholas. It was not, it may be remembered, till 1443 that the Rectory was appropriated by Bishop Nevill to the Hospital (Appendix A, p. 208). It will be seen in Appendix A, XIV, how in 1437 Bishop Langley visited the Hospital by commission; how in the same year, after such visitation, he acquitted Bukley of maladministration, and confirmed him in his office; how in 1439 Bishop Nevill did the same, but afterwards in the same year accepted his resignation on the ground of age and infirmity, assigning him a pension of 40 marks a year.

17

	Bishops.	Kings

calaureo sequestratori Episcopi in Archidiaconatu D., Domino Nicho. Hulme canonico ecclesiae prebendalis de Derlington, & Willelmo Raket clerico Cancellario episcopi. Reg. T. Langley, fo. 248 *a v.*

Et commissio custodiae Hospitalis praedicti concessa pro vita 29 Aug. A° 1437. Ib. fo. 249 *b.* — Tho. [Langley]. — H. 6.

JOHANNES LOUND[1] Clericus in utroque jure Bacc., Magister sive Custos Hospitalis praedicti. Constitutus 16 Oct. A° 2 Pontificatus Roberti [Nevill] Episcopi D. Anno 17 H. 6., 3 Reg., fo. 208, 9, 41 *b,* 68 ; 4 Reg., fo. 86, 4 Cart., fo. 191. Et vide Rotl. Cl. A° 14 Pontificatus ejusdem Roberti episcopi M in dorso. Et pensio 40 Marcarum concessa praedicto Ricardo Bukley pro vita per dictum Robertum episcopum Dunelm. A° 2 Pont. sui A° 1439, 3 Reg., fo. 242 *a.* Qui Johannes Lound Canonicus & Prebendarius de Hovedon in Ecclesia Collegiata de Hovedon fuit A° 1448, 4 Reg., fo. 63 *b.* — Rob. [Nevill]. — H. 6.

N.B.—quod praefato Hospitali appropriata annexata et unita fuit Ecclesia S[ti] Nicholai Dun. per praedictum

---

In the will of Sir John Lumley, Knight, we find, " Item lego Ricardo Bukley Clerico unum ciphum deauratum et x marcas argenti . . . Hujus autem testamenti mei facio ordino et constituo praedictum Ricardum de Bukley . . . executores meos " (" Durham Wills," Surtees Society, i, 62). In Bishop Langley's will, " Item . . . et domino Ricardo Bukley decem libras . . . executores ordino . . . et dominum Ricardum Buckley rectorem ecclesiae parochialis Sancti Nicholai civitatis Dunelm. . . . " (" *Tres Scriptores,*" Appendix ccxliv, ccxlvii). Among the *Soluciones debitorum* of Finchale there are, " 1423-4. Item domino Ricardo Buckley magistro de Kypiyer xxs." (" Priory of Finchale," Surtees Society, clxxxvii). Also, " 1446-7. Debita . . . Item executoribus Ricardi Bukley vj*l.* xij*s.* iiij*d.* (*Ibid.,* ccxlix). Also " 1447-8. Debetur . . . Executoribus Ricardi Bukley lxvj*s.* viij*d.* (*Ibid.,* clii).

[1] For his appointment see Appendix A, XVIII. In addition to what appears in the Mickleton MSS., the Rev. F. Thompson, in his notes on the Masters, has left the following notices of him : —" 8 June, 1455, he occurs as Master witness to the payment of £69 0s. 20d. offerings under an indulgence granted by Pope Nicholas V. In 1457 he was appointed one of the supervisors of Bishop Nevill's will, which was never proved. In 1446 he was witness to the instrument of election of Prior William Ebchester."

	Bishops.	Kings

Robertum episcopum 5 Junii 1443, 3 Reg., fo. 291 *b*.

Praefatus Johannes Lound fuit etiam temporalis cancellarius episcopi D. per patentes. Regis E. 4.

Ac etiam tempore Laurentii [Booth] episcopi D., ac ejusdem episcopi unus Justiciarius. Ac Aldermannus Gildae Corporis Christi in ecclesia beati Nicholai D. tempore Roberti Nevill episcopi. — Rob. [Nevill]. — H. 6.

Vide exemplificationem omnium veterum cartarum concernentium Hospitale praedict. per praedictum Rob. [Nevill] episcopum dat. 8 April A° Pont. ejus 7°. Vide Rotulos clausos ejusdem episcopi + 31, et Rot. Claus. ejusdem M in dorso, No. 69, eorundem.

Henricus Gillowe [1] (*Hunter MSS.*).

---

[1] Not mentioned in the Mickleton MSS., but placed in the Hunter MSS. and by Hutchinson and Surtees between Lounde and Booth. Surtees says that he resigned the Mastership in 1479, without giving his reason for saying so. Certainly in that year Ralph Booth, and not he, was Master, as will appear below. The late Rev. F. Thompson, in his notes above referred to on the Masters of Kepyer, doubts his having been Master at all, giving as a reason that Lounde was living and Chancellor in 1464, and that Bishop Laurence Booth (consecrated in 1457 and translated to York in 1476) seems to have given everything he could to his relative Ralph Booth, and was likely to have given him the Hospital. This, however, is but a weak argument: and Henry Gillow, who had followed the bishop out of Lancashire, seems to have been no less a recipient of his favours. He held the following preferments. He was (according to Surtees) Temporal Chancellor to Bishop Booth. Between 1470 and his death he was Rector of Houghton-le-Spring. On July 24th, 1476, he was installed prebendary of Tockerington at York on the presentation of the Archbishop Laurence Booth (*Reg. Capit. Ebor.*). He exchanged this for Fridaythorpe, to which he was collated on June 11th, 1479 (*Reg. Laur. Booth*, 7 *a b*). On March 5th, 1477 8, he was installed Sub-dean of York (*Regs. Capit. et Laur. Booth*, 5 *a*, &c.). This he held till his death, together with the Rectory of Gilling, in which he was installed July 18th, 1480 (*Reg. sede vacante*, 495 *a*). See Canon Raine's note on p. 281 of "Testamenta Eboracensia," Surtees Society, vol. xlv. In 1467 8, and in 1468 9, the house of Finchale paid him rent for certain lands at *Coken* (near Finchale across the river): for we find in the *Compotus domini Will. Byrden Prioris de Fyncall*, in those years, "Et solvit magistro Henrico Gillowe pro terris in Coken quondam Willielmi Redforth xxxiijs. iiijd." ("Finchale Priory," Surtees Society, pp. cccvi, cccx). Further, in 1475 he had a suit with the house of Finchale in the Consistory Court of Durham with respect to rights in coal mines "at Fynchale and Raynton." In letters relating to this dispute he is designated "Mr. Henry Gillowe parson of Hoghton," but not as Master of Kepyer (*Ibid.*, pp. 37, 38, 39). In his will (dated Feb. 8th, 1482-3, and proved April 29th, 1483), in which he describes himself as Sub-dean of York, prebendary of Fridaithorp, and

	Bishops.	Kings
	{ W. [Dudley].	E. 4.
	{ Jo. [Sherwood]	R. 3.
		H. 7.

RADULFUS BOOTH[1] Clericus, Magister sive Custos Hospitalis praedicti ac Archidiaconus Ebor. Vide Ro. W. D. B. in dorso. Qui etiam temporalis Cancellarius Episcopi D. A° 10 H. 7, Et tempore Johannis [Sherwood] Episcopi.

Indentura Dimissionis facta 12° Nov. A° 1479 per istum Radulfum Both Clericum Magistrum Hospitalis de Kepyer et Confratres ejusdem Hospitalis Richardo Both Armigero De toto dominio suo de veteri Dunelm., aldurham, pro 99 Annis sub redd. 10*l.* Vide exemplificationem hujus Indenturae in Rotulis clausis Episcopi Sherwood B., No. 7.

Johannes Langhorne Chapellanus seneschallus sub praedicto Radulfo

rector of Gilling and of Hoghton, he directs himself to be buried at Houghton near his mother; provides for the erection of a chapel over his body, and the foundation of a chantry in honour of the Blessed Virgin and St. Katherine with an endowment of 8 marks a year; leaves two silver thuribles and two silver candlesticks to the Church of Houghton, and several other legacies ("York Wills," Surtees Society, iii, 281).

[1] Master certainly in 1479, on the 12th of November in which year he leased Old Durham (which then belonged to Kepyer as glebe of the impropriated Rectory of St. Nicholas) to his relative Richard Booth for 99 years at a rent of £10. He was himself a relative of Bishop Laurence Booth, who was translated to York in 1476, and by whom he was made Archdeacon of York in 1477. He was afterwards, as is said in the Mickleton MSS., Temporal Chancellor to Bishop Sherwood and also to Bishop Fox. Hutchinson, in his list of Archdeacons of Durham, says that he was a prebendary of Norton, and occurs as Archdeacon in 1463. He was certainly Archdeacon of Durham in 1494, being so described in a commission to him and Prior Auckland for declaring the articles of the greater excommunication ("*Tres Scriptores*," ccclxxx). Also in 1496, as appears from an Appendix to "*Tres Scriptores*" to the following effect:—That on the 5th February in that year Thomas Swallwell, B.D., monk of Durham, offered at the shrine of St. Cuthbert, according to custom, the silver seals of the late Bishop Sherwood (who had died at Rome, July 12th, 1494) in the name and at the request of Ralph Booth, Archdeacon of Durham, who had been Chancellor of Bishop Sherwood during his life, and who was then on his deathbed at Kepeyre, Booth having further requested that at the time of the offering "quinque Pater noster cum salutatione Angelica" might be offered for the bishop and himself ("*Tres Scriptores*," ccclxxxvii). It is stated in the notices left by the Rev. Francis Thompson that in 1494 the bishop of Bath (Richard Fox, translated to Durham in that year) sent through him a licence for the election of a new Prior of Durham, that in 1495 Richard Booth and Ralph Booth were both witnesses to persons taking sanctuary in the church of Durham, and that Ralph Booth was named in a commission to pay Bishop Sherwood's debts out of the bishopric, *sede vacante.*

	Bishops.	Kings
Bothe Hospitii praedicti A° 1494. Vide Rot.		
Vide Indenturam pro Hosp. de Keepyere. In Rotulis clausis Tho^{ae} [Rowthall] episcopi.	Tho. [Rowthall].	A°. 1°. H. 8.

Thomas Colston, 1497.[1]   (*Hunter MSS.*)

Roger Layborn.[2]

Thomas Wytton.[3]   (*Hunter MSS.*)

John Boerius.[4]   (*Hunter MSS.*)

WILLELMUS FRANKLEYN Clericus L.L. Baccalaureus, Magister. Vide de eo Rotulos clausos. Tho^{ae} No. 56.

Iste Willelmus Magister Hospitalis de Keepyere, Et ejusdem loci confratres per Indenturam dat. 7 April A° 10 H. 8 dimiserunt Willelmo Hill et Elianorae Tempest Viduae Manerium

---

[1] Appointed by Bishop Fox in 1497. See Appendix A, XX. Omitted in Mickleton MSS., but inserted in Hunter MSS. Surtees says of him, "per m. Booth. Nephew to Bishop Fox; Archdeacon of Durham."

[2] Omitted in both Mickleton and Hunter MSS. Surtees includes him in his list as follows:—"1501. Roger Layborn, Rector of Stanhope and afterwards of Sedgefield. Archdeacon of Durham. Master of Pembroke Hall, Cambridge. Consecrated Bishop of Carlisle, 1503. Ob. 1509."

[3] "Thomas Wytton is mentioned as Master in a book of copied wills and instruments which I found J. Raine, jun., making extracts from in the D. and C. Library, Aug. 27, 1850" (*Notices of Masters of Kepyer left by the late Rev. Francis Thompson*).

[4] He was a Genoese clerk, Archdeacon of Durham from 1504 to 1515. In the list of Archdeacons given in Sanderson's "Antiquities of the Abbey of Durham" he occurs thus:—"Jo. Boerius Clericus Genuensis, who resigned in 1515." In a MS. list, written by Randall, in the Thorp Collection, vol. 49, p. 85, he is thus described:—"John Boerius, a Genoese clerk, intruded by the Pope . . . 1504. He res. . . . 1515, reserving to himself a pension of £50 p. a. during life."

One John Baptista Boerius, a Genoese, was eminent as a physician to Henry VII and Henry VIII for many years. There is frequent mention of him in "Domestic Letters and Papers of Henry VIII" (*Rolls Series*). Erasmus, as there appears, was well acquainted with him and corresponded with him during his stay in England (1510 to 1514), and at one time had a young son of his under his care as a pupil. There is a letter (No. 635) dated Rome, 28th June, 1515, from Julius Cardinal de Medicis to Wolsey, in which he promises to promote the cause of "John Baptista, the physician," and another (No. 634) of the same date from the same Julius to Henry VIII, adverting to one received from the King commending Bernard Boerius, son of John Baptista. It thus appears that solicitation had been made at Rome from high quarters in favour of the family of Boerius, so as to account sufficiently for the intrusion, as alleged, of some member of it into the Archdeaconry of Durham by the Pope; and it may have been under like influence that the same John Boerius got also the Mastership of Kepyer.

sive Grangiam vocat. est Grainge de Keipyere cum omnibus terris, &c., pro vitis Reddend. eisdem Magistro & confratribus & successoribus suis 20 marcas. Vide Rotulos clausos Th^{ae} [Rowthall] episcopi A. No. 83. Fuit iste Willelmus temporalis Cancellarius Dunelm. Episcopo Routhall praedicto A° 1513, &c. Ac etiam Cardinali Wolsey episcopo D. A° 1523-4, &c. Vide . . Fuit etiam Archidiaconus D. A° 1531.

Tho. [Rowthall].
Tho. [Wolsey].

Fuit iste Willelmus ultimus Magister praefati Hospitalis quando dissolutum fuit A° 1536, 27 H. 8, seu 1540, 31 H. 8, tempore Cuthberti Tunstall. Fuit ille Decanus de Windsore. Vide Rot. Wⁱ James 1, No. 1.

Datum [1] tempore H. 8 R. fuit isti Willelmo pro recuperatione castri de Norham e Scotorum manibus ejus potestate et astutia [his powers and policies]. Vide M.S.T., fo. 56.

II.—INCUMBENTS OF ST. GILES.

The following list down to A.D. 1828, with the exception of the names printed in italics, is as given by Hutchinson and Surtees, the differences between them being noted. Unfortunately neither of them gives his authority. What has been ascertained from other sources will be found in the notes. The additional notices in the text enclosed by square brackets with F.T. after them are from a list left among the papers of the late Rev. Francis Thompson, Incumbent of St. Giles, who was a careful and competent investigator of the antiquities of his parish.

Before the dissolution of religious houses the Master and brethren of Kepyer Hospital, being an ecclesiastical corporation, would no doubt serve the cure themselves, perhaps appointing usually one of their own body as parochial chaplain. Hutchinson and Surtees mention the

---

[1] *Hospitale* may be probably understood, the Mastership of the Hospital having been given him in reward of the services described. It would be during the Episcopate of Bishop Fox.

following three during this period as supposed to have held this office, of whom, however, one only is authenticated, as will be shown in the notes.

MELDREDUS,[1] 1131.

DOM. THOMAS WHITE,[2] } 1501.
DOM. W. DE EDEN,

———

After the surrender of the Hospital, there being no separate endowment for a vicar, the lay impropriator would be responsible for the cure. At first it is probable that the priest of the guild in the church, Richard Middleton, fulfilled the duties. See "Introduction" under "Parish Church and Living." After him (according to Hutchinson and Surtees) :—

JOHN KIRMAN, *occ.* 6 July, 1559.

DOM. GEO. COOKE, *occ.* 10 July, 1564.

DOM. OLIVER ESHE,[3] *occ.* 16 Oct., 1565.

———

[1] The only supposed evidence seems to be that a Charter of Agreement between Rad. de Nevill and the Convent for Staindrop (*Cartuar. II*, fo. 1866) is witnessed by "Meldredo p'sbit'o de S'c'o Egidio" among others. See Surtees' "History of Durham," vol. iv. pt. i, p. 149. But there seems to be nothing to connect him of necessity with the church of St. Giles which was attached to Kepyer.

[2] His name occurs as parochial chaplain of the Church of St. Giles in a Visitation of the city and diocese of Durham, A.D. 1501, by Thomas Savage, Archbishop of York, during the vacancy of the see after the translation of Bishop Fox to Winchester, thus :—"Ecclesia Sancti Egidii Dunelm. appropriata Hospitali de Kepyer. . . . . Dominus Thomas White capellanus parochialis, D. Willielmus Eden, praestiterunt," &c. See Surtees Society's Publications, vol. xxii, p. xiii). It does not thus appear that Sir William Eden was also a parochial chaplain, though assumed by Hutchinson and Surtees to have been so.

[3] This Oliver Eshe (or Ashe) was proceeded against after the "Rebellion of the Earls" in 1569 for compliance with it. See "Depositions and Ecclesiastical Proceedings" (Surtees Society's Publications, 1845, p. 137). He then confessed to having been in the Cathedral on some Sunday or Holiday in December, to having spoken to "Mr. Hoomes about sainge of service in the churche of St. Giells, who answered hym, that, for so moch as this examinate had bein a religious man, he coulde not absolve hym, sainge that he, this deponent, was excommunicat, and so shulde be for hym, the said Holmes, unto he had further auctoritie. And, at this examinate comming to the said Cathedral Church, the said Holmes was at the hynder end of his sermond, but he could not well hear or understande hym; and, after that, the said Holmes went to masse, and when the sacringe bell range this examinate loked towerd the priest, but he could not decern the elevacion; whereupon he loked up to Mr. Bromley" (John Brymley, the organist), "then in the loft over the queir door, and smiled at hym." Further he confessed that last Easter he had "ministred the bread and wyn to dyvers his parishioners, in their mowthes, and not in their hands, bycause they wold not take yt into their hands" ("Book of Depositions," 1565-73).

[Oliver Eshe was curate of St. Helen's Auckland in
1553 and to 1561. —F.T.]

CHRISTOPHER GREENE,[1] d. 1574.

ROBERT PRENTICE,[2] *occ.* 22 Jul., 1578.

[Rob[t] Prentisse was Curate of Whitworth in 1583, and
Rector of Dinsdale in 1588-98.—F.T.]

JACOB HOBSON, cur., *occ.* 23 Jul., 1578.

[Jacob Hobson was Curate of Hamsterley in 1578-80.—
F.T.]

JAMES PINCKNEY, cur., *occ.* 20 June, 1583.

WILLIAM MORROW,[3] 4 Feb., 1584.

JOHN WATSON,[4] *occ.* in Par. Reg., 1604 and 1621.

It appears from the above that Oliver Eshe had been a "religious
man," *i.e.*, belonging to some religious order, before the Dissolution. He is
described as being forty-one years of age at the time of his examination.
Probably he clung in his heart all along to the old order of things, as his
parishioners of St. Giles seem also to have done. For the Churchwardens
of the parish, with other parishioners, were accused also and confessed to
the charge of having set up altars in the Church, and that they "did burne
teare and utterly destroy the Holy Bible, the Apology, Homilees, Booke of
Praier, &c., in despite of God, the Quene Majestie' lawes, and damnation
of their own soules." Robert Corneforth of Gilligait, tanner, aged 46,
also deposed that "he had heard it reported that Sir Oliver maid
holly water and holly bread, but whether he had Latten service he cannot
depose" (*Ibid.*).

[1] Christopher Greene appears at Visitations in the years 1577, 1578, 1579,
as curate of St. Nicholas and of St. Mary Magdalen Chapel in Gilligate, but
not as curate of St. Giles. In 1577, and at a visitation of the Dean and
Chapter by Bishop Barnes in 1580, he is further described as under-master
(subpedagogus) of the Cathedral Grammar School (See "Ecclesiastical
Proceedings of Bishop Barnes," Surtees Society's Publications, vol. xxii,
pp. 46, 47, 73, 96, 103).

[2] *Alias* Prentize *or* Prentisse. For some account of him see "Parish
Registers," p. 123, n. 1. He appears at Visitations as Curate of St. Giles
in 1577, 1578, and 1579. On the first of these occasions there is appended
to his name "No Licence." At Bishop Barnes' Visitation of the Dean and
Chapter in 1580 he appears as seventh Minor Canon (Surtees Society's
Publications, vol. xxii, pp. 46, 73, 96, 103).

[3] *Alias* Murrey *or* Murray. For an account of him see "Grassmen's
Accounts," p. 15, note 4. It may be further noted here that his uncle,
Robert Murrey, Vicar of Pittington, whom he succeeded in that living, left
him in his will (dated 6th November, 1593) all his books except his Geneva
Bible and "Chemnius de Examinatione Tridentini Concilii." The latter he
had bequeathed to the Cathedral Library. The Bible was probably
reserved for his widow, Agnes Murrey, to whom he left his residue.
(See Surtees' "History of Durham," vol. i, p. 117). If the dates of his birth
and burial are given correctly in the Mickleton MSS. (quoted in the note
above referred to), he would be 103 years old when he died.

[4] Known as Sir John Lack-Latin. For notice of him see "Grassmen's
Accounts," p. 19, note 2, and "Parish Registers," p. 123. His son Robert
was christened in December, 1621, and his daughter Elizabeth buried,
having died of the plague, in September, 1604. See "Parish Registers,"
pp. 126, 133.

ELIAS SMITH,[1] 18 Apr., 1632.

[Elias Smith, A.M., Minor Canon of the Cathedral;
   Preacher of the Word of God; Vicar of Bedlington, 4
   Sept., 1643; ob. 1676; Master of the Grammar School.
   He was librarian to the Dean and Chapter.—F.T.]

HENRY SMITH,[2] A.B., 1665.

[p. res. of his father Elias Smith.—F.T.]

William CAM [3] [1678.—F.T.], bur. 2 Sept., 1682.

Thomas Teasdale.

Charles Maddison.[4]

RICHARD BEEL,[5] 1682 per m. Cam. (*Surtees*), 1685
   (*Hutchinson*).

Pexall Forster, A.M.[6]

---

[1] For notice of this notable person see "Introduction," p. 3, and
"Grassmen's Accounts," p. 62, note 2.

[2] Henry Smith was the only son of the above Elias Smith. Cf.
Mickleton MSS., No. 32. "Henricus Smith cl'icus Min. Can. 25 Martii
A⁰ 1673 filius fuit unicus Elie Smith. Fuit Sacrista pro aliquo tempore, et
Rector eccl. B. Marie in Ball. Australi." He is not there spoken of as
having been curate of St. Giles.

[3] Surtees gives his name erroneously as Thomas Cam. He is mentioned
next after Elias Smith in the Mickleton MSS., No. 30, p. 72. A Bond preserved
in the Vestry is attested, 11th December, 1678, by "Wm. Cam, Clerk." In
the "Grassmen's Accounts," A.D. 1680 (p. 83), he signs a parochial
document as "William Cam, Rector." In the Registers we find "Richard,
son of William Cam Rector of this Parish was Baptiz'd the 18th of March
in the yeare of our Lord God 1680-1" (p. 148). His burial, 26th September,
1682, is also recorded in the Register (p. 146), where he is described as
"Mr. Cam, Rector of Gyllegate." Maria, widow of Wm. Cam, Clerk, took
a house of the Lord of the Manor, 26th April, 1683 (*Papers left by Rev.
Francis Thompson*). Why he was designated Rector has not been made
apparent. See "Introduction," under "Parish Church and Living."

[4] These two names (not included in the lists of Hutchinson and Surtees)
are given in the Mickleton MSS. as succeeding Cam thus:—"Thomas
Teasdale Clericus A.M. Qui etiam unus Min. Can. Cath. Eccl. D."

"Carolus Maddison, Clericus A.M. Qui ab ista ecclesia ivit ad ecclesiam
de Chester in le Street."

[5] Surtees has got his date of 1682 from that of the death of Cam, on the
supposition that Beel (*or* Bell) had succeeded him; but erroneously, if
Teasdale and Maddison intervened. Beel is not mentioned as Curate of
St. Giles in the Mickleton MSS., but otherwise referred to thus: "Ric'us
Bell Clericus, Min. Can. 1682 filius fuit Ric'di Bell de Shinkliff prope
D. textoris. Ob. Londini." But that he was minister of St. Giles is proved
by the following entry in the Parish Register:—"Mr. Richard Bell
minister of St. Gyles was buried at London May ye 12, 1685."

[6] "Pexallus Forster A.M. Min. Can. 1686. Qui etiam minister
S. Egidii, ac postea Vicarius S. Oswaldi post deprivationem Johannis
Cock" (Mickleton MSS.). The deprivation of John Cock was in 1690.
It thus appears that Pexall Forster, having succeeded Beel, who died in
1685, was, on his transference to St. Oswald's, succeeded by Dunn (or Done),
whose entry in 1691 is recorded in the Register, as will be seen below.
Hutchinson, though he omits Pexall Forster, has given the date of Dunn's
entry correctly. Surtees, supposing the latter to have succeeded Beel, has
altered it erroneously to 1685.

WILLIAM DUNN,[1] 1685 p. mortem Beel (*Surtees*), 1691 (*Hutchinson*).

JOHN PERKIN,[2] A.B., *occ.* 1706 and 1708.

 [Curate of St. Nicholas, Vicar of Sockburn, 1722.—F.T.]

HENRY PORTER, M.A.

 [Curate and Lecturer of St. Nicholas, 1710; Vicar of Coniscliffe, 1718.—F.T.]

WILLIAM FORSTER,[3] A.M., 24 June, 1723.

 [Curate of St. Margaret's, Crossgate, from 27 Oct., 1719, to 1722; Vicar of Aycliffe and Curate of St. Giles, 1723 to 1725, both which he resigned for St. Oswald's, where he died, 1765.—F.T.]

ROBERT PIGOT, A.M., 1725, per res. Forster.

 [Pigot was Rud's successor as Librarian to the Dean and Chapter, 1725.—F.T.]

CHILTON WILSON, A.M., 1739, p. res. Pigot.

 [Vicar of Heighington, 1727, where he died, 1749; Curate of St. Giles, 1730 (from 1726 to 1745). Res. —F.T.]

---

[1] *Alias* Done; his name is spelt both ways in the Parish Register, in which are the following, among other notices of him :—" Michaelmas 1691, Mr. William Dunn, Minister of this parish " (p. 146).

" Memorandum that Mr. Wm. Done (*the name altered to* Dunn), Curate of St. Gyles, entered at Michaelmass 1691.

    Thomas Gelson, } Churchwardens " (p. 156).
    Walter Hair, }

" Mr. Wm. Done, Minister of St. Gyles, and Mrs. Elizabeth Davies of West Chester were married July ye seventeenth Anno D'ni 1692 " (p. 142).

" Burials in the year 1693, Wm. Done Curate."

" Baptismata in Anno 1693, Gulielmo Dunneo S'ti Ægidii Curato." So also (or " Gulielmo Done ") A.D. 1694 and A.D. 1695. A Memorandum, Easter, 1696, is signed Wm. Dunn, " Wm. Done Curate " being found in the following paragraph (p. 154).

" 1704. Frances ye daughter of Wm. Dunn Minister of this Parish was buryed on good friday ye 14th day of April. She was his second of that name " (p. 159).

A Memorandum dated April 2nd, 1705, is signed, " Test. Wm. Dunn Curate " (p. 156). Finally, " William Done, Curate of this Parish, was Buried Octobr 20th 1706 " (p. 160).

[2] His name occurs in the Parish Register as Minister of St. Giles in 1700:—" Mem. that Walter Haire was discharged from officiating as parish clark on Candlemas day 1709, & Richard Martin had orders to officiate from John Perkin, Minister of St. Gyles Durham " (p. 155).

[3] In Vol. iv of the Registers (1695—1749) there is—" Memorandum That I find there has been a scandalous neglect of registring Births, Burials & Marriages from the year 1711 to midsummer 1723, when the Curacy of St. Giles was entered upon by me, W. Forster."

ROBERT DAVISON,[1] A.M. (1749, *see note*).

[Curate of Croxdale, 19 Oct., 1742, Occ. Cur. of St. Giles, 1754.—F.T.]

RALPH GELSON,[2] A.B., 18 Feb., 1768, Bp. by lapse.

[Collated to St. Giles by Bp. Trevor by lapse ; Vicar of Merrington, 1760 ; died there, 1775.—F.T.]

JOHN ROBSON,[2] A.M., 22 Oct., 1768. RANDALL MSS. (*Hutchinson*).

The same, Line. Coll., Oxon., 1775 ; p. m. Gelson (*Surtees*).

[Presented by John Tempest, Esq. ; Vicar of Sockburn, 1759 ; Curate of St. Nicholas, 1783 ; died 1802.—F.T.]

JOSEPH WATKINS,[3] M.A., 1802, p. m. Robson.

St. John's Coll., Camb., Sept. 25, 1802 (*Surtees*).

[Presented by Sir A. V. Tempest, Bart. ; successively Vicar of Merrington (?) and Norham ; died 1828.—F.T.]

———

Here end the lists given by Hutchinson and Surtees. What follows, down to his own date, is from the list left by the Rev. Francis Thompson.

———

W. R. WYATT,[4] M.A., 1828.

Minor Canon of St. Asaph in 1836, and Perpetual Curate of Dyserth, Flints.

———

[1] On the back of the cover of the Volume of Registers for 1749–1789, is written :—" Robert Davison was nominated 8th Dec., 1749."

[2] Here, as in some previous instances, Surtees has corrected Hutchinson's date erroneously. The correctness of the date of Robson's accession as given by Hutchinson is proved by a note on the cover of the Parish Register for 1749 to 1789, viz. :—" John Robson, nominated 13th October, licensed 22nd, 1768." He appears to have had charge of the parish before his incumbency, the Registers being signed by him in 1760, and afterwards till 1789. Davison, who had become incumbent in 1749, probably retained Croxdale, and was non-resident at St. Giles.

[3] The date of his accession, as correctly given by Surtees, appears on the cover of the Register for 1749 to 1789, viz.:—" Joseph Watkins, nominated 21st Sept., licensed 25th Sept., 1802." " Parson Blackett," mentioned in the " Preface to Grassmen's Accounts " p. 3, as being remembered to have read prayers on " Whinny Hill " on Bounder Day, seems to have had charge of the parish during part of this incumbency, Watkins, who held other preferment, being probably non-resident. Blackett signs the registers in 1813. From 1820 to 1831, John Owen, Sub-Curate, signs every entry.

[4] In the Register Wyatt (28 Dec., 1830) signs the appointment of Thomas Tilly as parish clerk in succession to Richard Tilly, whose appointment by John Robson in 1801 to succeed John Tilly is also recorded. Successive generations of the Tilly family thus appear to have been parish clerks.

JAMES CARR.[1]
  Perpetual Curate of South Shields in 1831.
SAMUEL A. FYLER, M.A., 1831.
  Perpetual Curate of Cornhill in 1834.
THE HON. AND REV. ROBERT LIDDELL, M.A.[2]
  Vicar of Barking in Essex, 1836.
CHARLES BALSTON,[3] M.A., Fellow of Corpus Christi Coll.,
  Oxford.
  Licence of non-residence dated 26 July, 1836.
WILLIAM CASSIDI, B.A., Trin. Coll., Dublin, Oct., 1837.[4]
  Vicar of Grindon, 5 April, 1841.
FRANCIS THOMPSON, M.A., Univ. Coll., Durham, 1841.

JOHN GEORGE NORTON, M.A., D.D., Trin. Coll., Dublin,
  1872; Rector of Christ Church Cathedral, Montreal, 1884;
  Canon of Montreal, 1893.

ROBERT JOHN PEARCE, M.A., D.C.L., late Fellow of Caius
  Coll., Cambridge, 1884; Professor of Mathematics in the
  University of Durham; Vicar of Bedlington, 1895.

PONSONBY AUGUSTUS MOORE SULLIVAN, M.A., Keble
  Coll., Oxford, 1891.

[1] He signs the Register as "J. Carr, Curate," May 15th, 1831. But in the same year, Dec. 28th, he signs the baptism of his child as "Perpet. Curate of South Shields."

[2] He signs entries in the Register as Perpetual Curate from Jan. 25th, 1835, to May 5th, 1836. He became Incumbent of St. Paul's, Knightsbridge, and St. Barnabas, Pimlico, after the resignation of the Rev. W. J. E. Bennett.

[3] His Curate, in charge of the parish, was H. R. Bramwell, who signs the Registers to Aug., 1837.

[4] This name (though wrongly spelt "Cassidy") and those which follow have been supplied by the Deputy Registrar from the Diocesan Registry, where no record of any previous incumbents appears to have been preserved. Entries in the Parish Register confirm the list.

DESCRIPTION OF SEALS.

No. 1.   In green wax ; see p. 213.   *Insc.* ✠ SIGILLVM : SANCTI : EGIDII.

No. 2.   In white wax; see p. 213.   *Insc.* ✠ SIGILLV SANCTI EGIDII DVNELMIE.

No. 3.   In white wax, appended to a quit claim from Peter the master and the brethren of Kepier to Will. de Wetlawe and his heirs of an annual rent of 3s. 4d., etc. Kepier, 3 Non. Jun. 1291. Durham Treasury, 4ᵗʰ 14ᵐᵃᵉ Specialium, k. 1, No. 10. The seal is much damaged, especially round the edge ; the hind looking up to St. Giles is much better seen on the seal than in the plate : the saint is habited as a monk, and holds a crosier and a book. The inscription appears to have been SIGILLVM SANCTI EGIDII DE KYPIER.   On the back of the seal is a small *secretum* consisting of an antique gem, the impression of which is now too indistinct to be made out or photographed, with the words FRANGE LEGE TEGE round the margin.

No. 4.   In green wax, appended to the following document :—

> "Omnibus hoc scriptum visuris uel audituris. Radulfus rector et fratres hospitalis domus Sancti Egidii de Kippeyer, æternam in Domino salutem. Nouerit uniuersitas uestra nos concessisse et quietum clamasse fratri Radulfo sacristæ domus Sancti Cuthberti, et omnibus successoribus suis qui pro tempore fuerint, toftum et croftum quæ habuimus in Landa Dei[1] cum omnibus pertinentiis suis, in perpetuum, in excambium vnius mesuagii quod emit ad opus nostrum in balliuo de Dunelmo, scilicet illius quod Astinus Brachur et Annais filia Ede Tanai tenuerunt de Willelmo Croere ad feudalem firmam. Et, ut hæc nostra concessio et quieta clamacio futuris temporibus robur optineat, præsens scriptum sigilli nostri appositione roborauimus. Teste Capitulo Nostro." Durham Treasury, 2ᵈᵃ 3ᶜⁱᵉ Sacr., No. 1.

St. Giles in monastic habit holding a crosier? or an arrow? in his left hand, and a book in his right; the hind, as in No. 3, is partly behind him, and looking up to him. The inscription is SIGILL[VM SAN]CTI EGIDII : DE KIPPEYERE.

---

[1] Now Landieu, in the parish of Wolsingham. It is thus mentioned in "Le Convent" (*Feodarium*, Surtees Society, p. 216), "Locus autem qui vocatur Landa Dei, cum omnibus pertinenciis suis, concedimus et confirmamus in perpetuum Sacristariæ Dunelmensi, sicut illum locum habuit et tenuit frater Ranulfus, de dono Hugonis quondam Dunelmensis Episcopi." See above, p. 199.

No. 5. In black wax ; see p. 220. St. Giles in mass vestments, with crosier, book, and the hind. *Insc.* SIGILLVM SANCTI EGIDII DE KIPPIER.

The Conventual Seal of Durham mentioned on p. 220 is that which is figured and described in Raine's *St. Cuthbert,* p. 211, but more accurately figured, together with the reverse, in Surtees's *History of Durham,* Seals, Plate 6 (1). The seal is circular, and bears a cross a little expanded at the ends, with four short points in the angles. The inscription is ✠ SIGILLVM CVDBERHTI PRESVLIS SCĪ. About 1200 was added the reverse, consisting of an antique gem, with a beautifully cut head of Jupiter Tonans, let into a circular plate of metal bearing the legend ✠ CAPVT SANCTI OSWALDI REGIS. See above, p. xiii.

The Seals of the bishops mentioned, pp. 214, 217, and 222, are engraved in Surtees's Plates of Seals (*Hist. Durh.,* vol. i).

GLOSSARY.

ASSARTS (Lat., *Assarta*, or *Assartum*), forest land recently brought into cultivation.

AVERIDGE, apparently the same as *Averagium*, carriage, leading.

BANDELIER (or Bandoleer), a small wooden case covered with leather, carried by soldiers, containing charges for muskets.

BANNES, bands, strap-like plates of iron attached to gates for hinges. Usually associated with crooks.

BISANTIUS (Eng., Bezant, or Besant), a gold coin, said to be from *Byzantium*, where a gold piece, hence called *Byzantius*, was coined under the Emperors. The bezant was current in Europe; in England it was superseded by the noble in the time of Edward III.

BICK, a wooden bottle or cask for carrying liquor in. "A wooden bottle or cask in which beer is carried to the hayfield. *Norf.*"—(Halliwell).

BIGG, Barley, or a kind of barley.

BOON-DAYS (*precariæ*), days on which tenants, under feudal tenure, were bound to work for the lord of the manor in reaping his harvest, or other services.

BOUNDER-DAY, the day of perambulation of the boundaries of parishes or manors in Rogation week.

BOWE (for a bull), perhaps a wooden hoop put over his neck to tie him up by. See also *Saile*.

BOWER, originally a house, or chamber; later, an Arbour. See also *Maiden*.

BRANDED, Brinded, or Brindled. "Of a mixed red and brown colour with some black hairs among the red and brown" (Cleveland Glossary). *Cf.*, "thrice the brinded cat hath mewed" ("Macbeth," Act iv, Sc. 1).

BREARDING (for *bearding*) the dyke. "*Beard*—a hedge made by setting branches of thorns upright in the ground. Making hedges of this kind is called *bearding*" (Peacock's Lincolnshire Glossary).

CAP, or Capp (for a gate), a piece of wood placed over the top rail or post of a gate to protect it.

CARR, a pool in marshy ground. See p. 11, n. 2.

CASTING of dykes, pools, or trenches. Forming or clearing them by throwing out the earth. *Cf.*, "Thine enemies shall cast a trench about thee" (Luke xix, 43).

———— (for water at priers stabel, p. 103). Either digging for it, or possibly using some means for finding it, as, for instance, by the divining rod.

CAUSEY (Lat., *Calcetum, Calcea*), "a way raised and paved above the rest of the ground" (Johnson). Probably derived from late Latin *Calciare*, to tread.

CAVEING; see p. 116, n. 2.

CAVELL, a lot or share; see p. 65, n. 1.

CAYLIES, or Keyles (= Kyloes), a kind of cattle.

CHALLANWEAVER, a weaver of Shalloon, a kind of woollen stuff.

CHARE, a narrow passage. *Cf.*, "the Castle Chare," in Durham, and "chares" in other places in the North.

COTTRELLS, "small iron wedges or pins for securing bolts" (Brockett).
CUVA ; see p. 196, n. 1.

DALE, a deal board.
DIGHTING (the armour), dressing, furbishing, or repairing.
DIKE (or Dyke), a bank or mound for fencing. Also a ditch.
DIKER, one who makes dikes.
DISTRINGAS, a writ for distraint.
DRAWING (Straw). See p. 33*n*.
————— (the moor), the same as *Driving* (?).
DRIVING (the moor), driving together the animals upon the moor for any
    purpose.

ENTERCOMMON (*Intercommon*), a common right of pasturage.
————— Closes (called also Town Closes), enclosed fields, in which there
    was a right of entercommon only during the winter months. See
    p. 40, n. 1.
————— Breaking, entering on such closes at the prescribed time. See
    p. 83, n. 1.

FARMARY, Infirmary. See p. 242.
FLAGS, rushes used for thatching. "Sedge, a sort of rush" (Bailey).
    "A water plant with a bladed leaf and yellow flower" (Johnson).
    "Small pieces of coarse grass in meadows" (Halliwell). *Cf.*, "She
    laid it in the flags by the river's brink" (Exodus ii, 3).
FOREHEAD (of a gate), a piece of wood used in the construction of a gate.
    Perhaps the same as *Head-piece*, which see.
FOOTING (the stoops), probably in some way strengthening or supporting
    them at the foot.
FOOTSTONE, probably the stone under the hartree of a gate, in which it
    turns. See *Harr Tree*.
FOG, the after-math or second growth of grass after mowing.
FOUMART (foul marten), a polecat.

GAIT (or Gate), a run on a common or pasture-field for one head of cattle,
    as "a cow gait," a "horse gait."
GARLING, garland.
GARNEMENT ; see p. 237, n. 3.
GAVELL, gable.
GOODS (p. 106*n*.), cattle.
GOSPEL OAK ; see p. 3, n. 1 ; p. 8, n. 1.
GRASSMEN ; see p. 1.
GRIEVE, or Greeve (= Reeve, *A.S. gerefa*), the Bailiff of a Manor.
GRYPP, a ditch.
GUTT (p. 87), a wide ditch or watercourse.

HACQUETON ; see p. 55, n. 2.
HAINEING, hedging.
HANTING (the bull to the common), accustoming him to it ; getting him to
    feed quietly on it. "To hant is to practise or accustom to anything"
    (Jamieson).
HARNESS, Armour.
HAR, "the hole in a stone or the hinge on which a gate turns, the har-tree
    being the head of the gate in which the spindle is fixed" (Halliwell).
    In Mid-Eng., *Herre*. *Cf.*, "As a door is turned on his herre, so a
    slow man in his bedde" (Prov. xxvi, 14, in Wickliffe's Bible).

HARR KUTT ; see p. 55, n. 2.

HARR TREE (or Hartre), the upright piece of timber at the back of a gate, on which it turns.

HAYBOTE, an allowance of thorns for the tenants' hedges. (From *Hay=Hedge*).

HEAD, or Headpiece, the upright piece of timber in front of a gate, by which it is fastened when shut.

HEARTH-MONEY ; see p. 155, n. 1.

HEAST, probably in error for Hesp, or Hasp, viz., the loop which passes over the *staple* for fastening a gate.

HECKE, a manger or rack for cattle.

HOLLOW Thursday ; see p. 107.

HOULEWAY ; see p. 84, n. 3.

HOUSEBOTE, an allowance of timber from the lord's woods for support or repair of tenants' houses.

HOWSLING (for *Houseling*) people, people capable of receiving the Holy Communion.

HURD, a herdsman.

HUSBAND, a husbandman.

HUPE or Houpe (for *hoop*), for a gate (p. 91), probably an iron band round the top or bottom of a post to keep it from splitting.

INTERCOMMON ; see *Entercommon*.

INTOL, a toll levied on imports ; see U-tol.

JINGLE Pot ; see p. 117, n. 2.

JUG ; see p. 79, n. 1.

KAVEL ; see *Cavell*.

KEYLES ; see *Caylies*.

LAIRSTALL, a grave within a church.

LATTBRODES, nails for laths.

LETCH, "a small watercourse, ditch, or gutter" (Halliwell).

LIVERE ; see p. 237, n. 2.

LOOP (for gate), the hasp that passes over the staple (?).

LOUSSE (for the poundfould) ; see p. 77, n. 3.

MAIDEN ; see p. x.

MANGHE (= *Meyne?*) ; see p. 44, n. 2.

MATCH, "a sort of rope, made on purpose for the firing of guns" (Bailey).

MAYNE (Pain de) ; see p. 237, n. 4.

MAYTE ; see p. 237, n. 1.

MEREMIUM ; see p. 164, n. 2.

MIDDIN, a dunghill.

MORION (*or* Murrion), a sort of steel cap or head-piece (Bailey).

MOUDER ; see p. 61, n. 2.

MOULDING ; see p. 36, n. 1.

MULTURA, "Quod molitori ex frumento quod molit præstatur" (D'Arnis).

MURAGIUM, "Vectigal ad muros urbium aedificandos aut reparandos" (D'Arnis).

NOVALE, "Ager qui de novo ad cultum redigitur" (D'Arnis).

OUTMAN, a "foreigner," one not belonging to the borough of Gilligate.

18

OUT-TOLL ; see U-tol.

OVERSTINT, feeding animals on the common by people in excess of their legitimate *stints, q.v.*

OXGANG ; see p. 24, n. 1.

PAIR, a set of similar things arranged together, two or more.

PANAGIUM : " PANNAGIUM (1) Jus pascendi porcos in silva domini. (2) Tributum quodvis, præsertim vero quod pro *glandatione* porcorum solvitur " (D'Arnis).

PANT, a conduit for water ; see p. 13, n. 1.

PATE, a badger.

PARISHINGES, Parishioners, those who " parish " to St. Giles's. " I reporte me to awll the parysshyngby " (MS. Bibl. Episc. Dunelm., v, 1, 2, in Kalendar).

PICKAGIUM : " PICAGIUM—Tributi species quod ait Spelmannus in nundinis penditur ob veniam effodiendi soli, sic ut tabernacula ponantur nundinalia stationes et officinæ quas *stalla* vocant " (D'Arnis).

PICKE, or Pike (for a gate), possibly the spindle at the bottom of the *hartree,* which turns in the *har.*

PIETANCIA (*Pittance*), the monastic pittance was an extra indulgence in food and drink, often provided by the charity of some benefactor, for certain occasions.

POUNDLAWES, or Poundlouse, a payment for releasing (*loosing*) an animal from the pinfold. *Cf., supra* Lousse.

PRECARIA, Boon-days ; see *supra.*

PULMENTUM ; see p. 238, n. 1.

PUNDER, one who has charge of a pinfold, whose duty it is to impound stray animals.

PURVEY Money ; see p. 51, n. 2.

RISE (or Ryse), Brushwood.

ROOGE-MONEY (*Rogue-money*), a charge on parishes for the maintenance of gaols and the like.

ROUNGES (*e.g.,* " a burden of rounges for the gate "), apparently sticks or rods.

SAGERSTON or Seggerston, a sacristan, or sexten.

SAILE (" to the bull ") ; " Angl. Sax. *Sál* : a tie, band, rope, &c. A wooden hoop to put round the neck to tie an ox or cow in the stall " (Bosworth, Angl. Sax. Dictionary). N.B.—The occurrence of a " saile and band," p. 75, suggests the second of these two meanings. *Cf. supra* (Bowe).

SALTPETRE-MAN ; see p. 22, n. 2.

SCALING, scattering the deposits of cattle or other manure, etc., over land. *E.g.,* " scaling the moor " ; " scaling manure " ; " scaling ashes." See p. 36, n. 1. *Cf., Mouder.*

SEAVER or SIEVER (*Cf.,* κοσκινοποιός, p. 135, n. 4). A sieve-maker. " William Siveyer was born at Shinkley in this Bishoprick, where his father was a Siveyer or Sive-maker ; and I commend his humility in retaining his Father's Trade for his Surname to mind him of his mean extraction. . . . England neither before nor since saw two sive-makers sons advanced . . . this William in the Church, Sir Richard Empson in the Commonwealth " (Fuller's Worthies, Ed. 1811, I, 332).

SHEATH or SHETH, pp. 91, 114. Not explained.

SHELME, or SELME ; " A gate rail, *North.*" (Halliwell).

SHEROBALAVE, Sheriff's bailiff.

SOLDIER-MONEY, a charge on parishes for soldiers. (See Surtees Society's Publications, vol. lxxxiv, p. 19*n.*)

SPARTES; "*Spart:* the dwarf rush; *North.*" (Halliwell).

SPIKINGS, large nails.

STENT, or STINT (also *stinter, Stinting*). See p. 1.

STIE, a stile with steps. N.B.—In the North a ladder is called a *stee.*

STOBB (Stoup, Stoop, Stope), a post or stake driven into the ground.

STRASS, Distress; see p. 63.

SWALL, p. 12. Not explained.

SWERD, SWEARD, SWORD (also *Sword-tree*), a piece of wood used in the construction of a gate, placed across it transversely. A word still in use.

TENTER-RENT, a payment for bleaching ground.

THEKING (or *Thicking*), thatching.

THORNYNGE THE WICKE, protecting a new quickset hedge with thorns.

THRAVE, twenty-four sheaves, though some counties reckoned only twelve sheaves to the thrave. Jacob, Law Dictionary.

FRANCK (p. 86), not satisfactorily explained. The word is unknown, but possibly denotes here an excavated bit of level ground at some point in a narrow cart-road on the moor, for the carts to turn in. *Cf. supra,* CASTING.

TROUEKE (p. 80), not explained.

U-TOL, a toll levied on exports. *Cf.* Intol. Intoll and Uttol are mentioned in a charter granted by Henry I to the Church of St. Peter, at York. *Mon. Angl.* in Blount's Law Dictionary, 1691, under Toll.

VAYGE; see p. 66, n. 1.

VENNEL, a gutter, or a narrow passage. See p. 84, n. 3.

WACHERIA: "VACHERIA, ut VACCARIA, Ager seu prædium vaccarum numero alendo proprium. VACCARIUM, Stabulum vaccarum" (D'Arnis).

WAFE MEAR, a stray mare (?).

WEYSCALE, a weighing scale.

INDEX.

H

www.ingramcontent.com/pod-product-compliance
Lightning Source LLC
Chambersburg PA
CBHW031136120726
47905CB00006B/1705